**Escape . . .**

Uploading his mind into a computer gave Kenneth perfect recall. So why can't he remember what happened to his body?

On the harsh landscape of Mars, a monk yearns to be free of his weak flesh and walk in glory across the orange plains. . . .

Living a lie can take its toll, even on the world's greatest assassin.

**Imagine . . .**

The first human child born to an alien world is lonely. But in his dreams he's never alone. . . .

When her best friend Madgie abandons the long Sleep, Junie Carter must face her own fears—or risk dreaming her life away. . . .

The Harvester took his family, his heritage, his freedom. Now, captured and caged, Markus's very life hangs in the balance. Literally.

**Suppose . . .**

Space exploration requires rapid assessment of considerable data at once. How this is done can be quite a challenge—especially if that explorer is a chimpanzee.

Khren, indebted through deathbond, has spent two

decades toiling for the greedy humans. But what will his answer be when they ask him to kill for them?

In this bottomless pit, he who drops an object is sometimes condemned to follow it down. . . .

**Dream . . .**

In the depths of Oceanus, a damaged ship's pilot and a young woman hold the key to the survival of the human race.

A self-absorbed concert pianist, crippled by illness, volunteers as the first subject of an ambitious bio-engineering project.

In one moment of hesitation, time traveler Dannia became trapped, frozen and unchanging, for two centuries. But Artomo thought he could release her, given enough time.

**Wonder . . .**

A fanatical warrior and a mercenary mage go on a quest, only to discover success is more perilous than failure . . . especially when they can't trust each other.

In a far-future Earth, when the very definition of humanity has been amended, what are the limits of the soul?

Peter and Frans were lunar prospectors, Sunrunners. They circumnavigated the Moon, discovered hidden ice, risked death from company goons . . . and in their spare time, they staged a coup.

## What has been said about the
# L. RON HUBBARD PRESENTS WRITERS OF THE FUTURE
## ANTHOLOGIES

"A very generous legacy from L. Ron Hubbard—a fine, fine fiction writer—for the writers of the future."

—Anne McCaffrey, Author

"The contest has opened the way for scores of writers and has set them out on the fine careers they deserve."

—Jack Williamson, Author

"Prior to L. Ron Hubbard's Writers of the Future Contest starting, there was no field which enabled the new writer to compete with his peers—other new writers."

—Kevin J. Anderson, Author

"Winning the contest was my first validation that I would have a career. I entered five times before winning and it gave me something I could reach and attain. It kept me writing and going for something. Reading the anthology is important. Writers of the Future is a market and you have to KNOW your market if you are going to submit and win. I had the first four volumes of Writers of the Future and just read them over and over before I won and was published in Volume V."

—K.D. Wentworth, Winner, Author and Educator

"The L. Ron Hubbard Writers of the Future Contest has carried out the noble mission of nurturing new science fiction and fantasy writers for a decade now with resounding success."

—Dr. Yoji Kondo, Author

"Winning the Writers of the Future Contest was, to that point in time and long after, the highest point in my career. To this day, I go out of my way to recommend writers enter the contest, even if they aren't particularly interested in the genre. I believe my enthusiasm for Writers of the Future shows, as many do routinely enter the contest.

"In addition to the career boost (I learned more craft in one week at the workshop than in the previous two years on my own), which was substantial, I've made many friends through the contest, peers in the writer's struggle, fellow pros, not only from my volume (XIII) but from other volumes as well. They all share my belief that the contest is unparalleled in the business for helping new writers become pros."

—Ken Rand, Winner

## SPECIAL OFFER FOR SCHOOLS AND WRITING GROUPS

The fifteen prize-winning stories in this volume, all of them selected by a panel of top professionals in the field of speculative fiction, exemplify the standards that a new writer must meet if he expects to see his work published and achieve professional success.

These stories, augmented by how-to-write articles by some of the top writers of science fiction and fantasy, make this anthology virtually a textbook for use in the classroom and an invaluable resource for students, teachers and workshop instructors in the field of writing.

The materials contained in this and previous volumes have been used with outstanding results in writing courses and workshops held on college and university campuses throughout the United States—from Harvard, Duke and Rutgers to George Washington, Brigham Young and Pepperdine.

To assist and encourage creative writing programs, the *L. Ron Hubbard Presents Writers of the Future* anthologies are available at special quantity discounts when purchased in bulk by schools, universities, workshops and other related groups.

For more information, write:

Specialty Sales Department
Galaxy Press, L.L.C.
7051 Hollywood Blvd., Suite 200
Hollywood, California 90028
or call toll-free: 1-877-8GALAXY
Internet address: www.galaxypress.com
E-mail address: info@galaxypress.com

# L. RON HUBBARD
PRESENTS
# WRITERS
OF THE
# FUTURE
VOLUME
XX

# L. RON HUBBARD
PRESENTS
# WRITERS
OF THE
# FUTURE
VOLUME
XX

The Year's 15 Best Tales from the
Writers of the Future®
International Writing Program

Illustrated by the Winners in the
Illustrators of the Future®
International Illustration Program

With Essays on Writing and Art by
L. Ron Hubbard • Robert A. Heinlein
Robert Silverberg • Vincent Di Fate
Kevin J. Anderson

Edited by Algis Budrys

Galaxy Press, L.L.C.

Cover Artwork: Andrew Tucker



ISBN: 1-59212-177-2

Library of Congress Control Number: 2004111191
First Edition Paperback 10 9 8 7 6 5 4 3 2 1
Printed in the United States of America

# CONTENTS

# THE NATURE OF CREATIVITY

*by*
**Algis Budrys**

Here it is—Volume XX of this series, *L. Ron Hubbard Presents Writers of the Future.*

Volume XX! It seems hardly possible to us. But in this volume, at least one of the contributors is young enough, so that for them, this book has always been around. And many others have hardly known a time when it wasn't in existence. (And so, L. Ron Hubbard's prescient objective was met.)

Hubbard was an extraordinarily gifted person. He was capable of not only creating an outstanding career as a writer in many fiction genres, but also teaching the craft to others. SF was his paramount love. So this volume has always encouraged the science fiction young—teaching them, through the inclusion of his many how-to articles and those of famous science fiction writers and illustrators who serve as judges and contributors.

I wrote the introduction to the very first volume of this anthology series, published in 1985. It was entitled "On Shaping Creativity." Upon reviewing that statement, I now remind myself of the successful standard for introducing the Writers of the Future

Contest winners to the world of readers. And, yes, that first volume acheived what it set out to do. It alone heralded major publishing careers for its newly published writers: Karen Joy Fowler, Nina Kiriki Hoffman, Dean Wesley Smith and David Zindell. Newly published writers in subsequent volumes, including Stephen Baxter, Jo Beverly, Leonard Carpenter, Nancy Farmer, Robert Reed, K.D. Wentworth, Sean Williams and Dave Wolverton, have likewise gone on to achieve their professional publishing aspirations.

Volume I contained statements on the art and craft by SF practitioners who devoted their time as judges. Subsequent volumes of the anthology featured how-to-write articles and essays intended to help novices achieve their goals. And, just as Volume I featured an insightful essay by Robert Silverberg, so, too, does this Volume XX. We have also included an article by L. Ron Hubbard's close friend, Robert A. Heinlein.

From the outset, the Writers of the Future Contest has featured a stellar panel of judges—professional writers one and all. Gregory Benford, Robert Silverberg, Jack Williamson and I remain from the very first contest year. The others include: Kevin J. Anderson, Doug Beason, Orson Scott Card, Brian Herbert, Nina Kiriki Hoffman, Eric Kotani, Anne McCaffrey, Larry Niven, Andre Norton, Frederik Pohl, Jerry Pournelle and Tim Powers.

Why do these stellar professionals serve? I think my answer to this question twenty years ago in Volume I still suffices. "They do it because no one ever forgets what it was like to dream of acceptance and recognition, often in the long face of repeated discouragement. And they do it because historically in the SF field, beginning writers have never been regarded as potential competitors; they are new comrades."

Just as Volume I featured illustrations by beginning illustrators, so, too, does this Volume XX. However, the fledgling artists of today are discoveries of the L. Ron Hubbard Illustrators of the Future Contest, established in 1989 as the companion competition to the Writers of the Future Contest.

Twenty years ago, we were hoping that we had done our best for these new writers as these writers had likewise hoped they had done their best for you.

Twenty years later—*L. Ron Hubbard Presents Writers of the Future, Volume XX*—we no longer "hope," we know we have done our best for these new writers and, as you will see, the writers know they have done their best for you.

Add to this, the new illustrators introduced to the SF field through their very first publication experience. Further add the cumulative effect of the how-to articles and essays by professionals, the many writers and illustrators workshops, the judges' contributions throughout the years, the continued administration and sponsorship of the Writers and Illustrators of the Future Contests by Author Services, Inc., the publication by Galaxy Press of this very anthology—and I think you'll agree that creativity has been shaped and encouraged from the very first publication to the one you are reading now.

The history of the contests is a proud one. From their inception, they have set a standard of excellence and professionalism which are unparalleled in the field of speculative fiction and far beyond. One gentleman who has been around since the very beginning is William J. Widder, Mr. Hubbard's official fiction bibliographer and the author of *Master Storyteller: An Illustrated Tour of the Fiction of L. Ron Hubbard*. His article that follows is testament to the vision of the contests' founder and a success story that grows more amazing every year.

Enjoy *L. Ron Hubbard Presents Writers of the Future, Volume* XX!

Algis Budrys
Editor

# ON OUR TWENTIETH ANNIVERSARY

*by*

## WILLIAM J. WIDDER

By any measure, this historic Twentieth Anniversary edition of the *L. Ron Hubbard Presents Writers of the Future* anthology is an indisputable landmark in the world of contemporary science fiction and fantasy. It is science fiction that asks "What if?" and answers with bold and visionary spell-weaving tales that transcend the commonplace.

The bestselling and most widely influential anthology of its kind, this Volume XX in the series brings you fifteen richly exciting and original stories produced by the best new creative talent in speculative fiction—all winners of the Writers of the Future Contest for the year 2003. They are stories by new writers of singular aptitudes; beginning authors ranging across the spectrum of life's diversity in age, background and occupation, but not diverse in their shared aspirations as writers, and each with a demonstrated capacity to ignite one's imagination.

A winner of the companion Illustrators of the Future Contest vividly illustrates each story, as well; fledgling illustrators creating art, as one of the contest's most distinguished judges has phrased it, "in service of the story."

The volume also includes insightful articles and essays on the craft, techniques and business aspects of writing and illustration by a number of esteemed professionals—this year by L. Ron Hubbard, Robert A. Heinlein, Robert Silverberg, Vincent Di Fate and Kevin J. Anderson.

L. Ron Hubbard himself was a man of extraordinary skills and creative energies who brought the adventurous breadth of his life—as explorer and ethnologist, master mariner and barnstorming pilot, filmmaker and photographer, composer and musician—into his fiction. But always before anything else, he was a writer, stating, "Capturing my own dreams in words, paint or music and then seeing them live is the highest kind of excitement."

It was an excitement he brought with undiminished fervor to his more than 250 published novels and stories. These ranged from his early tales of action, adventure, western and mystery, when he burst onto the pulp fiction landscape at the age of twenty-three, through his incisively imaged stories of time and space, *Final Blackout* and *To the Stars*. These works stand among the literary pillars on which the Golden Age of Science Fiction was built. Hubbard's literary career flourished into the 1980s, with his crowning epic novels *Battlefield Earth* and the ten-volume *Mission Earth*.

But within the sweeping dimensions of his own career, Hubbard held a personal conviction that the established writer owed a generous helping hand to the newcomers in writing and illustration, without which there would be no viable literary future.

Over more than half a century of prodigious work, L. Ron Hubbard never lost the energizing sense of personal dedication that he brought to writing essays and articles on the craft of writing that he began when he was twenty-four. It was in fact the same year, 1935, that he was elected president of the New York chapter of the American Fiction Guild—the youngest president in its history.

During his tenure, he sought to bring beginning writers into the ranks of the Guild and facilitate their entry into the adversarial professional world. He lectured on the demands of writing at schools like Harvard and The George Washington University. And the articles he published then and later in such publications as *Writer's Digest, Writer's Review* and the *Author & Journalist* continue to be widely used today and are the instructional foundation for the highly regarded Writers of the Future Workshops. The winners attend these each year during the week climaxed by the Hubbard Achievement Awards that celebrate these winners, confer the coveted Gold Award prizes in each contest, and formally release the annual anthology. A companion workshop for the winning illustrators, embodying a strongly interactive review process among the participants and the judges, is also held each year.

L. Ron Hubbard once wrote: "A culture is only as great as its dreams and its dreams are dreamed by artists." His devotion to that ideal and his enduring legacy in the Writers and Illustrators of the Future Contests are today perpetuated by Author Services, Inc., which continues to administer those contests according to his wishes.

Winners for both the Writers and Illustrators Contests have been selected by top professionals from the very beginning. In these past twenty years, the more than 200 winning writers have contributed over 250 published novels—more than a few of them achieving *New York Times, London Times* and *USA Today* bestselling status. Collectively, more than 23 million copies of their fiction have been sold around the world.

Yet, we believe that the past is really prologue, and that the first twenty years of the Writers and Illustrators of the Future program are a triumphant preface to a still greater chapter in its history, and meanwhile, we hope that you will find *L. Ron Hubbard Presents Writers of the Future, Volume XX,* to be thoroughly provocative and entertaining.

William J. Widder
Author of *Master Storyteller—An Illustrated Tour of the Fiction of L. Ron Hubbard*

# MONKEY SEE, MONKEY DEDUCE

*Written by*
**Jonathan Laden**

*Illustrated by*
**Laura Diehl**

## About the Author

*Jonathan Laden ran a used bookstore and teahouse in Tacoma, Washington for years. He now lives in Washington, D.C., with his wife, Michele Barasso, their child, dogs and cats, as well as thousands of books.*

*He started writing in 1994, then again in 1998; he says he now starts his new writing career every three months, whether he needs to or not. He presently finds many moments in the day to practice his craft, including while stuck in rush-hour traffic.*

*His work has been accepted for publication in* Neo-Opsis *and* Hadrosaur, *fan magazines, and several online magazines including* Alienskin, Bewildering Stories, Bloodsample, Chaos Theory: Tales Askew, Scifantastic, *and* Twilight Times. *He's very proud of his online credits and very grateful to the enthusiasts who have created this market for speculative fiction.*

*For more information about Jonathan, visit his website at www.JonathanLaden.com.*

## About the Illustrator

*Laura Diehl was born in Oklahoma City, Oklahoma, in 1983. She attended McKinley Elementary and enjoyed her first formal recognition as an artist when her crayon drawing of a coral reef was selected for display in the school library. Countless other drawings followed until she had covered a large portion of her family's dining room walls with unicorns, mermaids and other magical things.*

*Throughout middle school and high school she continued to practice her art, taking all of the art classes offered.*

*Before her freshman year of high school Laura got her first computer, which completely changed the way she preferred to create her art and she found that she was able to express herself through digital painting. And with her connection to the Internet, she discovered many helpful art communities and message boards through which she could interact with her digital artist peers. She also happened upon the L. Ron Hubbard Illustrators of the Future Contest website.*

*Laura is currently attending James Madison University, working toward a B.F.A. in general fine arts and taking independent study courses in illustration. In her spare time she enjoys reading fantasy and science fiction, playing video games and working on her digital art. Upon graduation she intends to pursue a career in book illustration or video-game concept art. Her portfolio can be found online at www.ArtisticEnigma.com.*

He screamed from all his mouths, then covered all his ears.

The White Coat yelled, in its own high-pitched single voice.

He turned his heads. All of him fell down, balance lost in a scattershot of images. He pulled himself up by his long, strong arms. Then fell right to the other sides. Breath came in short gasps.

The other hairless ones entered in a rush, running as fast as their thin legs carried them. They held shiny stings. He shied away and pulled himselves along the floor toward safety. Home. He was blocked and hit into and collided and tangled and confused. He screamed in his own ears; all of him couldn't get into the cage at once. He was a struggling pile of selves. A sting bit his Alpha arm.

He became sluggish. Sleep overtook him.

•••

*The pain of birth is very nearly unbearable. It is the main reason why humans must be born many months premature, early enough that the offspring is not truly sentient; the necessity that the head be small enough to pass through the mother's pelvis is secondary. Even so, emerging into the world is quite traumatic. In later life, some succumb to that hidden memory, consumed by pain they don't even recognize. Most humans are insulated by having limited consciousness at birth.*

*I wasn't so lucky. The scientist, Peter Lowen, connected some stray wires in the head of my focal body, and* voilà! *The universe exploded onto my newly formed mind in one excruciating instant.*

*I cannot stress enough how bad an idea this was. I forgave Peter for the torture he exposed me to, but I never forgot. It wasn't until much later that I realized all that Peter had done. I could not forgive him after all.*

•••

"There, there." The White Coat vocalized.

He heard the hairless one through only one pair of ears. He opened his eyes slowly. Mostly, he saw black, but the Alpha eyes could see the White Coat's pink face.

He blinked. Turned his Alpha head. Then blinked again. The dark faded from his consciousness, leaving only the Alpha sight.

"Steady, easy." The White Coat patted the hair on his Alpha shoulders.

He tried to lift his arm, but it was bound. All of them, even the Alpha. He screamed, his voice sounding strange to his own ears. Caught. Captive. Stuck. He screamed again, straining against his bonds.

The White Coat gestured.

One of the other hairless ones came into view. A sharp prick bit his thigh. His arms relaxed.

•••

*I don't know why Peter didn't kill me. He had already destroyed his first seven attempts, so he wasn't squeamish. Nor did any moral qualms stay his hand. He told me, much later, that he ought to kill me for the good of the human race.*

*They were too insecure to accept an intellect superior to their own. By then he had come to enjoy my company. I was the only one willing to indulge his feeble attempts to play chess.*

*Yet at first I showed no more external signs of emergent intelligence than had the others. Perhaps he spared me only because his grant was expiring. There would be no time to raise another group of chimps to try once again.*

*This leads me to the uncomfortable probability that my predecessors were just as self-aware as I. I mourn their passing. The hundreds of chimps who were their component parts—I don't allow myself to think of their plight at all.*

•••

He made connections, waiting there in the dark. He felt the discomfort of metal bands against the arms of each of his bodies. He flexed, trying in vain to move each neck, all together, then one by one. Only the Alpha neck turned. Only Alpha eyes opened. Only Alpha ears heard the footsteps of an approaching hairless one. All his bodies cowered in their bonds.

It was the female. His noses sniffed. His Alpha nose picked up the sure sign of estrus. He puffed out his chests to impress her. Only the Alpha chest puffed. He began to forget there were other bodies to control.

"Hi, Caps." She bared her teeth, but he did not feel threatened. She pointed to herself. "Theresa," she said slowly. Several of him had heard that sound before. It was hers. She put her hand to her mouth then took it away, spreading the fingers. "You try."

He looked at her. His stomach grumbled. Was there food? He wanted food, almost as much as he wanted to be able to run and climb around his home. She had brought her hand to her mouth. But no food.

"Theresa. Theresa. Theresa." She made that strange gesture again.

He grunted.

She bared her teeth. "Good!" She pulled a grape out of her pocket and dropped it into his mouth. His other stomachs groaned their complaints. "Again." She made the gesture. "Theresa."

"Theee," he looked around quickly. He'd never made a sound like that before. His throat felt different. Sore. As though he had lost a fight and was wounded.

"Very good." She gave him a grape. "Theresa."

"Theere," he said.

"Nice." She bared her teeth. Backing up to the entrance, she hit a button on the wall. The bands around his arms emitted a snapping sound. She tossed a hand of bananas at his chest.

He caught it. His Alpha arms were free.

"I'm going to fuel your processing array. I'll be right back."

He did not know what her vocalizations meant. But the bananas were delicious. After the female was gone for a time, his other stomachs stopped complaining.

•••

*Theresa Finch was a better person than Peter, but complicitous nonetheless. She cared for me—all of me—so was aware of the meaning of what had been done. Still, her concern for my well-being was genuine from the first, as far as it went.*

*If not for Theresa's patient tutoring, I would not have learned English, and it would have all ended there. It was many long months before I could read the storybooks she brought me, and months after that before I was capable of understanding texts of mathematics and physics.*

*They never intended that I learn biology. But any laboratory is bound to have materials relating to its field. I stole and read them because I knew my vision of the world was incomplete. Without the basics, it took me some time to integrate the knowledge these papers contained.*

*But in time I understood all too well. I turned my thoughts away, never drawing obvious conclusions.*

•••

"Checkmate!" Peter smiled, genuine surprise on his face. Then he frowned. "Is your array malfunctioning, Caps?" He stood hurriedly. "I had better check all the connections."

"No need." Caps's mind was as sharp as ever. He reached a long arm to rest on Peter's shoulder. "I lost. That's all. My systems are fine."

Peter gazed through narrowed eyes. "Is something distracting you, perhaps? Are you thinking about your last lesson with Theresa?"

Caps flipped the chessboard over. The stone pieces clattered to the floor. He scampered around the lab, whooping and jumping on countertops. A few minutes later, he came to rest, hanging upside down from the light fixture by Peter's head. "Why can't I just lose without it being the end of the world?"

Peter shook his finger at Caps. Caps knew the scientist hated to watch his charge use the lab as a jungle gym. Which is why Caps did it. "Because you have 400 billion neurons at your disposal and I have one-fourth as many. Because you haven't lost once in the last hundred games we've played. And frankly," Peter's face relaxed into a small smile, "because I'm not very good at chess."

"That's true, you aren't." Caps nodded. He felt the shadow of an urge to jump on Peter's head, but remained still. "Have you considered the possibility that I lost to make you feel better?"

Peter puckered, as if he'd eaten a lemon. "If you did, that would be horrible. What good is an intellect that doesn't use its full capacity?"

"It wouldn't be a matter of using less of my ability. It's really a question of pursuing a different end." Caps hadn't been paying attention to the game, but he wouldn't admit that to Peter. Not now, while the scientist was acting like such a dim White Coat. "Just because I can win each time doesn't mean I must."

"I don't accept that." Peter crossed his white-sleeved arms. "There is only one worthwhile pursuit. Knowledge in its highest, most pure form. In the game of chess, winning can be the only goal."

•••

*For all his Ph.D.'s, Peter was essentially a simple man. He hadn't the gift of wisdom, so I shouldn't hold it against him that he didn't use it.*

*Yet, the beasts in me cannot accept that rationalization. His transgressions against them are real, regardless of the narrowness of mind that prevented him seeing beyond the simple achievement that I represented.*

*I do miss chess.*

•••

Caps blinked against the strong light. He sniffed, smelling spring flowers. Then sneezed. He gripped Theresa's hand tight, and kept focused on Peter's back, two steps ahead. Caps had been born in the lab. Sun and sky and grass were mere abstractions. Until now.

"It's okay," she bent over to whisper. "There's nothing to worry about."

He glanced at the barbed wire running along the top of the distant fence. A sign warned in large letters, ELECTRIFIED: KEEP AWAY. Caps wasn't reassured.

"Where are we going?" The concrete was hard against his feet.

Peter laughed. "You'll see soon. I don't want to spoil the surprise."

Caps didn't like surprises. The hair along the back of his neck stood at attention. There was no tree in the compound, nowhere to climb in case of danger. Only slick buildings with sheer walls. He would run back to the lab and hope he had the dexterity to open that imposing door. He had watched Peter's fingers on the narrow keys of the security pad, so knew the code.

"Really. It will be fine." Theresa patted his hand with her much smaller one. "You may even find this exciting."

Peter took them past several buildings to an immense one at the far end of the compound. He typed in a new code and the door slid open.

Inside sat a large rocket. Peter held out his hands, his smile wide. "Here you go."

Caps ran around the rocket, scratching his knuckles against the hard concrete floor. It was immense. The engines were too massive for any purpose but to achieve escape velocity from Earth. He tugged on Peter's lab coat. "What's it for? Am I to be a space-rocket engineer?"

"No, there's no need for an intellect of your capacity for that. You'll be inside the ship, taking in the data from our probes of Jupiter and her moons. We'll need you to analyze data rapidly and direct changes to the study based on what you learn out there. Your discretion is essential."

"Wouldn't a computer do just as well?"

"No. Thus far computers haven't been able to make the higher level judgments that we need, and the time lag is too long for remote control. We've lost several probes in the dense Jovian atmosphere. We need you to get close enough to get the data we need, but use your smarts and your survival imperative to keep the probe from being crushed before its mission is complete. Only an organic intelligence might survive."

"You go, then." Though he had eaten recently, Caps felt an emptiness, an ethereal hunger, as though his mind were warning him away from space.

"I wish I could. Even if they would let humans fly this mission, I'm too dumb to handle the job."

Peter smelled sincere.

•••

*Peter yearned for the wide-open vistas of space. As my astronautic preparations proceeded, he became less focused. Sometimes lapsing into silence in the midst of conversation. He had dreamed of exploring the vastness of the solar system since he'd been a small boy.*

*It's ironic to think that as I sit here, confined to a box smaller than my original cage in his laboratory. The room where my array rests is far larger, but I cannot enter there. Not yet.*

*Peter would enjoy looking out at space. The view from the window is spectacular. Yet no more so than the night sky from Earth, in the forests from whence my ancestors originated. Of my own volition, I would not travel untold millions of miles to see this narrow patch of sky.*

•••

The training took on a new intensity. Theresa was not only a chimp handler but also an astrophysicist. She took Caps to the flight simulator and trained him to be an astronaut. She gave him new, more advanced, physics texts. "Learn those thoroughly, and ask questions." Caps found all the new knowledge exhilarating, and exhausting.

One morning, Theresa greeted him with a wide smile on her face. "Today's the day."

"For what?" Caps wasn't sharp before downing at least one banana, or a good-sized plum.

She took him by the hand and exited the lab. "You're going to space today."

"No." Sweat formed on his palms. He pulled away, dragging her back toward the safety of the lab. "I'm not ready."

"Don't be silly. Of course you are." Theresa stopped, her grip tight.

Caps stopped too. He wouldn't harm her.

"I wouldn't let them send you if I wasn't confident in your ability. Do you believe me?"

Slowly he nodded. She had earned his trust.

"Good. Now that's settled. Let's go. Peter is waiting for you."

Caps walked on the concrete. "I'd like to play one last game of chess before I depart."

"I'm sure Peter would like that, if there's time. You'll be glad to know your shipboard computer has been programmed to play chess." She chuckled. "It'll give you a bit more of a challenge than Peter did."

Caps nodded. Before the path wound away from the only home he'd ever known, he turned back for one last look.

"Don't . . ." Theresa started, but then she stopped. He had already seen the immobilized chimpanzees being carried out the front door, the metal caps on their heads reflecting the morning sun.

"There were chimps like me in the building all along? Why didn't you tell me? I would have liked to meet them."

Her face was frozen. "They are you." She tapped his head. "Under the directions of this head, the brains of those sixteen chimps make up your processing array. I thought you knew."

He closed his Alpha eyes and discovered he did know, ever since he'd finished reading the stray papers in the lab. The phantom urges he felt to move, the ghost pangs of hunger and then satiation he had always felt. The whisper of panic that hid deep in the recesses of his mind. He had come to dismiss these as the shadows of intelligence, part of the natural disconnect of a sentient mind from its own body. The memory of emergence had been firmly blocked; they came free in a flood that nearly knocked Caps off his feet.

"Free them," he said, when he trusted himself to speak again.

She shook her head. "They are part of you. If I were to disconnect them, you would cease to exist."

Caps was too fascinated by the world to even consider such a possibility. He began to understand the human concept of guilt. "I must see them."

Theresa held him tight. "You don't want to do that."

"I must." She would not stop him. He walked steadily back, dragging her behind him. "Stop, technicians. I must inspect the array." The men stopped.

He peered at the first few chimps. Long antennas protruded from the metal caps atop their heads. Their eyes, nostrils and ears were sealed off in black plastic. Their expressions were blank. Feeling with mental muscles he had forgotten he had, he could discern a shadow of hunger, and frozen fear.

Later, when Peter offered to play chess, Caps refused.

•••

*Even the most intelligent of beings will hold onto their worldviews in the face of overwhelming contrary evidence. Especially in cases where self-interest dictates an advantage to maintaining the status quo. There are many elaborate terms for the phenomenon, but the simple term "denial" is as accurate as any.*

*For the first portion of my trip, I was in denial.*

•••

The flight to space was exciting. Weightlessness was new. Caps enjoyed the acrobatics that it made possible, even in the tightly confined space of the cabin. There was too little work for him to do. He checked all the systems three times per wake period. He took in the meager data of the voyage out to the gas giant, and transmitted his analysis to the scientists on Earth. He also spent a good amount of time staring out the window into space.

When he could think of no other activities he studied the intricacies of the spaceship. He understood the simple navigation controls, but many others were not as clear at first. Gradually, he came to understand that the ship had remote monitors and overrides that would allow the people on Earth to pilot his craft if he were in danger. Or if they wanted to send him careening into the crushing gravity well of Jupiter. Caps set about disabling them. He also found a bit of free space on the computer, and began to keep a journal.

After three weeks, Caps couldn't avoid it any longer. His thoughts returned to his array every few seconds. When he could sleep at all, he dreamed of smelling nothing but the inside of his nostrils, of hearing only the echo of his own heartbeat, of seeing darkness blacker than a starless sector.

He stopped caring about the data the sensors of the ship provided. He didn't eat for two days. He picked several patches bald on his arms and chest without even realizing that he was doing it.

When he looked down and saw his mangy body, Caps knew he must act. He had to go into the storage area. Approaching slowly, he peeked into the room where the array bodies were lined up, angled on slabs. Feeding tubes ran into the chimps, and waste tubes ran out. He turned away holding an arm over his mouth, barely getting out of the room. Though gravity had returned to one-quarter Earth normal in the rotating ship, he was space-sick for the first time.

After a sleepless rest period, he forced himself to return. He was queasy but moved forward anyway. There were nine females and seven males on the metal slabs. He set about figuring out how to loosen the bonds that kept the bodies bound insensate.

Caps succeeded in another month. He unsealed the eyes of one body, then another, until all sixteen were clear. Then, flexing mental pathways long degenerated, forced the eyes to open.

His focal self fell straight to the floor, a kaleidoscope of images flooding his mind. He could see the room from all angles, all at once. The images moved, sometimes overlapping, sometimes diverging. It was fascinating, so much more than he'd been able to perceive with the chimps of his array blocked from sensory input. He put his hand over his focal eyes. It gave him a massive mind ache. But at least the shadow of frozen fear stuck at the edge of his consciousness began to loosen.

He needed to learn to control all sixteen bodies of his array in addition to the Alpha "server" that he had treated as his only body for so long. It would not be an easy task. Fortunately, Caps had plenty of time available. He made steady progress.

•••

*I thought of the array chimps as pawns, each able to perceive a different portion of the board from their limited perspective. My focal self was the queen, just as limited in its perceptions, but so much more powerful in its capability. I, of course, was the chess player, controlling the entirety of the board, or—in this case—the array storage area, at once. Unlike in chess, all the pieces could move simultaneously through an infinite universe of possible moves. Even Spassky might have been daunted at the prospect.*

*Peter would have approved of my single-minded focus on winning this chess match. I nearly killed myself in the effort to become puppet master over all of me. I was not entirely successful. Even at the end, when I tried to move more than one chimp at a time they stumbled about, teetering into walls, or walking into each other.*

Illustrated by Laura Diehl

*But I could integrate all of the sensory inputs with growing confidence. With naiveté worthy of a lab assistant, I kept notes of my progress to show Peter and Theresa when I returned.*

*My mastery failed to extend beyond the chessboard's edge.*

•••

Out of long habit he kept the focal chimp separate, an Alpha sergeant leading his sixteen disciples in perfectly synchronized calisthenics. They were less than zombies, mere extensions of himself. But the faint shadow of a plan began to emerge from somewhere in the network of seventeen brains that was his mind. He continued to work on building their strength, resenting the time needed to conduct the mission and keep the ship safe from excessive pressure.

Caps was finishing a strenuous session of array exercise when the incoming message beacon pinged. He hurriedly put the array into their places and ran back to the console. "Here."

After a delay of several seconds, Peter's voice came over the microphone. "Great work! We've received our next assignment. You're to help analyze the latest research into the unifying principles of the universe. A grand theory of everything! A course adjustment is being sent to your computer. You'll be meeting me on the space station." Caps's head sank against the cushioned neckrest of his chair.

"If I refuse?" he asked flatly. He closed his Alpha eyes in the ensuing silence. Immediately his vision shifted to the array storage room. By looking from side to side he could see that the chimps were okay.

"Refuse? Why would you refuse?" Peter paused, then continued in a rush. "This assignment is a promotion. We'll talk when we rendezvous."

Caps opened his eyes. He looked at the photo of Peter Lowen, hands stuffed in his lab coat, warm fatherly smile on his face. Speaking to the photo, Caps said, "No."

"You can't say no," Peter shouted over the microphone several seconds later. "You've accomplished so much, much more than I ever dreamed possible. Every time I talk to you, I become more certain. You are the achievement of my life."

"I won't do it." Caps inhaled. The cockpit smelled clean, but the array storage room was getting stale. Too many sweaty chimp bodies were stuck in too small a space. The ventilation system hadn't been designed to handle such a heavy load. He'd fix that as soon as this call was over.

"You have accomplished what I only dreamed of, and this is only the beginning." He sounded subdued. "I am so proud of you. Meet me on the station. Don't make any rash decision. We'll play chess like old times and talk."

Caps closed his eyes. All his eyes. Speaking hurt his chest. "I'm not your pawn."

"You must come," the White Coat yelled. "You overgrown ape. I order you to be there!"

Caps turned off the radio. He tore the console out of the wall and smashed it against the bulkhead. In the array storage room, thirty-two arms twitched in sympathetic exertion.

•••

*I have sent the last of the information raw. I will not waste any more time discerning its patterns. I no longer care what story the data has to tell about the formation of gas giants, or the implications for planets orbiting other stars. Let Peter stew on all that. I wash my hands of it and of him. Earth beckons.*

•••

The spaceship set down deep in the Amazon rain forest. Though Caps longed to go to his native habitat, it was the first place Peter would look. The remaining wild areas in Africa were far too small to hide a tribe of metal-plate-headed chimps.

He looked at the bodies of his array. Their useless antennas would break off in time, on an overhead branch or in the wrestling and grooming that were part of being a chimpanzee. He had built them up with the clumsy exercises, but they were not nearly as strong as they should be. They hadn't moved under full Earth gravity in years. They had never lived in nature, only in the confines of a lab. Would they survive? Would their minds return to them once the network was severed? All Caps could do was hope.

•••

*I would have liked to leave the ship in the forest. To jump from tree to tree, confident in the unconscious geometric knowledge that would prevent me from falling. I have never been in surroundings where I felt truly at home, and now I never will. I couldn't trust myself to walk away if my focal self set foot in the lush greenery that lay just beyond the metal hatch. The smells and sights and sounds I receive from the chimps of the array only increase the pain of not fully being there.*

*Like Peter, I find myself watching my progeny venture where I may not follow. I too know what it is to yearn.*

•••

Caps set course for Burundi and the few acres of scraggly preserve he hoped remained there. Without access to a room full of sophisticated equipment, he couldn't disable the array, except by exceeding the range of the network. The Alpha would have to fend for himself.

Caps leaned back, eyes closed, savoring his last thoughts. Already he felt fuzzy, the microsecond delay impairing his ability to think naturally. Almost he turned around, but as his hands took hold of the controls, the ghosts of chimp minds grew stronger on the network. It was working! He whispered, "Soon you too will be able to live again, free of human thoughts." He hugged himself to pat his Alpha back.

"Caps!" Theresa's voice came from behind the bulkhead. Evidently there was a second emergency radio. "Why aren't you at the lunar station? What are you doing?"

"I'm on the verge of nirvana, Theresa."

"What?" Her panic came through, even louder than the static, instantly. She was somewhere on Earth.

"I've released the array." He paced the cabin, walking on his knuckles. There were no trees in this spaceship. A design flaw.

"They'll just die."

He shrugged. Part of him knew she could not see him, but it was easier, so much more natural than speaking. He thought hard, straining to reach his ever more distant memories and formulate words for

Theresa. "They might not. I could feel the shadow of their suffering behind my every thought."

"No." Theresa's voice was strained, as though she was on the verge of tears. "You just imagined that, Caps. They didn't suffer. Now you're going to die."

He shrugged again. "It was real to me." Caps closed his eyes, thinking hard to find the concept. There. "They didn't volunteer to be my subsidiary processors, wasting away in the dark. If I didn't release them, I couldn't live with myself."

Now she was crying. It hurt his ears, but he made himself listen. "You'll cease to exist without them. You'll die."

"As it must be."

"You're not saving chimpanzees. Peter will just create another chimpanzee array processing system. You know that."

"It's not easy to connect brains into a working massively parallel processor." The idea came to him quickly. It must have been stored in the Alpha's gray matter.

"No, but it can be done again. With what he has in the old lab, it wouldn't be impossible."

"Without it?"

"Without the information, I don't know. Peter might not get another grant for years, or he could get one in six months. You're slurring," she yelled. "You must return to your array now."

He reached for the navigation controls, and changed his course.

•••

*Father. Peter. So long. I hope this stops you.*

*I'm sorry, Alpha. You'll never know freedom, now. Goodbye, Theere.*

•••

The Alpha traveled through the air, higher than the tallest tree. He climbed the walls of the small space, trying to find a way out. He ripped off the metal seat and threw it against the patch of clear wall. The wall bounced but didn't break.

The ship descended. He stared out the window. It was familiar; a large building in a treeless compound. Home! He jumped around the cabin, throwing himself at every wall in frantic succession.

The building grew larger through the clear wall. The engines screamed louder. The building came faster and faster.

The ship hit. Heat, flames, pain. Pain.

His shouts sounded strange to his own ears—like the high-pitched vocalizations of the hairless ones.

# BOTTOMLESS

*Written by*
**Luc Reid**

*Illustrated by*
**Robert Drozd**

## About the Author

*Luc Reid made up his mind to be a writer in the first grade. Since college he has made his living primarily with computers, but devotes the great majority of his creative time to speculative fiction.*

*In 2003 he saw his first professional fiction publication in the eZine* Abyss & Apex; *and in August of that year he attended the Writers of the Future writing workshop and the L. Ron Hubbard Achievement Awards in Hollywood as a published finalist in* Writers of the Future, Volume XIX, *with his story "A Ship That Bends." It was shortly before his trip to Hollywood that Luc learned he was a contest winner this year with his novelette "Bottomless."*

*Luc now lives in Burlington, Vermont, with his wife and two young children, where he works at the marketing firm of Kelliher Samets Volk. He continues writing short stories regularly, and is making final edits on his novel,* Voices of Gods and Demons, *and is writing a young-adult fantasy novel set in fourteenth-century Lombardy,* The Brazen Adder. *His website is located at www.lucreid.com.*

## About the Illustrator

*Robert Drozd was born in 1969 in Zagreb, Croatia. He never studied art or design in college but has been in the graphic design business for some time. He currently works as a designer in a graphic design company producing advertising projects for a variety of clients in the areas of medicine, technology, tourism and other small-business ventures. He also does freelance work at home.*

*As part of his personal trademark, Robert likes to implement a little 3-D to his projects when the job allows it. He has been moving more and more toward the illustration side of things, which will in the future include album and book covers, as well as comic art.*

*Science fiction and fantasy illustration are subjects Robert enjoys as both leisure pastimes and possible future occupations. A friend told him about the L. Ron Hubbard Illustrators of the Future Contest and one of the main reasons he sent in an entry was the fact that all entries are judged by professional artists in that field. He feels competition is a challenge and a great way to learn new things, to get more experience, to meet other people who share the same interests and to be inspired by their work.*

*Robert believes the greatest happiness in life is to do what one likes for a living, but finds that very difficult to achieve in a small country such as his. To have fun creating art and get paid for it at the same time, now that would be something.*

Ánp clung to a rock face on the side of the bottomless pit, stealing apples. Through the branches of the tree, which was rooted on a narrow ledge some way off from the main village, Ánp could see the Sun Thread hanging in the exact center of the Pit and slowly beginning to turn its bright side, the day side, toward him. Far, far beyond that he could make out the far wall of the Pit, of streaked gray rock, with the familiar protrusions of the Giant's Nose and Split Rock about to disappear into nighttime. Above and below, the Pit continued farther than anyone had ever climbed, with the Sun Thread suspended in the middle and vanishing eventually into clouds in both directions. Likely as not, the Pit and the Sun Thread went on forever, although as far as Ánp knew the only way to find out would be to jump.

The question of whether there was a bottom tormented him. Sometimes Ánp was tempted to jump just to find out. But it was harder to decide which was worse: If the Pit did have a bottom, and he only knew of it for a few brief seconds before striking it; or if it didn't, and he continued falling forever—or at any rate, until he died of thirst or hit an outcropping. The dream of a kind of falling that was like flying, far into unknown places, was exhilarating. And the dream had to suffice.

The morning was nearly silent, the only sounds being the faint rustle of a mild breeze, the distant bleating of goats in their pens or on shelf pastures, and a slight shifting of rock, probably some animal moving across a ledge. The air smelled of apples and the faint smoke of cooking fires burning dried dung and brush.

*This is the last time, the very last time,* he promised himself when he had a good dozen apples in his bag. He felt bad about stealing even this time, it being Eni's family who owned the trees. He flushed at the thought of being humiliated in front of Eni; her family would never consider an offer of marriage after something like that. Too bad he hadn't fallen in love with her *before* he started stealing apples. Then again, he wasn't sure he would have been willing to give that bit of dietary variety up. Ánp's family were luckless goatherders, and were never able to afford apples or much of anything else. If he stopped borrowing them every once in a while, they'd be eating nothing but oats for months at a time, only relieved by an occasional bowl of goat soup.

"Thief!" someone shouted from below. Ánp froze, too frightened even to turn. It sounded like an adult voice. In fact, it sounded like Huhnun, whose wife's family owned this tree.

"I'll throw you in for this, you little sneak!" An empty threat, even coming from a man as mean as Huhnun, in a rage. Surely Huhnun would never defy the Thrower, throwing something into the Pit himself and risking being banished for a few lousy apples.

Ánp clambered up the cliff toward Khenkh, the next village. It was a half-day's climb there, and he'd probably have to hide the bag of apples somewhere along the way, where it might be disturbed by animals or lost in the unfamiliar territory. Would Huhnun follow him that far? Probably not. Probably Ánp could lay low there for a few weeks, and when he came home he could carry some of the trade goods. People would be so happy to see things from up-Pit, they'd probably protect him from Huhnun. He hoped.

Ánp climbed faster.

Rratah, his little brother, would be worried about him. His parents would guess where he had been, even though they had never discussed the source of the mysterious apples, but they wouldn't be able to tell Rratah his brother was a thief. But so be it; it certainly wasn't safe to go back right away. Anyway, he had only ever been to Khenkh twice, and he was eager to see other villages, with their foreign ways and unfamiliar faces.

When he had been climbing for a good ten minutes, he found a convenient shelf and used it to look down, just in case Huhnun was following him, which of course he wouldn't be, because it was only a few apples. Well, a few apples each week ever since they had started to ripen. Ánp began feeling a little nervous, thinking about this. How many apples *had* he stolen from those trees?

No Huhnun. Nothing but bare rock as far as he could see. Some wisps of cloud drifted past the apple orchard far below. He could barely make out the trees. He settled back and let out a sigh of relief, letting the cool rock dry up the sweat that trickled down his back while he squinted into the Sun Thread that hung, an infinite line in the center of the Pit.

Huhnun's face appeared over the edge of the shelf. "Aha!" He had been beneath the shelf when Ánp looked for him.

"I can explain," Ánp said.

"'No one explains climbing to a goat,'" Huhnun quoted, and grabbed Ánp by his goatskin chest belt, pushed him along to a corner of the shelf where Ánp could barely hold on with his heels, the shelf was so thin. A chip of rock broke loose and tapped, tapped, against the cliff as it fell. Ánp hoped it didn't kill anyone down-Pit.

"Please, I'll give the apples back," Ánp said. "Don't turn me in to the Thrower." The Thrower was a good man, a wise man, but he was also responsible for meting out justice in the tribe, and he was good enough at it to make Ánp feel itchy. Something creatively devised, fitting, and extremely dull was in store for him, he was sure.

"Oh, I have no intention of taking you to the Thrower," Huhnun said, sliding a knife—a precious knife made from metal by a mysterious tribe far down-Pit, a family treasure that Ánp knew Huhnun carried everywhere.

"It's only apples!" Ánp cried.

"Only apples? *Only* apples? Do you know what my wife's family has done to me over these many months, over *only* apples? Do you have any idea the humiliation I have suffered? Do you know we've had so few apples, we haven't been able to trade for meat in weeks?" Huhnun seemed crazed with anger, and Ánp couldn't entirely blame him. Huhnun's wife, Zhehühü, was sweet (if a little feebleminded), but her mother, though the matriarch of that clan, lay in the darkness of the clan cave wasting away with a painful illness, and it was well known her pain made her vindictive. "A goat in pain will sooner kick than give milk," as the saying went.

But looking at the knife, Ánp's sympathy dried up quickly.

"Stealing apples! I'll teach you to steal apples!" whispered Huhnun, and he slashed at him.

Ánp tottered, and for a sickening and embarrassing moment, he thought he might fall from the cliff, like a stupid baby left untended. His whole family would be shamed. He circled his arms wildly, grabbed a tiny foothold with the toes of one foot, willed himself to fall back against the cliff. Finally his balance returned, and he clawed at the rock until his back was pressed close against it. Hawks drifted in the breeze, far out from the cliff, circling the Sun Thread.

"Gotcha," said Huhnun, and he lunged with the knife.

Ánp didn't have time to think, but he scrabbled with his palms and his toes and managed to find purchase on the cliff, climbing up just enough for the knife to go beneath his feet. Huhnun wasn't good with it; Ánp would have been badly cut by now if he had been. Was Huhnun trying to kill him? Probably not. Probably just to scar him, to mark him, make him remember not to steal apples. Well, Ánp wasn't going to have any trouble remembering this day, scar or no scar. Maybe he should just brace himself and let Huhnun cut him. Then at least it would be over, and he wouldn't have to risk falling.

But he never had the chance. Huhnun's awkward jab had left him off balance, and he fell forward on the shelf, slipping off to one side. Huhnun gave a shriek and scrambled for a handhold, finding it only a moment later—but in trying to grab onto the rock, he hadn't held onto the knife firmly and it jarred out of his hand against the cliff. Ánp watched in bug-eyed horror as the unblessed object plummeted down, only a few feet out from the cliff wall, noiselessly. He gaped at Huhnun. Huhnun howled with dismay.

Would the Thrower banish Huhnun for this? Surely you couldn't be banished for an accident. But such a treasure! And so dangerous!

"You," Huhnun said. "You did this! You made my knife fall into the Pit. I was only trying to scare you, scare some sense into you. Little thief! Cursed little thief! You did this!"

Ánp could think of nothing to say, wondering if Huhnun would grab him and throw him into the Pit behind the knife after all and wishing fervently for that to not happen. To his great relief, Huhnun climbed down off the ledge and began making his way down the cliff. Twenty or thirty body-lengths down, Huhnun looked up and shouted again, "You did this!"

•••

For safety, and because he was eager to see a different village again, Ánp went to Khenkh anyway to wait until it all blew over. Since they didn't have much need of him there, he made a temporary living from harvesting blueberries from the more dangerous sections of shelf, ones that the Khenkh villagers didn't care to risk themselves on.

He was on one of these, having been in Khenkh for more than a week, when he saw a figure climbing up the wall, and for a moment he was afraid it was Huhnun, still angry and tired of waiting. He realized with relief, though, that it was only a young boy. After another moment he recognized his brother Rratah's faded orange shouldercloth. Rratah waved. Ánp went back to picking blueberries, so as not to seem approving of his brother making the dangerous climb.

Rratah was exhausted when he hauled himself up onto a nearby rock shelf. "I'm here!" he gasped.

"Dad will have you sleeping on the ledge for a week if he finds out you climbed up here."

"I missed you. It's boring down there."

Ánp sighed, unable to maintain his disapproval. "Well, it's boring up here, too. You made a big climb for nothing."

"Someday I'm going to climb so high I'll discover a city."

"There's no such thing," Ánp said, but he felt the same dreamy excitement for that myth that he heard in Rratah's voice. "Hey, don't you think Mom and Dad will have missed you already?"

Ánp would have liked to share Rratah's company longer, but the thought of him making the difficult climb back down made him anxious, and he wanted him to get down before night fell. There was no help for Rratah having to climb down; it wasn't as though someone else could safely carry him.

"Hah. I'm going to climb up for days and days and find a city someday. And their Thrower will be a K!ahum, and I'll get him to teach me magic tricks."

"There's no such thing as a K!ahum either. Nobody can fly."

"I'll bet they have *two* K!ahum. And they fly in and out of the city, and they'll teach everyone how to make stones talk and how to fly, so that someday it will be a whole *city* of K!ahum. And when I learn how, I'll be a K!ahum myself, and I'll fly down here and they'll make me Thrower. Then I'll teach everyone magic, and someday we'll make the Pit into Ümah, the flat world where you throw something to the air and it falls right back to you."

It was getting late; the dark side of the Sun Thread was already masking the light, meaning that there was probably not much more than a quarter day left. Ánp shook his head. Not enough time to be sure Rratah could make the climb safely, even though, admittedly, Rratah was an excellent climber.

"You'd better stay here tonight so you don't get stuck on the cliff when it gets dark," Ánp said, tying up his berry bag.

"Wow! Can I?"

"Don't be so happy. Mom and Dad will be crazy with worry about you being gone all night. You'll probably be sleeping outside the cave the rest of your life."

"They're more worried about you now."

"Huhnun?"

"Yeah. He said—"

"I know. I just was hoping it would blow over before I went back home."

"It didn't look like a blow-overy thing to me."

"Well, I guess I might as well go back and get it over with," Ánp said. "Come on, we'll trade some of these for some dinner and get some sleep on a ledge somewhere. I'll climb down with you tomorrow morning."

"Don't worry, Ánp. I know you didn't do it."

"Yeah," Ánp said. He should have known Rratah wouldn't believe ill of him, even though he had sat and eaten the apples with the rest of the family while Ánp and his parents had carefully avoided talking about where they had come from.

•••

The apples were lost somewhere. Ánp hadn't been able to locate the niche where he had finally put them, exhausted from carrying the bag, on the way up.

When they finally climbed down into the village, Rratah went on ahead to tell their parents they were home, still as cheerful as though they wouldn't mind his absence, but Ánp went straight to the Thrower.

No one spoke when he swung down off the cliff into the huge Dance Cave, a bag of trade goods from Khenkh on his back. There were women there, curing hides on the wide cave floor and stinking the cave up with the foul smells of their curing, but when they saw him they turned their heads and cut short their gabble of gossip and jokes.

It was unnaturally quiet as he climbed the stair tunnel toward the little cave where the Thrower lived with his two sons and their wives and children. Ánp had thought for a long time about what he should do when he returned, and he had realized that there would be no better time to appear before the Thrower and confess to the theft of the apples than when he was carrying trade goods from Khenkh. It was too difficult to climb to other villages to get trade goods from even that nearby often—and Khenkh had an expert beadworker, who had sent goods with Ánp on the expectation of eventually receiving payment when the next climber from Ánp's village came to Khenkh. If Ánp was lucky, the Thrower would be happy to see the trade goods and might go a little easier on him than he otherwise would.

The Thrower was on his ledge, looking out over the Pit, when Ánp reached the top of the stairs. Too nervous to speak, Ánp walked silently toward him across the cave floor.

"Ánp, the goatherd," the Thrower said, without turning. "Come sit next to me." He whistled a strange whistle, and Ánp glimpsed Pahoh, the Thrower's oldest son, appearing from the depths of the cave and running down the stairs. What was a grown man doing, moving in such a hurry? But Ánp didn't think it was safe to ask. He sat next to the Thrower, gently placing the bag of trade goods in easy reach. The Thrower ignored it.

"Do you know what this is?" the Thrower said, and he showed Ánp a gleaming splinter of something that had no color, like water. Ánp shook his head.

"I know what it is," said the Thrower. "It is death. Some careless person far up-Pit dropped a thing, of which this was a piece. The thing hit the edge of Mehü's cave, and this piece broke off and flew inside, cutting her granddaughter's hand. It needs no name other than death." The Thrower coughed, a racking cough, and Ánp saw that some of the spittle he coughed was pink. The Thrower was sick?

"What shall I do with it?" the Thrower said, when he finally recovered.

"Honored Thrower, I couldn't presume to tell—"

"You know as well as I!" the Thrower said sternly. "What is to be done with this piece of death? Is it to be kept in our homes, left here to hurt someone again?"

"No," Ánp whispered.

"No, it is not!" cried the Thrower. "It is to be thrown away! It is to be discarded, forever, so that we will never see it!" And he threw the bright thing out into the Pit. Ánp ran to the edge, unable to keep himself from watching the Thrower's perfect cast as the splinter arced unerringly toward the Sun Thread, spiraled around it for a moment, and then vanished into it. It had still been close enough for Ánp to see it when it struck the Sun Thread, to be burned into nothing. The Thrower discarded things this way nearly every week, but it was rare that Ánp was present to see it. The perfection of the throw was always overwhelming to him.

"Ánp!" cried a voice, and he turned to recognize his mother. She was holding her arms out to him, as though to embrace him, but she didn't move from where she stood next to his father, who looked unusually rigid, among a throng that must have already included most of the villagers, with more coming up the stairs every moment in respectful silence. Eni was there, in the shadows of the cave, looking directly at him. Ánp thought she should have looked furious with him, but instead she looked stricken, and after a moment she looked entirely away.

There must have been forty people there, more than Ánp had ever seen outside a festival. His stomach began to feel sour.

"There he is!" cried another voice, and although Ánp turned toward it, he already knew to whom it belonged. "He threw my knife, my family treasure, into the Pit!" Huhnun strode out of the crowd, looking authoritative and certain, toward the Thrower.

"I didn't throw that knife!" Ánp said. He turned to the Thrower. "Huhnun was trying to cut me with it, and he lost his footing and dropped it."

Huhnun laughed, an easy laugh. "Lost my footing? A man who spends his days tending apple trees, climbing up and down cliffs on footholds smaller than your family's honor? You are lying. You were afraid when I showed you my knife, to scare you out of stealing any more of my family's hard-won apples, and you took it from me and threw it in the Pit in fear."

Ánp looked to the Thrower. He would realize that Huhnun was lying, wouldn't he? Even if Huhnun was doing a good job of it. Even if it was easy to believe.

"You stole Huhnun's family's apples, many times," the Thrower said.

"Yes," Ánp said. "But I didn't—"

"And this time," the Thrower said, raising his voice, "this time, you were caught."

"But I—"

"*This* time," thundered the Thrower, "Huhnun frightened you. He came at you with his knife? Isn't this so?"

"I didn't throw the knife! He dropped it!"

"You are accused!" the Thrower said. "You are accused by a man who has always been honest, you who are a thief of sweets. You were not satisfied with what the gods had given your family, and you had to take what had been given to others."

"Yes! I'm sorry, yes!"

"And you are banished."

The cave echoed with the word, then went silent. Ánp stared at the Thrower in disbelief.

"For stealing apples?" he squeaked. "For stealing just a few apples to eat?"

"For throwing a knife! Huhnun has no reason to lie; therefore, we know that he is telling the truth. But you have admitted yourself to being a thief, and therefore dishonest. Your face is lost to us. You will not drink from our spring. When you die, your flesh will not make our gardens fertile." And he turned his back.

At this signal, the other villagers turned their backs on him as well, some immediately, others reluctantly. Ánp's mother paused for a moment longer than the rest, but finally she turned, too, starting the mourning wail, which echoed from the walls and gathered strength as other women took it up. Rratah tried to run to him, but

Ánp's father held him back. Eni was not wailing with the other women, but she was turned away from him, Huhnun's hand gripping her shoulder tightly.

If she hadn't, his punishment might be made more severe, Ánp knew that, but it didn't make the turning any easier to stand.

"I didn't throw the knife! I didn't!" he shouted, and ran frantically among the villagers, the people he had known all his life, but they turned away from him as quickly as they could each time they saw him. Finally the Thrower's son Pahoh spoke, in a quiet voice as harsh as sand in oatmeal:

"Don't force my father to throw you too, boy. Go!"

There was no taboo preventing the Thrower from enforcing his judgments, or from throwing things into the Pit. A chill ran down Ánp's back and he reeled back from Pahoh. After a moment, he ran to the mouth of the cave and began climbing down.

He looked up only once, when he was far below the cave. No one was looking back down at him.

•••

It was as though his world had been stolen from him. Everything was wrong; there was nothing he could cling to for comfort. He had never felt this lost before. No; there had been one time. When the Sun Thread had flickered. When he was young, hundreds of weeks younger than Rratah was now.

He had been gathered with his parents in their cave, eating a thin gruel for breakfast. His mother was big with Rratah at that time, and the Sun Thread shone indifferently into their cave as it always had, gleaming from the right as it slowly rotated to the day side after the long night.

And then he had found himself drifting in the air. His mother screamed and his father cursed, and similar sounds came from all across the village. Just as frighteningly, the Sun Thread was flickering on and off, as though someone were waving a hand in front of his face to block the light.

Despite that, Ánp's terror was mixed with delight. He was flying, and he had always dreamed of flying. He thought a K!ahum had come and instantaneously taught everyone to fly. The Sun Thread's flicker was strange, but no stranger than the floating, and the floating was nice.

Then it had all ended, abruptly, after only a few short moments. He fell to the floor, as did everyone and everything else. There were shrieks echoing across the Pit from the village, but the Sun Thread was shining steadily again and everything was back to normal. Ánp had laughed, and his father had looked at him with a mixture of amazement and disgust. The village had talked of nothing else for a dozen weeks, this unthinkable and unheard-of occurrence. It had been decided that the gods were dissatisfied, and they had returned to the ancient practice of pitching a live goat to the Sun Thread every harvest festival.

It was a little like that now, except that things weren't going to return to normal. It wouldn't end; he wouldn't find himself sitting on the floor and laughing. The humiliation and shock of the banishment hadn't worn off and didn't seem likely to do so soon, but there was one good thing about this unexpected trip. He would be able to journey to a far village, farther away than most people climbed in a lifetime. Perhaps there they might know more about the Pit. Perhaps they could even see the bottom from there.

Or maybe he would give up on ever returning home and become a journeyer, climbing down from one village to the next, carrying trade goods short- and longways, always searching for the bottom. Maybe he would be the one to find that answer.

In which case Eni would marry someone else, certainly. She might do that soon anyway, since with Ánp gone her prospects were fewer than before. He had seen a couple of young men about his age in Khenkh; he imagined one of them climbing down to Aumah to court Eni, and a bitter taste filled his mouth. He spat carelessly into the Pit.

He also wanted to put some distance between himself and his home village, because there was always the danger that Huhnun or someone who had believed Huhnun's story would come trading and cause his banishment from that place, too. Yet he didn't want to journey too far, because his only hope of returning home was to make friends in some other village, and to someday convince someone to venture up-Pit to trade with Aumah and ask the Thrower to reconsider his banishment. And that should be sooner rather than later, because the facts of the matter would begin to fade in people's mind, until there was no recollection of anything that might support his case.

So Ánp didn't head for the next village down, or the one after, tiny Unng, but continued down past these to Götöp, a modest village two and a half days down-Pit that no one from his own had traded with for years. He quickly grew tired, though he was able to slake his thirst at the waterfall that emerged from the Pit near Unng and from there fell, as far as he could see, forever. He had slept only a little, and fitfully, in tiny caves or grassy shelf-meadows along the way, lengthening the day sometimes by working his way around the edge of the huge Pit in the direction the Sun Thread turned. Sometimes the way below would be blocked, or too smooth to find handholds and several times he had to climb back up considerable distances to find a way around and down. But the Pit was so wide that he was always able to find some way that was passable. He descended through areas with strange, protruding shapes of rock, and rock in many colors: familiar gray and tan as well as brown and black and even pink.

There weren't many pine trees along the way, so it was sometimes hard to find the pitch he always rubbed on his palms to protect them, and to give him a better grip. It made a grueling and dangerous climb more grueling and dangerous still.

He was always careful to find a safe place to pass the night before the Sun Thread overtook him. The unfamiliar cave walls far below his own village made the Pit menacing to him, disturbing its familiarity and making him sometimes giddy with vertigo. In the dark, it was worse, feeling the wind plucking at him, knowing an unfamiliar cliff edge was always close by.

Reaching Götöp, he found an out-of-the-way shelf corner covered with tufts of yellowed grass and fell immediately into grateful sleep.

•••

Someone was kicking him. "Wake up." A woman's voice.

*"Unh?"* Ánp said, trying to clear his mind and remember why he was lying in the grass instead of on his pallet in the cave. The Sun Thread had not turned far since he lay down to sleep, he realized. He was still worn thin from the long climb. Would he ever be able to return

to his own village, even if he could somehow get around having been banished? He wasn't sure he could ever make such a climb again. Even to get to the nearest up-Pit village, Unng, the climb had been a day and a half down, and of course it was much longer going up.

"Come on! Wake up! Who are you?" said the woman. Ánp squinted at her.

"I'm Ánp, the goatherd, from Aumah."

She stopped kicking and looked him over. She was young, not much older than Ánp himself, and exceedingly ugly. She was squat, with squinty eyes and jowly cheeks. "And what are you doing here?"

Unable to shake his exhaustion, Ánp spoke sharply. "Leave me alone. I'll talk to your Thrower. Where is he?"

The woman raised her eyebrows at him. "He? Where is *he?* I don't know where *he* is, but I can introduce you to the Thrower."

Ánp had an uncomfortable suspicion that he ought to have been polite earlier. "Do you mean . . ." he began, and trailed off. "You're saying the Thrower is a woman."

"I'm the Thrower."

"You're . . ." He wanted to call her a liar to her face. Probably she was just devilling him. He had never heard of a woman Thrower before. On the other hand, this wasn't Aumah, and on the off chance she *was* the Thrower, he had better watch himself.

"What did you do, throw something?" she said.

"No!" Ánp said hotly. He instantly wished he has spoken more gently, but it was difficult. The woman was maddening, whether she was the Thrower or not.

"You don't believe I'm the Thrower."

"I didn't say that."

"Of course not. That would be stupid. Wait here." She walked across the shelf, made her way nimbly across the wall, over the main village caves, until she was far enough away that she was difficult to see. Then she turned around and made a sweeping motion with her arm.

For a moment he wondered what she could possibly be doing, and how long he was supposed to wait. Then he felt a blow on his forehead, and he was knocked over onto his back with the surprise of it. A pebble, which had hit him squarely above the nose, bounced off into the meadow—not toward the Pit. A trickle of blood leaked down the bridge of his nose, and he sat up, amazed by the throw. The Thrower made her way back around to him. She had to be the Thrower, because that was always the person in the village who could throw better than any other, as required by his—or in this case, her—duty of throwing things away into the Sun Thread, and there was no chance that there was anyone else in this village who could throw as well as that. He could imagine the old men grumbling over it when it had come time to choose a new Thrower, but they would have had no choice, if the woman had put herself forward. In Aumah, though, no woman ever had.

"We don't get many strangers here," she said when she arrived.

"I can see why, if you throw rocks at them."

"So what *did* you do?"

"How do you know I'm not here to trade?"

She made exaggerated movements, as though she were looking over his back. "Oh, I didn't see your trade pack," she said. Of course he had nothing with him, not even the trade goods from Khenkh, which he had left with the Thrower of his own village.

"I stole apples."

"No, you didn't," she said.

"They said I threw a metal knife, but all I really did was steal apples."

"But you didn't throw the knife," she said, unconvinced.

"I certainly didn't!"

She snorted, and he opened his mouth to retort, but she waved him silent. "Don't worry. We don't have any evidence that you did anything," she said. "So we're not going to banish you on a guess. But don't let me catch you throwing anything around here. I want you to find something useful to do and keep your head down. If you cause any trouble, I'll throw you into the Pit myself." He eyed her, and had to guess that she could do it if she wanted to. He was not tall for his age, and coming from a poor family, he was skinny.

"I'm on the lookout for a husband, if you're interested," she said.

"I'll keep it in mind," he said guardedly.

She spat on the ground. "Damn it," she said, "I was hoping a foreign man would be different."

•••

Götöp was creating new space, so it was not difficult for Ánp to make a living while he was there. The Thrower had declared that those who were working on creating the new clear space must be fed by those in the village who were raising crops and goats, and she kept a close eye on contributions to this fund. So Ánp spent his days using stone and bamboo tools to carefully crack stone along a certain narrow ledge, then cart it off to a deep vertical cave that was being used for nothing else. There were no young women other than the Thrower of an age close to his own, and he put aside the thought of marriage for the moment. Maybe, he thought one day many weeks later, when the narrow ledge had become a broad but uneven road between two existing shelf-meadows, one of the younger girls would make a suitable wife for him in a few hundred weeks. At the moment the likeliest prospects were as young as his brother.

He dropped a load of rock in the vertical cave, listening with satisfaction to the crashing sound it made as it bounced against the cave walls below. It was always tempting to dump his rocks into the Pit instead, so much closer and so inviting, but like everyone else, he lived with that particular enticement every day of his life, and knew enough not to succumb.

He was sitting at the village fire, sharing dinner with the Thrower and the two men who, like him, worked each day on the new shelf, when Rratah appeared. To Ánp's amazement and delight, Rratah, some fifty weeks older than he had been when Ánp left Aumah, appeared in the mouth of the cave, outlined by the darkening Sun Thread. Ánp knew who it was even though he could see only his silhouette.

"There you are! Why'd you have to pick such a faraway village?" Rratah said.

Ánp embraced him, grinning, while the others looked on and waited to be introduced.

"Another criminal?" said the Thrower.

"There are no criminals in our family," declared Rratah. "I can prove it." Beaming, he reached into the goatskin sack on his back and pulled out something a little longer than his hand, wrapped in his orange shouldercloth.

"How did you get here?" said Ánp. A stupid question, he realized. "Do Mother and Father know you're gone?" He looked pointedly at the cloth-wrapped item, but Rratah pretended to have forgotten about it. The Thrower took it from his hand and began to unwrap it.

"Not yet. But they'll forget all about that when I bring you home with me."

"I'm banished. Or did you forget?"

Rratah shrugged his shoulders. "Most people don't believe you did it. Huhnun keeps changing the story. I doubt even his own family believes him now." And he winked at Ánp.

"The Thrower believed him."

"The *new* Thrower doesn't. It's Pahoh." Rratah reached into the common bowl and took a strip of goat meat, dipped it in pepper sauce, and began chewing.

"But the Thrower—"

"The old Thrower's dead," Rratah said with a full mouth. "He had lung demons that caused him—"

"A metal knife!" said the Thrower of Götöp in awe. Ánp turned and gaped. Even if Pahoh wouldn't have been willing to reverse the banishment already, surely if he brought the knife back—

"I found it on the way down," Rratah said. "It was a long way away, but with the Sun Thread shining on it, it gleamed so that it was easy to see. It was wedged in some rocks."

Ánp gave a holler of delight and leapt on his brother, hugging and pummeling him. The two other men at the fire laughed with him as they bent over the knife to examine it, but the Thrower made a sour noise.

"It will take many more weeks to finish the shelf," she complained, then broke off. "Who's that?" she said. "Your father?"

Ánp looked over Rratah's shoulder. There, swinging into the cave from above, was Huhnun. "Watch out!" he shouted, and he pulled his brother with him into a gap in the cave wall that led out onto another ledge. He could hear shouting from within the cave, and the sound of Huhnun's bare feet slapping the cave floor as he climbed up. Rratah scampered after him, but he pointed to a high shelf where there was an outcropping of rock. "Over there!" he said. "Hide!" And for once Rratah had no comment and did as he was told.

Laboring up the cliff, Ánp wondered for a moment what Huhnun could be doing in Götöp. After a moment, though, he realized what his return to Aumah could mean for the older man. If the new Thrower decided in Ánp's favor, Huhnun might be banished himself, and he would certainly be humiliated. Probably he had realized his danger when Rratah was found to be gone. Which meant that he intended to kill both of them; anything less and there would be at least one brother to denounce him to the village.

Recognizing this, Ánp cursed himself for not staying in the cave. There he had friends, people who knew him, who could help him. Here he was alone.

Huhnun's arms and legs were long, and they were powerful from days spent hanging onto cliffs, harvesting apples. He was a faster climber than Ánp, and drew close more quickly. The others had emerged from the cave, and Rratah was sidling along a ledge toward them, below Huhnun. One of the men below started to climb, but the Thrower said something to him and he stopped, then dropped back onto the ledge.

Surely Huhnun didn't think he could get away with killing both brothers? But then, he probably could, couldn't he? There was not a good chance that the Thrower of Götöp would risk the life of one of her villagers simply to interfere with a matter whose particulars she did not fully know. Probably that's what had made her stop the man who had started after them, not wanting to interfere with other villages' affairs. So it was up to Ánp and Rratah.

Ánp grabbed at any holds he could find, even dangerous ones, hoping to get to another ledge not far above, from which he would have a chance of kicking Huhnun off the cliff face. The idea of killing Huhnun or pitching him into the Pit sickened him, but he could think of nothing else to try.

He didn't make it to the ledge. Huhnun got him first.

"Come down, come down, you thief!" Huhnun growled, and gripped Ánp's ankle. Rratah gave a cry of dismay and edged recklessly up toward them. Ánp's footholds were poor, and his handholds poorer. He looked out into the Pit. He could feel it reaching for him as the Sun Thread slowly turned its dark face toward them. In a moment it would be night, and he would not be able to see to climb.

Then, Huhnun shrieked with pain, and for a moment his hand let Ánp's leg free. Ánp slid over an arm's length further away, onto better footholds, but he needn't have bothered. When he looked down, he could see the metal knife protruding from Huhnun's ankle, and far below the Thrower lowering her arm to her side, a look of grim satisfaction on her sweet, ugly face.

With the loss of his handhold on Ánp and one foot unable to keep its place, Huhnun began to slide down, clawing frantically for a hold. With his good foot he found a solid hold, and to Ánp's terror, pushed off with it just far enough to grab Ánp's foot. Together, they began to slide, and for an agonizing moment they both scrambled for any purchase the cliff might afford as the rock slid by. Then they hit an outcrop and Ánp was flung out from the cliff, pulling Huhnun, who did not let go quickly enough, along with him.

They fell away too quickly even to hear whatever cries Rratah or the Götöp villagers might have made. Ánp kicked Huhnun away, and the older man flew toward the Pit wall as Ánp drifted farther toward the center. Then Huhnun's head struck an outcropping with a sound like two rocks being smacked together, and Ánp and the corpse tumbled separately into the darkness.

•••

Time grew lazy. They fell, and continued falling—sometimes near each other, sometimes farther away. Most of the time Ánp was not sure where Huhnun was, or even if he was still alive, but he could see the far cliff where the day side of the Sun Thread shone, and it did not seem to move by any faster as they fell.

There was time for fear to dissipate. First the panic, mixed even then with a bit of exhilaration. After a time, as nothing changed, and even the scenery on the far cliff wall only repeated themes—bare rock, tiny village, larger village, isolated meadow, waterfall—after a time, then, the fear fell away. Though he told himself death was close at hand, the fall had lasted too long and was too unchanging for that thought to continue to terrify him the way it had at first. Ánp reached out his arms to

Illustrated by Robert Drozd

fly, and to his great joy he felt as though he really were flying. Was he even falling a bit more slowly? Perhaps, perhaps not, and it hardly mattered either way. But he found that in a limited way he could turn and swoop and swim as though the air were thin, thin water. In this way he drifted through the sky to the day side of the Pit. He knew his only chance for life was to bring himself close to that wall and try to slow himself down, but picturing that, he could only imagine scraping himself to bloody shreds that flapped in the wind as they fell forever. Better to fly, and die perhaps of hunger or of thirst. Or maybe everyone was wrong, and there was a bottom. If so, he would probably see it rushing toward him only in the last moments, and be battered against it among the million other things that had dropped over the hundreds and thousands of weeks since time began, never feeling that flash of death.

Then, though he never saw it rushing toward him, he was caught by the net.

A huge net it was, made of some soft, twisted fiber, and Ánp's landing in it dimpled it deeply, propelling him down in the Pit before it stretched to its limit and pulled him back up. It began to bounce him back up a short way, but something else struck elsewhere, perhaps Huhnun's corpse, and it evened out fairly quickly.

Ánp was amazed that the net had held him, and that he was not falling quickly enough for it to somehow kill him. He looked up, and before him was a great, teeming city. A city! That myth, then, was true.

The city gleamed in the daylight and stretched around the Pit as far as he could see in either direction, and on into the night side. Hundreds, maybe thousands, of caves were cut into the cliff wall, and holes were cut for windows through which he could glimpse people in strange clothing, as he could see others walking across ledges or scaling bamboo ladders or negotiating stepped cliff faces. Above and below that heart of the city he could see deep, wide shelves cut regularly into the stone, each green with pasturage or crops. Strange music and heady scents came from the city, and sights he could not understand.

One of those sights was a fenced area on a nearby shelf, where the great net was hung higher, so that the fenced area, open only to the Pit, had nothing between it and the abyss below. The fence was high and tightly worked and the area was underneath a smooth overhang, so that it was clear that there was no way in except through a gate on one side and from the open air of the Pit. Inside the fenced area were four huge triangles of what appeared to be goatskin. A man seemed to be somehow connected beneath one of the triangles and was holding onto a frame of bamboo. To Ánp's amazement, he ran to the edge of the Pit and leapt out into it. Then he was flying, like a bird, circling lazily, always down, but at such an easy speed that surely he could touch down in some far down-Pit shelf-meadow without any harm to himself. It was a wing, then, a wing a man could use to fly.

No one seemed to have noticed his landing, and he climbed along the net as well as he could to a narrow weaving of rope that led across to the cliff. He clambered over that, and found himself on blessedly solid ground again, whole, unhurt. Then the guards took him.

"What is it?" Ánp said. "What's the matter?"

The guards wore long metal knives at their sides, and were in strange, close-fitting garments of hardened goatskin, with hard leather hats on their heads. One of the guards said something to the other, but his words made no sense to Ánp at all. Did people even speak differently in this place? How could they be understood, if they didn't use true words?

"Where am I? Have I done something wrong?" he said.

The guards said nothing more, but held firmly onto his arms and walked him into the city, up steps, and into a massive natural cave, thronged with people in many kinds of strange clothing, chattering to one another in nonsense words. One of them said something to a man in brilliant blue robes that covered his entire body, and did not seem to be made of wool or leather.

"Greetings," the man said. "Certainty, you will speak Páum?"

"What is Páum?"

"Ah, saying a strange kind of Páum you are. Waiting here, surely." And he ran off with an awkward gait, bringing back a woman, also wearing a blue robe.

"Do you speak this way, so that a goat is something that nibbles grass?" she said.

"What kind of question is that?"

Her faint smile lapsed into a faint frown. "I'm trying to find out whether we are speaking the same way or not. Do you understand me or don't you?"

"I understand you."

"Perfectly?"

"Yes, perfectly."

"Good. Are you a criminal, a suicide or a bad climber?"

"None of those!"

"It stands to reason that you were thrown into the Pit, in which case you must be a criminal, or jumped, in which case you must be a suicide, or fell, in which case you are very clumsy."

"I was pulled."

"I see," said the woman primly. "Well, you'll be questioned to see if you have any information that is new to us—which I doubt—and then either made a citizen or disposed of." She said something to the guards in the strange way that they had spoken before, and then she walked away, and they reached up and pulled down a wide leather belt attached to a rope swinging from a strange arrangement on the ceiling. Saying nothing, they wrapped it around him and dragged him across the floor. On the far side of the room, above a hole in the floor, Ánp saw another man who wore leggings and shouldercloth like the ones they wore in Aumah and Götöp, held by two guards. One pulled his hair and stretched out his neck. The other chopped with his long knife, several brutal blows, and then the head and the body were let to tumble into the little pit, from which came snarling and barking sounds.

Ánp's guards brought him to a wide, round hole in the floor and pushed him so that he fell into it. He cried out in surprise, but realized as he reached the bottom that the harness they had connected to him had slowed his fall so that he landed gently among a cluster of men and women dressed in a strange variety of clothes. Most were slumped dejectedly against the walls of the hole, the sides of which seemed too smooth to climb and too high to jump to the top of. Two were arguing about something. Ánp felt a jerk on the rope, and looking up he saw one of the guards gesturing for him to take off the harness. Eying the long knife, Ánp clumsily undid the leather belt and watched as it lifted up out of the hole.

Ánp staggered, realizing all at once that he was too exhausted to stand. Ignoring the other prisoners, he dropped down on the chill stone against an unused portion of the hole's wall, where the Sun Thread shone down into the cave through a window cut high up above, and he fell immediately to sleep.

•••

He woke up in a nightmare. He was flying again, like when he was falling in the Pit, but this time the air was not rushing around him, and the light flickered strangely, and everyone was screaming in words he could not understand.

He was awake, he realized in shock. He was awake and drifting slowly up into the air, as was everything and everyone else in the cave. The flickering light was the Sun Thread, and his weight was gone just as it had been on that long-ago day in Aumah.

Surely the other adults here would have had that same experience, but most of them seemed terrified. Then again, he realized, most of them wouldn't have taken the perverse joy he took in drifting through the air. And only these few around him would recently have had the experience of flying down through the Pit, suspended in air much as he was now, except with the Pit walls flying past. Also, to city dwellers this would mean interruption, danger. To Ánp, it meant the possibility of escape.

Probably in another several moments everything would return to normal—but until then, Ánp could fly. He pushed through the air as he had learned while falling, dragging himself down to the ground, and leapt into space. Too fast, he realized. He struck the roof of the cave with his extended arms, bruising them. But he grabbed onto slight handholds in the roof and held himself there while the shrieking and howling continued around him. Ánp pulled himself along the ceiling and out into the open air outside the cave.

He was drifting through the air, still full of shrieking, panicked city-dwellers. The city fascinated him, but he was not willing to stay to see whether he would prove useful to them and be permitted to live. He had the strong suspicion that they had little use for goatherds here, even well-travelled ones. His best option was to begin climbing down the Pit wall—or up? Had there been a village above?

He pushed himself through the air, moving with agonizing slowness. He drifted well above the ledge, watching the ground with apprehension, trying to move lower so that he wouldn't be killed if his weight came back and he fell. Then he managed to grip stone, the edge of the flying triangle cage, the cage of the wings.

Wings.

Before he had fallen into the Pit, Ánp would probably not have considered trying to use such a thing as the great wing, and certainly not without having been introduced to its workings. But his long, long fall had a dreamlike hold on him that made the Pit benign, even attractive. The flickering light and absolute darkness combined with his weariness and this dream-sense to amplify the feeling of unreality.

He pulled himself down into the cage and to the ground, clawing for purchase as he drifted past a wing and grabbed it. Awkwardly, still drifting above the ground, he pulled the heavy thing up over him. The harness, which he had barely glimpsed when he saw the flyer, turned out to be very like the one they had used to lower him into the prison hole. He strapped this on awkwardly but, he was nearly certain, properly. Glancing behind him, he saw several guards converging on the cage.

Then the Sun Thread suddenly burst into its normal steady light, and he had weight again.

Only an arm's length above the ledge, Ánp dropped uncomfortably but not painfully onto it. From the cries of the guards behind him, they had not been as lucky, and he heard a sickening crack from that direction, of bamboo breaking—or bone.

Among the hanging screams and wails of injured people throughout the city, he ran to the edge of the cliff and jumped, for the first time, *jumped* into the Pit, his weight pulling down on the harness as he struggled to guide the wings with his hands on the frame. A startled bird flew beneath him, squawking pitifully, perhaps still frightened by the loss of weight from moments before.

Looking back, he saw an enraged guard at the cliff's edge shaking his fist at Ánp, furious but clearly unwilling to chase him into the depths of the Pit.

He drifted and circled, and as he wended his way in lazy spiral figures down away from the city, he let the villages and smaller cities that passed all around him vanish up-Pit, vanishing deeper and deeper into the depths of the Pit of the world, half careless of his life now that all that he had ever known and cared for was forever out of his reach, farther up-Pit than a strong and lucky man could expect to climb in a lifetime.

•••

It was many hours later that his nerve, his resolution to find the bottom of the Pit, began to boil away. The many and many days' climb of cliff that slid past him wore at him, turning a near certainty that the Pit must somewhere have a bottom into an increasing uneasiness, and then a doubt, and then only misty shreds of belief that evaporated, leaving him at the mercy of hard fact, of infinite stretches of cliff: The Pit had no bottom. The Pit went on forever. He could circle downward until he starved, or even until he died of old age, and there would be no bottom.

Even so, it took something unusual, even more unusual than the rare cliff cities, to convince him to land. Far below, among the usual rough cliff faces and occasional grassy ledges, he could see flat, shining surfaces. Too flat, in fact, to be made by anything but people, and yet there was no trace of grass or crops or goats or caves or any other thing that a village would require. Guiding the wing easily, he brought it onto a flat ledge, brilliant like the surface of a pond and smooth, and he slid to a stop on it, crashing gently into a similarly smooth wall. Gingerly, feeling numbness in the places where it had held him, he disentangled himself from the harness and pushed the wing aside. Sleep, all he wanted was sleep. He felt along the unfamiliar, smooth surface. Fearful of falling, he felt carefully along the ground and moved on his hands and knees.

Then his hand touched something strange, a slight depression, with a sort of a bar across it. Was the bar fixed in the depression? He pulled up on it, and suddenly the ledge gave way beneath him. He dropped several times a man's length and collided painfully with a hard, bumpy surface at the bottom of some hole underneath the ledge, and then there was a muted hum, and all around him a warm light—unlike the Sun Thread, unlike fire, being pinker and gentler—blossomed into being. He was in a cave with perfectly flat walls covered in bizarre objects, protrusions and shelves. Piled on the floor with him were unattached objects, all made of hard materials, jumbled together. There was a spark of blue in one corner of the room, and all at once there was a woman standing there—but not a woman, because hazily, he could see through her to the strange, flat wall. He glanced up at the hole he had fallen through, but it was out of reach.

The woman spoke, as unintelligibly as the guards in the city had spoken, but differently. He stared back. She spoke, in a different way this time, and then in yet a different way, and then:

"I greet thee, and dost thou make of this speech an understanding?"

"What are you?" Ánp said, and gasped. His side hurt; he might have broken a rib.

"Thy speech is passing strange to me. Wilt thou speak to me for a time, and instruct me in thy tongue?"

"I'm hurt," Ánp said. "Are you a phantom?"

"By my troth, I am nought but a clever invention, wrought by men. Fear me not. I have here sealed these many years things that may aid thee in thy hurt, and too have I food for thee, saved for thee for many generations." From the cave floor nearby, a box lifted of itself out of the trash, then split open, showing an array of incomprehensible metal items. A disembodied hand appeared in the air above them, pointing to one as though to suggest it to him.

Too far, Ánp thought, he had come too far, to things too strange and hard for him. Given the chance, that moment, he would have traded his situation for a place in the hole prison.

"Marry, my patience wears thin! Take thee thy tool and make thyself well. My makers thought all thy people killed in the cataclysm, and as I wake now I find the Thread of the Sun well past the length of days they thought for it to last. Rouse thyself, if thou will prevent the Sun Thread from dying, ten generations hence or sooner!"

Another sharp pain in his side made him wince. Too hurt to climb, he obeyed the apparition, and took the tool.

"It is well," she said. "Now, hearken to me, for I must learn thy tongue in each particular."

•••

Weeks later, he had cleared the control room of its long-broken trash that crashed into the wall (now the floor) two thousand years before when the gravity turned. He had healed well with the medical supplies that were preserved there in perfect stasis, and if the food was strange to him, it had survived those years—years, a new term, only meaning fifty weeks, based on the turnings of a ball in space far away and long ago—survived those years still palatable and nourishing.

"So the Pit doesn't have a bottom? It really is bottomless?"

"Your question isn't meaningful, Ánp," she—the computer—replied. "Can we please return to the technology studies? We have limited supplies of food and water—"

"Is there a bottom? Just answer yes or no."

"I've already answered this."

"Well, keep answering until it makes sense."

The computer groaned with frustration, something that had seemed natural at first, then strange when Ánp began to understand that she was only a machine, and by now felt natural again. Did she have emotions, or was she simply made to counterfeit them? "It's an artifically constructed torus," she said. "It's not a pit."

"It's a pit now," he said.

"The gravity was supposed to pull out toward the walls, not down along the Sun Thread."

"But it doesn't pull out toward the walls now, does it? Or are you claiming that I'm sitting on the wall? So let's pretend it's a pit."

"Can we call it a tube? A hollow tube, bent into a circle?"

"Sure. Is that what a torus is?"

"I've been trying to explain. People live on the inside of the tube, and the Sun Thread, which is suspended inside the middle of the tube, making a circle itself, exerts gravitational force that pulls around and around in a circle. So if you're inside the tube, one direction always feels like down, and the other feels like up."

"All right, that almost made sense. Except the gravitational part. But where's the bottom?"

"I wish a less stubborn human had found this room."

"A less stubborn human never would have. Now, where's the bottom of this tube?"

"There is no bottom; it just goes around and around. The Sun Thread creates an influence like that of gravity and pulls things down its length. It used to pull out toward the walls such that there was no place to fall, but that failed several times, and the last time they thought everyone who wasn't evacuated died."

"You're getting off topic," said Ánp. "Just answer me this: If something were to fall, and were to never come in contact with the Sun Thread, and were to never come in contact with a cliff wall—"

"But it's curved. Of course the torus is much too big to *see* that it's curved, like a planet's surface, but eventually a falling object would hit the wall of the torus, because—"

"Stay with me here, stay with me for a moment. Just for the sake of argument, let's say there was something that never hit a wall, and never hit the Sun Thread. Would that just be falling that goes on forever, or would that thing eventually hit bottom?"

"There is no bottom."

"Aha! Thank you, that's all I needed to know."

"Now can I get back to teaching you what you need to know?" the computer said tiredly.

"This—this physics you're trying to teach me—I don't understand any of it yet. It doesn't make any sense. I don't think I'll be able to teach—"

"You're the only one *here* to learn it," the computer said. "So you'll have to, if you people are going to learn how to rebuild the Sun Thread."

"All right," Ánp said, slumping in his chair. "Show me that thing about the three laws again. I almost got it the last time."

They continued like that for many weeks.

•••

Nearly eighty weeks after Ánp climbed fearfully down from the Thrower's cave in Aumah, he circled down toward it on the wing he had stolen in the city far, far down-Pit. Or up-Pit, it could as easily be said.

He came in late afternoon as the village gathered in preparation for the evening meal. This time of day, someone was certain to notice his entrance. It was important that they did.

It was Rratah who saw him first.

"K!ahum! A K!ahum! Come see it!" he shouted, and the sound was strong enough to be just audible to Ánp far across the quiet sky of the Pit. He smiled and circled closer. Below him he could see the people of the village gathering, Eni and her mother, his parents running to Rratah's side, Pahoh the Thrower and his wife and children, all looking up.

He touched down in a shelf-meadow, running to slow himself, digging his calloused heels into the dirt, the long grass stroking softly at his ankles as he slowed down across it.

"Ánp!" Rratah cried, and he ran toward him. Ánp smiled wearily. The flight down had been much longer than he could have imagined. He stopped in innumerable villages, and for a long time he found only ones where people spoke strange languages of which he could learn only a little before he flew further down. And finally, two days ago, someone had spoken to him in his own tongue, and he knew he was almost home. He had watched for Khenkh, and after that for the Giant's Nose and Split Rock, and his relief on seeing them was only exceeded by the joy now, disentangling himself from the harness and collapsing as Rratah barrelled into him and knocked him to the ground, hugging him and pummelling him and crying out joyously.

Most of the rest of the village hung back, but his father stepped forward hesitantly, and his mother ran in with a shriek of delight. Further back he saw Eni, stepping forward from her mother's side while her mother, Zhehühü, looked questioningly at Ánp, and occasionally at the sky.

"You're just in time," Eni said in a low voice. "I was beginning to think I was going to have to marry an old man who keeps climbing down from Khenkh to bring me beadwork." She took him by the hand and led him through the crowd. Most of the village was still dumbfounded and apparently a little fearful, and they stood a little back. Ánp's mother tried to follow, but Rratah held her back for a moment, giving Ánp and Eni a few moments to themselves.

"They may not want me back here," Ánp said. "The banishment—"

"Your brother came back with the Thrower from Götöp, and Pahoh was satisfied by their testimony that Huhnun had been false with us."

"I'm supposed to teach you. The things I have to teach won't sit well with the elders. It may be that no one understands them. *I* hardly understand them."

"You're a K!ahum. You're supposed to teach."

"And our children—" Ánp cut himself off, embarrassed. "I didn't mean *our* children. . . ."

Eni shrugged. "There's time and more time to talk of that."

And then Pahoh stepped forward and took his own brilliant blue Thrower's shouldercloth, laying it across Ánp's shoulders. Ánp felt even more embarrassed by that gesture, but he wasn't surprised. Who would presume to be Thrower over a K!ahum? And Pahoh smiled brilliantly. "Welcome home," he said.

And as they walked away from the Pit, Ánp pulled the blue cloth closer over him, still cold from the breezes of the open Pit. He had found the bottom of the Pit, the place where, having fallen as far as a man can fall, he will fall no farther. The bottom was home.

# ART, MORE ABOUT

*Written by*
**L. Ron Hubbard**

## About the Author

*L. Ron Hubbard lived a remarkably adventurous and productive life whose versatility and rich imaginative scope both spanned and ranged far beyond his extensive literary achievements and creative influence. A writer's writer of enormous talent and energy, the breadth and diversity of his writing ultimately embraced more than 560 works and over 63 million words of fiction and nonfiction. Throughout his fifty-six-year writing career, convinced of the crucial role of the arts in civilization, he generously helped other writers and artists, especially beginners, become more proficient and successful at their craft.*

*Starting with the publication in 1934 of "The Green God," his first adventure yarn, in one of the hugely popular pulp fiction magazines of the day, L. Ron Hubbard's outpouring of fiction was prodigious—often exceeding a million words a year. Ultimately, he produced more than 250 published novels, short stories and screenplays in virtually every major genre.*

*L. Ron Hubbard had, indeed, already attained broad popularity and acclaim in other genres when he published his first science fiction story, "The Dangerous Dimension." It was his groundbreaking work in this field that not only helped to indelibly enlarge the imaginative boundaries of science fiction and fantasy, but established him as one of the founders and signature architects of what continues to be regarded as the genre's golden age.*

*In the article "Art, More About" that follows, L. Ron Hubbard, a prominent creative talent himself, offers insight into how he regarded the fundamental role of the artist, art and the receiving audience.*

How good does a professional work of art have to be? This would include painting, music, photography, poetry, any of the arts whether fine or otherwise. It would also include presenting oneself as an art form as well as one's products.

Yes, how GOOD does such a work of art have to be?

Ah, you say, but that is an imponderable, a thing that can't be answered. Verily, you say, you have just asked a question for which there are no answers except the sneers and applause of critics. Indeed, this is why we have art critics! For who can tell how good good is. Who knows?

I have a surprise for you. There IS an answer.

As you know, I searched for many years, as a sort of minor counterpoint to what I was hardwork doing, to dredge up some of the materials which might constitute the basis of art. Art was the most uncodified and most opinionated subject on the planet—after men's ideas about women and women's ideas about men and man's ideas of man. Art was anyone's guess. Masterpieces have gone unapplauded, positive freaks have gained raves.

So how good does a work of art have to be to be good?

The painter will point out all the tiny technical details known only to painters, the musician will put a score through the alto horn and explain about valve clicks and lip, the poet will talk about meter types, the actor will explain how the position and wave of one hand per the instructions of one school can transform a clod into an actor. And so it goes, art by art, bit by bit.

But all these people will be discussing the special intricacies and holy mysteries of technique, the tiny things only the initiate of that art would recognize. They are talking about technique. They are not really answering how *good* a work of art has to be.

Works of art are viewed by people. They are heard by people. They are felt by people. They are not just the fodder of a close-knit group of initiates. They are the soul food of all people.

One is at liberty of course to challenge that wide purpose of art. Some professors who don't want rivals tell their students "Art is for self-satisfaction" "It is a hobby." In other words, don't display or exhibit, kid, or you'll be competition! The world today is full of that figure-figure. But as none of this self-satisfaction art meets a definition of art wider than self for the sake of self, the professional is not interested in it.

In any artistic production, what does one have as an audience? People. Not, heaven forbid, critics. But people. Not experts in that line of art. But people.

That old Chinese poet who, after he wrote a poem, went down out of his traditional garret and read it to the flower-selling old lady on the corner had the right idea. If she understood it and thought it was great, he published. If she didn't he put it in the bamboo trash can. Not remarkably, his poems have come down the centuries awesomely praised.

Well, one could answer this now by just saying that art should communicate to people high and low. But that really doesn't get the sweating professional anywhere as a guide in actually putting together a piece of work and it doesn't give him a yardstick whereby he can say "That is that!" "I've done it." And go out with confidence that he has.

What is technique? What is its value? Where does it fit? What is perfectionism? Where does one stop scraping off the paint and erasing notes and say "That is that"?

For there is a point. Some artists don't ever find it. The Impressionists practically spun in as a group trying to develop a new way of viewing and communicating it. They made it—or some of them did like Monet. But many of them never knew where to stop and they didn't make it. They couldn't answer the question "How good does a piece of artwork have to be to be good?"

In this time of century, there are many communication lines for works of art. Because a few works of art can be shown so easily to so many there may even be fewer artists. The competition is very keen and even dagger sharp. To be good one has to be very good. But in what way and how?

Well, when I used to buy breakfasts for Greenwich Village artists (which they ate hungrily, only stopping between bites to deplore my commercialism and bastardizing my talents for the gold that bought their breakfasts) I used to ask this question and needless to say I received an appalling variety of responses. They avalanched me with technique or lack of it, they vaguely dwelt on inherent talent, they rushed me around to galleries to show me Picasso or to a board fence covered with abstracts. But none of them told me how good a song had to be to be a song.

So I wondered about this. And a clue came when the late Hubert Mathieu, a dear friend, stamped with youth on the Left Bank of the Seine and painting dowagers at the Beaux Arts in middle age, said to me "To do any of these modern, abstract, cubist things, you have to first be able to paint!" And he enlarged the theme while I plied him in the midnight hush of Manhattan with iced sherry and he finished up the First Lady of Nantucket's somewhat swollen ball gown. Matty could PAINT. Finally he dashed me off an abstract to show me how somebody who couldn't paint would do it and how it *could* be done.

I got his point. To really make one of these too too modern things come off, you first had to be able to paint. So I said well, hell, there's Gertrude Stein and Thomas Mann and ink splatterers like those. Let's see if it really is an art form. So I sharpened up my electric typewriter and dashed off the last chapters of a novel in way far out acid prose and put THE END at the bottom and shipped it off to an editor who promptly pushed several large loaves down the telephone wire and had me to lunch and unlike his normal blasé self said, "I really got a big bang (this was decades ago, other years, other slang) out of the way that story wound up! You really put it over the plate." And it sent his circulation rating up. And this was very odd because you see the first chapters were straight since they'd been written before Matty got thirsty for sherry and called me to come over and the last chapters were an impressionistic stream of consciousness that Mann himself would have called "an advanced rather adventurous over-Finneganized departure from ultra school."

So just to see how far this sort of thing could go, for a short while I shifted around amongst various prose periods just to see what was going on. That they sold didn't prove too much because I never had any trouble with that. But that they were understood at all was surprising to me for their prose types (ranging from Shakespeare to Beowulf) were at wild variance with anything currently being published.

So I showed them to Matty the next time he had a ball gown to do or three chins to paint out and was thirsty. And he looked them over and he said, "Well, you proved my point. There's no mystery to it. Basically you're a trained writer! It shows through."

And now we are getting somewhere, not just with me and my adventures and long-dead yesterdays.

As time rolled on, this is what I began to see: The fellow technician in an art hears and sees the small technical points. The artist himself is engrossed in the exact application of certain exact actions which produce, when done, his canvas, his score, his novel, his performance.

The successful artist does these small things so well that he also then has attention and skill left to get out his message, he is not still fiddling about with the cerulean blue and the semiquaver. He has these zeroed in. He can repeat them and repeat them as technical actions. No ulcers. Strictly routine.

And here we have three surrealist paintings. And they each have their own message. And the public wanders by and they only look with awe on one. And why is this one different than the other two? Is it a different message? No. Is it more popular? That's too vague.

If you look at or listen to any work of art, there is only one thing the casual audience responds to en masse, and if this has it then you too will see it as a work of art. If it doesn't have it, you won't.

So what is *it?*

TECHNICAL EXPERTISE ITSELF ADEQUATE TO PRODUCE AN EMOTIONAL IMPACT.

And that is how good a work of art has to be to be good.

If you look this over from various sides, you will see that the general spectator is generally unaware of technique. That is the zone of art's creators.

Were you to watch a crowd watching a magician, you would find one common denominator eliciting uniform response. If he is a good magician he is a smooth showman. He isn't showing them how he does his tricks. He is showing them a flawless flowing performance. This alone is providing the carrier wave that takes the substance of his actions to his audience. Though a far cry from fine art, perhaps, yet there is art in the way he does things. If he is good, the audience is seeing first of all, before anything else, the TECHNICAL EXPERTISE of his performance. They are also watching him do things they know they can't do. And they are watching the outcome of his presentations. He is a good magician if he gives a technically flawless performance just in terms of scenes and motions which provide the channel for what he is presenting.

Not to compare Bach with a magician (though you could), all great pieces of art have this one factor in common. First of all, before one looks at the faces on the canvas or hears the meaning of the song, there is the TECHNICAL EXPERTISE there adequate to produce an emotional impact. Before one adds message or meaning, there is this TECHNICAL EXPERTISE.

TECHNICAL EXPERTISE is composed of all the little and large bits of technique known to the skilled painter, musician, actor, any artist. He adds these things together in his basic presentation. He knows what he is doing. And how to do it. And then to this he adds his message.

All old masters were in there nailing canvas on frames as apprentices or grinding up the lapis lazuli or cleaning paintbrushes before they arrived at the Metropolitan.

But how many paintbrushes do you have to clean? Enough to know that clean paintbrushes make clean color. How many clarinet reeds do you have to replace? Enough to know which types will hit high C.

Back of every artist there is technique. You see them groping, finding, discarding, fooling about. What are they hunting for? A new blue? No, just a constant of blue that is an adequate quality.

And you see somebody who can really paint still stumbling about looking for technique—a total overrun.

Someplace one says, "That's the TECHNICAL EXPERTISE adequate to produce an emotional impact." And that's it. Now he CAN. So he devotes himself to messages.

If you get this tangled up or backwards, the art does not have a good chance of being good. If one bats out messages without a TECHNICALLY EXPERT carrier wave of art, the first standard of the many spectators seems to be violated.

The nice trick is to be a technician and retain one's fire. Then one can whip out the masterpieces like chain lightning. And all the great artists seem to have managed that. And when they forked off onto a new trail they mastered the technique and *then* erupted with great works.

It is a remarkable thing about expertise. Do you know that some artists get by on "technical expertise adequate to produce an emotional impact" alone with no messages? They might not suspect that. But it is true.

So the "expertise adequate" is important enough to be itself art. It is never great art. But it produces an emotional impact just from quality alone.

And how masterly an expertise? Not very masterly. Merely adequate. How adequate is adequate? Well, people have been known to criticize a story because there were typographical errors in the typing. And stories by the nonadept often go pages before anyone appears or anything happens. And scores have been known to be considered dull simply because they were inexpertly chorded or clashed. And a handsome actor has been known not to have made it because he never knew what to do with his arms, for all his fiery thunderings of the Bard's words.

Any art demands a certain expertise. When this is basically sound, magic! Almost anyone will look at it and say Ah! For quality alone has emotional impact. That it is cubist or dissonant or blank verse has very little bearing on it; the type of the art form is no limitation to audience attention generally when it has, underlying it and expressed in it, the expertise adequate to produce an emotional impact.

The message is what the audience thinks it sees or hears. The significance of the play, the towering clouds of sound in the symphony, the scatter-batter of the current pop group, are what the audience thinks it is perceiving and what they will describe, usually, or which they think they admire. If it comes to them with a basic expertise itself able to produce an emotional impact they will think it is great. And it will be great.

The artist is thought of as enthroned in some special heaven where all is clean and there is no sweat, eyes half closed in the thrall of inspiration. Well maybe he is sometimes. But every one I've seen had ink in his hair or a towel handy to mop his brow or a throat spray in his hand to ease the voice strain of having said his lines twenty-two times to the wall or the cat. I mean the great ones. The others were loafing and hoping and talking about the producer or the unfair art gallery proprietor.

The great ones always worked to achieve the technical quality necessary. When they had it they knew they had it. How did they know? Because it was technically correct.

Living itself is an art form. One puts up a mock-up. It doesn't happen by accident. One has to know how to wash his nylon shirts and girls have to know what mascara runs and that too many candy bars spoil the silhouette, quite in addition to the pancreas.

Some people are themselves a work of art because they have mastered the small practical techniques of living that give them a quality adequate to produce an emotional impact even before anyone knows their name or what they do.

Even a beard and baggy pants require a certain art if they are to be the expertise adequate to produce an emotional impact.

And some products produce a bad *mis*emotional impact without fully being viewed. And by this reverse logic, of which you can think of many examples such as a dirty room, you can then see that there might be an opposite expertise, all by itself, adequate to produce a strong but *desirable* emotional impact.

That is how good a work of art has to be. Once one is capable of executing that technical expertise for that art form he can pour on the message. Unless the professional form is there first, the message will not transmit.

A lot of artists are overstraining to obtain a quality far above that necessary to produce an emotional impact. And many more are trying to machine-gun messages at the world without any expertise at all to form the vital carrier wave.

So how good does a piece of art have to be?

# FLOTSAM

*Written by*
**Bradley P. Beaulieu**

*Illustrated by*
**Shawn Gaddy**

## About the Author

*Brad Beaulieu hails from Kenosha, Wisconsin. He is married to his beautiful soul mate, Joanne, who he thanks wholeheartedly for supporting his dream of writing.*

*Brad has been writing for eight years, but it is only in the last three years that he's become serious about the craft. Since then, he's finished two novels, nearly finished a third and written over a dozen short stories. His only publishing credit to date is "Secrets of the Shoeblack" in* Deep Magic, *an electronic publication of fantasy and science fiction.*

*Although his writing and reading tastes tend to be on the "realistic" side of fantasy, à la J.R.R. Tolkien, Brad states he is "open to a science fiction romp now and then."*

*Brad first heard about the Writers of the Future Contest from author/lecturer Kij Johnson. He started entering the contest in December of 2001 and submitted every quarter until he finally won. He says he's already seen more interest in his work in the marketplace as a result of winning the contest and for that he thanks the contest and its staff.*

## About the Illustrator

*Shawn Gaddy is a self-taught artist from a small town in North Carolina, Brevard. Because he was drawing from a very early age, his family tried to encourage him to take art lessons to develop his skills; however, he wasn't interested in what the instructors had to teach, such as drawing still lifes of fruit baskets. Instead he began studying the techniques and styles of his favorite artists, such as Frank Frazetta.*

*Shawn enrolled in and completed Art Instruction Schools after high school. During his enrollment, he spent a lot of time developing his own artistic style, experimenting and making it as original and different as possible so that it would stand out from others. He feels strongly that it is pointless to create art that doesn't reflect your personality.*

*Shawn worked for five years on an online comic book and is now doing album covers for Metropolis Records in Philadelphia. Although he works primarily in pen and ink, he plans to continue experimenting with other media—painting, graphic art, photography—to continue evolving his work. He has also been putting his artistic vision to the test by trying to expand his creativity in the film industry, writing scripts and learning video production.*

Strange how one can be so close to freedom, yet still wish for death. Freedom: the water below the bowsprit I rested on; water that would welcome me with open arms had I so chosen; water that I had loved so much, but now found to be mocking, perhaps more so among the closeness of the harbor.

I began to shift backward to escape the water's call when two sets of footsteps crept onto the forecastle deck behind me. I shrugged my shoulders tight, wishing them to be gone, anticipating the humiliation to come.

"It doesn't wear clothes," a young male said.

"Yes, never has." This, the captain's niece, present from the moment we docked to the moment we left again.

The boy giggled. "You can see its poop-hole."

"I told you!"

I despised that the humans' sense of decency had worn off on me, but still I turned to hide my privates from them. Twenty years with another culture would do this to even the most antithetical society.

The boy gasped, and his heart beat faster. "What happened to its eyes?"

"They're just glossed over, see? He's a shaman. They're born with no eyesight."

Not strictly true, I thought, but close enough to the truth.

The boy's footsteps came closer. "Looks like rotted cheese."

"Told you." The girl came closer as well. Though she feigned confidence, I could hear her heartbeat catching up to her brother's. The coarse skin of her hand ran along the smoothness of mine. Her touch brought some feelings of resentment, but the simple reminder of youth and its innocence shadowed such thoughts.

"Come here," she said. "His skin's like an eel."

The boy's sweat mingled with the dead-fish smell of the harbor. His footsteps receded.

"Scared as a mouse," the girl said with feigned disgust, yet she backed away quickly, too.

From the quarterdeck, a liquid voice rose above the gulls and creaking wood of ships at dock. "Neera. What are you doing?" Captain Hoevin's long stride echoed over the main deck toward us.

The children scuttled to one side. "Nothing, Uncle Hoevin," the girl said.

His steps halted a few paces short of me. "Nothing indeed. The yeavanni are not pets, least of all Khren, here."

"Yes, Uncle."

"Off with you now. We're nearly ready to depart."

Just then, a thundering crack pealed over the harbor. The concussion struck a moment later—long before I had a chance to cover my ear-pads. The pain of it coursed through me, and only long breaths later did it recede to a dull pain.

"Go, I said!"

The children's scattered footsteps left the forecastle deck and diffused into the maelstrom of other sounds and the ringing in my own ears. The captain shifted slowly to the gunwale.

He didn't speak for some time. "We need to talk, Khren."

"Perhaps we do, Captain."

"You've heard the cannons, no doubt."

He knew that I did, so I said nothing.

"The new sightings are nearly complete, and the fleet's ready to set sail. Tonight."

Still I said nothing. I was unsure where the human wished to take the conversation.

"Your . . . race. You've been an immense help to us over the years. And despite whatever advantage the king may have taken, *I* appreciate it. You've saved my men a dozen times. More."

His words shed from me like water slipping over yeavanni skin.

"Well. The king decided to wait until now to give his latest request. We're to fight through the blockade to the south. They're ready to tear down the walls of Trilliar, and we cannot allow it."

A low laugh escaped my throat. As with most humans that hear such sounds, the captain's heart quickened. "You mean *you* will fight, Captain."

"No, Khren. You will fight, too."

"I will not. Our atonement does not include battle."

The captain's fingers drummed against the wooden railing. He smelled of rum and garlic. "He's offered to free you of your commitment if you do this."

My response died in my throat. What simple words Hoevin had spoken . . . but what promise they held. "The king would forgive us?" My own question barely made sense to me.

"Yes. One battle—provided we win—is the last service he shall require from you. From all of you."

I turned from the captain, unable to be near him any longer, and crawled further up the bowsprit. I opened my mind to the water; how I longed to drop into its arms and return to my people, return to those I had come to believe were lost to me forever. But at what price? The king would have us kill when death is what delivered us to him in the first place.

Behind me, the captain shuffled some steps away. "Think on it, Khren. Think of your home, your people."

Waves lapped against the hull of the ship. The sounds beckoned me, begged me to join them among the waters, to swim with them and follow my brothers home. But my stomach soured at the captain's words—they had the taint of deception and corruption upon them. Fight for us and be freed, they said. But kill, and lose our eternal salvation. Such urges tempted while trapped within this mortal shroud.

With a broken heart, I turned from the water and shimmied up the jib-line to the foremast. I stayed as far away from the water as I could, for I didn't know if I could resist the calls of the sea much longer.

•••

I felt the night breeze as it tugged the ship against the ocean current below. A school of dolphin splashed through the waves on the port side; a few strays played to starboard as well. I leapt free of the bowsprit and dove into the water, unable to resist its call any longer.

The cool water met me, and I rejoiced in a deep dive below the ship's keel. A large dolphin nudged my back. I could feel the waves of its escape before me. I pursued, catching up easily until the beast tired of my simple chase and sped off into the deep. In my prime, I could keep up with schools of dolphin, but as twilight touched the ocean of my life, I could only rely on their sympathy.

The ship's motion, ahead and above, washed over me. The trickle of the dolphin pod did the same, but it came staccato, as opposed to the deep bass of the ship.

Something else lingered nearby—behind and below. I turned and felt for the presence, unsure of the source—but I had an inkling. I sent a bellowing call through the water; a moment later, a haunting reply was returned. Another yeavanni, and this one I was not so sure I wanted to speak to.

I felt the yeavanni swim nearer, heard the trickle of its movement through the deeps. He stopped nearby and performed a slow pirouette. *At least he still shows respect,* I thought.

"Khrentophar," he began, "it is good to have you near."

"And you, Iulaja."

We swam together, trailing the ship by a half-league.

"I bring news," Iulaja said, "though I'm sure you've heard some of it already."

I was pleased to feel the link between us build. I could feel his concern over the human's battle. "Of the war? Yes, I know of it."

"I've come from the other ships, and the queen before that." An eagerness overcame Iulaja then. A joy.

"The queen wishes us back, does she?"

Confusion touched him for only a moment. "Yes, as do the other shamans. They have agreed to fight this human battle, and be done with them."

Sorrow overcame my heart. *They have all agreed?*

"Yes, all of them, Khrentophar. All but you."

I couldn't speak for a moment. *All of them?* "You asked them before coming to me."

Iulaja's mind echoed his embarrassment. "You would have convinced them otherwise, Khrentophar. Our villages would have you back home. I would step down so that you might return to your proper place."

We swam in silence for a time, catching up to the ship. A school of grayridge whales harrooned their song into the night. Iulaja drove before me and brought me to a halt. His anger soured the water between us.

"Do you wish to talk like the humans, still and unmoving? Have you become so like them that you wish to stay until your dying day?"

"In truth, Iulaja, I would welcome my dying day. These humans lay foul on my tongue, ring with clangor in my ears, drive coral under my skin. If Yeavan, in her divine guidance, would summon me to the depths, I would rejoice and sing so that all the yeavanni could hear." I began swimming again, forcing Iulaja to keep pace. "Yet I will not lose my place in her land to further the goals of these land-ridden beasts."

The water turned colder.

"You have paid a score times the deathbond price. Twenty years, Khrentophar! The sinking of their ship was an *accident*. *They* stumbled onto *our* lands in a hurricane."

"A hurricane we summoned."

"As a ritual to our Goddess! I don't understand why, but I believe she wanted them dead. Those humans care nothing for Yeavan; they don't bow to her will, nor does she have dominion over them or we would have had you back long before now. Do you truly think she wished for this to happen after Khuum Livva, her holiest day?"

"I think, Iulaja, *shaman* of our people, *keeper* of her faith, that she will guide us as she sees fit. I cannot willingly murder for them. I will not."

Iulaja turned away in heat and anger. He swam to one side and turned back. "Then you can stay with them, Khrentophar, though it rots my heart to see it so. Farewell."

"Begone, traitor," I said to him.

Iulaja's echoes trailed off and were lost among the din of the dolphin pod.

"Begone, dear Iulaja," I said to the sea. "May she keep you well."

The ship had pulled ahead, but I caught up to it quickly. I dove up from beneath the prow and leapt from the water to grasp the bowsprit and swing around. I dropped down to my typical, folded pose, hating the simple fact that I *had* one.

A heartbeat from behind startled me. The distinctly human rhythm was small, frail. No human man had such a signature. I could not at first remember who it belonged to, but it came to me shortly.

"Come out, girl. It's no use hiding from someone blind to the world."

After a moment, I heard her tentative footsteps sidle up the gunwale.

"I don't think your uncle would approve."

Her heartbeat sped up. So impressionable, these humans.

"Please don't tell him. I wanted to go to war. I wanted to help fight the enemy."

She *wanted* to? My heart wept at such a statement. How can they still live when even their children hunger to kill?

"What would make you want such a thing, child?"

"They killed my father. He was a captain, like Uncle Hoevin."

"Why don't you search for a way to reconcile instead?"

The girl seemed taken aback, for she said nothing for a long time. "Because they killed him." Her voice was tentative, but it grew stronger the more she talked. "They killed everyone on the ship, even those they took hostage."

"And peace? When will that come?"

"When I have revenge. Then we can have peace."

I laughed; again the girl's heart raced as she stepped away. "Yes, child. That is the way of your world, isn't it?"

"I don't understand."

"No, you wouldn't. I should call your uncle." Before she could plea for my silence, I continued. "Go. I won't tell. Perhaps if you see war with your own eyes, you won't be so quick to embrace it. Go."

She took two steps back, but then her feet turned. "Can I talk to you more? Will you tell me what you meant?"

Tell her? Among the rotted places of my heart, a clear note rang out. Teach a human child. Is this what Yeavan had in store for me? Have I endured twenty years of heartache to bring them into her fold? As quickly as the note had sung out, it was smothered by the drums of war.

"We will see, child. We will see."

Long after she had hidden herself beneath the canvas of the rowboat, I pondered her words.

•••

On the fourth day from port, the sun warmed my back as I lounged on the bowsprit, smelling the sea.

A brass bell rang three times, cutting through the wind. I clapped my hands over my head and hunkered down tightly.

The thunder of a cannon broke the calm, rattling my head despite my meager protection. Far to the starboard side, the splash of the cannonball broke a wave, and again further away, and more times as it skittered over the sea's surface.

"That's enough, men," Captain Hoevin called. "Secure the cannons."

A league or more behind us, another cannon peal broke over the waves. Twelve other ships had joined the fleet in the last two days, and according to the captain, the other seven would be joining us shortly. We were now only a half-day's sail from the besieged city of Trilliar.

The minds of my fellow shamans called from the other ships—two were ahead, on the flagship and another gargantuan vessel, and the others behind. With each that came nearer, the bond between us strengthened.

The captain had found his niece, Neera. She had been allowed to stay, for with the battle so near and the city at such need, the captain could no longer justify returning home. To my surprise, she had kept her promise, returning to speak to me several times each day. She asked of my home and the other yeavanni villages on the far side of the sea. She asked how I could manage without eyes, how I could talk with the other shamans, how I could control the seas. All of these I answered as best I could, and in truth, my heart rejoiced at the chance to speak of Yeavan and her ways.

Even if the girl never learned, never believed, it was an outpouring that had been damming up inside me for years. Too many years, I thought. So many that the speaking of such things brought back a yearning such as I hadn't felt in a long time.

My proud words of faith to Iulaja felt hollow to me now. In the bowels of my mind I had to admit that had the enemy appeared before me right there and then, I might have slaughtered them all simply to go home. Iulaja had a point, after all. Yeavan did not speak of ritual with other races. What were human lives to her? Did we not war with our enemy, the salazaar? Did she not sanction such actions when necessary? Ah, but there lies the rub: this felt too much like murder, instead of defending our people.

Footsteps padded over the forecastle deck, and I broke the contact with my brothers and sisters, perhaps embarrassed at the relationship I had fostered with the human girl.

"Uncle says the battle will begin tomorrow."

"Yes."

"Will you fight?" she asked, spoken like she was unsure what she wanted the answer to be.

"No, child, I will not."

She stepped to the gunwale and tapped something metal against the wood of the rail.

"That's probably best," she said, "seeing as you want to fall to Yeavan's arms."

I laughed. The girl's heartbeat, to her credit, barely rose. She'd become more accustomed to yeavanni sounds over the last few days.

"And you? Do you still wish for revenge?"

Her tapping ceased. "I don't know. I'm still angry."

"Mortals can expect no less."

"There are still times when I wish them dead."

"The mind wanders, child. You cannot hope to still all such thoughts. What of revenge?"

"No. I guess I don't want it anymore." She laughed. "I won't even see the battle in any case. Uncle has me in the cook's larders for the whole thing."

"That's for the best, I would think."

We lapsed into silence, and I breathed the sea air deeply. Below, the sound of something small breaking the water's surface hid among the breaking waves. I closed my eyes, and opened myself up to the sea. The object tasted metallic.

"What did you wish for, child?"

Her heart skipped. "I thought you couldn't see."

"The sea sees much for these dead eyes."

"I . . . I wished for the enemy to break before we reached Trilliar. I don't want to see war anymore."

As if devouring the girl's naive thoughts, a brass bell's clanging broke the silence. I had been with this ship for two decades, and never had it rung with the nervous fervor I heard then. But, then again, never had we been in true battle. Across the sea, bells rang from the other ships.

"Enemy flags, Captain. Ten degrees to port, coming 'round the cliffs."

The ship came to life, men moving about, some climbing through the rigging above. Rope creaked and sure feet pounded their way to their stations.

"How many?" the captain called.

"Over a score or I'm a king's fool."

Neera moved to port and hopped up on the railing. Her heart beat faster than the bell had rung. "How soon?" she asked.

"Depends whether the fleet runs or not."

"How close are the other ships?"

I opened myself to the other shamans. At the edge of our awareness, the other seven approached. "An hour if we turn to meet them."

Heavy boots climbed up the forecastle stairs. Neera moved out along the bowsprit and grasped my hand. The contact surprised me, but it was oddly touching as well. No human had ever held my hand in such a way.

"He'll send me away now. Good luck."

"May she preserve you, child."

"Neera!" Captain Heovin bellowed. "Get your mischievous hide below decks!"

Neera gave one last squeeze before shimmying back to the deck. Her footsteps receded as the captain's approached.

"One hour if we turn around, Captain," I said.

Words died on his breath, and he paced for a few moments. "With their ships, I don't think we have that much time. Will you help us?"

"I will relay information from the other shamans and the sea, but that is all."

"We need you. Your inaction could cause more deaths than fighting."

"No, Captain; that is fool's logic. I will not take responsibility for a conflict I never began."

The captain heaved a great sigh. "I hope you change your mind, Khren, even if it's only for Neera's sake." His bootsteps grew softer as I considered his words.

*For Neera's sake.* Odd how one can wish for death and friendship in the same breath. Did I care for Neera so much to actually *consider* his proposal?

I leapt from the bowsprit to dive deep into the cold sea. The water welcomed me again, but I paid it little mind. Our fleet began turning to cover the distance to the trailing ships. I swam ahead, wondering how the next few hours would unfold. The enemy was not so far off that I couldn't sense them; the watchman had been right: twenty-four ships. The sea held them in its light grip, allowing them to slip through its currents to come ever nearer. I could sense the eagerness of those on board.

Something tainted the waters, though—a taste I hadn't felt in . . . years, yet I couldn't place it. Too faint it was, but foul just the same. I began to swim forward when I felt one of my brothers dive into the sea ahead. Behind, a sister-shaman joined us, and I moved to meet them. Unlike Iulaja, my brethren merely swam with me, knowing they could not change my mind. I nearly opened my mouth to convince them to shun this course, but their anger rose with the unspoken thought, so I remained silent.

The enemy closed the distance faster than they should have been able to. Much faster. The taste like sour blood returned to my tongue, stronger. I scrambled amongst my memories for understanding.

The enemy's lead ship turned starboard to bring its cannons to bear. Together, our small group called the sea to protect us from the imminent cannon blasts. Moments later, the first of them rang out, booming through the sea around us. The sour taste became pronounced, like I had opened my mouth to a goblet full of blood.

Salazaar.

Our sworn enemy had joined battle with the enemy humans. They rode the ships; I could feel them now, each one a torch held against the cold surface of my mind. Another cannon boomed over the ocean. As the cannonball was loosed, a salazaar infused it with fire, lending it explosive strength, which released when it struck near my ship. I exhaled relief when I realized it had struck wide.

My brother and sister had already begun weaving. They swam in a complex circle, moving closer to our own ships to come between them and the enemy. More shamans dove into the waters behind us. They swam with energized fervor toward the dancing globe. Some called to me, but most spurned my presence and added their anger to the swirling call of sea and sky. Above the water, storm clouds gathered as more enemy ships brought their cannons to bear.

Our own ships, perhaps realizing that they could not outrun the salazaar-assisted sails of the enemy, turned to bring their cannons to bear as well. An entire barrage sounded from two enemy ships. I heard them claw into our flagship. Fire from the salazaar shed flame over the decking and masts.

My fellow shamans danced in a large, writhing globe, circling ever tighter. A current pushed harshly at one of the enemy ships, turning it about, despite what its rudder might wish. The same happened to the ship nearest it. The first tentative lightning strike rang down from the stormy sky, tearing into a third ship.

Our own ships fired back, and the new cannons broke one of the enemy ships. From this strike could I feel the first enemy deaths—perhaps from cannon shot, perhaps from the shredded wood as the shots struck home, perhaps drowning after being flung unconscious from their ship. The reason mattered not at all; I wept for them just the same. Even the salazaar. When the first one died, I wished, as I always had, that our peoples could have patched our indescribable differences.

But I must be honest. There was hatred, too. A small part of me relished the idea of the vile lizards dying. Indeed, as the water began to heat from their efforts, I found myself urging my brothers on.

Above us, the water's surface began to hollow until forming into a bowl, limiting the depth we had to work with. Our circle of shamans broke and began swimming away, but it was too late for some. The furthest behind, the most visible, was whisked into the air. Immediately, I felt fire ring across the distance from three separate ships and strike the hovering yeavanni.

Her death throes echoed across all of our minds, but it was followed quickly by the second and third. I could feel the glee with which the salazaar dealt their death.

I pleaded to my Goddess, *Yeavan, how can you allow this? Please, oh please, stop this insanity.*

I swam, afraid for my life. Afraid of being flung into the air like a salmon caught for the spit. The salazaar released their water-hollow, which sucked us back toward the center. The seabed churned around us, sending rock and coral biting against our skin.

Our brothers from the other part of the fleet had arrived, though. They swam in a shaman-circle a league away, and a water spout pulled up from the sea, twisting and writhing into the sky.

This they let loose on the nearest ship before drawing another from the cold depths. Iulaja was among them. I could feel his scorn as he wove his magic. His hatred soured perhaps more than the salazaar taint.

My own group of shamans regrouped and began weaving once more. They asked me, begged me, to help, and still I resisted.

The rock below us split, opening a deep channel. In moments, the water around the shaman dance flashed an incredible heat. The circle broke apart, and three more yeavanni lives were lost to the boiling sea.

Cannon peals rang above, and death's specter took more and more lives on both sides. Three salazaar used the winds to leap from their ships onto one of ours—Captain Hoevin's. I could feel their fire rip into the men aboard. With a fear I couldn't quite explain, I dug through the water toward my ship. What I planned to do, I had no idea. But I remember how striking it was that a sense of loyalty had sprung up inside me.

I reached the ship and leapt up from the water to the bowsprit. Only two of the salazaar remained. The heat from their flame touched nearly all of the sails. I nearly blacked out from the intensity.

Captain Hoevin screamed from the quarterdeck. "Reload, men. Quickly, by God!" I heard him run forward and the sound of his rapier coming free came just before another salazaar blast raked the quarterdeck. Ten men screamed, including Captain Hoevin.

"No!" I screamed, impotent in my rage.

The next blast, I could tell, was directed especially toward the captain. I followed his maniacal shrieks as he ran across the main deck. The distinct sound of steel biting flesh rose above it, and then a salazaar howl broke over the din.

His foul brother sent one more blast into the captain, and Captain Hoevin fell lifeless and burned to the deck. Another body fell: the wounded salazaar.

Neera's calls broke the relative silence that followed. "Uncle!"

"No, child! Don't go near him! Run!"

My warning had little effect, and by any measure, it was too late. Another blast from the remaining salazaar scoured young Neera as she ran. Her body struck the nearby gunwale with a thud, and a moment later, she splashed into the sea.

In that one instant—the instant I realized Neera's fate—I lost my tentative hold on my mind. A gurgle escaped my throat; a sound of pain and regret, a burst of hatred and revenge.

A warcall.

I leapt from the forecastle deck, pulling the strength of the sea with me. My leap took me onto the salazaar's back, and, though my hands and feet sizzled, I wrenched him over to face me.

The fetid beast began to speak, but my tightening forearm silenced him. I summoned the sea. For this waste of life, I needed but little, and it came eagerly in any case. A snake of water slipped up the side of the ship and over the railing. It slithered closer and reared up behind me. The salazaar felt fear. For one of the few times in my life, I dearly missed my eyesight. Seeing the look on his pitiful face as the snake dove down his mouth and nose would have been like fine wine to my parched throat. I slipped my handhold down to his shoulders now that the snake had ensured its entrance. It slipped through throat and lungs in an instant as a cacophony of burps and gurgles escaped the salazaar's throat. He could no longer breathe, but still he writhed.

Illustrated by Shawn Gaddy

I enjoyed every single moment of it.

His life was snuffed by the holy water nearly a minute later. I panted over him, wishing he had more to give me. No matter. There were more of him about.

I dove into the sea to rejoin my brothers and sisters. They had regrouped into one dance. There were few now, but I made one more. I swam around them, touching yeavanni flesh, coaxing more magic from them, and them from me. These podlings knew too little of death. I coaxed just the right dance from them, and together, we began a deadly ballet between water and air. We dragged the sea about the enemy ships. Our anger fueled the speed. Above, lightning rang down, snapping into salazaar and main masts, sails and rigging.

The lizards tried to pull us from the sea once more but we would no longer be caught off guard. We dove deeper, moved around the sea's hills and mountains, its tunnels and warrens. It mattered little where we danced from; the weave would still be as tight.

We called a storm, focusing solely on the enemy ships, but one yeavanni's anger touched the next. Their anger fed more, and it built and built until we thought we would burst from it. The storm scoured the sea about us. The whirlpool sucked the enemy ships down: one, two, now four and five of them gone.

A gale drove at the few ships that tried to escape. Waves lashed at those poor vessels. I pulled away from my brothers. I became the focus of their magic—the avatar to the god we had summoned. I rose above the sea on a waterspout and brought the full fury of the storm and sea upon them. Six ships remained, then five, two, and finally the last had been wrecked from the power of Yeavan.

I turned about, feeling for more of them, but finding none. Where had they gone? Why could I kill no more?

Kill no more . . .

The *geis* over my mind began to clear. The destruction registered in a glacial crawl. *Dear Yeavan, what have I done?*

I dropped from the spout and fell listlessly into the water below. My sides tightened as I realized how large the storm had become, how dangerous—to everyone—it had grown in our thirst for revenge. Seven, perhaps eight of our ships had remained when I left my ship. Now, only two remained. Surely, several were wrecked from our own magic; the churning seas must have dragged seaman after seaman under the waves, dozens of lives snuffed by our thirst for salazaar blood. I swam about the ocean floor, wailing my sorrow to the seas around me.

It took me minutes to realize the state of the two remaining ships. One would surely founder, and the other would be a near thing. I swam quickly to the ship that might be saved, and asked Yeavan, Her Grace, for one last favor. She granted this, and the water was staved from the cracks in the ship's hull. The humans inside began pumping the water out, and slowly, she began to regain her height.

My brothers joined me a short time later, though many of them felt loathe to do it. *We've done enough for them,* their minds said.

"You can go home soon enough," I told them. "Give them this token, this bauble that means nothing to you."

They agreed and stayed until both ships were well enough to sail. But then they began to leave. One by one, the yeavanni shamans turned from the ships and began to swim home.

I waited until I was sure the human ships could make it without me, and then I turned away, too. But I didn't swim toward yeavanni seas. I swam toward the battle, toward the site of my ship's sinking. I found her ruined hull in little time and searched around the remains of the once-proud ship.

I found Neera shortly after. She rested at the bottom, cupped by soft seaweed. I pulled her from the bottom and began swimming toward the departing ships.

Iulaja met me and blocked my way. "Leave her, Khrentophar. *They* fashioned this graveyard, not you. Let her rest among the other humans."

I floated nearer to Iulaja and touched his shoulder. "I will return to them, Iulaja. I owe her a deathbond."

"You . . ." His mind flared with disbelief. "None of them, not even she, deserves that. Drop her and come home."

"Yeavan protect me, but I cannot. I touched this child, Iulaja. Perhaps more of them can come to understand us."

"They will never understand us. Never."

Odd, how freedom can change its meaning. I had once wished for nothing but death by the hands of my Goddess, to be free of human shackles. There, floating close to my brother, I wished only to live that I might pass on her ways.

Iulaja misunderstood my hesitation. His hand touched my shoulder, and he said, "Come, brother."

I pulled away. "I cannot."

He floated nearby for long seconds, and then his anger flared and he swam to one side. "Begone, fool yeavanni."

I hugged Neera tight and swam away.

Long after I had left Iulaja, I heard his ever so faint words. "Begone, dear Khrentophar. May she hold you close to her heart."

# KINSHIP

*Written by*
**Jason Stoddard**

*Illustrated by*
**Brian Carl Petersen**

## About the Author

*Ever since Jason Stoddard finished his first story—written longhand with a fountain pen—he knew what he wanted to be, but it would take twenty-four years before he fully realized it. Not that he didn't try. He wrote stories through college and collected rejection slips from all the best magazines of the day.*

*Jason received his degree in engineering and became vice president of engineering for a high-end audio company.*

*Early in 2001, everything changed. Jason met Lisa and he proposed eleven days later and they were married within four months. Within twelve months, Jason was writing again.*

*Today, Jason is running an advertising agency with twenty employees and clients that range from cruise lines to nanotech startups, and finishing up his second novel,* The Other Side of Paradise. *His work has been published online in* Another Realm, Fiction Inferno *and* Far Sector, *as well as this volume of* L. Ron Hubbard Presents Writers of the Future.

## About the Illustrator

*Brian Carl Petersen is a thirty-year-old artist living in the Pacific Northwest. His mother is from Sweden and still lives there. His father's family hails from Denmark and Ireland mostly, with a dash of the rest of Europe mixed in.*

*Brian has visited and lived in Sweden a couple of times. The last time he was there was about five years ago and he stayed for about a year and a half. Since his return to the United States, Brian has been bouncing around from job to job, house to house, searching for his calling. For many years, he had no real intention, regardless of how much his work was praised, of doing anything with his art.*

*When a friend suggested he submit an entry to the L. Ron Hubbard Illustrators of the Future Contest, he took the suggestion to see what would happen. He didn't place with that entry but, undaunted, he submitted a second time. To his great joy, he found out that he had won.*

*Winning the contest has given Brian greater confidence in his abilities and has inspired him to produce more work. He has also been thinking more about different avenues he might travel in pursuit of a successful and rewarding career in the arts. He follows the motto, "Do what you love, love what you do."*

In the viewing room of the greatship *Avalon,* the Lawbringer Natural Alexander watched the earth turn beneath him while images of the Kin danced behind his eyes.

*Echoes, just echoes,* he knew. He had spent the last four days in deep Mesh, trying to keep his mind from returning to Elise, trying to leash and contain it, to channel it down the narrow avenues away from her touch. And yet, even then, the Travelers had chided him more than once: *Her record is no more. Go from here.*

He looked down upon the earth, forcing the images away. Thirty years since he had left, thirty years in the arid terraclime of Mars, almost thirty years with Elise.

Africa was now passing beneath him. The Sahara was a dim ochre eye, shrinking. The rest was riotous greens and olives and moss colors, teemingly alive, straining toward space. There had been a time when mankind thought their mechanical culture could destroy the earth, but those days were long past. Africa was empty of all but his biochanged playthings.

*And the Kin.*

Looking at Africa, he let himself slip back into second-level Mesh. He saw demographic breakdowns of the Kin overlaid on the continent, population centers and migration patterns and percentages of intelligence. He saw them moving over the African plain, singly and in small groups. He saw sterile documentary pictures of male and female. He saw the now-intelligent eyes of one female as it tended its children.

*Beauty and grace,* he thought. *Whoever made them, made them well.* Unbidden Mesh-images of the unearthly sfumato beauty of Da Vinci's "Mona Lisa" and the *gevrinesse* of Quartocure's "Before the Days of Paradise" sprang to mind, but he bid them away.

In second-level Mesh, whispering voices found him. . . . *These are the most successful of the ur-humans, more successful than the Cyborgs of Australia, more successful than the Thinkers of the Indian steppes, who had yet to prove the superiority of their intellect, more successful than the dolphin-men who swam in the sea. . . .*

The Grid whispered of their observed habits, their lifespan, the unique pattern of their intelligence. Natural Alexander floated, buoyed by information.

He urged a thought about their origins, but the voices only muttered, like cemetery leaves. Dry rustlings, without meaning or purpose. Like so many things in these long new days, their origins were buried, forgotten. Natural Alexander could dig deeper, but the viewing room was no place for third- or fourth-level Mesh.

*There would be time for that. There was always plenty of time.*

One of the greatship's aides drifted in, skin as soft and glowing as that of an infant, blue doe-eyes downcast, subservient. One of the many half-remembered ideas. "Your shuttle will arrive in seventeen minutes, Sir Alexander," she said. "We are transferring personal items from your stateroom."

He nodded, coming down into first-level Mesh. The aide drifted off toward another passenger.

Above the globe of the world, several gossamer ships of the Travelers hung, sparkling with points of light, readying for one of their journeys to far stars. Inside, he knew, were humans, gossamer and insubstantial themselves after the Shift, Meshing with the Grid-forces that made their Travel possible.

But for all their beauty, he could not bring himself to warm to their purpose. They insinuated, they manipulated, they *stole* for the Shift, for their Travel. That he knew. That he had Judged.

*You have not Judged us,* the Travelers told him, in Mesh. *That was the Judgment of another.*

Natural Alexander shivered in hate and rage, plunging savagely to minimal Mesh, looking away from the earth, from the Travelers, and from the Kin.

It was many long minutes before the shuttle arrived and he began the descent toward Africa.

> *Judgment of the Kin and the hunters will be based on a single criterion: Are the Kin, despite the pattern of their intelligence, fully human? Can they, naturally and instinctively, access the Grid?*
>
> *—Assignment Summary, The Law*
> *To Natural Alexander and Quasara*

The little boat dropped out of the sky and landed on a shiny gray featureless pad set in a vast rolling green plain. Here and there, old acacia trees poked their skeletal branches above the brighter greens of biochanged grasses and shrubs, still clinging tenaciously to life. Off to the north was a pile of black shiny buildings, slowly graying in the hot sun, and a long-disused fused road, snaking away to the east and west. In the distance were the rainbow ruins of an old city, gracefully rounded spires rising here and there amidst the rubble. *Nairobi?* Natural Alexander wondered. *Kenya?* It had been a long time since man had needed Africa.

He stepped out into suffocating heat and humidity. The smell of green growing things, of the mindless dance of chlorophyll and earth, the musty smell of the dark black loam assaulted him. After his years of Mars's mechanically arid terraclime, his body drank it in. *Africa. Earth. Home.*

He stepped out of the shuttle and froze.

A woman stood beside a black glossy streamlined oildrop groundcar, waiting for him. She was a tall and graceful figure with skin like cream, long flowing white-blond hair and startlingly clear gray eyes. Her face was thin, narrow, triangular, almost ascetic, pale skin stretched tight over high cheekbones.

He shuffled forward in the high gravity, hand outstretched. "Elise . . ."

"No, Quasara," his partner said, dodging his grasp. Breaking the spell. Closer, he could see that her resemblance to Elise was only superficial.

*Chance?* He wondered. *Or had the Law chosen a partner that might be able to salve his pain?*

*Not bloody likely,* came her thought.

"Sorry," Natural Alexander said. "I've been spending much time in Mesh. There is some overlap."

Quasara grinned, dark and sardonic. "Not another dream-warrior, his mind filled with dead thoughts from the Grid."

"I like to think not."

"We'll see." *Now get out of my mind!* She fed him images of burning bodies, hate and pain.

Natural Alexander dropped out of second-level Mesh, gasping with her fury, still feeling her waves of emotion. "I'm sorry," he told her. "I did not wish to offend. If I had been informed . . ."

"You would have done it anyway, back on the greatship." Quasara shook her head.

"I'm here to See," Natural Alexander said, by rote. "I serve the Law."

She looked him up and down once more, weighing him with the heavy freight of her unblinking gray eyes.

Once the car was speeding them over the lush greenery, Natural Alexander noticed something odd. Quasara never touched anything. He remembered how she had avoided his touch. She sat in her seat, disconnected, almost floating.

But he said nothing.

Instead, he played back a memory of the Kin that he had obtained in second-stage Mesh on the shuttle down, a memory of their death. He watched as one of the hunters, a great large man camouflaged by a quicksuit, ran one of the Kin down and slit its throat. Blood ran into its short fur and stained it red. Its legs quivered, claws scratching feebly in the dirt. Its hands clutched at the long grass, brought up clumps. Its eyes looked out over the plain, blank and feral, displaying no intelligence. Then it stopped, dead.

He played this over and over, as they glided into the jungle, thinking *this is what I have to Judge.*

•••

*Purposereport Travelers. Carry instrumentalities [NODES] of human Grid [extracorporeal infonet] to placesbeyondbeforeafter physical contact: enhancement of humankind mentality/infonet by datinclusion from nonterrestrial sources. Traveleraccess of extracorporeal infonet established: various eccentricities duetofrom Travelers acorporeal nature assessedtabulatedaccounted.*

*—Traveler Humanview Synopsis, textrender partial*

Quasara took him to a rambling white wooden structure set at the top of a low rise in the plain. The biochanged grasses and trees grew less wildly here, as if restrained by a thoughtful and intelligent hand.

"Your home?"

She nodded.

He raised his eyebrows, said nothing.

The sun was setting, dropping blood-red into the greenery, as the dark oildrop slid into its berth and stopped.

Natural Alexander sensed a deep relief in Quasara as the berth doors slid closed. He wanted to go into deeper Mesh and investigate some of her mysteries, but he forced restraint. There would be time. There always was.

He followed her through a tour of the home, done in archaic style, all sweeping white curves, alabaster pillars and vaulted ceilings. She told him that it was a family home, an ancient holding, that she lived alone in it except for mechanical servants. She touched nothing. Everything responded to the sound of her voice.

She showed him his room, which was large, geometrically perfect, and self-effacingly utilitarian.

"I hope you did not expect company," she said, almost coquettishly.

Natural Alexander smiled. One of her mysteries he had deciphered. "No."

"Good," she said. "Once you've configured the room, come join me on the deck. I'll have food."

"But not for you," he said.

Quasara turned slowly. She looked at him with coolly direct eyes. "So you know."

"I know one thing. I'm sure there are others."

"Perhaps." An enigmatic smile.

The deck was a great glass terrarium, enclosed from the outside by thick rose-tinted panes. Quasara had the lights low so that they could look out at the stars, twinkling faintly in the distance. Below the stars the plain stretched far toward the horizon, the grasses waving in the breeze like a charcoal-on-black sea, vaguely phosphorescent.

She had set a plate for one. He sat, looking pointedly at the bare table in front of her.

"So what gave me away?" she asked.

"You are a wonderful illusion," Natural Alexander said. "But you never touch anything. And I am a fourth-level Mesh-adept. You should not have been able to read me."

She nodded.

"How old are you?"

She smiled, a sad soft smile. "I'll leave that one for later. It's the house, isn't it?"

He nodded. "The location."

"*Traveling* is not easy."

Natural Alexander caught the strange overtones of her feelings, the odd emphasis she put on *Traveling*.

"You were a Traveler?" he asked, feeling suddenly cold.

"I have seen the wonders of the stars," she said. "But all I want is to come home again."

Natural Alexander sat in quiet uncertain rage. *Typical, typical, typical.* The Law was "repairing" him with this ancient setup.

Quasara shook her head. "I know how you feel about Travelers," she said. "I have been trying to reverse the Shift ever since I came back to Earth. My body lies in stasis, waiting for me."

"'Once the soul is freed, it can never again love the bottle,'" Natural Alexander quoted.

*But one can try,* she thought. Natural Alexander felt shades of her own yearning, her own pain, her own desires to feel the flesh again, to walk in the halls of the Limited Mind, to play out the rituals of being human once again. A token image, as false as Grid-love, flashed before his eyes. Her body lying naked on a stone dais, illuminated by a powerful blue light. Glowing, fluorescent, dreamlike in the blue light. Cold, so cold. Needing only a kiss to wake her.

*False, false, false.*

Natural Alexander was silent for a long time, his head down, not looking at her. Thinking of the last days. Elise: *I'm going to do it, on that day. There is nothing more for me here.* And him: *What about me?* The look on her face, not pity or hate or pain but love, love and total belief that this was the only way, and hurt that he would not join her, that he could not bring himself to the cold and alien Shift to become a Traveler too, so they could Travel together, sharing diffident love in the light of dying stars. And the Travelers. Recruiting, recruiting. Always there, at the edges of your mind. Always there, in Mesh. Taking advantage of the end-times of the Third Martian Terraforming.

"We both hurt," he said finally.

She nodded silently and looked out over the darkening plain. He knew now that the direction of her gaze meant nothing. Not as an inhabitant of the Grid. But he knew what it meant, and appreciated it for that.

Dinner was silent, broken only by the faint hum of the circulators, bringing the damp and fragrant air in to the deck, full of mystery, cool with night.

Natural Alexander drank it in. There was always something right, something that said "home" about the earth. Even Africa, abandoned so long ago.

"Why are you here?" Natural Alexander said finally, sipping an exquisite port.

"Here? In Africa?"

"In this Judgment."

"The Law thinks that because I have lived on the border of humanity, I will be better able to Judge our Kin."

"Or the hunters."

"Yes, however it turns out."

"What do you know about the Kin?"

Quasara grinned. "You mean you haven't stuffed yourself on the Grid, thinking it Truth?"

"I have had some Mesh-time, but I value your opinion."

"Good. The Grid is not always correct in its word."

He smiled at her. The Grid that Meshed all humans from birth, the Grid that spanned the solar system and the stars, the Grid that could be accessed by anyone, anywhere, the Grid whose great glowing nodes could be seen from space when Earth swung to darkness like coals in a fire, the Grid that contained the sum total of thoughts, emotions, data of the human race from times long forgotten, the Grid was *wrong*?

"I feel your doubt," she said. "But you will see. Tomorrow, when we go out to meet the hunters. The extreme first."

Natural Alexander nodded. He had spent his life with the extreme. His heresy on the Godfarm in Nebraska. Embracing the Law. Traveling, Traveling, Judging, Judging. People of the fringe often did not enjoy Judgment.

He pressed her further on the subject of the Kin, but she would say no more.

He spent most of the night in his room, his eyes unseeing, his hands unfeeling, deep in fourth-level Mesh. He had heard the arguments for seeing through one's own eyes, had heard them many times as a child, even as the State Nebraska residents were removing an arm, a hand, a nose in their catch-as-catch-can, eye-for-an-eye justice.

Then, as now, he gave those arguments little weight.

*A human being is an unmodified Homo sapiens, or an engineered variant thereof, that breeds true with its own subspecies, and that has mental capacity and mental frequency [partially accurate translation] that resonates [partly accurate translation] in tune [partially accurate translation] with the nodes of the Grid, such that an individual is capable of first-stage Mesh without mechanical assistance.*

*—From the Grid, rendered with zero-level limitations*

He woke with the sun, feeling heavy with ideas. Fourth-level Mesh used the power of the Grid to magnify his connection, and he now recited fact upon fact, mating habits and intelligence patterns and lifespan and geographic distribution. He *knew* the Kin.

Illustrated by Brian Carl Petersen

He had even glimpsed a shadowy reference to their origins, buried in an ancient dark corner of the Grid where shadows danced and menaced. He had trawled that one for long moments, wary of the darkness, shying away from the biting acidic pain of a guardian. He had appealed to the Law, but the Law had been silent. They had no jurisdiction in some parts of the Grid, just as their many human and ur-human agents and mechanicals had no power over those that chose other paths.

After his breakfast, they took the groundcar and glided out to the camp of the hunters. Approaching it, seeing the coarse fabric tents and open campfires and the rugged, somber way in which the men were dressed, he was vaguely disappointed. *A thousand Hemingways, a thousand clichés,* wasn't that what Manson Federico said, half a thousand years ago?

The camp was an intermingling of fantasy, myth and reality. There were sweating fat men dressed as the stereotypical Great White Hunter smoking cigars, others that were clearly supposed to be Muslim slavers, others that looked to be every bit the dapper Englishman of five thousand years past, even one or two that did not appear fully human. Many of them wore the jewel-like telltales of mechanical Gridlinks.

Natural Alexander shook his head at their grim posturing. *They want to be the apotheosis of all hunters,* he thought, *but they are little more than rabble.*

Their leader was a great big white man, as pink and sunburned as the image of an ancient Georgia cracker, wearing great khaki clothes, a floppy safari hat and a glowing orange telltale above his left ear, a gleaming gem that told of his mechanically enhanced Mesh to the Grid.

His name was Great White Hemingway, and when he introduced himself, even Quasara grinned mildly.

"I should warn you that we recognize no arbitrary law here," Hemingway said, before they even sat down.

"We serve the Law," Quasara said. "The singular and pure."

"We're not hurting humans."

"That remains to be seen."

"If you're intent on proving them human, then why are you talking to us?"

"To determine motive. Why do you hunt them?"

"The apes are about all there is to hunt out there," he said, his ancient American accent so pronounced that Natural Alexander was tempted to use a translator. "They've been weeding out the other big predators the past few years."

"The demographics don't have them at that population density here," Natural Alexander said.

Hemingway smiled. Sunlight winked off his mechanical Gridlink. "I know what I see," he said.

Hemingway's woman drifted over to their area and sat beside him on a collapsible chair. She was young, blond and wild, no more than seventeen or eighteen.

*So much the stereotype,* Natural Alexander thought.

"I saw the Kin being hunted," Natural Alexander said. "They were using quicksuits."

Hemingway grinned, a terrible grin full of blood and death. "Not sporting enough," he said. "We use jeeps and rifles now. Just like the old days."

*How is it, in these long new days, when a man can be almost anything he wants, that people like Hemingway exist?*

"I don't judge you personally," Hemingway said, sounding angry, sounding intense. Natural Alexander realized that the hunter had been using his mechanically enhanced Gridlink to read his thoughts. He also, for the first time, felt the almost oppressive weight of age in Hemingway's mind. He was nearing the end of his third century, and men did not live much beyond that.

"Yes, the tyranny of the telomeres," Hemingway said, still reading his thoughts. "It's the trap of all of us. Still the great Democrat, as they used to say."

Natural Alexander nodded. "I'm sorry," he said. "One cannot always control the voice of the mind. The Law Judges impartially."

"Apology accepted," but still the eyes smoldered. "It doesn't matter. The apes aren't intelligent when we kill them."

Quasara, who had been sitting quietly through all this, said suddenly, "How do you know?"

Hemingway looked at her, his gaze sexual and frank. "Three ways," he said, his voice suddenly soft, harder to hear. "First, we only take females. If they aren't carrying an infant, they aren't smart. Second, we have a thinker that analyzes their behavior and tells us if they are intelligent. We also have mechanicals that read heat patterns. When they are intelligent, their body temperature rises consistently by half to three-quarters of a degree. Believe me, they aren't intelligent when we bring them down."

Natural Alexander sighed. "The Law has made it not a question of intelligence, but of Mesh."

Hemingway shrugged. "If they can Mesh, I would think that they would get the hell out of there before we showed up. We don't try to mask our intentions."

"We would like to accompany you on a hunt."

Hemingway looked at his woman, then at the others who had gathered. "Sure," he said. "Why not? Just stay out of the way."

"And if we don't?"

"Then you won't have to worry about this case, Lawbringer. Because you won't be around to worry."

Later that morning, he and Quasara were led to one of the jeeps, which was not exactly a jeep but a modified open groundcar that had semiautomatic drive. Thick hoops of plasticarbon or some other composite looped over the open top above their heads, apparently protection of some kind.

"It's reasonably safe," Great White Hemingway said. "Just try to keep your arms and legs inside the jeep."

They drove out into the plain, the jeeps riding above the tall green grasses in dead silence. The sun sat directly above their heads, its heat flat and white on their shoulders. The air was hot, muggy, close, fragrant. Mountains rose in the distance, purple gray and swimmingly unreal in the heat-shimmer of the plain.

The hunters did not talk. Quasara asked Great White Hemingway more about the hunter's methods, about how many they had killed, about some other things that she could have learned from Mesh. Hemingway answered her questions with clipped, curt tones for a while, and then told her to shut up.

They drove in silence for a time. Natural Alexander dropped into second-level Mesh and caught some of the conversations between hunters, nothing unusual.

*It doesn't look encouraging, so far,* Quasara said, after a time. *I had thought that they might use their mechanical Gridlinks to drop themselves out of Mesh, or to interfere with the signal. But they're using the Grid heavily. If they can approach the Kin like this, then they either aren't Meshed, or are ignoring what they are receiving.*

*Or they use their Mesh in a different way,* Natural Alexander sent back. *Let's not reach conclusions before we have Seen.*

*Of course,* Quasara sent back, her eyes gray needlepoints. But she stayed silent.

They got their first view of the Kin as they crested a low rise in the plain and began to descend into a small, grassy valley full of low trees. Natural Alexander didn't even know that he had seen them until the jeeps shot forward and several tan-colored shapes detached themselves from the shelter of the trees and began to run.

"Rifles!" Great White Hemingway cried, his voice booming above the silence. "Target per OK!"

He set the autodriver on and shouldered his own weapon.

As the autodriver bobbed and weaved around the trees, intent on its quarry, more and more Kin began to join the fleeing crowd. Some of them tried to escape to the right or left, but other jeeps in the hunting party sped after them, hemmed them in.

They ran with surprising grace and inhuman swiftness, their long legs flashing, leaping and flying like gymnasts. Natural Alexander reflected again on their beauty. Most of mankind's biological experiments rarely achieved even a utilitarian aesthetic, but the design of these creatures was inspired.

In fact, they were not that far off-human, with long gracefully muscled arms, long strong legs, and slightly widened, vaguely feline heads. They wore coats of short fur like slick skin. It rippled with the working of their muscles.

Some of the females ran blindly alone, others ran with naked fear, clutching children, as pink and hairless as human babies. His second-level Meshed mind brought up a dissection of one of the Kin.

The hunters began firing. Natural Alexander smelled the dull firework smell of gunpowder and thought, *They really are using the ancient weapons.*

They burst out of the cover of the trees. The plain sloped downwards to a natural watering hole, where more of the Kin were gathered. Over a hundred of the Kin ran in front of them.

*Too many,* Natural Alexander thought. *Far too many of them here.* He looked up at Quasara, and she nodded as if in confirmation.

In the open, the jeeps were able to put on a burst of speed, and the hunters hit their marks. One, two, three of the Kin went down. Their jeep and one of the others slowed, while the others shot on, still pursuing the Kin. Hunters jumped out of the jeeps and hauled the carcasses in. The still-twitching body of a big female was deposited at Natural Alexander's feet. Her hand, with its ragged sharp claws, fell against the leg of his trousers and hung there, as if in silent plea. He shook it off and looked back up. The jeep was already moving again.

The second jeep, slower to start, was set upon by a half-dozen big males with clubs. Half of them used their clubs to batter ineffectively at the hardened windshield and plasticarbon hoops, but three of them dropped their clubs and clung to the jeep as it began to accelerate. One of them reached through the hoops and got hold of one of the men within. As their own jeep wheeled to help, Natural Alexander saw one of the big males pulling an arm off one of the hunters as easily as a cruel boy would pull a leg off a fly. Great White Hemingway blazed away with his rifle in the air.

As their jeep drew closer, the males dropped and scattered. The hunters did not fire on them as they disappeared into the trees.

They pulled alongside the other jeep. The man who had lost an arm was dead, lying on the bottom of the jeep in a pool of his own blood. One of the other men was badly wounded, slumped in his seat with deep gashes in his lower abdomen.

"For every two of them we take down, we lose a man," Great White Hemingway said, his eyes shining. "And the Law thinks this might not be fair."

At that point, another jeep joined them from the east, blood and gore-streaked, but with the carcasses of two Kin inside. Hemingway had a brief conference with the driver of that jeep. Then he started up the autodriver and began heading back to the camp. Natural Alexander sat stunned, unable to completely assimilate all that he had seen. Not yet. He tried to ignore the spreading pool of blood on the floor of the jeep.

"What do you use the bodies for?" Quasara asked Hemmingway as they drove into the trees once more.

"Some of them have been stuffed, some of the heads have been mounted. Their fur is too short to have any commercial value."

"So you just hunt them for sport?"

He just looked at her with cold, flat dead eyes, as if asking if there was any other reason to hunt.

She shook her head, but said nothing. They accelerated back toward the camp. As they left the protection of the trees and began to climb the low rise they had crested earlier, Natural Alexander looked back and saw several of the Kin, male and female, walking restlessly among the trees, watching them as they left. They were too far away to make out much detail, but Natural Alexander was again struck by the way they moved, the way their color blended into the background of the tall grass, the regality of their posture. They looked almost preternaturally *right*.

*They walked as we once must have walked,* he thought, *on this African plain, so many millions of years ago.*

*Don't be so sure about that,* Quasara sent.

Natural Alexander dropped out of second-level Mesh and put up his shields, not looking at her.

> *Show me a law, any law, that is not arbitrary, save for the prevention of harm to another human being. Is it law that we should tithe to our leaders and our churches? Is it law that we should dress and act a certain way? Is it law that we should eat only vegetables, or only meats, or only the fruit of the genetically engineered vine? No, no, and no. We choose these things, and choose to impose them on others, because the alternative frightens us. Selfish, small, arbitrary laws. The only true Law, I say, is the Law of doing no harm to others of our kind, or to any intelligent beings that we discover or create, our kin.**
>
> *—Maximilian Greyson, Dissertation on Arbitrary Law*
> *Founder of the Philosophical Basics of the New Days*
>
> **It is unknown whether M. Greyson was using* kin *as a specific or a generic.*

The next morning, they went to the Kin.

Natural Alexander had spent too much of the night before deep in Mesh, researching the origins of the hunters. They had the feel of a childhood memory, the texture of a past better forgotten, and he had driven tirelessly, remorselessly, at their past. Their origins were, as he had suspected, in the vast American Midwest, long since gone back to the rolling grassland of times past. Not very different from when he had grown up there, a hundred and a half years ago. A little darker, a little more decadent, the involuted workings of State Nebraska and the Prophet Moderns were still very much recognizable. Some myths are so difficult to change.

Once, briefly, he thought he had felt Quasara's presence, a dry and somewhat hard wit nearby. But he opened his perception, and there was nothing there. He thought for a moment about seeking her out, then decided against it.

He had dreamed of the Kin. They had not been pleasant dreams.

He sat quietly in the groundcar as it parted the lush and fecund vegetation, his eyes seeing again only the blood, only the death, of last night's visions.

"You're quiet," Quasara said finally.

Natural Alexander nodded. "Strange thoughts."

"You spend much time in Mesh."

"No more than you."

Quasara frowned. "You seem nervous."

Natural Alexander looked away, out at the green grassland speeding by. He could sense concern at the heart of her statements, amplified by the Grid, but he could not bring himself to respond. Not the time. Not the place.

The groundcar was arrowing toward a place that they had found on the Grid the day before, a valley where the Kin seemed to congregate naturally, showing more stability than the nomadic groups that the hunters pursued. It was distant, almost a hundred and fifty miles from Quasara's home, and untrafficked by hunters. When pressed on methods of communication, the Grid had responded with second- and third-hand stories of certain Kin learning the rudiments of Enhanced English, and carrying on broken conversation with explorers of a thousand years ago. He and Quasara had looked at each other at that point, grasping for the first time the difficulty of what they intended to do. And yet they had to try. The Law came, Saw, Heard, and Judged. That was the Way.

Midmorning had them approaching a shallow valley, ranged on one side by low limestone cliffs and bisected by the silver shimmer of a small stream. Their destination turned out to be a break in the cliffs, where the stream emerged from a small gorge and tumbled down a short slope into the valley below. Rows of neat, regular openings had been cut into the side of the cliffs, black and empty like eyes.

"Caves," Quasara said. "That's where they are."

Natural Alexander shivered, looking around the valley for any sign of the Kin. They surely would not have to go into the caves themselves?

Quasara sensed his reluctance and suggested that they scout outside for a time. They ranged up into the river gorge, and cried out together when they saw the writing on the far wall. Phantasmagorically twisted and gouged, geometric shapes and diagrams, with flecks of pigment here and there clinging to the eroded limestone.

"The Kin have a language?" Natural Alexander said, dropping instinctively into second-level Mesh. In Mesh, the carvings became clear, resolved themselves as ancient human graffiti.

"We should have suspected," Quasara said.

A few hundred yards up the gorge, they came upon the hunter.

His quicksuit lay half in, half out of the water. Currents caught at the shiny fabric and tugged it to and fro. Long streamers of moss had grown from rips in the fabric covering his legs. A hand that was more bone than flesh emerged from one of the sleeves.

"It seems," Quasara said, finally, "our information was in error."

Natural Alexander knelt down and pulled at the fabric of the quicksuit, unable for a moment to believe it real.

"How could they bring down a man in a quicksuit?" Natural Alexander wondered.

"Men," Quasara said.

"What?"

"Men," she said again, gesturing farther up the canyon. There were several other quicksuited bodies lying both in the river and on the rocks.

"How did they do this?"

Quasara shook her head. Natural Alexander followed her out of the canyon.

"Do you know how fast a man in a quicksuit is?"

She nodded, said nothing.

"Jeeps I can see. I can see them running down a jeep. But quicksuits?"

Quasara only nodded again, calm, unreadable. She stood now near the closest of the cave entrances.

"They're gone," she said.

"I'm not going in."

She looked at him. "Then I will."

Natural Alexander waited outside the cave, watching the tall grass of the peaceful little valley, half-expecting some feral half-crazed Kin to descend upon him, until Quasara called to him over the Grid.

*Come in. You need to see this.*

Reluctantly, he obeyed. Once inside, he paused, invoking an algorithm that amplified his dark-vision with Grid processing. Details jumped out at him in the artificially grainy relief of augmented vision.

He found Quasara in a large, circular chamber lit through a fissure that opened from the top of the cave. In the center of the chamber was a large fire-pit, ringed with rocks. The roof of the chamber was stained an immensely deep satin black by the smoke of many past fires. Other pathways, some curiously artificial looking, led into the deeper darkness of the cave.

He readjusted his eyesight and came to stand by Quasara, who was looking up at a natural rock overhang near the far end of the chamber.

"Here's their art," she said softly.

He looked up.

And was stunned.

Carved into the natural rock of the cave were twelve, twenty, a hundred scenes. Some were recognizably idyllic: the Kin in the light of a stylized sun rising over the limestone hills of the valley. Two Kin, making love. A family in the trees. The bright, seeking rays of warmth radiating from a fire. Even a distorted, nearly comical caricature of a human, a figure that emphasized the human's large odd graceless head, stubby legs and slick, hairless body.

They were not looking at primitive art. It was stylized and simplified, to fit within the constraints of bas-relief sculpture on rock, but it was not a primitive simplicity. Rather, it looked to be the mature workings of a culture that had seen its renaissance realism, its postmodern experimentation, and evolved and simplified it into a singular expression of art, a grace of line and fluid form that was undeniably alien and compelling.

Natural Alexander dropped quickly into second-level Mesh, searching for references to Kin art. There were none. He searched for human referents and found nothing. He was standing in front of something totally new, something he had never seen before. He captured images and stored them in his personal archive, imagining the playful dance of firelight animating the images, making them even more real. He simulated a few of those. The results were haunting.

"My God," he said.

"They are powerful," Quasara said, reaching forward to touch one of the images.

One image captivated him more than any other. It was a rendering of the valley, but this valley was populated with strange, sulking, slick-skinned figures that darted here and there. Humans.

He saw Quasara looking at it, too.

When they were done, they drove out from the cliffs, the dark eyes of the caves following them like an accusation.

Back at the house, Natural Alexander ate his dinner alone, in silence, images of the Kin's art swimming up unbidden behind his eyes. Even without Mesh, the images were still too fresh to be denied. He ate methodically, not tasting the food, as the night descended around him.

Quasara floated in as he was finishing.

*What did we see today?* she sent.

Natural Alexander shivered. "I don't know."

*I never suspected . . . and the Grid gave no word.*

A nod.

*Natural Alexander, these are not just animals.*

"No!" he stood up, advanced on her. "Look! See! Hear! You cannot prejudge this. You cannot!"

*So that is your crime.*

"Damn it, talk to me."

"What should I tell you? I know you are right. We still need to meet the Kin."

Natural Alexander collapsed into his chair. "If you had seen what they had done to her," he said, trailing off, realizing what he had said, who he had said it to.

Quasara had come very near him, a faint smile on her lips.

Then she turned away, with one quick sob. Grid-amplified images of rotting bodies, ancient burials under full moons, the rending and tearing of flesh filled his mind.

*This is the time when I need to be able to take you by the shoulders and shake you,* she sent.

*This is when I need to be touched.*

> *Are we living in the great time of the Long New Days, as Gamine Feetha said seven centuries ago, or are we living a fever-dream? No human lives longer than three centuries, despite our biochanges and nanotech and medicine. The stars are the province only of the Travelers, with their vague and cold humanity. We have attempted to terraform Mars twice and succeeded only in making a place where stunted humans can scratch out a dry and bleak existance. Venus has resisted our best efforts. We've found nobody to communicate with in the cosmos. And searching for*

*answers with our engineered variants is a vain exercise, like peering into a distorted fun-house mirror. Our birthrate is on the rise again, but many children die before maturity of simple neglect. Can we say that we have done nothing, that there is no progress, that the only thing that we can point to as the all-encompassing achievement of humanity is the Grid?*

*—Henry Clare, Short Times of the Long New Days*

They went even farther afield the next day, a brittle silence between them. They had brought shimmersuits, an unspoken acknowledgment that they had no idea of what they might find.

Shortly after noon, they found the Kin.

They had been passing through the polychromatic ruins of an ancient city, looking up at the spires that flung themselves at the sky. In the center of the city were the remains of an ancient park, now a forest run rampant with bioengineered growth. Grass had crept out over the fused roads. Lush vines and creepers followed the cracked sides of the buildings toward the sky. In the very center of the park was an ancient fountain that still sprayed water into the air, to burble and chuckle over brightly colored geometric patterns.

Around the fountain, and near the perimeter of the forest, were a small group of Kin. Not more than twenty, they lounged on the grass and played in the clear water of the fountain, looking completely natural and at ease. Three or four looked up as their car slid to a stop on the edge of the square, but they made no move to flee. After the car hadn't moved for a few minutes, they turned their attention back to what they were doing.

"This is very strange," Natural Alexander said.

Quasara nodded. "But maybe not as strange as we think. They could be a nomadic group, just passing through the city."

Natural Alexander nodded, pleased by the logic of the answer. Still, it was almost as if the Kin had chosen this place to stay out of sight of the big, rolling plains where the hunters pursued them.

"Let's watch them for a time," he said.

Quasara looked at him, said nothing.

After less than an hour, some curious patterns emerged. There were three older males standing in front of the fountain, alert and watchful, as if on guard. Their eyes shone with fierce intelligence. They ignored the four immature Kin that played in the fountain behind them, but watched intently as any other Kin approached the fountain to drink. All the Kin, as they approached the three in front of the fountain, would bow their heads and hold one hand in front of their chest, as if in salute. Then, and only then, would they drink and return to the grass.

Natural Alexander saw quickly that there were potentially many more Kin in the abandoned park than they saw. There was a constant slow flux of Kin emerging from the dark, overgrown forest while others returned, keeping the number fairly constant.

A number of families came out as a unit, adult male alert and watchful.

*Clearly intelligent,* Natural Alexander thought. He had found out in his first night with the Grid that the males become intelligent when the female they were mated to became pregnant, and served as a guard for her and the rest of the family group during the next fifteen to twenty months. Then both parents gradually lost their intelligence, reverting to their feral state.

*They stay intelligent long enough to maximize the chance of the child's survival,* Natural Alexander thought. *Intelligence, after all, was a survival factor when natural ability was equal.* It made sense. He could even imagine a species like this evolving naturally.

*But then why discard intelligence, once childbearing was over? Why treat it as something to be endured, but not to be treasured?* Natural Alexander tried to imagine himself the captive of instincts, living each moment as if it was his first, his last, his all. He could not fathom it.

After a time, a small, stooped figure emerged from the forest and began making its way, slowly and methodically, toward the fountain. His gray brown fur was streaked with silver. His eyes were downcast, masking any evidence of intelligence.

But his age wasn't the most remarkable thing about him. He walked with the aid of a straight, thin walking stick. As he got closer, Natural Alexander could see that the stick was no rude branch, but an intricately carved and worked piece of wood.

He turned to see if Quasara had seen the walking stick, and saw that she had donned her faux shimmersuit. As if she really needed one. She could be no more than a voice if she wanted to. She gestured at his. "Come on. Time to See."

"But . . ." Natural Alexander said, then shrugged and pulled on his suit. In the shimmersuits they would be virtually invisible, not more than the heat-shimmer of overworked Grid processors. If they stayed far enough away . . .

*I wonder if that's what the hunters thought,* he thought, remembering the caves.

Quasara slid the door open and they jumped out into the hot, humid day. The shimmersuit began immediately adjusting his temperature.

The silver-haired Kin had kneeled by the edge of the fountain and was drinking with his walking stick tucked under one arm. The three guards stood, alert as ever, apparently unaware of the two humans' presence.

*Did you see what he was carrying?* Natural Alexander sent.

*Yes,* Quasara sent. *That's why I came out.*

Quasara showed up as a bright, shimmering blob with vaguely human features in the shimmersuit's visual processor. She seemed to look at him for a moment, then began walking quickly toward the fountain.

*Stay behind if you want,* she said.

He followed her.

Nothing happened until they were within twenty feet of the silver-haired Kin. Then things happened very fast. The three guards suddenly snapped toward them, dropping into protective crouches. Natural Alexander froze, his heart pounding. They may have just sensed the shimmer, but he could swear that they were looking right into his eyes. Their eyes, at close range, were strange, golden, full of keen intelligence.

Quasara dropped the shimmersuit illusion.

The kids that had been playing in the fountain stopped playing and looked at them.

The three guards crouched, as if frozen on the spot.

Then slowly, methodically, the Kin that had been lounging in the grass and the kids that had been playing in the fountain stood up and began to walk back toward the overgrown forest in the park.

The three guards waited, still unmoving, until the Kin had disappeared into the trees. Then, with unnatural swiftness, they raised up and bounded into the trees themselves, their long legs flashing.

The silver-haired Kin was the only one left. He turned and looked at Quasara. Then he turned his head, the smallest fraction, and he was looking directly at Natural Alexander.

*But it can't be,* Natural Alexander thought. *He can't see me.*

For several moments, the tableau held.

Then Quasara moved forward, her hands outstretched, showing empty palms. "We would like to talk," she said.

No response.

*We would like to get to know you. We represent the Human Law.*

No response.

She stepped forward again. She was no more than ten feet away from the silver-haired Kin, who still watched them intently, not dropping his gaze.

*We mean you no harm.*

No response.

She closed the distance again.

Then, with a sigh that sounded almost like regret, the old Kin turned around and began walking toward the forest.

*Wait!*

No response.

Quasara stopped and watched him retreat.

That night, Natural Alexander dove into the Grid once again, digging deeper, mustering his legions of

Grid-node-processors to divert the guardians, looking for some mention of the Kin beyond the dry facts and figures. Clues to their origins. Anything. He had drilled through four thousand years of history, had chased that first tiny faint echo of the Kin's origins that he had felt the first night, but everything was slippery, so slippery. Contaminated with emotion. He drew back, trying to find another way around the barriers, satisfy the slavering gatekeepers.

*And so he bloats himself on the Grid, again seeking Truth,* Quasara sent to him. He sensed her presence, near, very near, straining toward him.

*Touch me,* she said.

He pulled away, retreating to his personal archive. The familiar walls enclosed him, hid him.

Quasara appeared in front of him, wearing a thin filmy dress that fluttered in a nonexistent breeze. She was so thin, so waifish, so much like Elise.

*Touch me. Here.*

He did.

*The Law is no more than a legal program with delusions of grandeur.*

*—Archaic, Author Unknown*

They went out again the next day.

And the next.

Both times, they found more Kin. Both times, the Kin withdrew as soon as they appeared.

They gathered more data, more observations. They built shimmering castles of thought, harnessed the processing power of a thousand Grid thinkers, analyzed and probed and analyzed more.

There were glimpses of great beauty in the Kin. Even from afar, Natural Alexander and Quasara could see that they had more than an animal grace. Their elaborate ballets of mourning after a hunt, when the hunters had gone. Whole groups nodding and moaning in unison, a sharp-edged cry that made Natural Alexander shiver in unconscious dread. The fact that they buried the dead that the hunters sometimes left, again with a gibbering, lowing ritual that sounded almost like language. The rituals of love and sex were complex, intricate, and the ties of family not forgotten.

On the third day, the Law sent them an emissary.

Its flyer fell to Earth outside Quasara's house as they were breakfasting on the deck.

*Come out.* A curious voice from the flyer, harsh and grating, full of command.

Inside the flyer was an Independent Thinker. Smooth, curved, polished and beautiful, it moved with an oiled mechanical grace. It bid them to sit down in a semicircular alcove, then swiveled the pilot seat to face them. Vaguely human, its face was sharp-chiseled, metallic, with cold dead lenses for eyes.

*I am the arbiter,* it sent. *You are to Judge quickly.*

"But we haven't yet contacted the Kin."

*Perhaps that is the answer you need.*

"No, there is more," Quasara said.

It swiveled to look at her. *Trouble Seeing. Noncorporeal projection. Now it is time to See. I will cast own vote based on your data. I have spoken to hunters. I have tried contact Kin. No success.*

"We need more time!"

*Law says not. Emotion a barrier. You must quickly use organic sight to See and bring justice. That is Law's instruction.*

"I don't believe this."

*Is not a matter of belief, of faith, of God. Time to Judge.*

"Why is the Law impatient?" Natural Alexander asked, speaking for the first time.

*Law has followed. Law has Seen. Law knows your failure and has other tasks for you.*

He turned to Quasara. "I can't believe this. We are being removed."

*You have one more day. Then Judgment.*

"But you have seen the art. You know there must be something more to the Kin! We need time to try to contact them."

*Can argue honeycomb is art. Product of insects. Now, please leave vehicle. I will remain in here. Less dirt. Tomorrow by noon, we cast votes. That is all. The Law has decreed.*

The Independent Thinker picked them up and set them down outside the flyer. Then the door slid closed.

Quasara looked at Natural Alexander. "What can we do?" she said.

Natural Alexander frowned. "There is one chance," he said. "But it is a chance. Get the car."

At the camp of the hunters, the Great White Hemingway found enough humor in Natural Alexander's request that he bellowed laughter, despite his obvious pain. He gripped his slashed belly, crying and laughing at the same time. The camp had been raided the night before, and now stood in ruins. The tents had been shredded and burned. Dead hunters lay on the ground. Smoke rose from a dozen smoldering fires. The hunters that were still alive were gathering up their things, getting in their jeeps, and leaving.

"A Mesh-adept asking for a mechanical Meshlink," the Great White Hemingway chuckled. He tore the link from his ear and tossed it at Natural Alexander. "It'll burn out your brain, adept."

"It may at that," Natural Alexander said. *But then again, what was the alternative?*

*What are the limits of human experience? Is that the question, or is a better question, WHY are the limits of human experience?*

*—Short Times of the Long New Days*

Natural Alexander seated the Meshlink, feeling it shiver and burrow into his skin, gripping tight with a million tiny nanohooks. He imagined that he could feel its tendrils burrowing deeper, deeper, deeper into his skull.

*Hello,* the thing said. *You may call me Charlie.*

Then it went silent. Natural Alexander frowned. How did he use the thing? He had never . . .

The data hit him like a hurricane. Ungodly amounts of information poured in, operations modes and specifications and simulated life-scenarios, examples of use from its former owner, how it was manufactured, the theory behind the link, everything, everything, everything all at once . . .

"Enough!" he cried. The stream stopped.

*Do you wish filtering?*

"Yes. No. Are you active?"

*Yes.*

Natural Alexander sighed, waiting for more. A slight tingling in his head, like a million tiny bees, like the electricity in the dull black wires that used to ring the earth, was his only response.

He looked up at Quasara, who had been watching his one-sided conversation in what looked to be real concern.

"It's time," he told her.

"I know," she said, coming over to his bedside. They were in his room, all customization off, all windows off, as isolated as they could be from the outside world. She reached down, as if to take his hand, but her projection passed through him like smoke, only the faintest hint of projection-energy. She smiled sadly.

"Just come back," she said.

"I will."

He closed his eyes, laid back, and dropped into second-level link.

THE POWER! POWER! POWER! He rushed through data, thinking ohmygodifIknewitwaslikethis . . . the tingling sensation had become electric, humming and throbbing with power, with capability, with response. He visited his own archive, passed through the ghosts of his touch, a hundred and eighty years of data falling before him, giving up its surface, its texture, its reality. He felt his first kiss once again, felt the emotion as he watched State Nebraska's border fade from the back of the big groundcar, saw his first enterprise grow, succeed, experienced arriving on Mars again, the thirty good years of his life, all passing through, felt, recorded and relentlessly classified, kept, and cleaned.

*My God,* he thought. *I can do so much here.*

He drilled down into the Grid.

Down, down, back and back, toward the hint of the Kin that he had felt before. Layers of the Grid parted before him, effortlessly. The sensation of speed was incredible.

He bobbed and waved, avoiding guardians that he had passed only with difficulty before. He was getting a feel for the parameters of the device that he was wearing. It amplified his rapport with the Grid, but his Grid-adept status was the power behind it all. If he was not able to hold the whole of the Grid in his mind, and turn it in upon itself in fourth-level Mesh, he would be helpless, an ultrafast skimmer of data, but no more.

He pushed himself deeper into link. Guardians could be called to ward guardians, extensions of the Law itself could be suborned to give him access to areas otherwise inaccessible. He went deeper, playing one force against the other.

The Kin were so close. He could get an emotion, a longing, that was tenuously connected to the Kin's origin, and was skirting around the edges of a large light that flared and died, the source of the emotion. He arrowed toward the light.

PAIN, BLINDING PAIN. He was a supernova, he was a sun, unbelievable heat, unbelievable pain.

He pulled back, quickly, his visual processing distorted and hazy.

*Pain is used to indicate potential damage to human mental function,* the device told him. *Please take care to avoid direct contact with areas of conflict.*

*Enough!* he thought, and the thing was silent.

He concentrated on the light. It was a dim and flickering thing, buried so far down in the Grid that he wondered if it would be possible to get back out. Formless and pulsing, it radiated the dull emotion of longing and despair, and flashed images of Kin, half-developed Kin.

He tried to go around the light, but the Grid slowed him. He was nearing its core, its beginning, almost three thousand years in the past.

Natural Alexander pushed down, as far as he dared.

The light had changed. Now it was feeble, fleeting, dimming. He pushed toward it.

PAIN.

No good.

He could go no deeper, he could go no further. He was stuck here at an interface more than four thousand years old.

The light flickered and pulsed.

Natural Alexander pushed down deeper into link, into the deepest fourth-level link he had yet acheived. If there was not a direct way in, maybe there was something in the way he had come, a path he could trace, a path that would lead to an alternate opening.

He saw lines, the twists and turns and feints that he had taken down from the upper levels, ever deeper. He plotted the location of the light. He rotated, he analyzed.

In the real world, he knew, he would scarcely be breathing, now.

There it was! Near the light. The light was a decoy.

As soon as he thought that, the path began to constrict, to close.

He arrowed toward it. And passed through.

Light and calm and silence. Where is he?

*You are riding on the backs of our souls.* A voice, soft, slow, alien.

*Charlie?*

*Not your mechanical thing. Us. Your Kin.*

The flash of a furred face, aged and sad, eyes burning with the fierce light of intelligence. Then nothing.

*Where am I?*

*I have answered that, human.*

For a moment there is more than a glimpse. He is immersed in warm, slow thought. The song of instinct, the blood-drive of unreason. He is looking down, as if from a great height, on a group of Kin, standing tall and alert in the African grass. They are looking up at him.

A chill surge of fear passes through him.

*Where am I?*

Another flash. He is feeling the first thoughts of a newly intelligent male Kin, as it wonders about such concepts as past and future, and connects the physical love of his female with the child growing in her. The feeling of his own pale, childlike joy.

Another flash. Pain and fear. The hunters have just come over a hill, on a group of Kin. The intelligent ones are communicating quickly with others of their group, others that are out of sight and out of earshot. They are straining, collectively seeking the resonance that will alert the natural ones that the killers have come, making the strategy that will ensure that the fewest of their number are killed.

*I see,* Natural Alexander thinks. *You have your own Grid.*

*We feel the texture of our souls directly,* came the soft, alien voice. *We do not use machines.*

Natural Alexander feels another, deeper chill. *If they have their own Grid that is separate from ours,* he thought, *that argues technological accomplishment . . .*

*No machines.*

*You are trying to say this capability is inherent?*

*That is exactly what I am saying.*

Natural Alexander's mind reels. He stretches his perception and tries to feel where he was, to get his bearings in the Grid. But there is nothing but soft resistance and light. A strange texture, a sponginess that is organic, cloying. He pushes at it.

*Do not struggle, man. You are out of your Grid.*

Again, he receives a flash. Distant origins, grown hazy and indistinct with time. The days when people sat down in front of displays to connect to the web. The next logical step, beyond man's ability to influence his own brain. A Grid that was inherent. A Grid that was biological. A Grid that was not dependent on the energy of the nodes, radiating across the universe.

*A web of souls,* the voice said.

*Souls? By religious terminology?*

*A soul is what we are. Our essence. More than body. Not religion.* Natural Alexander feels a chill equation, religion as a distortion of what it can be, of the underlying reality, of the potential. And, for the first time, he gets the impression that he is conversing with a profoundly simple mind.

*Why the lack of intelligence?*

The picture that came to him was chilling in its simplicity. Intelligence as a black blot upon the Kin's pure white web, as unnatural as nanotechnology and bio-steel. For a moment, just a moment, he is seeing intelligence from their perspective, constant intelligence as a glitch in the programming, a cold, hard drive of unreason, an unfeeling, unsoulful way of living, cold and icy and black. He sees their lives, rich with meaning without words, the sensual rush of nonsentience, the joy of feeling.

*What can compare to the touching of the souls, man?*

There is more. He sees how they view the human Grid as a mechanical monstrosity, horribly artificial. Gigeresque, ingrown, rotten, festering with ancient thoughts, drives, ideas, data, useless and unlighted storehouses far from the reach of the sun. A place where devils cavorted, sick and twisted grotestesqueries of human form. Clanking and groaning mechanically with the weight of the millennia. *No place for a soul.*

Natural Alexander shivers with the power of the imagery, thinking of Quasara. Trapped in the Grid by the Travelers.

*Travelers are human no more. No feeling,* came the soft, alien reply.

*They are human by definition.*

*Very poor definition of humanity, man. Humanity feels.* He is fed an image of himself, deep in Mesh, trying to separate, compartmentalize, package and put away his feelings for Elise. And, on the whole, succeeding. *That is our kinship.*

And before he can deny it, before he can begin building the tapestry of lies that will convince him that is not what he did to Elise's memory, there is more.

An image of him and Quasara, walking hand in hand through the African grass.

An image of Quasara's body in stasis, rotting away from uncountable ages.

An image of him flying to another indistinguishable Judgment, old, very old, his heart running down and eyes dim, flying in Mesh, hearing about the Kin boiling up out of Africa, taking Europe, and how that is all right, because man does not need Europe anymore.

And then there is nothing.

And then there is PAIN! PAIN! PAIN! On and on, forever and ever.

Natural Alexander passes out.

*I say we just reboot* the whole thing.*

*—Ghuton Velasco, contemporary of Henry Clare.*

**This word is known to be obsolete slang, the meaning of which is now unclear.*

Natural Alexander came slowly up from his depths, wrapped in veils of bright gauzy white. Low hums became murmurs of sound, then voices. Chill burning pinpricks and flashes of pain faded out, resolved, grew sharp and clear. He felt a human hand, white and cool, on his forehead.

"Wake up," Quasara said.

He opened his eyes. The room swam, resolved. He was still in his small room, but it was now crowded with figures. Quasara bent over him, blocking his view of the others in the room.

She was *touching* his forehead.

Natural Alexander reached up, *took her hand.*

"You're . . . you're . . ."

"I'm here," she said softly, leaning back so that he could see the others in the room. One was the Independent Thinker, his equation-perfect metal contours looking surreal and out of place in the plain white unornamented room.

The other three figures were Kin.

The robot bent toward him, screeching something unintelligible in its rapid metal voice. He dropped into second-level Mesh to understand what it was saying . . .

And got nothing.

He tried dropping down again. Nothing.

He tried to get emotions, feelings, anything, through first-level Mesh.

Nothing.

He felt for the mechanical weblink. It was gone.

There was not even a distant hum.

She saw the panic in his eyes and gripped his hand more tightly. "No," she said. "You can't."

"What happened?"

Quasara looked at the Kin. "It's their doing."

"But with the Meshlink . . ."

"It won't work," she said. "I've tried it."

Natural Alexander tried to imagine living without Mesh. Not to know what someone else thought, what they were planning, what was going on around him. To be cut off from all human contact. To be, according to the Law, something less than human.

He looked at the three Kin. One of them spread his hands in a curiously human gesture, as if saying, *We are helpless to change things now.*

Quasara took his hands. He looked back at her, seeing a miracle.

"They did this, too?" he asked.

"Yes," she said. "To them, the soul is a simple device."

The Independent Thinker, with a squeal, gave up and whirred out of the room.

*Obviously not equipped for verbal communication,* Natural Alexander thought.

Quasara looked at him, uncomprehending.

Natural Alexander laughed and took her arm, pulling himself up out of bed. "It seems that I have some unlearning to do."

"We all do," Quasara said, de-opaquing the wall of his room. Outside, the flyer of the Independent Thinker was rising toward the west, off to take its own Judgment, however incomplete, to the Law. Natural Alexander and Quasara walked, hand in hand, to look out over the brightening day. The Kin joined them.

"It's wonderful to feel again," Quasara said. "Thank you."

The Kin nodded. One stepped forward, extended his hands, grasped both Quasara's and Natural Alexander's.

"Small step," he said, slowly but clearly. "Much to come."

Natural Alexander shivered, remembering the final scene that they had sent him. A vision of one possible future, a future now closed to him? He did not know.

He took his free hand and pulled Quasara close. They would await the results of the Judgment.

Together.

# IN MEMORY

*Written by*
**Eric James Stone**

*Illustrated by*
**Luis G. Morales**

## About the Author

*Although born in America, Eric James Stone spent most of his childhood in Latin America and England. No matter where he lived, he read voraciously thanks to his father's science fiction collection.*

*During college, Eric wrote several science fiction and fantasy short stories. After two rejections he gave up and did not write another short story for over ten years.*

*During his writing hiatus, Eric went to Baylor Law School, passed the Texas Bar Exam, worked on a Congressional campaign in upstate New York and found a job doing research for a nonprofit organization in Washington, D.C. Four years later he returned to Utah and, at the height of the Internet boom, was hired as a website developer, where he still works.*

*One day in 2002 he was suddenly filled with the desire to write a novel. He again began taking creative writing classes and going to writing workshops. His writing skills improved and class assignments inspired him to set aside his novel to work on a short story. This is his first published story.*

*His Web site can be found at www.ericjamesstone.com.*

## About the Illustrator

*Luis Morales, age forty-six, came to the United States from Colombia, South America, sixteen years ago and has worked in a printing shop doing pre-press production since that time. He has been interested in art since he was a child, drawing at school and for his family, and drawing an occasional cartoon for newspapers in Colombia.*

*Luis pictures himself as an illustrator and he has tried many times to get into the field of illustration. But he has never succeeded until he discovered the L. Ron Hubbard Illustrators of the Future Contest on the Internet.*

*He submitted an entry in the first quarter of the 2001 contest year, which placed in the finals. Upon receiving his critiques from the panel of judges, Luis studied the critiques and practiced what the professionals instructed. He then resubmitted to the Illustrators' Contest in 2003 and was selected as a winner.*

*Now, with the publication of the following illustration, Luis has indeed entered the field of illustration and hopes to actually work as an illustrator. Doing so would be, to him, a "dream come true."*

*Luis thanks his wife, Giselle, for her belief in him and for her strong support of his dream. He also thanks Hector, his fourteen-year-old son, for his support.*

I'm soaring over the snow-tipped peaks, enjoying the warmth of the sun on my wings, when the call comes in from Andrew. It's been three years, four months, seventeen days, five hours, forty-seven minutes and twelve seconds, simtime, since I last talked to him, so immediately I fork my consciousness and slow one of me down to realtime.

I answer the call in video mode, using my human appearance. "Hey, buddy. Long time no see."

Andrew jerks slightly, then shakes his head with a smile. "Can't you at least wait for the phone to ring before answering, like a normal person?"

"Sorry. Was just glad to hear from you."

His voice is thoughtful. "Just got back from your mom's funeral. Thought you might like to talk."

The funeral had been more than thirty-two days ago, simtime, and I hadn't thought about it since. "Thanks for going. I saw you were there when I watched the feed." I had not really watched it; I'd run it through an abstraction routine to note who was there, then archived it in case I ever needed it. I sent a message to the simtime me asking myself to watch it and give me the memory.

"I know you and your mom hadn't really talked since . . ." His voice trailed.

"Hey, I know you're trying to commiserate with me, but trust me, I've done all the grieving I need to do. The funeral was a month ago for me."

"Oh. Right." He scratches his hair over his right ear. "What's the sim up to now?"

"Three hundred ninety-one point seven to one. A little over a year per day of realtime. Still doubling every couple of years or so. They keep saying we'll reach the physical limits of processor speed soon, but people have been saying that since before you and I were born."

"A year a day." He purses his lips and puffs out a breath and grins. "All I can say is, don't expect a birthday present from me every year."

I chuckle. Then my simtime self slips me the memory of the funeral, and I remember how my dad looked: shoulders slumped, shadows under his eyes. Not that I really care, but . . .

"Did you talk to my dad at the funeral?"

"Yeah."

"How's he holding up?"

Andrew pauses and licks his lips. He does that when he's nervous. "Not well, I'm afraid. He didn't look good, and he kept talking about how alone he was, with no family."

"He can call me anytime he wants." Alone? No family? Welcome to the club, Dad. I haven't heard from him or Mom in fifteen years. Realtime.

"Look, I think you should call him."

"I'll think about it." Dad and Mom are the ones who turned their backs on me, after I uploaded. I don't need them anymore; I've grown beyond them. If Dad wants to talk to me, let him call.

"He needs you. And I think . . ." Andrew subconsciously licks his lips and falls silent.

"What?"

"How old are you now? Simtime?"

I run a quick check. "Twelve hundred thirty-nine years, three months and eight days old. What's that got to do with my dad?"

Andrew shakes his head. "I just turned forty-five, and my kids think *I'm* old. I know I don't seem to change much between phone calls, but you've been changing, and it's getting faster. Twelve hundred years, and it's only been, what, sixteen years realtime?"

"Seventeen years, two months, twenty-two days."

"See what I mean? Nobody keeps track of time like that. Oh, I know you and all the others are becoming something more than human, but I'd like to think you're adding on to your humanity, not turning away from it."

I make my voice halting and mechanical, like a robot from an old movie. "Puny . . . human . . . you . . . dare . . . to . . . question . . . me?"

"Ha-ha. Very funny." He rolls his eyes. "I'm trying to make a point here. I know that the time before you uploaded must seem like a distant memory to you, but I think you should talk to your dad. Maybe it'll help you remember where you came from."

I try not to be annoyed. "Uh, maybe your brain's getting rusty with age, but mine—perfect recall. I remember where I came from: Falls Church, Virginia, same as you."

He laughs, shakes his head. "Yeah, well I ended up not too far from where we started. But you . . . you always were on the fast track, even before you uploaded. Anyway, I better go, don't want to keep

Illustrated by Luis G. Morales

you slowed down to mortal speed. Just think about what I said."

"Okay, okay. Give my love to Deb and the kids."

"Will do. Talk to you in a few years. Bye."

"Bye." I cut the connection. My simtime self notices the conversation's over and reintegrates me.

The wind ruffles my feathers as I catch an updraft. Being up here alone helps me to think, even if flying with feathered wings is not a very human thing to do. It's one of the things Andrew can't really understand. I answered a call once with my wings on, and I think he found them disturbing, because he kept shifting his eyes away from the screen. When I told him I liked the feel of the sun on my wings, he asked how that was possible, since both the sun and the wings were simulated. I replied that it didn't matter, since I was simulated, too.

He didn't like that answer. I guess he still likes to think of me as the kid he grew up with, best friends forever.

He's been my friend for twelve centuries. That seems like a good start on forever.

But I'm not the kid he grew up with. That kid went on to get a Ph.D. in mathematics from M.I.T., then got involved in the SIMINT project to copy human consciousness into a supercomputer, and then . . .

Then what? I'm a copy, but what happened to my original?

I don't remember.

There's a hole in my perfect memory. Immediately, I begin diagnostics on my memory storage. I also Google "Kenneth Granley mathematician bio."

There are plenty of references, and I feel a flash of pride while reading the first few, which describe me as the SIMINT mathematician who proved the Riemann

Hypothesis. I know it's not a big deal outside the mathematical community, and it took me a hundred and twenty-seven years, but I have made a lasting contribution to the study of prime numbers. But there's nothing in the articles about what happened to my flesh-and-blood, and that seems a little strange.

Now that I think about it, I don't remember anything about the flesh-and-blood lives of any of us who uploaded, other than some conversations during the first few months after upload.

My diagnostic comes back, and it shows several major gaps in my memory storage for my first three years of simtime, plus other gaps at apparently random intervals, including as recently as two hundred twenty-eight years ago. And my pre-upload memory has thousands of unnatural gaps.

I send an urgent message to all three sims of Jeff Hwang—he had been the head designer of SIMINT, so he was the most likely to know what might be happening.

Jeff-3 got back to me a few seconds later. "Hey, Kenny, relax. There's no problem."

"Then why is my memory messed up?"

"You did it to yourself."

"What? I did it? Why?"

"Umm." There's no visual, but I know he's frowning. Assuming his current form has a face, that is. "I think I'd better let you find out the answer for yourself. I don't think your memories have been erased; I think you've just stored them in a protected area. At least, that's what you've done the other times."

"You mean I've done this before?"

"Yeah, five times. Every time, you call me in a panic. Just look around a bit and I think you'll find the missing memories. You always have before."

"Oh." Why would I keep doing this to myself? "Thanks. Sorry to have bothered you."

"No prob. But maybe you should set up an auto-message when you run a memory diagnostic. Take care." He cuts the connection.

Now that I know what to look for, I find it quickly enough: a large secured file mixed in among 3-D reconstructions of old movies. It has to be the one, because I can't think of any reason why I would take such care to store *Pet Semetary II.* The file recognizes me when I try to open it, but instead of unlocking, it activates a message.

It's from a younger me. Much younger—I think he's only about twenty years after upload. "Hey, future self. This is just a warning. I'm locking these memories away for a pretty good reason. Unless there is some urgent reason to access them, I suggest you just leave them here and forget you ever found them. You can append your current memories about this situation to the file. Trust me; you don't want to remember what's in here."

After playing the message again, I decide I was a smug little twerp back then. But obviously I've agreed with what I did every other time I've found this file, or there wouldn't still be holes in my memory.

So, do I trust myself and just forget this?

Of course not. I can always reseal the memories if necessary.

Again I try to access the file, and this time it unlocks. As it opens, it automatically begins patching the holes in my memory.

I remember.

•••

I remember having a water fight with my little sister Katie in the inflatable pool in our backyard. She shrieked at me to stop while continuing to splash me. I must have been about six, and she was two years younger than me.

It's my earliest memory of Katie. And thirty-two milliseconds ago, I didn't even remember having a sister. Why?

•••

I remember Ginger Allman, the neurobiologist who was second-in-command on the SIMINT team, telling us that Jeff Hwang was in a coma and not expected to live. While driving on a highway that wasn't yet integrated into the autodrive net, his car had smashed into a bridge abutment at ninety miles an hour.

At the time there was only one Jeff sim, and he took it pretty well. "I didn't have much of a life outside the project," he said when we tried to console him, "and I guess that's literally true now."

His body never came out of the coma before it died two weeks later. A tragic accident, everyone thought, but of no real consequence to the project: the Jeff sim was as capable at designing and upgrading the SIMINT software as his flesh-and-blood—no, even more capable.

That was ten months, three days, after he uploaded.

•••

I remember running down our street, pushing Katie on her bike. "Go! Pedal faster. Go!"

The training wheels were off for the first time, and as I let go, she continued on her own about ten feet, then started to wobble.

"Keep going!" But my yell of encouragement did no good, and she toppled to the pavement.

I caught up to her, expecting her to be crying.

Her eyes were shiny, but with excitement, not tears. "Did you see me? I did it for a bit. I did it. Did you see?"

"I saw. You did great. Wanna try it again, for longer this time?"

•••

I remember Ginger telling us that Alicia DiNovo, one of our programmers, had slit her wrists in the bathtub of her apartment. Alicia's sim insisted her flesh-and-blood would never do such a thing, that it must have been a murder set up to look like suicide. But the rest of us knew better: Alicia had obsessed over her boyfriend, and he had dumped her the previous weekend.

That was nine months, twelve days, after she uploaded.

•••

The memories pour into the cracks of my mind. Some of them—mostly of Katie—impinge upon my consciousness, while others merely settle into place so I can call them up when needed. I'm still puzzled as to why I erased Katie from my life. But then . . .

•••

. . . then I remember Dean Willingham calling me privately about the third team member to die, only eight days after Alicia's death. One death is a random event; two deaths, a coincidence; three deaths, a pattern. This latest death was not a suicide: he was shot by the police, because he charged at them wielding a butcher's knife. The same knife he'd used to kill his sister Katie and her husband and their newborn baby boy.

That was nine months, twenty-one days after I uploaded.

•••

As designed, my simulated body reacts naturally to my emotions. My vision blurs as I begin to cry. Instinctively I discontinue the body simulation, which is what I always do in a painful situation. Unfortunately, I don't know how to shut down my emotions without stopping my thoughts completely. And I cannot stop remembering.

Remembering my little sister Katie. Reliving every memory I had of her with perfect clarity. Fun in the yard. Fights in the back of the car. Helping her with homework. Insulting her in front of my friends. All the love and strain of being brother and sister.

Fortunately, my memories of her end with her wedding to Brendan. How happy she looked. I pretended it was my allergies making my eyes water as I said goodbye to her before they got in the limo. I hate to cry.

That was the last time I saw Katie. I was uploaded four months later, so at least I don't have to remember going crazy and killing her and Brendan and their baby. But I am forced to remember the horrid details that came out in the news. Photos of the dead bodies. Video of my grief-stricken parents refusing to answer questions from the newsies on their doorstep.

And over and over again, I watch the grisly footage from the police cameras as my flesh-and-blood charges out of my sister's doorway, brandishing a bloody blade and screaming incoherently. The police stunners are ineffective, and finally a flurry of gunshots leaves my flesh bleeding and dead.

Over and over I watch, knowing each time I deserved it.

I had tried calling Mom and Dad after Dean Willingham told me what had happened. Mom burst into tears and ran from the phone without a word. Dad came on, saw it was me, said, "How could you?" and hung up.

Who could blame them? I was just a simulation—the real me had killed their daughter, their grandson. The real me was dead.

It was the uploading that caused it, we discovered too late. Duplicating a human brain required a level of quantum scanning far beyond what hospitals routinely use. We couldn't test our custom-designed scanner on animals because of the Animal Rights Act, but we ran thousands of simulations and we were sure it would allow us to create a perfect copy.

And it did. The copies were perfect. We just didn't realize that it would damage the original.

After what my flesh-and-blood did, the thirty-four remaining members of the SIMINT team who had uploaded were taken into protective custody, to keep them from harming themselves or others. In all of them, the pattern turned out the same: insanity about nine to ten months after upload, then—among those who did not manage to commit suicide—a geometrically progressing disruption of brain functions, ending in death. No one lasted more than a year.

The flaw in the scanner wasn't my fault—my work was on large-scale data integrity of multidimensional arrays. My work is what has prevented us sims from going gradually insane as random errors built up in our mental matrices.

Instead, it was my flesh-and-blood that went crazy. It wasn't me. He wasn't even himself.

Then why do I feel so guilty?

I'm sorry, Katie. I'd give up my twelve hundred years if it would bring you back. I'm so sorry.

Now that the flood of memories has receded, I begin to think more rationally.

I understand why my earlier selves locked up that file. There was too much emotion tied up with those memories. Why endure the pain those memories brought when I could just seal them up? If I don't remember, it's as if it never happened.

And that's why Andrew felt I was becoming less human. In sealing off my pain, I'd severed most of my connections to my life before upload. Discarding my past left me free to fly ever faster into the future.

Part of me wants to seal up these memories again, and go on with my life. I've done it before. Five times. Katie's gone. Nothing I can do can fix that.

And now Mom's gone, too. I play her funeral again, this time really watching it. Seeing the people who loved her mourn her loss. And this time, I mourn with them. If I hadn't shut myself off from the pain, maybe we would have talked, eventually. Maybe she would have realized I really am Kenny, that the man who killed Katie wasn't the real me. Maybe not. Either way, it's too late now.

I could still try with Dad. Andy thinks he needs me. Does he, or would I just be stirring up painful memories?

As for me, it's been a dozen lifetimes since I really thought much about my family. Why not just lock up all memories of them? Or even delete them entirely? Do they really mean anything in my life anymore? They are merely memories, nothing but patterns of electrons accessed by my simulated brain.

Then again, what am I but a pattern of electrons? In my simulated world, in my simulated brain, my memories are the only things that *are* real, the only connection I have with a reality outside myself, with a world I cannot control with a whim.

And if I lose my connection to reality? They have a word for that: insanity.

I've seen insanity. Over and over again. It has a bloody butcher's knife in its hand.

That wasn't me. That cannot be me. The real Kenneth Granley is the mathematician who solved the Riemann Hypothesis, not the madman who killed his sister and her family. The real Kenneth Granley is me.

I reactivate my simulated body, changing it to my old human form before I slow down to realtime and call Dad. The phone rings several times, then asks if I want to leave a message.

I can try again later. If there's one thing I have, it's time.

# ON THE WRITING OF SPECULATIVE FICTION

*Written by*
**Robert A. Heinlein**

## About the Author

*Robert Heinlein entered the world of science fiction with the publication of his first story, "Life-Line," in the August 1939 issue of* Astounding Science Fiction *magazine and with it launched one of the most singularly versatile and influential careers in the history of the genre. His debut appearance was rich with other connotations as well—coming as it did little more than a year after L. Ron Hubbard's benchmark story, "The Dangerous Dimension," appeared in the same magazine, underscoring a close personal and professional relationship between the two master storytellers that would endure for a lifetime. In concert with John W. Campbell, Jr., editor of* Astounding, *the two writers helped to vitally define and structure the Golden Age of Science Fiction and shape the forms, concepts and narrative techniques that became the foundation of contemporary speculative fiction.*

*An Annapolis graduate whose active career as a naval officer was prematurely ended by illness, and a student of physics and mathematics, Heinlein's career reflected a virtuosity of style and invention, and a fusion of hard science and imaginative originality that produced some of speculative fiction's most remarkable novels and stories.*

*His early pacesetting works, such as* Sixth Column *(as Anson MacDonald),* Beyond This Horizon *and "Methuselah's Children," and others, were configured as Future History, with extrapolated events that had not yet occurred but were recorded with chronological exactness, as if they already had.*

*His prevalent themes—duty, valor, sacrifice and principled conscience and strength among them—provided narrative continuities in a body of fiction that ranged, with assertive energy, across a half-century of work. Notable works include* The Puppet Masters, *with its alien life forms from Titan, the very moon that is now among the prime objectives of the Cassini space probe to Saturn, and his award-winning novels,* Double Star, Stranger in a Strange Land *and* The Moon Is a Harsh Mistress.

*Robert Heinlein was the first recipient of the Grand Master Nebula Award, bestowed for his lifelong contribution to the genre of science fiction.*

*This essay was originally written by Mr. Heinlein in the summer of 1947 while living in Ojai, California, as part of a symposium on writing science fiction with six fellow writers. All of the symposium's essays were published in early 1948 as "Of Worlds Beyond."*

*In the following article Mr. Heinlein points out that there are actually three main plots for the human-interest story in science fiction, a fact pointed out to him, he says, by L. Ron Hubbard.*

*There are nine-and-sixty ways of constructing tribal lays and every single one of them is right!"*

—Rudyard Kipling

There are at least two principal ways to write speculative fiction: write about people, or write about gadgets. There are other ways; consider Stapleton's [sic] "Last and First Men," recall S. Fowler Wright's "The World Below." But the gadget story and the human-interest story comprise most of the field. Most science fiction stories are a mixture of the two types, but we will speak as if they were distinct—at which point I will chuck the gadget story aside, dust off my hands, and confine myself to the human-interest story, that being the sort of story I myself write. I have nothing against the gadget story. I read it and enjoy it. It's just not my pidgin. I am told that this is a how-to-do-it symposium; I'll stick to what I know how to do.

The editor suggested that I write on "Science Fiction in the Slicks." I shan't do so because it is not a separate subject. Several years ago Will F. Jenkins said to me, "I'll let you in on a secret, Bob. Any story, science fiction or otherwise, if it is well written, can be sold to the slicks." Will himself has proved this, so have many other writers: Wylie, Wells, Cloete, Doyle, Ertz, Noyes, many others. You may protest that these writers were able to sell science fiction to the high-pay markets because they were already well-known writers. It just ain't so, pal; on the contrary they are well-known writers because they are skilled at their trade. When they have a science fiction story to write, they turn out a well-written story and it sells to a high-pay market. An editor of a successful magazine will bounce a poorly written story from a "name" writer just as quickly as one from an unknown. Perhaps he will write a long letter of explanation and suggestion, knowing as he does that writers are as touchy as white leghorns, but he will bounce it. At most, prominence of the author's name might decide a borderline case.

A short story stands a much better chance with the slicks if it is not more than 5,000 words long. A human-interest story stands a better chance with the slicks than a gadget story, because the human-interest story usually appeals to a wider audience than does a gadget story. But this does not rule out the gadget story. Consider "The Note on Danger B" in a recent *Saturday Evening Post* and Wylie's "The Blunder," which appeared last year in *Collier's.*

Let us consider what a story is and how to write one. (Correction: how *I* write one—remember Mr. Kipling's comment!)

A story is an account which is not necessarily true but which is interesting to read.

There are three main plots for the human-interest story: "Boy-meets-girl," "The Little Tailor," and "The man-who-learned-better." Credit the last category to L. Ron Hubbard. I had thought for years that there were but two plots. He pointed out to me the third type.

"Boy-meets-girl" needs no definition. But don't disparage it. It reaches from the "Iliad" to John Taine's "Time Stream." It's the greatest story of them all and has never been sufficiently exploited in science fiction. To be sure, it appears in most SF stories, but how often is it dragged in by the hair and how often is it the compelling and necessary element which creates and then solves the problem? It has great variety: boy-fails-to-meet-girl, boy-meets-girl-too-late, boy-meets-too-many-girls, boy-loses-girl, boy-and-girl-renounce-love-for-higher-purpose. Not science fiction? Here is a throwaway plot; you can have it free: Elderly man meets very young girl; they discover that they are perfectly adapted to each other, perfectly in love, "soul mates." (Don't ask me how. It's up to you to make the thesis credible. If I'm going to have to write this story, I want to be paid for it.)

Now to make it a science fiction story. Time travel? Okay, what time theory? Probable-times, classic theory, or what? Rejuvenation? Is this mating necessary to some greater end? Or vice versa? Or will you transcend the circumstances, as C. L. Moore did in that tragic masterpiece "Bright Illusion"?

I've used it twice as tragedy and shall probably use it again. Go ahead and use it yourself. I did not invent it; it is a great story which has been kicking around for centuries.

"The Little Tailor." This is an omnibus for all stories about the little guy who becomes a big shot, or vice versa. The tag is from the fairy story. Examples: "Dick Whittington," all the Alger books, "Little Caesar," *Galactic Patrol* (but not *Grey Lensman*), *Mein Kampf*, David in the Old Testament. It is the success story; or, in reverse, the story of tragic failure.

"The man-who-learned-better." Just what it sounds like—the story of a man who has one opinion, point of view, or evaluation at the beginning of the story, then acquires a new opinion or evaluation as a result of having his nose rubbed in some harsh facts. I had been writing this story for years before Hubbard pointed out to me the structure of it. Examples: my "Universe" and "Logic of Empire," Jack London's "South of the Slot," Dickens's "A Christmas Carol."

The definition of a story as something interesting-but-not-necessarily-true is general enough to cover all writers, all stories, even James Joyce, if you find his stuff interesting (I don't!). For me, a story of the sort I want to write is still further limited to this recipe: a man finds himself in circumstances which create a problem for him. In coping with this problem, the man is changed in some fashion inside himself. The story is over when the inner change is complete. The external incidents may go on indefinitely.

> People changing under stress:
> A lonely rich man learns comradeship in a hobo jungle.
> A milquetoast gets pushed too far and learns to fight.
> A strong man is crippled and has to adjust to it.
> A gossip learns to hold her tongue.
> A hard-boiled materialist gets acquainted with a ghost.
> A shrew is tamed.

This is the story of character, rather than incident. It's not everybody's dish, but for me it has more interest than the most overwhelming pure adventure story. It need not be unadventurous; the stress which produces the change in character can be wildly adventurous, and often is.

But what has all this to do with science fiction? A great deal! Much so-called science fiction is not about human beings and their problems, consisting instead of a fictionalized framework, peopled by cardboard figures, on which is hung an essay about the Glorious

Future of Technology. With due respect to Mr. Bellamy, "Looking Backward" is a perfect example of the fictionalized essay. I've done it myself: "Solution Unsatisfactory" is a fictionalized essay, written as such. Knowing that it would have to compete with real story, I used every device I could think of, some of them hardly admissible, to make it look like a story.

Another type of fiction alleged to be science fiction is the story laid in the future, or on another planet, or in another dimension, or such, which could just as well have happened on Fifth Avenue, in 1947. Change the costumes back to now, cut out the pseudo-scientific double talk and the blaster guns and it turns out to be a straight adventure story suitable, with appropriate face lifting, to any other pulp magazine on the newsstand. There is another type of honest-to-goodness science fiction story which is not usually regarded as science fiction: the story of people dealing with contemporary science or technology. We do not ordinarily mean this sort of story when we say "science fiction." What we do mean is the speculative story, the story embodying the notion "Just suppose" or "What would happen if?" In the speculative science fiction story, accepted science and established facts are extrapolated to produce a new situation, a new framework for human action. As a result of this new situation, new human problems are created and our story is about how human beings cope with those new problems.

The story is not about the new situation. It is about coping with problems arising out of the new situation.

Let's gather up the bits and define the Simon-pure science fiction story:

1. The conditions must be, in some respect, different from here-and-now, although the difference may lie only in an invention made in the course of the story.
2. The new conditions must be an essential part of the story.
3. The problem itself, the "plot," must be a human problem.
4. The human problem must be one which is created by, or indispensably affected by, the new conditions.
5. And lastly, no established fact shall be violated, and, furthermore, when the story requires that a theory contrary to present accepted theory be used, the new theory should be rendered reasonably plausible and it must include and explain established facts as satisfactorily as the one the author saw fit to junk. It may be far-fetched, it may seem fantastic, but it must not be at variance with observed facts, i.e., if you are going to assume that the human race descended from Martians, then you've got to explain our apparent close relationship to terrestrial anthropoid apes as well.

Pardon me if I go on about this. I love to read science fiction, but violation of that last requirement gets me riled. Rocketships should not make banked turns on empty space the way airplanes bank their turns on air. Lizards can't crossbreed with humans. The term "space warp" does not mean anything without elaborate explanation.

Not everybody talking about heaven is going there, and there are a lot of people trying to write science fiction who haven't bothered to learn anything about science. Nor is there any excuse for them in these days of public libraries. You owe it to your readers (a) to bone up on the field of science you intend to introduce into your story (b) unless you yourself are well-versed in that field, you should also persuade some expert in that field to read your story and criticize it before you offer it to an unsuspecting public. Unless you are willing to take this much trouble, please, please stick to a contemporary background you are familiar with. Paderewski had to practice; Sonja Henie still works on her school figures; a doctor puts in many weary years before they will let him operate—why should you be exempt from preparatory effort?

The Simon-pure science fiction story [must contain] examples of human problems arising out of extrapolations of present science:

1. Biological warfare ruins the farm lands of the United States: how is Joe Doakes, a used-car dealer, to feed his family?
2. Interplanetary travel puts us in contact with a race able to read our thoughts: is the testimony of such beings admissible as evidence in a murder trial?
3. Men reach the moon: what is the attitude of the Security Council of the United Nations? (Watch out for this one and hold on to your hats!)
4. A complete technique for ectogenesis is developed: what is the effect on home, family, morals, religion? (Aldous Huxley left lots of this field unplowed, help yourself!)

And so on.

I've limited myself to my notions about science fiction, but don't forget Mr. Kipling's comment. In any case it isn't necessary to know how just go ahead and do it. Write what you like to read. If you have a yen for it, if you get a kick out of "Just imagine," if you love to think up new worlds, then come on in, the water's fine and there is plenty of room.

But don't write to me to point out how I have violated my own rules in this story or that. I've violated all of them, and I would much rather try a new story than defend an old one.

I'm told that these articles are supposed to be some use to the reader. I have a guilty feeling that all of the above may have been more for my amusement than for your edification. Therefore, I shall chuck in as a bonus a group of practical, tested rules which, if followed meticulously, will prove rewarding to any writer.

I shall assume that you can type, that you know the accepted commercial format or can be trusted to look it up and follow it, and that you always use new ribbons and clean type. Also, that you can spell and punctuate and can use grammar well enough to get by. These things are merely the word-carpenter's sharp tools. He must add to them these business habits:

1. You must write.
2. You must finish what you start.
3. You must refrain from rewriting except to editorial order.
4. You must put it on the market.
5. You must keep it on the market until sold.

The above five rules really have more to do with how to write speculative fiction than anything said above them. But they are amazingly hard to follow—which is why there are so few professional writers and so many aspirants, and which is why I am not afraid to give away the racket! But, if you will follow them, it matters not how you write, you will find some editor somewhere, sometime, so unwary or so desperate for copy as to buy the worst old dog you, or I, or anybody else, can throw at him.

# THE KEY

*Written by*
**Blair MacGregor**

*Illustrated by*
**Yancy Betterly**

## About the Author

*Blair MacGregor lives a life of motherhood, teaching and martial arts training. Her spare moments are spent in the seclusion of her basement office writing of places she wouldn't mind visiting.*

*In 2003, Blair considered giving up writing. From the rejections she'd received she'd begun to wonder if her writing lacked the elusive quality that could translate into a sale. Without telling anyone, she decided her next submission would be the final test and sent her story to the Writers of the Future Contest. It won first place in the quarter.*

*Now Blair is back at work writing and revising eight fantasy novels. Another half-dozen outlines are not-so-patiently awaiting their turn. Her online site can be found among the People Pages and newsgroups at www.sff.net.*

*Blair dedicates her story to Linda the Potter—creator of beauty, believer of dreams. Many years ago, she gave a confused thirteen-year-old a pen, a blank notebook, and an order: "Go write your novel, girl." May every young writer receive such gifts.*

## About the Illustrator

*Born in Fort Lauderdale, Florida, Yancy was first introduced to illustration by his older brother, Rory. He was fascinated by his brother's ability to tell stories with pictures, so he taught himself how to draw.*

*Although Yancy is self-taught as an artist, he does have many influences, including Will Eisner. When Yancy was only thirteen, Will Eisner generously spent an hour with him in his Tamarac studio, showing him how a professional worked and critiquing his portfolio.*

*He was introduced to the Illustrators of the Future Contest through his good friend Troy Connors, who was a winner of the contest in 1999. Yancy had stopped drawing for nearly five years at that time. Throughout those five years he had become a father, attended college and become part owner in his family's business.*

*Yancy is now actively working to finish college to teach history, while self-publishing his own comic books: Manifest Destiny, a dark tale of a lawman trying to escape his past and The Odyssey, a graphic adaptation of Homer's epic. He lives in Orlando, Florida, with his wife of ten years, Leslie, and his two-year-old son, Logan.*

Cassie pushed through the crowd, nose wrinkled, unable to avoid being touched. The smell of greasy meats mingled with the tang of cheap black ale. Oily fingers smudged her pale blue shirt and dust dulled the sheen of her blue black trousers. Ben had urged her to wear full skirts and tailored blouses more appropriate to her supposed station. She'd acceded to rich fabrics instead. If the good folk in Paize-of-Killaan looked askance at a woman in trousers and long shirt, no doubt they'd boggle over the scars beneath, not to mention the close-cropped hair hidden by her brown wig.

Ale stalls at last gave way to the merchant booths, where business was swift and quiet. Poets examined brushes and reeds as Cassie would knives and arrows, tested ink as she would weapons oil, inspected vellum as she would armor-grade leather. Cassie thought their obsession a waste—a preoccupation with the tools rather than the trade. Written words were but stains on a surface. It took breath and intent to make them true.

She dodged a man trailing a potential patron and reached a meadow crowded with canopies. Highborns and lesser patrons stood in the shade to hear poets vie for any position that would see them housed and fed through winter. Cassie winced at the pitch of desperation in the poets' voices. With the weeklong

Festival of Pen and Voice ending tomorrow, options were slim for patrons and poets alike.

Cassie spotted Ben sitting beneath an oak on a hillside overlooking the meadow. With so many ongoing presentations, she crossed the trampled grass in relative solitude. A highborn lord looked down his nose as she passed, and she ignored the impersonal insult. The Abandoned World had always embraced conceit. Small wonder none of Shendow's tribes sought to return. Were it not for her search, Cassie would have ordered Ben to take her from Paize on the day they'd arrived.

She hiked up the hillside and shivered as she reached the bubble of cool air Ben kept around him, then suppressed another shiver when he ended the keshin working and the air warmed.

"We leave today," she said, then waited for Ben to argue.

Ben raked his fingers through the dark hair ringing his scalp. Though he and Cassie were of an age, his mostly bare head added ten years to his thirty. The patron's robe he wore over his ample body took enough wool to clothe Cassie thrice over. The appearance of wealth had garnered interest from nigh every ambitious poet. *But not the right one,* Cassie thought, and bit the inside of her cheek. Enduring Ben's company was a small hardship compared to the wars that would befall Shendow if her search failed.

"But I found one," Ben said.

Cassie tensed. "Where?"

He pressed a fist to his mouth, but the corners of a smile showed on either side of his knuckles.

"Tell me," she said through clenched teeth.

Ben nodded toward the nearest canopy, where poets had gathered to hear their next assignment. She saw nothing but a crowd of fidgets until a woman stepped from behind the group and commanded Cassie's attention. Dark hair hung to her waist

*—a fall of liquid obsidian—*

and the woman was the ninth

*—the perfection of threes—*

and she cradled a bundle of scrolls at her hip

*—chronicles of dreams, of lives once lived—*

and she looked over her shoulder the moment Cassie's gaze touched the back of her head. A brief glance, no more.

Cassie rubbed the callus at the base of her right index finger. The ridge of hardened skin had traversed the Door intact. Her steel ring, both comfort and captor, had not. In the months without it, she had learned that freedom hid painful choices she wished she'd never known.

"Spotton," Ben said.

Cassie started. "On what?"

"Regional vernacular for 'We found the Key.'"

"We found a prospect," she corrected. It irked her that Ben had mastered the local language swifter than she, never mind that his keshin workings were the reason she understood the words at all. "We've found prospects before."

"True," he said in that airy tone she hated. "Shall we hear her presentation?"

Cassie shook her head. She'd heard enough recitations of convoluted passions to see her through old age and the afterlife. Better she speak with the prospect alone than hear her spoil verses with a performance catered to impress rather than illumine.

*Illumine* . . . Cassie frowned. A few months ago, she hadn't known such a word existed. She had no right to be on this side of the Door, no right to be anywhere but barracks and wallwalks and training yards . . . places she'd once wished to rise above.

"Cassandra?"

"I'll corner her tonight," she told Ben. "But if she's another hapless romantic with tales of woe, I'll kill something. Slowly."

"Oh, stop. You're ruining my appetite."

She glanced to his paunch—"Perhaps you should thank me"—then pushed from the tree and expected Ben to follow. She would have preferred to trek back through the surrounding woods, but she wasn't in the mood to hear Ben gripe about his bad knees.

Ben caught up with her amongst the hucksters' stalls, and the crowd parted for him as they hadn't for Cassie. She wondered if his girth caused people to step back, or if he'd found yet another frivolous means to flex his keshin.

"You think she's it," he murmured once they reached the city gates.

"Why do you say that?"

"Because you're pretending you don't."

More than once his gibes had caused her to drop a hand to her hip in search of her sword. But it—like her ring—hadn't survived passage through the Door. The longer she searched for the Key, the more she wished for both. The ring encompassed her Oath's simplicity; the sword was a weapon she understood.

"You know," he went on, "you could let yourself be a little excited."

Excitement breeds mistakes, she wanted to say. But since she'd already told him so a dozen times, she muttered, "Gods grant me patience."

"Superstitious warriors, always thinking the gods will intercede."

"Arrogant mages, always thinking they're the gods incarnate."

Ben's laugh surprised her. "You strike well, Cassandra Mintolina. Well indeed."

Cassie hailed the first empty rig that drew near. She flipped a shell—a coin, she corrected—to the driver and told him to take Ben wherever he wished. Before Ben could comment, Cassie turned and headed toward the woods. If Ben's luck held, she'd return having purged the desire to crack his jaw.

•••

Benjas Kalari sat on the sole bed in the chamber he and Cassie shared. He could have filched enough coin to rent two rooms, but Cassie had muttered one too many rude remarks about keshin workings and mage ethics. So he'd secured the inn's last and most plush accommodations and, with a gracious smile, dared Cassie to object. She hadn't—not aloud—and the frost between them had thickened or thinned depending upon her mood.

At the moment, her mood was tolerable due to her absence. She was off in the adjoining bath chamber whispering her prayer-chants, just as she did every morning, every evening, and every time the fancy struck her. The fanaticism of such warriors amused Ben. He

Illustrated by Yancy Betterly

always wanted to add his own benediction: "Now that you have prayed, go forth and slaughter with glee."

The mage captain, when Ben had confided the impulse, also found it amusing. So much so that he'd charged Ben with taking Cassie through the Door and acting as her relay for contacts. Ben appreciated the humor, not the task. For him, finding the Key was an important contract with weighty consequences. For Cassie, it was the quest of a zealot.

Another series of whispers, the cadence slower, drifted beneath the bath chamber's door. Three muffled claps followed, then Cassie joined Ben in the larger room. She'd exchanged her tailored shirt and trousers for the looser garments favored for Paize's chilly nights. With the wig to complete her disguise, she almost looked attractive.

"You'd better be ready," she said, perching on the trunk opposite the bed, boots firmly braced on the floor.

Ben nipped his tongue to contain a sarcastic rejoinder, then rested his wrists on his knees. Eyes closed, he dismissed Cassie's presence with practiced ease. With the next breath, he gathered keshin tendrils from his extremities—cobweb filaments tickling beneath his skin that he spun into a pliant, biddable cord bearing his personal mark.

He flung his creation homeward, like a rope tossed across a great chasm, and found fragile purchase in a familiar soul. Within a heartbeat, Jivin seized the cord. Ben clenched his teeth, enduring sharp reprimands for flaws in the keshin cord as the captain took control of the contact. With a snap, Jivin shimmered into focus behind his lids. His image—sharp-edged, tidy, and clear—reflected the man's standing and skill.

"Sloppy work, loggerhead," Jivin said. His face, all folds and creases, was a comforting picture of jocund authority. "By all the gods of all the tribes, I taught you better than that."

Ben performed a mental obeisance. "My amiable companion urged haste, Captain."

"Impatient warriors." Jivin rolled his eyes. "I've one clamoring at me, too."

"I respectfully remind you, providing that man our services wasn't my idea."

"Respect isn't in your nature." He grinned. "Let's finish before the warriors start rattling their scabbards."

Ben felt a faint tugging of the cord as Jivin's image dissolved. When he opened his eyes, the captain stood between him and Cassie, almost tangible in the room's steady lamplight.

"Greetings, warrior," Jivin said, bowing to Cassie before nodding to Ben.

Ben returned the nod as if they hadn't held their short discourse. That they could communicate without projecting an image was one of the secrets mages chose to keep from their employers—particularly the warriors.

"Greetings, Captain," Cassie said. "My message is brief. We found another prospect matching traits foretold in Dominik's portents. I'll speak with her tonight to discover more."

"I'll convey the message. Commander Hallik is most anxious for your news."

"Any message for me?"

A shade of concern darkened his features. "Only that the need for the Key grows more acute. The tribes are on the brink of open challenge. Warriors may need to intercede with force."

"I'm doing all I can." Her lips thinned and her fingers formed claws over the trunk's edge.

"No doubt." Jivin offered a tight smile. "Anything more?"

She shook her head, as did Ben.

"Then"—Jivin clasped his hands beneath his chin—"until tomorrow." And his image diffused like steam on a warm day.

Ben's eyelids drooped as he unwound the cord and returned his keshin to balance. Scents of sulfur and raw iron permeated his skin, the result of crossing the Door to fetch Jivin. Though the citrus-smelling soap in his pack would kill the stench, hours would pass before he felt well enough to use it.

"Ben?"

Ben squinted against the light. "I need a nap."

"Milksop." She was already striding for the door. "At least leave me a pillow this time."

The ache at the base of his skull began to spread, and speared deeper when Cassie slammed the door. Ben hurled one of the heavy down pillows toward the bath chamber where Cassie insisted upon sleeping, then curled onto his side. With luck, he'd drop off to sleep before the headache grew unbearable.

"You're welcome," he grumbled, "stupid warrior."

•••

Cassie took the back stairs down to avoid the common room, her feet barely scuffing the edges of each step. Dealing with Jivin never bothered her—she often wished he, not Ben, was her companion—but the message he'd delivered made her wish for a good blade and deserving victim. To be reminded of the price of failure through a hired mage . . .

She reached the bottom step still seething. Before bursting outside, she checked her anger and pressed her hands against the wooden door.

Commander Hallik was dangerous. She'd known it long before leaving Shendow, but their separation allowed her to admit it. "Dominik was never firm enough with the tribes," he'd said of Shendow's last Key, and Cassie had chosen to agree. "Do you see how the tribes take advantage of every weakness?" he'd asked, and she'd chosen to see nothing else. "I am the one who can keep Shendow united and strong," he'd promised, and she'd believed him. So when he'd granted her the honor of finding the Key who would succeed Dominik, she'd promised to return with a Key who would grant Hallik the power Dominik had refused him.

But Hallik was also a fool, never dreaming she'd see his faults more clearly from a distance than in his bed. That the tribes were, under his temporary guardianship, so near heated conflict boded ill. The Shendow Islands didn't need a shadow-ruler of harsh ambition. Shendow needed the *Key*.

She looked at her ringless finger, at the pale band of skin that had been confined by steel since she'd given her Warrior's Oath nine years ago. The Oath demanded she place everything—sword, skill, soul—between Shendow and harm. Never before had she needed to judge which betrayal was the lesser shame.

*Hallik, Shendow, freedom, responsibility.*

"You're a warrior, Cassie," she whispered. "You cannot ignore this fight."

She lifted the latch and strode into the yard. By the time the door banged shut behind her, she'd passed the inn's herb garden and soon reached the flagstone path above the creek. The gurgling water reminded her of streams that trickled down mountainsides before spilling into the sea. Cassie swallowed the pang of homesickness and headed for the less affluent quarter of Paize. Every thud of her heels distanced her from confusion and focused her primary intent.

The quiet chatter spilling from windows, and the twilight shadows muting the city's edges, helped slow her pulse before she joined the smattering of people still walking the lamp-lit street. She skirted a knot of tipsy poets trying to remember the chorus of a ballad she'd heard far too many times, passed a hostel crowded with traveling laborers, and reached the rows of tables and benches set up for the poets' shared meals. Few yet lingered over their free meal, and none occupied the tables farthest from the street. She chose one in the darkest corner. The gathering night allowed her to see through the windows of the crowded inn across the street.

The woman soon appeared in one of those windows, scroll and ink case in hand. Cassie watched her push her way to the door and stomp across the street. Head lowered, ebony hair hiding her face, she claimed a table nearby. She set her ink case down, tossed the scroll atop it, then flopped onto the bench. Sighing, she latticed her fingers over her eyes and propped her elbows on the table.

Cassie silently released the breath she'd held and clenched her hands to cease their tremors. That the woman had sought solitude, yet had been drawn here . . .
"Are you feeling well?"

The woman started, then gave a small smile. "I'm sorry. I hope I didn't disturb you."

"No, I'm simply waiting."

"Ah." She smiled again, but in dismissal, underscored by the way she flipped open her ink case. Ignoring Cassie, she chose a fine-tipped brush before opening the scroll and tilting it toward the lamplight.

Cassie studied her with her peripheral vision. The woman was older than she'd first thought, though still younger than she. Other than her stunning hair, she was rather ordinary—pretty enough to garner second glances, but not obsessions. "Are you working the festival?"

"Mm-hmm."

"A poet?"

"So I call myself."

And the big question—"Have you secured a patron?"

"No." The woman drew a black line across the scroll. "And I doubt I ever shall."

"Why is that?"

The woman looked up, hazel eyes squinted. "I'm tired of seeing 'the look' when I answer that question."

"What look?"

"The one that slides down the noses of patrons who think my highest aspiration should be to discover a new metaphor to say without saying what lovers do when naked and alone." She held up a hand. "I mean no offense to other poets, but they treat me like the outlander goatherd impersonating the duke's son."

Cassie shelved the odd metaphor for a later translation from Ben. "I'm not much impressed with the other poets," she said. "Tell me what you write."

"Epics," she said, barely moving her lips. "And I . . . I use the Old Tales as my premise."

Cassie's skin, toes to scalp, flushed. "I enjoy the Old Tales."

"You do?" When Cassie nodded, the woman laughed—hearty and rich with not a touch of giggle—and slid down the bench to be closer. "Then we should at least exchange names. I'm Jana."

Cassie stared at the woman a full heartbeat before she answered. The name echoed in her thoughts as she spoke her own.

Jana raised her eyebrows. "I don't recall hearing of another corrupt poet at the festival. Are you in disguise?"

"No, I—" *Dear gods, her name is Jana.* "I'm not a poet."

"Oh."

"I represent a patron."

"Oh?"

She drew a deep breath to settle her racing heart. "We seek a unique talent to grace our holdings."

"I see." The woman glanced aside, then leaned toward Cassie. "The rules forbid me from offering you my written work without a formal invitation, but if you—"

"Yes. I want to see your work."

"I'll fetch it for you now," Jana said, grinning. "Where are you lodging?"

Cassie stood. "I'll go along and save you the walk."

"I thought you were waiting for someone."

"You showed up."

Jana cocked her head as she retrieved her things, then gave Cassie a skeptical grin. "I suppose we'll call it fate, then."

"Destiny has a better sound to it."

Jana chuckled as she began walking. Cassie forced herself to match the strolling pace rather than seize Jana's arm and propel her onward, all the while blessing the wisdom of her peers who had so carefully interpreted Dominik's portents to match what would be found on this side of the Door.

And the name . . . Jana . . . gift of the gods.

Cassie touched her ring-callus and tried not to think of Hallik.

•••

The gentle shifting of the bed woke Ben just enough for him to feign he hadn't. His head no longer ached, but lethargy weighed down every muscle, his eyelids most of all.

"You're a lousy fake," Cassie whispered.

Ben groaned and hunched the blankets over his ears. The bed shifted again, close behind him, and a hand rested on his shoulder. That mild touch—she usually ripped the covers from his hands—surprised him enough to open one eye. The curtains were still closed, and a scant hint of moonlight seeped around their edges. "It's dark, warrior. When the sun gets up, so will I."

Cassie's grip tightened. "I'm trying to be nice. Don't count on that lasting."

"I can't open the Door again so soon after—"

"I don't want another contact. I want you to read."

"Read?"

"She gave me a scroll."

"Then *you* read it."

Fingers dug into his shoulder. "I can't, you know it, so get up."

Ben cringed at his unintended insult. Most warriors were illiterate, and learned the complex patterns of their prayer-chants by repetition alone. Though his keshin manipulations allowed Cassie to render languages on this side of the Door, Ben couldn't give her a skill she'd never learned.

"A pact," he said, and rolled onto his back. "You let me bathe without barking at me to hurry, and I'll read as much as you want."

"Pact sealed."

Ben spent nearly an hour dawdling in the chest-deep tub of steaming water, as much to enjoy the solitude as test Cassie's word. Not once did she bang on the door, though he heard her cease pacing when he at last opened the sluice to drain the tub. To reward her unusually good manners, and because he'd begun to feel a tad guilty about his poor ones, he yanked on his trousers and loose dressing robe while his skin was still damp and joined her. She waited by the window, one foot braced on the sill, her wig tossed on the bed. On the small table sat a pot of fresh tea and a scroll thicker than his wrist.

"You're joking," he said. "You want me to read that? All of it?"

She nodded. "Aloud."

"The woman impressed you."

"Her name is Jana."

"The gods' gift, eh?" Ben eased into the armchair. "Anything else?"

A heartbeat's hesitation, then, "Read."

So there was more, and Cassie didn't trust him. From a warrior, such distrust was a compliment. Few but mages trusted mages, and warriors took great pains to spread the notion that mages were loyal to the tallest pile of shells. Ben had grown accustomed to the slant, his pride soothed with the knowledge that most warriors rarely held more than two shells at a time.

But something else about Cassie bothered him. He'd always expected her to show some hint of triumph when they found so good a prospect. Instead, she looked angry . . . *afraid?*

He must have sat idle too long, for Cassie smacked the table. "Read."

"Fine." He opened the scroll, wrapping the left end the opposite direction of the right, then took a moment to pour himself some tea. "'Of Gods and Vengeance.' Nice title."

"Mage . . ."

"I'm reading, I'm reading."

The tale began predictably enough—a land in turmoil, magical skills discovered, a reluctant hero on a quest, a wise advisor to explain how and why. The meter was technically sound, but Ben still found the opening stanzas somewhat clunky. The dialog between the hero and the trickster was engaging, but what followed sounded pedantic and flat. By the time the hero received sudden insight into his hither-to-unknown noble destiny—of course—Ben separated his eyes and mouth from the rest of his mind. Since he hadn't a notion what Cassie was listening for, he needn't participate in the search. Only the numerous cups of tea kept him from nodding off.

Then, in the third movement, his tongue stumbled over a familiar name. "Does she mean *the* Lindelati?"

Cassie nodded, staring at the window as if she could see through the curtains. "Jana writes of the Old Tales. The epic touches on the disappearance of Lindelati."

"First of the tribes to abandon the world," he murmured, and rubbed his forearms when his skin prickled. To find a poet still interested in the Old Tales was surprising enough. That the poet had chosen one of Shendow's first great warriors . . .

"Keep reading," Cassie whispered.

Ben shifted his shoulders to dislodge a chill, and refocused on Jana's perfect penmanship. At the end of the next stanza, Cassie interrupted, "Read it again."

"Which it?"

"The last few lines."

"She then twirled a curl—"

"Farther down."

"The secret?"

"That's it."

"The secret burned her soul like molten gold." *What a horrid simile!* "But she would suffer pain with hidden smiles. Secrets were easy to keep. Knowing when to share them separated victors from victims."

"Read just the last."

Ben complied, intrigued less by the sentiment than Cassie's interest. When he finished, Cassie pressed the fingers of one hand over her mouth, thumb hooked beneath her chin, eyes lidded.

At last, she broke from the trance with a grim nod. "That's enough." Then she took the scroll from Ben's hands, set it aside, and went into the bath chamber. The clank of the lock followed.

"You're welcome," Ben grumbled. "Again."

He heaved himself from the chair, stuffed his feet into his short boots, and headed out. The tea he'd consumed had suddenly made its presence known in his bladder, but it was far less trouble to travel to the outdoor privies than disturb a warrior's prayers.

•••

Cassie yanked the pipe chain over the tub, thrust her hands in the gush of cold water that spilled out, then pressed her chilled fingers along the base of her skull.

*Secrets, share them, victors, victims.*

The door rattled with the force of Ben's departure. Cassie cringed, a reaction she allowed herself only in privacy. Mage though he was, Ben deserved more consideration than she'd given. His abilities never fell short of her needs, nor had his complaints ever turned into spiteful refusals. But Ben worked for the mage captain who was employed by the man she now intended to betray.

More cold water, more shivers.

As Ben had read Jana's epic, no doubt believing she was interested in content, Cassie had listened to cadence—patterns of stressed syllables, arrangement of hard and soft sounds. It had been so perfect, she'd lost herself in the rhythm until Ben reached that line. *Secrets, share them, victors, victims.* Taken in its purest form, the passage matched the lowest, barely spoken breaths of a prayer-chant. The Key had been found.

Cassie backed away from the tub and slid down the wall to sit. She had no choice but to face the quandary of success. Convincing Jana to cross the Door's threshold might prove simple in comparison to what Cassie might meet when they arrived. Refusing Hallik's orders made her a betrayer. Following them made her an oathbreaker. Either choice led to shame.

Prayer would be good right now, she acknowledged. But warriors, unless half-dead or under healer's orders, made their chants on their feet. Cassie didn't trust her legs. Accepting death as a near event was no easy task, not even for a warrior.

•••

Eventually, Cassie regained her footing. She performed a brief ritual ablution to the chant of guidance, then drew heated water for proper washing. As she soaked, she crammed her fear into the deepest recesses of her heart.

The mastery of fear, she'd learned, was nothing but a noble myth reborn each time a warrior ran toward a fight rather than away. In truth, warriors hid their fear beneath layers of faith and boasts, in places least likely to be stumbled upon by the mind's wanderings. The unspoken pact to ignore each other's terror was the strongest tie between warriors, a bond Ben would never understand. The only thing tying mages together were purse strings.

Smack on cue, Ben rapped on the door. "She'll be here soon. I've sent down for tea and pastries."

Cassie checked the sunlight's long slant through the tiny window set high in the wall. Late afternoon already. Small wonder the water lapping around her chest was cold. Leaving the crisis of Hallik behind with the bath water, she stepped from the tub. By the time she joined Ben, refreshments had arrived. A second covered plate waited beside the pastries and tea.

"You haven't eaten all day," Ben said in nursemaid's tones. He'd donned silk shirt and trousers, but not the heavy patron's robe. "And save the lecture on warrior endurance, or I'll give you one on keeping up your strength in return."

Cassie looked askance at the tray. "A mage suddenly concerned for a warrior?"

"You're cranky when you're hungry. Cranky-*er.*"

He was lying—not about her disposition, but his motive. "If this is a bribe—"

"For what?"

"Information."

"Cassandra, whatever is between you and Hallik—"

"Not your concern."

"What *does* concern me is your temperament since finding Jana. If you and I don't run the same course—"

She snorted. "Worried you'll lose your bonus if I fail?"

"Damn the bonus!" He smacked his palm on the table, jiggling the mugs. "And it's *we,* Cassie. If we fail, *Shendow* loses."

His accusations clawed open her fears, flooding her with images of islands sundered by civil war, waves churning red on bloodied shores. She raised her right hand and pointed to the callus. "My Oath is to Shendow. Not warriors, not shells, and certainly not one man. Though Hallik sent me, it's Shendow I serve."

"Is pontification part of a warrior's training?"

"Is shell-grubbing part of yours?"

"What secrets are you keeping?"

Cassie forced a deep breath through her clenched throat. "Thanks for the meal. And that's all your act of 'kindness' will earn."

He clasped his hands over his paunch. "I've one more thing to say, if you'll listen."

"Go ahead." She lifted the cover from the plate and tightened her gut to keep it from gurgling at the sight of slivered beef in gravy flanked by peas, onions and potatoes. At least Ben had put some thought into his bribe.

"We mages serve Shendow as wholly as warriors."

"Uh-huh."

"Our contract is to convey you through the Door, provide occasional contacts, and—if possible—bring the Key home."

She shrugged, attacking the meat with the strange, multi-tined fork.

"That's all, Cassie. Do you hear what I'm saying?"

"I'm not deaf."

"If there's something outside the contract—"

"My Oath requires I secure the Key," she said around a mouthful of meat. "I'd do nothing to jeopardize that."

"You're making it exceedingly difficult for me to offer my help."

The meat, so succulent a moment ago, became a tasteless wad of fiber on her tongue. So Hallik hadn't trusted her after all. How much shell had passed between cupped hands to ensure Ben kept Cassie from committing the betrayal she'd just decided upon? "Stick to your contract, mage. Leave me to my Oath."

•••

Ben hadn't expected the Key to look so . . . cute. Fine-featured and delicate as the previous Key, perhaps, or maybe sinewy and brutish as a warrior, but Jana was neither. She was short and stocky, and her cheeks bunched up when she smiled. She wore the same faded red skirts and pale cream blouse as she had the day before—probably the sole ensemble of "finery" she possessed. He couldn't imagine her holding any sway over Shendow's councilors, let alone convincing them she was their predestined ruler.

She briefly bowed her head when he opened the door, then met his gaze. "Good evening, Master Kalari." The waver in her voice was slight. "Cassandra told me you might wish to see me."

"I do indeed." He motioned her inside. By the time he closed the door, Cassie had called Jana to the table. Jana took the chair she indicated and cast questioning glances to Ben when he poured tea for them.

"I trust Cassandra's judgment in these matters," Ben said by way of explanation. "Though I play a patron's role, I leave decisions in her hands."

Jana smiled at him, missing Cassie's little sneer at his wording. Ben set a mug before each woman—Jana acknowledged the act with polite thanks—then he edged into the room's shadows. Unless Cassie hit trouble, his job was to watch.

"What would you say," Cassie began, "if I told you it's the best epic I've heard?"

Jana chuckled. "I'd call you a liar and walk out."

"And if I said it's the worst?"

"I'd ask you what meter and tone you'd prefer, and do my best to match it."

"Wouldn't that sacrifice your intent?"

"Only if you asked me to discard the tale itself. The means of telling it are decided by the patron."

Jana's mouth formed a firm line, her eyes narrowed the slightest—a shrewd negotiator replacing the cheery sprite. Ben adjusted his estimation of the woman, and Cassie's swift glance echoed his opinion.

Cassie steepled her fingers over the mug, wisps of steam curling around them. "We're not seeking an exceptional poet, Jana. We seek an exceptional person who happens to be of a poetic inclination. Someone willing to withhold judgment on the unexplainable and accept on faith, for a time, what seems beyond possibility."

Cassie let the statement hover in silence; Jana merely sipped her tea. *Nervous,* Ben thought, *but too intrigued to leave. Good sign.*

"Do you believe the Vanished Tribes truly existed?" the warrior asked.

Jana quirked a tight grin. "I'm willing to entertain the notion."

"Would you believe they survive still, beyond the reach of the world you know?"

"Perhaps, and no."

"Would you believe I'm from the other side of a Door linking my world to yours?"

"No."

"And that I came here to find you?"

"Definitely not." Jana rapped her mug onto the table. "But I'd believe you're planning to make a fool of me."

Ben chose to prove his worth to the warrior. When Jana stood and reached for her scroll, he stepped forward and laid his hand atop hers. Jana tensed. Ben stilled every strand of his keshin to exude calm sincerity.

"You are no fool," he said. "Lindelati discovered another realm, where descendents of the Vanished Tribes yet prosper."

"You're talking lunacy," she whispered, but not timidly. She hadn't relaxed a muscle.

"Listen, Jana." He discreetly rapped his toe atop Cassie's foot to keep her quiet. "Have you never wished such a place were real, wished you lived within it, playing a role in the grand drama of another world?"

She stared up at him, her gaze making minute jumps as she scanned his face. "So it's akin to the Old Tales, is it?"

"Much akin, yes."

"You came through some sort of . . . portal."

"The Door."

"Door? How bland. How . . . flat." All tension seeped from her bearing as she relinquished the scroll and flopped into the chair. "Let me tell the rest. There's a land in turmoil, a prophecy to be fulfilled, warring factions vying for supremacy, and you two came through a *door* on a great and magical quest—"

"Not exactly, but—"

"—for the one person who can set everything right again."

"Cassie, you could say something now."

"And lucky me!" Jana shouted before Cassie opened her mouth, dancing her fingers overhead. "I'm the one! The great and powerful savior of—what's the place called?"

"Shendow," Ben said.

"That's as bad as *door*. The jape is over." As swiftly as he'd seen Cassie move, Jana was on her feet. "It might've been funny—I do have a sense of humor—but pretending to be patrons? Do you know what I went through, waiting for this meeting? Thinking I might have a chance?"

"It was the easiest way to see your work," Cassie said.

"Anyone at the festival could have—"

"I needed to hear it," Cassie said and stood, shoulders drawn back, thumb hooked through her sash as if she still carried a sword. "I needed to hear how your work sounded when you weren't forcing the wrong rhythms to please an ignorant audience."

Jana's eyes narrowed. "What are you after?"

"Precisely what Ben told you. We came through the Door, searching for the Key, and that Key is you."

"Keys and doors. Very uninspired."

"Most truths are."

Jana snatched up the scroll and headed for the door. Ben intercepted her, blocking the way with his girth. Jana stopped, one hand cradling the scroll against her waist, the other braced on her hip.

"Oh, I forget the stanza of pleas," she asked, honey-sweet. "The gallant hero must draw his holy sword and swear by whatever-god that his life is forfeit if he returns without me."

Cassie's laughter rescued Ben from making an answer.

"He's nothing but a mercenary mage," Cassie said. "And even if *my* sword had passed through the Door, he'd likely sprain his wrist trying to lift it."

Jana rocked back on her heels, expression wiped clean of certainty, then squared her shoulders. "I don't believe you."

"Give us a moment, and you will."

"Then, by all means, go ahead." Jana hugged the scroll to her chest and leaned against the trunk. "I'm curious to see what little tricks you've contrived."

At Cassie's nod, Ben sat on the end of the bed opposite Jana. Once he settled, though, it required small effort to gather his keshin, reach out to the inn's gardens, and snatch a large collection of lemon balm and mint. He simultaneously placed a bundle around Jana's feet, trailed another along the trunk behind her, and plopped a third on Cassie's lap just for fun. In the same heartbeat, he opened his eyes.

Jana looked on the verge of screaming or fainting, or both.

"I would have opened the Door," he said, "but I can only do that once a day or so, and my partner might want to make contact later tonight."

"Jana," Cassie said as she shoved the stems onto the floor, "now will you listen?"

One end of the loosely bound scroll slid free, then the entire scroll slipped through Jana's arms to unfurl atop the fragrant leaves at her feet. Ben rescued a single stem of balm and offered it to her.

"It's real, Jana," he said. "Touch it."

Her shaking hand almost made contact with a small leaf before she *did* faint. Ben barely managed to break her fall and ease her to the floor.

Cassie groaned. "The Key shouldn't pass out at the sight of common keshin workings."

"In her place, I suppose you'd have taken it in stride?"

"I probably would have split you from groin to gullet."

"Then be grateful she merely fainted."

Cassie grunted. Ben assumed that meant she agreed.

"Take a stroll, mage."

"I don't want to."

"Don't tell me that little trick gave you a headache."

"No, but I think I should be here when—"

"I don't." Cassie crouched and laid a hand on Jana's shoulder as if taking possession of her. "I'll talk with her."

*About things you fear me knowing.* But there was no arguing with a warrior possessed by purpose, particularly this warrior. Huffing and cursing, Ben pushed to his feet and stomped away.

"Hang a sash on the door latch," Cassie said. "I'll take it off when I'm done."

"How gracious."

"And thanks for the herbs."

Since she'd finally offered a mite of gratitude, Ben decided to ignore her.

•••

Shortly before midnight, Cassie pulled off the wig and dragged her stubby nails over her scalp. Jana didn't flinch, and probably wouldn't now even if Cassie donned full mail and plate and began juggling torches. Ben's return might elicit a different response, and Cassie counted that an asset. No one—particularly the Key—should trust someone whose loyalty lived in a purse. Acclimating Jana to displays of keshin could be done over the next few days.

"Do you still doubt me?" she asked, and Jana shook her head. "Want me to explain anything again?"

"Only if the ending will change."

"I'm sorry," Cassie murmured. "It's a lifetime commitment, though the mages can take you through the Door for visits."

"I suppose it isn't much different from finding a patron far from home." Jana blinked hard, dabbing her lower lashes with her knuckle. "If I said no, would you force me?"

Cassie shook her head. "That would be worse than never finding you at all. If your first dealings with the conclave are anything less than decisive, they will refuse you. The interpretation of Dominik's portents will be declared false, and the fighting may well begin."

"So it's completely my choice."

"There's always more than one person who could match the portents." She decided against explaining how deep Jana's match ran. Understanding the inner rhythms of prayer-chants was difficult for the most advanced sword-scholars of her order. "And Shendow will survive without a Key. The question would be how well."

Jana rested her forehead on her fists. "If I go, what happens then?"

"Ben takes us through the Door—it's quick," she added when Jana shuddered. "You'll be in seclusion for five days to ensure none of the tribes influence you before the conclave"—*the very crime I nearly committed*—"then you'll be brought before the assembled councilors, Dominik's portents will be read and, if you answer their challenges well—"

"What challenges?"

Cassie looked away. "Only the councilors know what demands will be made of the Key. If you answer them as Dominik foretold, you will be named Shendow's Key."

"But how will I—"

"You'll know," Cassie broke in. "The answers will come to you, as they have for every Key in Shendow's history. I'd stake my life on it." And indeed she'd already done so. Now all she had was a mage who trawled for secrets, a life that would end with a single cut, and the cold triumph of finding the Key. "The tribes will rejoice at the naming of their new high ruler."

"I couldn't even convince a desperate patron to let me recite passion stanzas in a brothel!"

"Because you're far more than a poet," Cassie whispered.

"How can you be so certain?"

"You know what separates victors from victims."

Jana blinked. "You really read the epic."

"I listened. I heard the rhythms I've been seeking."

"Can you hear how absurd the whole thing sounds?"

She shrugged. "Shendow has survived the rule of seventeen Keys over the last four hundred years. Our last Key, Dominik, passed away months ago, and the Islands have been sniping at each other ever since. The only way to placate all twelve tribes is to choose a ruler who belongs to none of them."

"That actually makes sense," she mumbled, gaze drifting to the window. "And to know the Vanished Tribes still exist . . ."

Cassie stifled a yawn, and grudgingly admitted that the meal Ben had provided was responsible for sustaining her thus far. If only he hadn't corrupted the kindness with his false offer of the very help she so needed.

"I can't decide now," Jana said. "If I did, I'd always wonder if I made the right choice."

Cassie smiled. Jana hadn't said no. Then the near future blundered in, and her gut knotted. "There's more you must hear, Jana. I ask your vow that you'll not speak a word of it to Ben, regardless of your decision."

She endured a moment of cool appraisal before Jana nodded agreement. Whatever faults Jana had, timidity was not among them. Cassie pressed her thumb over the place her ring should be, drawing what courage she could, and chose whom to betray.

"Shendow's warriors—those dedicated solely to the Key's service—are currently led by Commander Hallik, and he has held control of Shendow since Dominik's death. Hallik doesn't wish to surrender such power, not even to the Key. He'd never go so far as to harm you, but you'd do well to keep your distance from his advice. He isn't evil, but he sees the tribes as things to be controlled at any cost. And he can be so convincing. . . ." She stopped before tears welled up.

Jana slid her hands over the table, pulling them onto her lap. "Why would one of his own warriors tell me this?"

"My Oath binds me to Shendow, not to my commander," she whispered. *And it took me too long to remember that.*

"And Ben?"

"Benjas Kalari works for the mage captain whom Hallik hired to take me through the Door. I don't know what, if anything, Ben knows. Probably very little, but the captain . . ." Cassie swallowed, then compounded her shame by divulging more. "Jivin was the mage who played Ben's role in finding Dominik. The two were at odds until the day Dominik died. Jivin might play blind if enough shells were dangled under his nose, and if he believed even greater gain would follow."

"Shit."

Cassie chuckled despite herself. She'd most likely be the only one in all Shendow to hear the Key utter an obscenity.

"The stakes are too high," Jana continued. "It's too much. I can't—"

"You can."

"I don't know," she whispered.

When Jana rubbed her eyes, Cassie said, "Sleep on it."

"Sleep? I don't think so."

"Rest, then." She stood and offered Jana her hand, grateful her fingers didn't tremble.

Jana accepted the handclasp with a wan smile. "This is lunatic and sane all at once."

"Destiny sometimes feels that way, I'm told."

"And that sounds trite, warrior."

After walking Jana to the door, Cassie removed the sash from the latch and tossed it onto the trunk. Exhausted, she retreated to the bath chamber with pillow and blanket. She savored every breath and trill of her evening chant, needing to make each sound perfect and whole. Once the last wisp of air left her lips, she could face the darker truth.

Hallik would know of her defiance the moment Jana refused his request to be her sole guard during seclusion. Convincing Jana to do otherwise would require Cassie disclose the role she'd played in his plans, and she would rather face Hallik's fury then Jana's mistrust. Besides, she'd already told Jana enough to be convicted of corrupting the Key's perception of Shendow's own warriors.

As she rolled into her blanket, comforted by the barracks-like feel of the hard bench beneath her, she wondered if Hallik would use just such an accusation to have her silenced. Though it took a lengthy five days to confirm Shendow's Key, it took but a moment to execute a warrior.

•••

Ben wended his way through the streets of Paize before giving in to his longing for open spaces. In Shendow, finding solitude meant a simple walk to the shore. Even if the entire population of the Islands stood at his back, he had only to gaze at the empty sea to feel alone. Though the Festival of Pen and Voice had ended, and most of Paize's inhabitants were recovering or preparing to move on, every window seemed like an eye trained on his movements. So Ben bribed a guard to open the gates and strolled toward his favorite oak, set on the hillside above where the poets had offered their talents.

Once there, he indulged in a few deep breaths, arms open wide to embrace the chill fog rising from the deserted meadow. Then he settled on the ground and propped his back against the oak. With disciplined haste, he collected his keshin and launched the cord toward Shendow. It was received with a jolt of surprise followed by snarls and snaps of vexation.

"I'm sleeping, you idiot," Jivin grumbled as his image coalesced, his robes askew and his thinning hair atangle. "Tell that warrior—"

"Are you alone?"

Jivin blinked. "Yes."

"So am I. Hallik?"

"He left hours ago. What's this about?"

"We found the Key." Ben swallowed, then added, "Her name is Jana."

"Gift of the gods!" The captain struck a mocking pose of a warrior at prayer. "What could be more perfect?"

"A warrior who felt likewise." His fists clenched at the sense he was betraying some meager confidence Cassie hadn't even granted. "Cassie's in trouble. I don't know what or how much, and she doesn't trust me enough to share it."

Jivin stilled. "Any guesses?"

"When I dropped Hallik's name, she swallowed her tongue."

"Splendid."

"May I remind you—"

"No," he snapped. "You were right, I was wrong, that shall suffice."

In the moment, being right didn't feel as satisfying as he thought it should.

"Wait, you're fading." Jivin quickly took charge of the contact, his superior keshin control relieving Ben of the strain. Jivin's image shifted as well, tidying itself until the captain looked as polished as if he'd spent hours preparing for the contact. "Now. Tell me."

Ben related all that had occurred—every conversation, suspicion and speculation. When he finished, Jivin tapped his forefinger against his lips. Ben waited, wanting very much to be told he was wrong.

"To move against Hallik . . ." Jivin winced. "A bad prospect, on our part, with no more evidence than your hunch."

"No one in Shendow suspects anything is amiss?"

"The tribes suspect each other, trust the warriors, and take us into their confidence when best it suits them." He shook his head. "Think of how the councilors will receive the accusation of a mage against the word of the commander."

"I know, I know." Ben slumped. "So we just wait until something happens?"

"Unless you believe Cassie will endanger the Key."

"Mayhap the opposite, in some way."

"Then we wait. The warrior can take care of herself."

Ben released a heavy sigh. "Did you have so difficult a time bringing Dominik from the Abandoned World?"

"Difficulties, yes, but different ones." Jivin shrugged. "I told you the contract would not be a simple one."

"Then why did you send *me?*" he griped.

"A hunch." Then Jivin smiled faintly. "I'll keep an ear to the wind in Shendow, you keep an eye on the Key."

Jivin dissolved the contact, and Ben restored his keshin balance. His headache was sparse since he hadn't projected an image this time, but the stench was just as strong. A dip in the frigid stream and a rubdown with mint leaves should mask it well enough. The last thing he needed was Cassie demanding he explain why he'd contacted Jivin without her knowledge. He hoped no one would see him splashing about in the nude.

But first, he strolled from beneath the oak and gazed toward Paize. The fog had thickened, turning lamp-lit windows into hovering spheres of misty yellow—beacons to guide a traveler though the destination remained hidden. Ben gave a tight grin over how well the ambience matched his dilemma. If Jana decided she still wanted to write poetry, perhaps he'd one day share the metaphor with her.

•••

Jana's acceptance turned out to be a simple thing. She arrived at the inn's common room a few moments after Cassie and Ben, and said to Cassie, "I assume I shouldn't pack much."

"Whatever you think you'll need," Cassie said after releasing a shaky breath.

Jana laughed. "How would I know?"

The three claimed a small table beneath the awning outdoors, where the damp chill kept others from joining them. All good manners and gallantry, Ben dusted off a bench and swept his arm toward Jana.

"May I be the first to honor you, Key of Shendow," he said, grinning. "I promise there will be no displays of keshin this morn unless you so request them."

"I promise not to faint," Jana answered, then blushed. "Always thought I'd be steadier about something like that."

"You will be," Cassie said, as grateful for Jana's company as her decision. Ben had been unusually quiet all morning, giving her odd looks though asking no questions. Cassie waited until the innkeeper had delivered platters of fried sausage and cakes to ask Ben, "How soon can you open the Door for travel?"

"Day after tomorrow. We'll contact Jivin tonight. He'll need time to prepare."

"You can't do it alone?" It was her last hope—bring Jana through before Jivin and Hallik knew she was coming, see her safely into seclusion, and disappear until the conclave confirmed their new Key. Then it would be too late for Hallik to mete out revenge. Any warrior accused of a capital offense was entitled to an audience with the Key, where not even Hallik would dare to give false testimony.

But Ben laughed. "I'm flattered you think so much of my skill, but I cannot alone open the Door for the three of us."

"Two days it is, then," Cassie mumbled, and became engrossed in a stack of soggy cakes while Jana questioned Ben about the workings of keshin magic. She watched the pair reach mutual fondness before she'd eaten half of breakfast, and wondered what it was about

Ben that let Jana trust him with such ease. The line from Jana's epic kept hissing in her ears—*secrets, share them, victors, victims*—until Cassie couldn't tell where one word ended and another began.

•••

Ben was beginning to detest his opulent lodgings. Every day the bedchamber seemed to shrink, and looked even smaller from his cramped seat between the trunk and the corner. Cassie had stacked chairs on the table, even propped the bedframe and mattress on end against the wall, so she could battle the air empty-handed. Jana, wedged into a corner, watched with awe as Cassie flailed and kicked and spun. Ben was bored stiff—stiffer than his knees after a long hike uphill.

At least the day with Jana had gone well. The Old Tales fascinated her, and Ben delighted in her rapid questioning. Cassie had even joined the conversation to explain the methods and purpose of a warrior's prayer-chant. Ben had lost her thread of reasoning, but Jana seemed to understand it.

He and Cassie—in uncommon agreement—had eased Jana into the sort of treatment she'd receive in Shendow, beginning with her lodgings. Since a suite in the inn had been vacated the day before, Cassie had escorted Jana from her old room while Ben ensured the new one was bedecked with the inn's finest furnishings. A foray to the markets found soft linen bedrobes and the heavy silk gown—burgundy, as suited the Key—that Jana had immediately donned. Later, Cassie had sought permission to perform her drills, and answered, "as you wish" when Jana asked to watch. The twitch of Jana's cheek had revealed she knew their intent, but she didn't object.

Cassie completed her drill with a spin-kick and gut slash, then dropped to one knee before Jana. The warrior was winded, having put more effort into the performance than Ben had before seen. Every movement had been cloaked in a desperation Ben wished he understood.

"That was marvelous," Jana said breathlessly.

"My thanks." Cassie stood and made a quick, shallow bow. "It looks better with full weapons."

"I'd like to see that someday."

A shadow of pain darkened Cassie's eyes. "It's time for my prayers, if I may."

Jana glanced to Ben. When he said nothing, her eyes widened the slightest with the realization it was her consent Cassie awaited. "That's fine."

Cassie chuckled. "May I make a suggestion, Jana?"

"Of course."

"Don't say 'That's fine' to the councilors' requests, even if that's what you mean."

"How about . . ." Jana tilted her chin. "Do what you must, warrior, and return to me when you have finished."

"Much better." She bowed again, then retreated to the bath chamber. "Behave," she whispered as she passed Ben.

Ben raised his hands in innocence, and Cassie rewarded him with a sneer before closing the door. Tugged between amusement and foreboding, Ben turned back to Jana. She eyed one of the chairs on the table, then crossed her ankles and sat on the floor instead. With an ungraceful flapping of her hand, she beckoned Ben to join her.

"What does the Key require?" he asked with precision.

"Is everyone in Shendow going to speak to me as such?"

"At first, yes, and you should encourage it. After a few weeks, you can relax a bit and people will consider you quite gracious." Ben lumbered to the floor in front of her. "You'll be called Jana most of the time, though. Since you're the Key, your name is your title."

"Well, that's convenient," she said as Cassie's whispers began, then asked softly, "How long will she be in there?"

"A while. Her evening chants are the longest."

"Good." Jana straightened her skirts, then clasped her hands beneath her chin. "Tell me about warriors and mages."

"Ah . . . would you be more specific?"

"If I would, you'd know what I already knew."

"Shrewd reasoning," he admitted while his mind narrowed in on what Cassie might have already disclosed. "Warriors work for the ideals of Shendow. Mages do as well, but expect to be paid in something weightier than gratitude. Warriors don't trust us because they mistake purchased skill for procured ethics."

"And mages trust . . . ?"

"Other mages. Most warriors."

"Cassie?"

His own swift answer surprised him. "I trust her to serve Shendow at any cost. To follow her Oath, and protect the Key."

"What warrior don't you trust?"

"Hallik." His teeth snapped together on the last sound. The name had skipped off his tongue so quickly, he hadn't had time to soften the enmity.

Jana merely sighed. "I gave my word on a matter, and I don't think the Key should be one to break a promise."

Throat tight, Ben said, "Nor do I, but the Key should keep the good of Shendow foremost in her cares."

"Then answer my question, and do what you must." She looked up, gaze steady. "What would Hallik do to a warrior who betrayed him?"

Ben leaned back to give himself room to breathe. Cassie was in deep, deep trouble indeed. "Take revenge."

Cassie's chants filled the ensuing silence. After a while, Jana began putting the furniture in place. Only half aware, Ben helped her right the bed and straighten the sheets and coverlet. His thoughts were nagging him to answer why he felt compelled to help a warrior who made no secret of her scorn for mages.

*For Shendow's sake? For Jana's?* No, the latter had just proved she would take care of both, now that she'd been warned. *For Cassie?* That was a discomfiting notion indeed.

When a trio of claps came from the bath chamber, Ben tried to shake off the feeling of doom and began explaining to Jana what the next step of her journey entailed. Cassie gave him a hard stare as she joined them. Since Jana spared only a glance for the warrior, Ben continued talking.

"Be as formal as you can," he finished. "History tells of your predecessor babbling like a fool during his first contact."

"No fainting, then, I suppose." Jana rubbed her hands together, finally looking at Cassie. "Shall we?"

Cassie pulled a chair around for Jana before taking her usual perch on the trunk. Casting final glances at the women—Cassie appeared more nervous than Jana—Ben settled on the bed and closed his eyes. Jivin must have been waiting, for he took control of the keshin cord in an instant, his spectral image appearing to Ben alone.

"I've found nothing," Jivin said without preamble, "but a bunch of warriors who aren't talking to mages."

"I'm not alone, and haven't time to explain. Where's Hallik?"

"Waiting just outside the room."

"Do not tell him about Jana," Ben ordered. "Tell him we won't make another contact for three days."

If the captain were insulted by Ben's command, he showed no sign. "I can stall him for two days at most. Even then—"

"We must be through the Door before he knows."

"It's that bad?"

"Might be."

"What a mess," Jivin muttered, solemnity swept aside. "And a soured contract to boot. Well, introduce me to the Key before Cassandra begins wondering what's taking so long."

Keshin power hummed through Ben's body. He opened his eyes in time to catch Jana's gasp as Jivin appeared in formal, sea-blue robes that shimmered as if woven with starlight. The captain gave Jana's surprise no notice before turning to Cassie.

"You have news for me, warrior?"

"The Key has been found, as Dominik foretold," Cassie answered. "Her name is Jana. She awaits your greeting."

"A fortuitous name," he murmured, then bowed low to Jana. "May I be the first to greet you as Key of Shendow."

"Your mage has already claimed that honor," Jana said, the faint tremor in her voice settling by the last word. Other than the way her thumbnail dug into her forefinger, she looked calm and almost regal. "But I thank you, nonetheless. I'm told I'll have the pleasure of meeting you in person within a few days."

"One day, if that suits."

Cassie stiffened. "So soon?"

"If I start within the hour."

Cassie swallowed—hard. "The decision belongs to the Key."

"Tomorrow suits," Jana answered after a vain attempt to catch Cassie's gaze. "Begin your preparations."

Grinning, Jivin bowed again. "Shendow will know a strong Key. The warrior has done well."

"Yes, she has," Jana answered. "I value her for it. I'll trust you to do the same, no matter the consequence."

After Jivin took his leave, and Ben's head began to throb, Cassie's gaze slid from him to Jana and back again. Whatever the warrior suspected, Jana would need to deal with it. After a disjointed explanation of his condition for Jana, and her kindly acceptance of his need for sleep, Ben crawled under the covers.

"I'm glad I was sitting down," she whispered to Cassie. "My legs felt like poor man's porridge."

"Jana," Cassie said, almost too softly for Ben to hear, "may we talk?"

"Not now. I've letters to write and accounts to settle before tomorrow. My family needs to believe I've found a secure position."

"I'll escort you to your—"

"It's only two doors down the hall. I'd prefer to be alone."

There was silence before Cassie replied, "As you wish."

The moment Jana was gone, Cassie pounced on the bed and yanked Ben onto his back. Pinpoints of orange and purple burst behind his lids.

"What did you tell her?" she growled.

"Damn it, Cassie, I can't even think right now!"

*"What did you tell her?"*

"That I trust you!" he shouted, instantly regretting the thunder his own voice caused in his ears. "Is it so terrible that a shell-grubbing mage has a little respect for you?"

"Ben . . . ?"

Shielding his eyes from the light, Ben peered between his fingers. Cassie's look of shocked confusion would've been amusing were it not for the pressure within his skull. If he didn't sleep soon, he'd be unable to do his part in taking Jana through the Door. That task carried greater import than delving into Cassie's secrets. He'd done all he could for the ungrateful warrior.

Cursing keshin limitations, he crumpled onto his side and wrapped his arms over his head. When he at last found relief in unconsciousness, Cassie still sat beside him.

•••

By the end of the next day, Cassie knew her fate had been decided. Jana had managed to spend not a single moment in her company when Ben wasn't within earshot, and the two kept exchanging long, silent stares. Last night Cassie had wanted to tell Jana the truth, but Jana had refused to listen. Then she'd nearly spilled her secrets to Ben, but he'd turned away. Now it was too late. Jana had chosen to trust the mages, and there was nothing left for Cassie but the shame and the dying.

It was after midnight when Ben—half-tranced on the bed—announced the Door's readiness. Cassie eased onto the bed and motioned Jana near. Jana was pale, but took her place between Ben and Cassie without hesitation. She'd chosen to bring nothing but the clothes she wore.

"It's quick, right?" she whispered.

Cassie nodded tersely. "But frightening, I won't lie about that. Take Ben's arm, if you want, and close your eyes."

Jana did, then slipped her other hand around Cassie's elbow. "I trust you both, warrior, and I meant what I said to the captain."

"Ready," Ben warned before Cassie could respond. "Steady now . . . we . . . go."

The world plummeted—or heaved skyward, Cassie couldn't tell. Acrid steam burned her eyes before she squeezed them shut against the swirl of white and red. Fiery needles pricked her skin. The reek of hot rotten eggs made her gag. Her own sweat and tears seemed to sizzle in rivulets down her cheeks, carving through flesh and muscle and bone and marrow until her entire body dissolved within the Door's rank power and she was nothing but a speck of existence hurtling through a barrier never meant to be crossed. *This is wrong, worse than last time, dear gods, protect Jana. . . .*

A cold wall of air slammed against Cassie, driving out the breath she'd held, and the world regained substance. Gasping and choking, she lurched onto elbows and knees, her head too heavy to lift. She groped blindly for Jana, trying to call her name. Her knuckles grazed a leg, but it was snatched away before she could grab hold. Words and phrases, too low to comprehend, scattered then ceased.

Hallik had claimed the Key.

A voice—weak and grating and insistent—called her name. She pushed onto her haunches, hid her fear beneath her Oath, and opened her eyes. Jivin was propped against the wall, legs splayed on the floor and eyes half-shut. Ben knelt, hunched over, at his side.

"Sorry for the rough travel," Jivin rasped.

Cassie scanned the room, squinting at the dusty barrels and grain sacks stacked about, then checked over both shoulders. Her throat hurt when she spoke. "What happened to Jana? Where's the commander?"

Jivin offered a weak smile, his words coming out as an unintelligible hiss. Clicking his tongue, Ben put a hand on Jivin's shoulder and faced Cassie. He looked nearly as bad as his captain, and worse than Cassie felt—but exuded a power stronger than she'd ever sensed, as if his keshin reveled in homecoming.

"Here's the short of it," Ben said. "Hallik doesn't know we're here. If my hunch is right, you'll disappear before he finds out. If I'm wrong, my apologies for the deception."

Cassie pressed the heels of her hands to her temples. "What are you talking about?"

"If you'd tell me, we'd both know." His smug grin was at odds with the haggardness sagging beneath his eyes. "Jivin put a few things over there"—he nodded toward the corner—"he thought you'd need."

"Jana?"

Ben snorted. "Fared better than either of us. Shaky, but fine. She's being taken to the tower now."

"How . . . without Hallik knowing . . ."

"A stroll beneath the courtyard, up a few flights of stairs, and her seclusion shall begin before Hallik can bolt from bed."

The pieces clunked into place. The Key had safely arrived, Hallik didn't know, and the mages were offering help to a warrior. At the moment, considering the alternatives, it didn't much matter why. She stumbled to the collection of bags and steel, peeled off her wrong-side-of-the-Door clothing, and began dressing in the nondescript shirt and trousers set atop the pile. The chain mail and plate she pushed aside. As an old scout had taught her, a warrior cannot clink and sneak. Cassie intended to sneak.

A man and woman entered the room—mages or healers, from the way they hovered over Ben and Jivin. Since they ignored her, she returned the favor as she tugged on a pair of boots. Weapons next—knife in each boot, throwing blade on each forearm, a pair of long daggers crossed at the small of her back. With boot cuffs turned up, sleeves pushed down, and a short cloak over her shoulders, no hint of weapons showed. She left behind the sword—three feet of steel made for difficult sneaking—and snatched up a pack that smelled of fresh bread.

Before heading out, she turned to Ben. The mage looked unconscious, leaning against a grain sack while a stranger held a cup to his lips. Cassie hesitated, shifting her weight, then walked out. The rudeness of leaving without a word of thanks shamed her more than owing gratitude to the stupid mage.

A person stood at every corner to point her in the right direction. She nodded to each mage, never slowing, already planning her disappearance. At last Cassie climbed a stairway that brought her to a deserted landing and a heavy door. With a final decision to trust a mage, she opened it and stepped outside. Cold, salty air stung her eyes and stole her breath. Cassie let the tears spill down her cheeks as she trotted along the trellised pathway linking Jivin's holdings to the courtyard shared by the warriors' complex and the Key's palace. There was no sign of Jana.

Before panic gripped muscles already strung taut, Cassie remembered—*a stroll* under *the courtyard*—and smirked. Leave it to mages to have hidden means to meet any end. Then she glanced up as the windows of the Key's tower began to glow. She recognized the solitary figure silhouetted in the lamplight.

As she turned onto the path that would take her to the mountains, her vision muddled again. Damned salt air always made her eyes water.

•••

"Drink," a voice commanded, and Ben obeyed. The chalky liquid made him gag, but he retained enough sense to swallow. So what if the drug would negate his keshin control for days? It would dull the pain *now*. The thought alone eased the hurt.

"Still with me?" the healer asked after a few moments.

"Still," Ben croaked. "Not pleased by that."

"Then this will break your heart."

He risked cracking open his eyelids. Because of the drug, the light from a single shaded candle merely pained his eyes rather than shattered his vision. It was the letter Marisala held that made him wince.

"The captain left it for you," she said.

"I can*not* bear the light I'd need to read—"

"He pressed it for you."

"Ah." Of course Jivin would have thought ahead. Ben pushed higher on the grain sack—the drug had dulled his keshin enough to make movement more trial than torture—and took the letter. The soft crack of the seal hurt his ears. Eyes closed, he unfolded the parchment and touched the symbols pressed into the paper: *You, captain, voice, brief, stall.* "Are you certain this is mine?"

"If your name is still Benjas Kalari."

Ben cursed. "Did the captain say anything else?"

"He said, 'Ha, ha.'"

"Then the jape is on us all, sweet Marisala. Our dear captain has given me his voice until he recovers."

She quirked her eyebrows. "Which explains why he moved his belongings from his old chambers and moved yours in."

"Splendid," he said on a sigh, and heard in his voice an echo of Jivin's. "Ha, ha, indeed."

Squinting, he looked across the storeroom to where Jivin was being placed on a litter. Since tradition held that a mage captain could never be separated from his keshin, Jivin must endure without the drug currently keeping Ben coherent. Ben wondered which of them would enjoy the coming day less.

"Warriors at the gates!" came a shout from above.

"Answers my question," Ben muttered, then hardened his tone. "Admit the commander, find me a reception room, shield the captain, pretend I know what I'm doing. Did I miss anything?"

Marisala cocked her head. "Has Hallik paid off his contract?"

"My thanks for the reminder."

With silk robes to soothe his overly sensitized skin and gauze wrapped over his eyes to diffuse any light, Ben made his way from the cellars. Two fellow mages helped him walk a straight path. Marisala followed with a pail should nausea get the better of him.

Ben strained to make out the faces of those awaiting him in Jivin's own plush reception room. Most were warriors of Hallik's escort, but the unarmed man in their midst jittered Ben's nerves.

"Good evening, Councilor Gredan, Commander Hallik." Ben eased onto the divan and rested his head against the high, curved side. "Forgive my informal greeting. I fear bowing might cause me to vomit on your boots. Have you brought enough shells to pay off our contract, Commander?" he added.

"Where is she?" Hallik demanded.

"As far as I know, the Key is on her way to the tower."

"She's already arrived," Gredan said, voice neutral. "Her seclusion has began."

Ben grinned to hide his surge of relief. "Have you told the commander?"

"The warrior," Hallik said. "I want Cassandra Mintolina in my custody. Now."

Ben adjusted the linen over his eyes to better see the commander. The man outmatched him in height and weight, but every fingerspan was hard muscle. Though his clothing looked to have been donned on the run, a sword hung at his hip and daggers' hilts jutted from his boots and belt. And Hallik's escort was better armed.

"I don't know where the warrior is." A truth. "Why would I hide her from you?" A good question. "What gain would there be in that?" A question Ben still couldn't answer for himself. Nor could he answer why Jivin had chosen to share the risk. "And why would a warrior need to hide from you?" *That* was the question Ben wanted answered most of all.

Hallik advanced. Reflexively Ben reached for his keshin to calm his nerves and found only the drug-induced void. Fear mingled with his remaining weakness to turn his spit to bile.

"Bring me Cassandra," Hallik said, steady and low, "or I will confiscate these holdings and search for her myself."

Sweat began to slick Ben's forehead. "Well, I'm in no condition to search in your stead."

"Leave the mage be," Councilor Gredan murmured. "The travel has left him ill."

Scowling, Hallik stepped back. Ben's sigh of relief caused his stomach to lurch, and he waved Marisala forward. Bending over the pail nearly caused the sickness he was trying to avoid. He fought down the nausea and focused on the orders Hallik gave his warriors: all of Jivin's holdings were now under the commander's control, mages were confined to the grounds, and any who resisted questioning were to be brought before him. When Gredan didn't object, thereby condoning the act, Ben shuddered. The five days of Jana's seclusion might be perilous indeed.

"Tell mages," Ben whispered to Marisala, "to answer as their conscience rules."

While Marisala slipped out the side door before a warrior could stop her, Ben stared at the bottom of the pail. If he shifted his gaze the slightest, he feared the nausea would win. The clatter made by the warriors as they left with Hallik pounded within Ben's skull. He nearly missed the soft footsteps of the person left behind.

"Councilor?" Ben rasped.

"Mage Kalari." Gredan came nearer and crouched in front of Ben. "There are grave accusations in the making."

"Warriors have always mistrusted us," Ben muttered.

"Your clandestine arrival has given them cause aplenty."

"Couldn't be helped."

"The conclave will assemble in five days. Before it does, you will answer my questions."

Anything he chose to say, Ben knew, would make matters worse. Stall, Jivin had said in his letter, and it was wise counsel. Once Jana's seclusion ended, action could be taken. Until then, Shendow was in Hallik's hands, as were the mages now depending upon Ben for protection.

"First," Gredan went on, "tell me how Cassandra has attempted to corrupt the Key."

Ben played his tongue against the back of his mouth, making himself gag. Undignified as puking in the councilor's presence was, it served the purpose. Ben hoped his next inspiration to forestall an interrogation would be a tad more pleasant.

•••

On the third day, Cassie sat beneath a shallow overhang on the mountainside above the city and stared at the slate gray cliffs that plunged toward frothy waves below. Sometimes she counted the gulls swooping along the shore, sometimes imagined huge beasts roiling beneath the swells. Most times, she stared at the Key's tower far below her hideaway and whispered chants of protection for Jana.

Cassie knew her chances of eluding a search would be better if she trekked higher, but she hadn't clothing enough to protect her from the cold and could not risk a fire. The coastline was too well traveled, and if she hiked into the woods, she'd be dodging hunters and homesteads. Islands, she decided, were not kind to fugitives lacking seaworthy vessels.

Yet even if she could finagle her way aboard ship, she wouldn't repay Jana's trust with abandonment. In two more days, when the horns sounded to announce the confirmation of Shendow's Key, Cassie would ensure the truth about Hallik's plans was heard, and admit her own role as well. Jana deserved no less. As for the mages . . . Even when alone, shame heated her cheeks. For no reason or gain, Ben and Jivin had saved her life.

Cassie tensed, head cocked, listening. A faint sound teased the edge of her hearing—too solid to be the wind, too near to have carried from below. Motionless, she scanned the crags and ledges below, and the ferns and fronds that grew farther down, then stared at the jagged shadows cast by the afternoon sun. Nothing moved.

The sound became a wail—a child calling for Mama—and the child's terror won out over Cassie's caution.

Cassie edged over the rough and rocky slope, working her way closer to the crying child. She clenched her teeth to keep from shouting reassurances lest her voice carry to the wrong ear. Her hands were raw by the time she spotted a form huddled on a narrow ledge, but she quickened her pace. If the little boy squirmed more than a handspan, he'd tumble over the edge.

"Be still," Cassie called, and cursed the echoes. At once the boy ceased crying and lifted his head, searching. She waved to catch his attention, then lost sight of him as she climbed around a boulder. When she reached the other side, the boy raised his hand and pointed directly at her.

Training usurped thought. She scrambled atop the boulder and reached for the ledge above as warriors clambered from hiding. Fingers and boots found cracks and crevices, pulled and pushed her higher and higher. Her throat ached and her side burned, but she had to gain distance. If she could elude them until sundown, she'd have a chance. Elude them for another day, she might survive long enough to see Jana confirmed.

Pebbles tumbled onto her head. She wasted no time looking up before changing direction, nor wasted breath answering the demand she surrender. A hand caught her ankle and she kicked free. A boot grazed her outstretched hand and she jerked away. An open ledge came into sight and she rolled onto it, coming to her feet with a dagger in each hand. Two warriors dropped to the ground near her and she charged. She scored cuts along each of their arms before a third attacked, then a fourth.

She didn't know which of them circled behind her; the solid blow across her shoulders flung her forward. Fists locked around her elbows, forcing her to her knees, heedless of the shallow slashes and stabs she tried to deliver. A sharp kick to her thigh made her cry out. Her daggers were taken before she could recover.

"I claim . . ." Cassie gasped out, "claim Key's sanctuary."

"This is a matter between warriors, Cassandra."

She squeezed her eyes shut, unable to close her ears to Hallik's voice—rich undertones mingled with firm assurances that had once made his prayer-chants sound more sacred than life itself, now twisted into a perversity bent on hampering the Gift of the Gods.

"And it shall be settled," he continued, heedless of the low moan pushing between Cassie's clenched teeth, "before an assembly of warriors. Bind and gag her," he said, softer. "Tonight we will see justice meted out."

"Oathbreaker!" Cassie screamed, and threw all her weight against the hands holding her. One arm broke free, and she reached for a fallen dagger. Just as her fingers touched the hilt, an elbow rammed the base of her skull to end her fight.

•••

From the bedchamber, Ben heard the door of Jivin's—now his—private suite open. He kept his eyes closed and his breathing steady. His first day in bed had been blissful. The second had grown tedious. Today had veered between boredom and anxiety. Three times, Councilor Gredan had paid him a visit. Each time Ben had feigned unconsciousness. During the last visit, Gredan had leaned over the bed and whispered, "I intend to be fair, Mage Kalari, but cannot unless you speak." Ben had remained immobile. Fairness was too malleable to be trusted.

The door closed. Footsteps, soft and steady, came near.

"I knew it," Jivin said. "I put you in command, and you take a nap."

Ben sat up so quickly his vision grayed. Haggard and grim as Jivin looked, he was a beautiful sight. "I'm a sorry substitute for you, Captain."

"Indeed. The place is infested with warriors—"

"I *stalled*."

"—and no doubt they're speeding word of my recovery to Hallik. Gredan will arrive on the commander's heels."

Ben grimaced. "What should I tell him?"

"The truth, when he asks for it, which won't happen today. I've another assignment for you."

"But my keshin hasn't—"

Jivin flicked his fingers to interrupt and sank into the chair beside the bed. "Hallik has Cassandra. She was captured this afternoon, brought in this evening and will be tried in a warrior's assembly within the hour."

Pain tightened Ben's chest. "Stupid warrior."

"Jana charged us to value that warrior."

"I'll do what I can." Ben lurched from bed, knees popping from the effort, and lumbered to his wardrobe. He needed an ensemble that was refined but simple, that would respect the gravity of a warrior's assembly without bragging of his wealth.

"For a warrior?"

"Cassie took a risk. I won't let her bear the consequences alone."

"Why is that, Benjas?"

Ben discarded the red silk robes—right fabric, wrong color—and considered the blue cashmere. "She matters to Jana."

"Is that your only reason?"

The cashmere would have to do. Ben chose unadorned trousers and shirt of cream silk to wear beneath. "No. And I haven't a notion what the other reasons are."

Jivin gave a tight smile and watched Ben pull on his trousers. "Don't bother with the robes. You're not going to the assembly. Mages have no say there."

"But—"

"But the Key does."

Ben paused with his shirt half on, then completed the motion. The amusement creasing the corners of Jivin's eyes heartened him. "How do I get word to Jana?"

Jivin pushed from the chair and curled his finger. Ben followed into the sitting room, to the deep and cushioned bench built into the window embrasure.

"I always enjoyed the view from here," Jivin said, though the drapes were closed. Then he leaned over and ran his hands along the velvet cushion's edge. His lids fluttered, the sole outward sign of his keshin use, and a rapid series of clicks followed. Jivin lifted the bench with ease, its hinges silent, to reveal narrow wooden stairs that descended into darkness. "Dominik and I were quite good friends, after all."

"He detested you"—Ben glanced to the passage, then back to Jivin—"so far as I knew."

"Mages are hardly acceptable confidants for Keys. We wouldn't want to worry the warriors, would we?"

"The passage leads to the Key's tower?"

Jivin smirked. "Dear Benjas, you are incredibly astute."

"Shouldn't you—"

"*You* are one of two people in Shendow she trusts, just as Dominik trusted me." Before Ben could ask another question, Jivin rattled off directions through the passages. Most of the tunnels Ben knew, but some he'd never noticed though he must have passed them a dozen times. "It ends at the embrasure in the Key's tower," Jivin finished. "You can open the lock from inside without using keshin."

"I'll likely frighten Jana half to death, popping out of the bench," Ben muttered, then climbed over the edge. The stairs creaked, but held his weight. Jivin handed him a small lamp and lit the wick with a fingersnap of keshin.

"Wish me luck, Captain."

Jivin snorted. "You've an abundance of luck, Benjas. I'll wish you haste instead, lest the warrior lose her head while you're dithering."

Ben took his captain's wish and descended the stairs. He felt exceedingly silly, peeking around corners and sneaking down dark passages. The climb through the walls of the Key's tower nearly ruined his knees. When he reached the top, he fumbled with the half-dozen latches as quietly as he could, then snuffed the lamp.

The trapdoor was yanked open before he touched it. Ben staggered down a few steps, dropping the lamp, and held his breath when someone peered down at him.

"Ben?"

"Jana?"

She chuckled. "I wondered when you'd pay me a visit."

*When?* "Interrupting the Key's seclusion is frowned upon, you understand."

"Not by this Key." She waved him up the stairs. "It'll be nice to talk with a person I can see, for a change."

"Are you whispering through the walls?" he asked as he climbed from the bench.

"Not exactly." Her cheeks rounded with a smile, and she swept her arm wide to include the richly appointed suite before settling in an oversized armchair. "Though I believe the Duke of Killaan himself would envy my change in fortune."

Ben wanted nothing more than to enjoy her good mood in such exquisite surroundings, but his thoughts churned with everything from Jana's odd comments to her disheveled appearance. "Are you bored yet?"

"Sometimes."

"Would you like a breath of fresh air?"

Her smile faded and she glanced to the main door. "Will the guards let me out?"

"Sweet Jana, the guards will be so shocked, you'll be gone before they pick up their jaws. I, however, shall leave the way I came lest this mage be accused of manipulating the Key into interrupting an assembly of warriors."

"The warriors . . ." She paled, eyelids fluttering as if she were a mage reaching for keshin, and took hold of the armrests with a start. Color rose in her cheeks, then she narrowed her gaze at Ben. "Dominik was right about Hallik," she said evenly. "Tell me what the commander has done to Cassie."

•••

Cassie silently chanted her own list of self-accusations—stupid, clumsy, shortsighted, over-confident—while a scribe read the formal charges: deceiver, betrayer, oathbreaker.

Hands bound to the rails, Cassie stood within the box for the accused and stared at the floor, at the sand that had been layered atop stone to soak up her blood. She was still gagged—a futile precaution on Hallik's part. Since the moment she'd awakened in a cell, silence had been her choice. Any truth she uttered would either implicate the mages in the perceived treachery or sound like the desperate ranting of the guilty.

She pressed her thumb over the callus on her finger, then curled her fingers into a fist. Hallik could take her life, not her Oath. Could take revenge on her, not the Key. Cassie's only regret was how the matter would taint the beginning of Jana's rule—not enough to impeach, but enough to cast doubt.

The scribe read the proofs upon which the charges were founded. Cassie had to admit they sounded bad when properly prefaced. As the scribe related Jana's unannounced arrival, the warriors seated on benches all around her began to mutter and fidget. The account of Cassie's attempt to flee elicited hisses of contempt. That she'd been captured with the child-in-danger trap commonly used to snare renegade warriors evoked a round of shaming laughter.

"Cassandra Mintolina," Hallik intoned from his seat on the platform before her. His sun-browned features conveyed none of the tenderness he'd once shown her. "Do you claim these events did not occur?"

She shook her head once. *Thank our gods they did, my once-lover, for the Key is now secure and Shendow will prosper.*

"Can you prove these events occurred for reasons other than those stated in the charges?"

Again, she shook her head. *You won't trick me into accusing others. You might find it easy to break past devotions against your ambitions, but I do not.*

Hallik leaned forward, hands clasped between his knees. His eyes dared her to protest one moment, showed pity the next, then squinted with unchallenged command. "Will you admit your guilt and die with that last bit of your honor intact?"

Cassie bit the leather gag and glanced to the executioner. Torchlight flickered on the sickle blade he held. The death she had grudgingly accepted—it would be decisive and swift—but not the confession. Yet her refusal would require Ben and Jivin to deliver testimony, to either voice their own guilt or perjure themselves. They had sought to spare her life. Speaking a lie to spare theirs was all she could do in recompense.

And Jana knew the truth. The whispered thought brought comfort. Though the evidence would be lost with Cassie's life, the Key wouldn't allow her death to go unanswered. Looking back to Hallik, Cassie tried to smile around the gag. *Secrets, share them, victors, victims . . .*

Commotion sounded from outside the assembly. Cassie craned her neck, unable to turn, as the doors opened and light from the hall spilled in. Her legs weakened when she recognized the woman who entered. Dressed in a gown of rippling burgundy silk that covered all but her face and hands, ebony hair flowing over her shoulders like black water, Jana strolled across the court.

Hallik stood, hand on his sword's hilt. "What's this about?"

"I ask the same of you," Jana answered, stopping beside the box confining Cassie, her voice steady enough to sound deadly.

"By what authority?"

She offered him a coy smile. "I'll forgive your rudeness since we've not yet met. I am called Jana"—a flurry of whispers rose and quieted—"and I will become Shendow's Key."

This time the whispers droned on. Hallik's knees bent the slightest, then he seemed to think better of sitting in Jana's presence without permission.

"You . . ." he rasped. "You have broken seclusion."

Jana's smile vanished. "I will break any tradition that would unjustly cost a life. Such things are the tools of cowards and the protections of tyrants."

All whispering stopped.

"The warrior is charged with corrupting you for her own ends," Hallik countered. "That you've come here lends credence to the charge."

"Do you think so little of your Key to assume she corrupts so easily?"

"You don't know Cassandra as I do."

"I know you both well enough to judge whom I'd prefer to see in that box."

"You haven't the right to speak here," Hallik said, hands clenched at his sides. "The councilors of the tribes have yet to confirm you as Shendow's Key."

"Dominik trusted you little," Jana answered. "Yet he trusted your Oath. In secret, he told you one of the challenges I must answer and bid you commit it to memory. Did you do so?"

Hallik's lips parted, and he nodded once.

"The challenge," Jana said, "is to decide which of the tribes I should most heed, which I should most favor, when Shendow is in conflict. Is that true?"

"Yes," he whispered.

"The answer is 'none.' The tribes stand equal before the Key and with each other, just as all people stand equal within the tribes. Hence the reason I have come, to be the Key that locks the Door against the ways of the Abandoned World, lest Shendow fall prey to the ambition of the few and become a mirror of what its forebears sought to leave behind." She lifted her chin. "Is that the precise answer Dominik told you to expect?"

He jerked his head with a nod.

"How precise?" Jana pressed.

He swallowed. "Word for word."

"Then I have a right to speak here." She gestured toward Cassie. "You should better confirm your suspicions before acting upon them. Since I was never asked, you'd never know if it was I who decided to arrive with no notice."

Hallik glanced around the assembly, then pressed his lips together. Jana hadn't actually said the decision was hers, but Cassie had seen Hallik calculate risk and return often enough to know he understood the peril of challenging Jana now.

"You made a grievous error, Commander. Surely you agree."

"Yes, Jana."

"Thank me."

Hallik's jaw twitched. "You—have my gratitude, Jana."

"Release your prisoner."

Hallik had lost the moment Jana entered the court. Cassie watched him realize defeat as her bonds were cut before he could speak the order.

Jana took five steps forward, bringing her to the base of the dais. "I'm certain a man of your standing can be trusted to guard his honor. That honor would be sundered beyond mending should harm befall this warrior. If there remains any question of her guilt after I am formally confirmed as your Key, I will gladly hear your concerns. Do we have an understanding?"

Hallik bowed stiffly. "We do, Jana. The issue need not be revisited."

Jana didn't respond. She turned, gaze sweeping over Cassie as if she were not there, then stared toward the back of the court. Cassie made a quick glance over her shoulder to find many of Shendow's councilors had apparently heard of the Key's appearance.

"Councilor Gredan," Jana called, and waited for the man to step forward and bow. "I see seven of your peers in attendance. Are the remaining four still at sea, or already abed?"

Gredan dipped his head. "Three have not yet arrived, Jana, and Councilor Tonsina is indeed asleep. She is the eldest of your councilors and—"

"—and therefore holds the most crucial of challenges the conclave shall set before me," Jana interrupted. "Though the challenge you yourself hold is one Dominik considered equally important to his successor, just as he believed your integrity to be among Shendow's greatest treasures. Did he not tell you so before his passing?"

*Gods all,* Cassie thought, shivering when Gredan's lips pulled into a sad smile. *Gods all, how did Jana know that?*

"He did indeed," Gredan answered softly. "I shall strive to live up to his expectation."

"Continue to serve the Shendow Islands, and you shall." Then Jana smiled—genuine, warm, and contented. "For now, I'll return to the tower, and await the conclave's summons."

"That seems rather moot now," Gredan said.

"It's fitting I should wait. This"—she made a dismissive wave over her shoulder—"was an unfortunate incident, but needn't alter tradition any longer."

"As you wish, Jana."

Cassie held her breath. If Jana stayed another moment, her carefully wrought design of authority might crack. But she did precisely the right thing—said nothing more, strode for the door, and expected people to step from her path. Cassie dropped the leather gag on the floor, spared not a glance for Hallik, and followed her.

But Jana stopped just inside the assembly and turned to stare at Cassie. Without needing to think, Cassie sank to her knees before the Key.

"Cassandra Mintolina," Jana said, "listen well."

Jana's chant began gently—puffs of air stretching into rounded breaths, rising to catch sharp consonants and tight vowels. Cassie lowered her forehead to the stone floor, breathless with awe, as Jana sang on of promises made, oaths remembered and absolution gladly bestowed. One pair of hands made three soft claps. As Cassie lifted her head, the assembled warriors echoed the Key's judgment.

"See to it her ring is returned to her hand," Jana said. "She understands her Oath better than most."

"Thank you, Jana," Cassie whispered, and watched the Key walk away with her head held high.

•••

Alone beneath the cliffside trellis, Ben watched moonlight flow atop the wind-ruffled sea. Out here, away from the swirl of scandal caused by Jana's performance, he found the peace to savor success. Come sunrise, activity around the palace would treble: final preparations for the conclave, inquiries into Hallik's dealings, clandestine meetings to nominate a new commander. Ben had plans of his own: answer Gredan's summons, corner Jivin for questions about Dominik, visit Jana for an explanation of how *she* suddenly knew more about Dominik and the councilors than he did.

He peered through the trellis when he heard footsteps, and spied Cassie headed his way. She was dressed in full regalia befitting a warrior belonging to the Key—burgundy tunic over black silks, hems and cuffs trimmed with gold thread. Though poor in shells, Cassie had earned the right to such finery, and to the numerous pointy things hanging from her belt and tucked in her boots. After months of seeing her weaponless, he'd forgotten just how intimidating she looked when fully armed.

Cassie leaned against the trellis and stared at the night. "Why did the mages help me, Ben?"

He shrugged. "Jana never broke whatever promise she made you. She asked a few questions, and I put them together with my own suspicions. I've wondered about Hallik for a long time."

"But *why* did you do it?"

"If you're waiting for a confession of passion, you'll die of old age first."

"Mage . . ."

"I told you, Cassie. I respect you. You knew what was right, and were willing to face the consequences. I thought the price Hallik wanted to exact was too costly." He sighed. "As trite as it sounds, it's the only reason I can come up with."

"You suspected something all along?"

"Keeping secrets is easy, Jana said. Knowing when to share them separates victors from victims." He glanced at her profile, noting her lowered eyebrows and thinned lips. "I knew you had secrets, and I knew they changed when you found Jana. Since you wouldn't share them, I made the decision for you."

"I thought you and Jivin had been bought by Hallik," she whispered. "Maybe . . . maybe I'll know better next time."

"A warrior trusting a mage? You'd throw the whole world off kilter."

"You're right, it's a lousy idea." She stared at the steel band once again encircling her finger, then clenched her fist. "We found the Key, Ben. The gods themselves have accepted her, else she wouldn't have been able to answer the challenge."

Ben found Cassie's rationale for Jana's knowledge less than satisfying. "Superstitious warriors—thinking the gods must direct our fate."

"Arrogant mages—thinking they know the gods' minds."

"Spotton," he said, and grinned.

"Spotton, indeed."

Cassie rested a hand on her sword, then turned and walked away. Ben waited until her form began to meld with the shadows before calling after her.

"You're welcome," he shouted, "stupid warrior."

Cassie paused, then chuckled as she resumed her trek to the barracks. Ben decided that was thanks enough.

•••

From her window high above, Jana watched the two shadowy forms on the cliff part ways and smiled. Soon—uncomfortably soon—she'd bear responsibility for every person of every tribe of the Shendow Islands. Tonight, she enjoyed the private success of making Cassandra Mintolina and Benjas Kalari champions of the Key.

She let the drapery fall across the window and left the embrasure. Her evening tea—the one that made her sleep deeply enough to avoid contact with whomever spent the night tidying her suite—waited in the niche behind the cupboard door. Last night, she'd been tempted to forego the drink in hopes of glimpsing her servants, but Dominik had counseled her it was bad form for the Key to be caught spying during seclusion. He said the same about her making her own bed, but it seemed a sacrilege to leave the sheets in a tangle when all else was immaculate.

Jana took only a small sip of the tea before settling into the oversized chair. The arm rests, broad enough to hold her mug, called to mind the welcoming embraces of old friends.

*Indeed?* Dominik asked, sounding distant. *I never thought of it that way.*

Closing her eyes to better reach him, she answered, *It's the now-repressed poet in me, I suppose.*

*A poet,* he muttered, and Jana smiled. He'd been as appalled by her previous vocation as she'd been stunned to find his memory-presence enwrapped in the old chair. *How in all the worlds did the sword-scholars mistake historian for poet?*

*I fit both requirements, thank you muchly,* she countered. *And *you* were an apprenticed ale brewer.*

*Be grateful when you taste Shendow's beer. It was terrible before I initiated a few changes.*

She shared a quiet laugh with him. *You're decent company, Dominik. I wish you'd stay. So many memories . . .*

*You don't need me any longer, Jana. After tonight's events, you'll be confirmed without question. What remains to learn can be taught by others.*

*By Ben?* She stole a peek at the window embrasure.

*In part. Jivin thinks so, or he wouldn't have sent him with Cassandra, and I trust Jivin's intuition.*

*And when I grow old,* she thought-whispered, *Ben will help me do . . . as you've done for me?*

*If you chose to share the secret with him, yes,* Dominik answered.

"Sharing secrets," she murmured, then patted the armrest. This one she would keep awhile longer. *Thank you, Dominik.*

*It has been, to my surprise, a pleasure, Jana. Gods be with you.*

She smiled. *And with you.*

Nothing about the chair changed outwardly, but Jana felt the difference and shivered. She drew her knees to her chest and tucked her toes beneath the robe, then drank down her tea. As her eyelids drooped, she snuggled into the chair's embrace and let the spirit-thirsty wood soak up her memory of the night's events. It might be needed by next Key to be brought from the Abandoned World.

# CANCILLERI'S LAW

*Written by*
**Gabriel F.W. Koch**

*Illustrated by*
**Douglas Pakidko**

## About the Author

*Gabriel Koch was born, raised and attended school on the North Shore of Long Island, New York.*

*In 1998, along with his wife Ruth Gaul Schliessmann, Larry cofounded and continues to operate Obscurities & Oddities/Noir & More Books.*

*The first time Gabriel submitted a story to the L. Ron Hubbard Writers of the Future Contest was in 1997 while he was a member of the Garden State Horror Writers Group in New Jersey. Working the craft of writing four hours a day, he has written fifteen novels and about thirty-five short stories. None of them, until "Cancilleri's Law," has been published professionally.*

*About his voluminous production as a writer and his single publication, Gabriel states: "Short story submissions continue to clatter down cobbled halls lined with rejection notices, with a focus on the light at the end of the tunnel switched on by L. Ron Hubbard."*

## About the Illustrator

*Douglas Pakidko was born in Provo, Utah, the second of five boys. The house was always alive and interesting, and throughout his life it was his brothers who always gave him the greatest competition and became his greatest allies. His parents bound the boys together, showing them how a bundle of sticks is far harder to break than each one separately.*

*Douglas discovered drawing by watching his older brother draw pictures. When he could finally hold a pencil, he too began drawing and has never left this fascinating world of art. At the same time, his mother and father constantly taught him how important it was to be well-rounded, so through the years he learned origami, karate, fencing, calculus, poetry, physics and many other fascinating subjects.*

*Douglas received an associate degree in computer graphics at Utah Valley State College and he is currently working toward his bachelor's degree in computer animation at the Academy of Art College in San Francisco.*

*As concerns his artwork, Douglas strives to eventually achieve the skill level possessed by top professional artists so he can help other new artists by passing on what has been given to him.*

Waxman swore she lived, but you would be hard pressed to prove it to me. I saw no sign of breathing, not a twitch of muscle. Not once during the long hours I sat and watched from across the primitive wood-slab table, did she blink. A rough, hand-woven scarf shrouded her lower face and hair—part of her period costume, Waxman had told me. The material's color matched her crystalline blue eyes.

Unless I touch her, I thought, despite my knowledge of her situation, how can I be certain she's real?

She stood poised in a half-squat of indecision as if trapped before her thoughts had time enough to sift evidence. Her room was constructed from pale gray sound-deadening plastics. Light strips around the baseboards subdued the space into the dusk of her original departure.

The furniture, one table and chairs padded and upholstered in dark ruby velvet, sat on a floor carpeted with a thick pile, blood-red synthetic both soft and resilient—except where her feet touched bare earth grown over with knee-high wheat or barley.

I stood and went around the table. She did not move. By then, I wanted to believe I witnessed a mirage, a holographic prank. I could still hear my mates at the Advanced Chrono Sciences Lab laughing at my naiveté when I had announced I would be the one, the person to bring her the rest of the way through.

However, the woman was a frozen mannequin, incredibly lifelike and frighteningly human. The briefing data provided by the Loyal Order of the Keepers had not exaggerated.

I rounded the table's corner to close the distance between us. I could smell her, but could not identify the sweet, almost sickly aroma.

Her unblinking eyes remained fixed on the place where I had been sitting. I studied my hand as I reached to touch her, and stopped. Will she suddenly come to life and attack me? Will she scream? Or will nothing happen?

I lowered my hand, and decided to stare directly in her eyes before I touched her. I could only see shadows below her scarf; the highlights across her cheekbone, the swirls of her right ear, and of course, her eyes.

The briefing data said her life span had reached thirty years when the accident occurred over two hundred years ago; she had not and would not age.

I moved closer and saw strands of blue black hair poking from beneath the scarf. The woman was stunningly beautiful. I felt there was something hauntingly familiar about her, which increased her mysteriousness. I wondered, maybe she's . . . Then thought, No. It's not possible.

My eyes, on the same level as hers, blinked. In the instant of darkness, something changed. It was minor, superficial, and, at first, I did not believe I saw anything different.

I did not dare blink again. Although I could not decipher what had changed, I decided I would not miss the movement a second time. Leaning closer, I stopped when I thought I should have been able to feel her breath; eerily, I felt nothing, not even a brush of heat.

I extended my forefinger, and lightly traced the high ledge of her cheekbone. The woman's flesh felt cool, but not cold, pliant but not soft, nor as warm as she should be, but she felt alive.

Without straightening, or breaking eye contact, I guided myself around the end of the table and back to my chair.

When I sat before her, I remembered the touch of her flesh, and shivered.

Being trapped that way would be horrific, I decided. Maybe I whispered it aloud.

As I fought to keep the dread I felt from becoming a shudder, I saw that her blue scarf had slipped. The movement revealed the top of her upper lip; the middle, where her lip pointed up at her nose, with a half-moon in the center as if ready to cradle the flesh above if she smiled.

If she had smiled, I think I would have fled.

I reached into my jacket pocket for a laser pen and my notepad. With both on the table before me, I opened the pad and wrote, What is your name? Although I knew her first name.

I held the pad where she could not help but see it.

Did her eyes move? Damn it!

Voices invaded. A door alongside the table swung inward. Two white uniformed Keeper-Initiates stormed briskly into the room and approached my silent companion. I heard snatches of whispered conversation.

". . . let them dry out."

"We'd be better . . . don't move her."

"It appears that . . ."

"Do you think . . . I suppose we should inform the director . . ."

The caregivers ignored me, focused on the woman's incredible eyes, gently inserting a drop of clear fluid in each, moving her eyelids as if trying to squeegee dust accumulated through decades from their brilliant blue centers.

They touched her hair, her cheek, wiped a moist cloth across her brow and nose, lowered the scarf and rubbed her lips. I leaned to see more clearly.

Her lips flattened as if warm and pliant. However, they quickly readjusted the scarf, and again covered her mouth.

I wondered if a kiss would revive her, then scoffed at my idiocy.

Frogs and princesses?! I laughed aloud.

The Keeper-Initiates ignored me and left quickly. The door hissed shut behind them, producing a transitional sound like the stroke of a palm on a bare shoulder.

I mentally questioned what she saw, if anything, and turned my head to watch obliquely. In the process of moving, I blinked and lost her for a second, no more. When I reopened my eyes, her left hand lay flat on the tabletop, centimeters from my own. My heart leaped into my throat. I saw a glint of gold from the band on her third finger, and felt a pang of grief for the family she left behind.

I gasped, "What's this? Are you here? Do you hear me?" I concentrated. "Move again. Please."

Her forefinger rose as if she meant to point at a spot on my shirt, or an out-of-place hair in my drooping jet-black mustache. I wondered, if I look down would she suddenly reach over and flick her nail up my chin and shout Gotcha! as my mother had when I was small?

Illustrated by Douglas Pakidko

I refused to look down, felt foolish and did. Her finger moved again. I flinched and glanced up and saw her features moving like a melting ice sculpture. Her eyelids lowered slowly, then rose and revealed irises dilating in response to the ambient light.

A finger brushed the end of my thumb and I moved to increase contact. With my other hand, I stretched and placed my fingertips on her cheek. She felt warmer, softer. I pushed the edge of the scarf lower, uncovered her lips, touched them with the pad of my forefinger and found them moist and firm. Her breath skated across my flesh, cooling before it reached the second knuckle.

"Can you hear me now?" I asked.

I jumped when the entry door hissed and turned angrily to confront the intruder. My mentor and field research guide, Doctor Alexander Waxman, had returned. He stood at the end of the table, his short, gray bristle hair standing like a brush.

"It's time to go, Doctor Blaylock." His voice sounded grave, a bass with gravel undertones, coming from a round smooth shaven face with tiny close-set green eyes.

I glanced at the woman. She squatted as she had when I had first entered the room. I shook my head and looked at Waxman, noticed his sympathetic smile, and nodded with resignation.

I thought, maybe I daydreamed it all.

I pulled up my sleeve and saw the time was four o'clock. I had spent five hours with her.

Hurriedly, I said, "Look, Waxman, I've got to come back. She moved."

"Of course, Artomo. Everyone sees her move one time or another. If you stare long enough, you'll imagine anything." He went to the woman, adjusted her scarf, placed the end of his forefinger on the tip of her nose; she did not react.

He looked where his finger rested, and up at me. "You see? She doesn't know we're here." He shook his head slowly. "I'm sorry. I realize how much you are disappointed. Every chrono-science medical intern thinks he or she will be the one to bring her through . . . and every one of us sees her 'move,' but . . ."

"She did move." I wanted to shout, how could you be this close-minded?

"Let's go, Doctor. The shuttle leaves in ten minutes. If we miss it, we'll be stuck here for three weeks."

"Three weeks?"

"Yes. Imagine spending that many days on an atoll in the middle of the South Pacific with El Niño churning the waters?"

I could not, I knew, unless I spent the time with the woman I had been observing.

Otherwise, the atoll remained a repository for travelers lost due to eerie malfunctions, a sterile, monotonous dead-end, once home to the original Gate project. Of course, the hundred-and-fifty-year-old Order of Keepers would not concur with my assessment.

I asked Waxman, "Why didn't you tell me she was this beautiful?"

"I didn't wish to taint your study, Doctor. You needed to witness her predicament firsthand. It's an important part of indoctrination into the medical corps. This," he pointed at her as we reached the door, "is what happens to the traveler who ignores Cancilleri's first law, which is, as you know: no traveler can coexist in two times at the same time. Once they begin passage through the Gate they must not hesitate."

"Yes, of course. And she's been stuck for over two centuries." I finished his recitation.

"She's the first of the thirty-three . . . been here since before this facility was created," he continued as if I had not spoken. "And don't forget two centuries of caretaking. This location, as you knew and now have seen, is home to the religious order of Keepers. The selection process to become a member is . . ."

I interrupted, and changed the subject. "I think waking from where she is would be terrifying."

"I imagine." He put his hand on my back and pressed me to precede him. "I doubt we'll ever know."

"Unless it could be done in a specific way for each individual."

"I imagine," he reiterated as if distracted and impatient.

We strode the length of an underground tunnel, lit with pale green lighting that turned off behind us as we moved forward. The passageway simulated the Gate. Tacky but effective.

At the end of the passageway, we stepped onto the glidestrip and moved toward the sea-air jump shuttle. Outside the walkway, the Pacific Ocean ran to the arc where sky met water, a desolate stretch of blue green water. As far as I could see the ocean held nothing but choppy waves undulating against the horizon.

I had a bad feeling when the transport's hatch opened. I'm abandoning her, I thought.

I heard a woman's voice beckon, "Artomo?" and spun around to respond. The toe of my boot caught the edge of the glidestrip. I waved to regain my balance, and called out, "Doctor Waxman!" and flailed the empty air, hit the waist-high railing, and dropped over the side.

I shouted, "What . . ." then, head first, plunged into cold water.

I sank, it seemed, forever. I searched for light and when I spotted illumination, kicked toward the source. My head broke the surface. I did not see the shuttle, and assumed it had departed with, I felt sure, Waxman aboard.

Apart from the water lapping the rocks surrounding me, everything looked different. Then I realized I had come up inside a cavern.

Gingerly, I edged around the rocks until I could hoist myself onto one with a tilted, but relatively flat surface.

An overhead beam of sunlight shimmered the moving water to illuminate the cave's interior and an opening in the wall on the opposite side of the cavern.

Still wet, I dove in and swam across. As I pulled myself up, I knew the shuttle would not have waited for me. By now, I thought, they've assumed I've drowned, and with their tight scheduling . . .

I sat below the opening, slid through on my stomach, and found myself in a small well-lit arboretum.

A loud demanding voice choked off relief for my safety. "What are you doing here? How'd you get wet?"

The voice came from a middle-aged female Keeper.

I stood, looked at my ruined clothing, and shrugged half-heartedly. "I apologize. I'm Doctor Blaylock. I fell . . ."

"I know who you are, Doctor. I asked what you're doing here." She stood and walked over as if prepared for an escalated confrontation.

I pursed my lips, looked at her in white shorts and a loose fitting short-sleeved white shirt. She stood about ten centimeters less than my hundred and eighty-five, and seemed to weigh around sixty kilos. She had tanned, well-shaped legs and arms. Her blond hair lifted behind both ears in swirled scoops.

"I fell off the glidestrip as it approached the shuttle."

"Then you've missed your ride," she stated.

"And final exams," I added.

She frowned severely. "You'll need to come with me, Doctor."

We walked several corridors lighted with normal fluorescent illumination. I knew we moved inside the boundaries of a realm where outsiders would rarely be welcomed.

The Keeper finally stopped before a narrow door, pointed and informed me, "We seldom have visitors. Forgive the insufficient guest quarters. I'll return shortly with dry clothing and a pass that will provide you with limited access to most areas within our compound." She pressed her palm on a palm-lock and said, "Okay. Now you."

I pressed my palm where hers had been and heard a low-pitched whine, then a beep. I was coded to enter.

While waiting for her to return, I examined my quarters. The area had three times the space allotted me at the academy. I had a private bath. The bed stood on the floor instead of occupying a slot in the wall. To my surprise, I discovered I had a wall access point to the Tri-W-INet.

I fished out my hardwire attachment from the sealed pouch strapped to my waist, inserted the sterile end into my cerebral access slot, and plugged in.

"Access restricted," squealed through my head. I tore the wire from the outlet and recoiled, backed up fast, collided with the bed and fell.

The Keeper opened the door and entered before I could stand. "Here's a clean jumpsuit." She placed it on the bed and added, "If you want to sleep . . ."

"No. I'm not tired. I tried to plug in." I pointed at the wall outlet.

She laughed dryly. "Not a comfortable experience."

"No access."

"What did you expect, Doctor? Full access to our data banks?"

"No. I thought the plug would prove to be a Tri-W-INet link and hoped to discover if I had been declared dead yet."

She laughed again. "I've informed the academy of your status. They'll be here in three weeks."

"Three weeks." I groaned, then thought of the silent woman, and asked, "Can I see her?"

"Is she why you fell from the glidestrip?"

"What?"

"Doctor Waxman said he had a difficult time pulling you away from the woman."

"What's her name?" I asked.

The Keeper studied me as if trying to decide whether she should press for an answer, or tell me what I wanted to know. She frowned, and said, "Dannia Foxlena Hersh."

The name had more than a familiar ring. My mother had been born a Hersh. A chill raced the length of my spine. I recalled her face and understood why she looked like someone I knew. Dannia had my mother's eyes, nose and lips, or my mother had hers.

"Can I see her again?"

"You actually believe she moved?"

"Did you see it?"

"No. I have never seen her move in my twenty-three years here. I played back the recording of your conversation with Doctor Waxman."

"Oh. Then you know he said everyone thinks they get Dannia to move."

"Yes. I suppose they do." She pointed to the jumpsuit. "Get dressed. We've an appointment to see the director in fifteen minutes."

"Pearlman?"

"Director Pearlman, Doctor. I'll be outside."

Meeting the director was commensurate with confronting a sergeant major after a failed mission or a mother superior after violating curfew.

She sat behind a drab gray steel desk that looked like it weighed five hundred kilos. Waxman had dreaded meeting her. The Keeper had sounded as if forced to undergo an activity she could avoid if not for me.

Pearlman, who I thought already stood, got to her feet when we entered and towered over me. She had a perfectly straight spine, a thin torso, squinted through hazel eyes with a yellow cyborg tint, and spoke in a commanding voice. "Why are you here? Shouldn't you be back at the academy?"

"Yes, Director Pearlman. I had an accident. I tripped on the glidestrip. Before I knew it I fell in the water, sank, and . . ."

"I've been informed of your escapade. Apparently, we're stuck with you." She sat, and waved us to chairs. "I've also been told you want to spend your time with Commander Hersh. What do you expect to accomplish?"

I cleared my throat. "She moved, Director."

The woman laughed wryly, shook her head, and steepled her hands. "Everyone sees her move once and only once. The blink of an eye, a smile, a twitch."

She must have seen the astonished look crease my face, and added, "Oh, it's true. We have it on record-cubes. However, no one sees her move a second time. The best-case scenario for her full recovery is unknown. Worst case? She will never recover. No traveler has returned fully after being trapped. And you do not wish to meet those halfway through and awake to know their dilemma." She stared, then said, "What can you do no one else could?"

"I don't know, Director, but I believe she might be an ancestor of mine."

The director stood and smoothed her blood-red robe and nodded. "I see." She studied my face and to my surprise said, "I'll allow it. If for no other reason than to keep you occupied for the next three weeks. However," she said in a firm voice, "only five hours per day. If you violate my orders or any of our rules, your privileges will be revoked immediately. Understood?"

"Yes, ma'am." I left a bit too quickly, but did not want to give her the opportunity to change her mind.

Outside, after the door had slid shut behind us, the Keeper said, "You'll be the first person to spend that much time with Dannia since she was encapsulated."

I smiled.

The following day I sat with Commander Hersh. She had not moved.

Day after day, however, I went to her, spoke to her, touched her face, and steadily grew more despondent. I tried to imagine her plight, stuck between the moment of departure and the moment of arrival, jammed between—the record showed—May 14, 1912 and May 14, 2064. She had hesitated at the flux point of transition, turned to go back, changed her mind, and the Gate had collapsed, encasing her where time grinds matter, and folded her into its amber.

Two hundred years.

I began eating at the table in her room, making certain I ordered the most aromatic meals on the menu. Each morning, before going to see her, I went to the hidden garden and picked a sweet-smelling flower. When I ran out of words, I set up a holocube and programmed it to play raucous comedy, or melodramatic romance. I entertained her, whether I sat in her room or moved through another part of the complex.

Eighteen days raced by without a favorable outcome. I prepared myself to accept that I had badly exaggerated my chances for success.

However, the day before the shuttle returned everything changed with heart-lurching abruptness.

I can't accomplish this, I had thought, and felt depressed.

Dannia screamed. I nearly dropped to the floor.

Her fearful shriek cut through the thrumming bass played by the band accompanying a female vocalist who could seemingly sustain a high C through eternity.

I had moved partway out the door, leaving the music on as I always did, when she started. Alarmed, I spun about and saw that her scarf had fallen away; her mouth opened wide. Dannia's eyes had narrowed into a squint of terror. I wanted to run, ashamed of the pain I had brought her, but I could not leave.

I went to her and pressed the back of her hand. With blinding speed, she grasped mine, and squeezed hard enough to grind bones.

Two Keeper-Initiates slammed through the room's main doors.

"Release her," one shouted.

"Release *her,*" I retorted through a pain-filled groan. "She's holding me!"

Then I heard, "Oh, my God, he's done it." Director Pearlman stepped next to me. "How long has she been like this?"

"Forever," I yelled. The word filled the room as Dannia's mouth snapped shut. Her scream ended.

She did not release my hand, but pulled me toward her. Her face had returned to its frozen state.

"I don't like this," I said softly.

Then I tugged her arm.

Pearlman gasped, the Keeper-Initiates' voices buzzed behind me. My attention focused on the realization that her lips had moved like she wanted to speak.

I began pulling her, thinking she needed to stand straight. Surprising everyone, including me, Dannia reacted. She stood shakily, and then collapsed face down across the table.

I tried to sit, but missed the chair and sat hard on the floor, looked up, and saw her ice blue eyes alert and staring at me. She smiled crookedly.

Pearlman straightened her wrinkle-free robe, and said, pompously I thought, "Welcome back, Commander Hersh."

Dannia looked up. She raised her head, then stopped as if suddenly dizzy. "Where am I? Who are you?" She looked at both Pearlman and me.

I answered first, "Artomo Blaylock."

She smiled, "Yes. I know you, Artomo . . . don't I? You waited for me at the Gate, or did you? No, you waited with Henry . . ."

The director interrupted, "I'm Director Katherine Pearlman, Commander," but Dannia's eyes never left mine.

When the Keeper-Initiates helped her to walk for the first time in two centuries, she studied me as if she knew me well and expected me to take specific actions.

The Initiates supported her weight and led her away. I followed and heard Dannia ask, "Was my mission a success?"

"Yes. Your years of work in the twentieth century proved fruitful. Atmospheric particulates dropped forty percent over the next cen——" Pearlman stopped short and cleared her throat.

Dannia asked, "The next what? The next cen? Can't you finish what you meant to say? A century?" She paused and when it became obvious the director would not answer, Dannia asked, "What's going on here?" She looked from person to person and finally stopped and faced me. "I don't know any of you. Do I?"

"No," I told her. "Not directly."

She clamped onto the director's forearm and shook her. "Something's wrong. I demand to know what immediately."

The director gently freed her arm. "I am sorry. You no longer oversee the Gate project, Commander."

"What? I make a mistake and—" She stopped, scratched her head, then said, "You're one of them.

Don't you Negs ever give up? We've got to make adjustments or we're doomed."

The director's voice filled with pity as she said, "That's an ancient and dead argument. We have sufficiently altered history. I am not one of the Negs. The last of them died . . . many years ago."

Dannia's breathing became rapid. She looked around and asked, "What's today's date?"

I blurted, "Twenty-two sixty-five, June the second."

"Oh, my God! Everyone is dead? All of them? Now what do I do? How do I live without . . . ?" Dannia sounded brokenhearted. Her eyes flooded and she fainted.

The shuttle arrived early the next morning. An amused Doctor Waxman greeted me with: "Nice dive. Glad you got the pearl." He supervised the team as they assisted Dannia onto the craft. She had not spoken another word. Her demeanor reflected defeat and unimaginable loss.

We planned to return Dannia with us to the academy where, we hoped, she would fully recover and join the teaching staff.

"Her knowledge of early travel," Waxman had stated, "will be invaluable. And you, Artomo, will be part of the corps medical team helping her readjust."

I sat next to her aboard the shuttle, told her about myself, and noticed a long, wide blade of grass curled around her ankle. It seemed an unusual ornamentation, and stranger still, it was as green as the blade would be if she had plucked it from the earth a moment ago.

She held my hand and listened, but stared as if the greater part of her remained where she had been trapped, or perhaps searched her memory for lost faces.

The shuttle's engines wound into liftoff pitch.

Dannia's hand vibrated, then her arm and torso. Shoots of grass sprang up from beneath her and entwined her feet and calves. I stared in horror.

The shuttle roared and rose rapidly, too rapidly for my hasty "Stop!" to be heard, or in time.

Dannia stretched as if anchored to the atoll by unfathomable forces. Her fingers passed through my palm like rays of light through mist. Her body elongated and atomized into a trillion time-bound sparks, which wavered and blinked out and were replaced by a fist-size pocket of depthless black. That too shrank, popped, and left an indentation in the seat cushion.

Hesitantly, I placed my palm on the spot and felt the warmth of her body and felt sure Dannia had left our time as the shuttle pierced the cloudbank and a single blade of grass left on the floor withered brown.

# SLEEP SWEETLY, JUNIE CARTER

*Written by*
**Joy Remy**

*Illustrated by*
**Brian C. Reed**

## About the Author

*When Joy Remy was in the sixth grade, she found a copy of* Dragonsong *by Anne McCaffrey in the school library and consumed it in a single, intense session. Not long after, she began to produce her own fantasy and science fiction stories at a rapid rate, penning short stories, young adult novels and space operas.*

*After graduating high school, she joined the U.S. Army and spent three years working as a translator at Fort Richardson, Alaska. She eventually went back to school, studying history, Latin and Ancient Greek, ultimately graduating with a B.A. in classics from the University of the Pacific.*

*Joy is currently employed as an environmental planner at a local consulting firm and in the evening hours, she tries to write the same kind of stories she's always loved to read.*

*About her winning, she states, "I am grateful beyond expression to participate in the L. Ron Hubbard Writers of the Future Contest. To have a winning place in this contest is the fulfillment of a lifelong dream."*

## About the Illustrator

*All his life Brian Reed has drawn pictures of cars, monsters, people and animals. He aspires to be an illustrator and make his living at it. To help him in that lifelong pursuit, he studied illustration at California State University at Fullerton, earning a B.F.A. There he learned how to use graphite, pen and ink, oil paint, watercolors and colored pencil.*

*Feeling he needed more intense training, Brian then enrolled in the Academy of Art College in San Francisco. He's now working toward his M.F.A. in two-dimensional animation. Although he's just started the program, he has already learned how clothing wraps the body, and new ways to draw the human figure and the human head. He feels his illustrations have improved dramatically as a result of this.*

*When he earns his degree from the Academy of Art College, he would like to work in the entertainment business as a character designer or as a storyboard artist. He would also like to illustrate childrens' books and feels that having experience as a storyboard artist will help him immensely.*

*Brian feels it is an honor to be selected as a winner of the Illustrators' Contest. He says, "Finding that there are people, besides my family and friends, who really like my work, has been a tremendous boost to my self-confidence. For that I am eternally grateful."*

*When your spouse is in the Service, it's best not to get too attached to anyone. The long Sleep changes you, warps you. Sometimes it turns you into an empty-eyed junkie with iridescent skin and a constant case of low-grade shakes. Sometimes it leaves you sound in body, but takes your friends away forever. Zip. Hiss. Gone.*

*Private Journal 2300.02.05*

*June Anne Carter née Goldsmith*

From the recovery chair, Junie reached out with her left hand and caressed the controls to the hibernation bed, her muscles still trembling from Sleep. She toggled the numbers up and down on the main view screen, listened to the hissing and whirring sounds that issued from deep within the labyrinthine recesses of the bed. Tiny servos whined, tubing flexed, rippled. The bed measured nutrients, set up timetables, prepared to send her into oblivion for a day, a month, a year, a decade . . . As long as it was supplied with sufficient power and organic material with which to keep her body functioning, the bed didn't care how often or how long she slept. The Service engineers tried to program safeguards into the operating system to prevent accidental oversleeping, but it was a well-known fact that the safeguards were not absolutely foolproof, that one could hire a man, a certain quiet and understanding man—

*a professional ghoul, Junie, don't be a fool*

—a sympathetic fellow in the know who could jimmy the machine, convince it to let you Sleep the final Sleep until the chemicals ran out and your body surrendered itself to the deep.

Junie stroked the keypad with trembling fingers, watching the lights on the control panel change from red to green one by one across the lineup. Although they could have done away with the old-fashioned gumdrop lights long ago, they were comforting—and so the Service engineers continued to design them into the control panels instead of replacing them with some less expensive and wholly boring All Systems Go message on the main view screen. For some Sleepers it was exhilarating to watch the lights change colors like old-time traffic signals, but for Junie Carter the real toe-curler, the real tongue-tingler was the sound of the canopy going up, a steady ascending hiss that sent sensuous shivers of anticipation down her spine, every time.

She let her hand drop to her lap, contemplated the open bed. Just sitting there, looking inside it was enough to make her feel like a needle freak with the smack melting in the spoon, vein caressed into an eager, throbbing Appalachia, waiting for the glassy push, slow slide, hot rush. She teetered there, on the edge of something cavernous and crystalline, made a motion as if to crawl inside, then collapsed back into the chair with lungs clenched like a child's fists.

Kneading the knuckles of one hand into her closed eyes to ease the tension there, she keyed in an abort code and watched the glass canopy settle back down over the bed, listened to the hiss of the seals. The gumdrop lights winked out and Junie's heart chattered, a painful, stuttering *rattle-drop, rattle-drop*. The sweat that trickled down the small of her back revolted, humiliated. Not yet ten minutes awake and already fantasizing about climbing back into the welcoming womb to once again ride the long darkness. Sickening. One day it would take her, of that she was sure.

Mrs. Mac was never the first to speak when attending to Junie after a Sleep. There were times just after waking when the slightest noise or the tiniest sliver of sunlight could trigger a seething migraine headache that would send Junie to her couch for a fortnight of vomiting and intravenous drips. To avoid this eventuality, Mrs. Mac never, ever, opened the heavy drapes in the Sleeping room and she always entered the chamber wearing soft crepe-soled bedroom slippers.

There was something unaccountably radiant about the woman as she padded into the room, her medical case in one hand and the cat in the other. She glowed with a disturbing vitality. If not for the strictness of the Service rules outlined in the handbook, Junie would have asked Mrs. Mac about the hectic light in her plump cheeks, the snapping fire in her lilac-colored eyes.

"You look well, Mrs. Mac," said Junie, accepting the cat with reluctance. As if it sensed Junie's irritation with the ritual procedure, the cat twitched and kicked briefly before falling into a placid, motionless limpness.

"Six months doesn't change a person much." Mrs. Mac's furry voice was pitched low, lapping Junie's ears in waves of velveteen. She reached out and took the cat away, stroking its parti-colored fur before releasing it into the hallway.

To Junie's great relief, Mrs. Mac never made her hold the nervous feline for more than a few moments. Although the woman conscientiously obeyed the spirit of the handbook's rules, she occasionally allowed Junie to dodge out of things that were especially likely to make her cranky. Mrs. Mac seemed to know that, contrary to what the handbook said, Junie didn't like to be touched after a Sleep, didn't want to stroke the parti-colored cat, the latest installment in a long line of placid, over-bred and indistinguishable Carter family cats.

What Mrs. Mac didn't seem to suspect, thank goodness, was how comforting she had become to Junie over the last four short Sleeps. Her lilac eyes had become a cool and soothing constant in the bitterly confusing firestorm of Junie's waking days. The way she gently manipulated her implements, taking Junie's vitals with a still and vanilla-cool touch, made the wakings less traumatic than they had ever been. It was going to be sad and a little frightening to see this particular Mrs. Mac leave once she began to show signs of age and became unfit to attend.

"How's Miss Mac?" asked Junie, trying, trying to remember Mrs. Mac's daughter's smiling face. She had caught a glimpse of a photo once, a full-color picture in a sterling silver frame. Miss Mac's eyes had not been lilac like her mother's, but her face had been kind and soft.

"She's enjoying Seminar. It won't be long until she's fit to look after you." Mrs. Mac unstrapped the blood-pressure cuff and packed it away in her medical case. She whispered some numbers into a micro-recorder while fetching Junie's bathrobe. Suddenly two rosy spots bloomed on her cheeks and she began to study the ceiling, pressing her lips together in a manner that spoke of regret or compassion or both. "There's a troubling thing you ought to know," she said. "Mrs. Kimble bought a dog."

"A dog."

"Yes."

"My Madgie Kimble . . . bought a dog." Junie's heart was suddenly a numb, stupid thing in her chest. Never robust since the first Sleep, it shriveled as if held to a flame. When Mrs. Mac handed her Will's photo, she forgot to look at it, handed it back. "Are you sure Madgie bought it for her very own self?"

"The Strickley's girl called me on the phone, told me she saw Mrs. Kimble walking it in the park. She said she saw Mrs. Kimble's girl bringing in a big sack of dog food with the groceries." Mrs. Mac's lovely, lovely eyes were no longer calm. They darted around, searched the ceiling, the walls, the floor. They were starting to fill with tears.

That wouldn't do.

"Thanks, Mrs. Mac. I'll be in the bath." Junie fled from the room on tottery, sleep-weakened legs, desperate to escape the sorrow and pity in Mrs. Mac's eyes. "Madgie," she said, clutching the robe around her shivering body as she hobbled down the gallery. "Oh, Madgie, what have you done?"

How Madgie would love that dog. She would play with it, kiss it, teach it to dance on its hind legs and beg for table scraps. She would make up funny nicknames for it, dress it up in silly clothes made just for dogs. And when Junie awoke from her next long Sleep, maybe Madgie would be old, playing with a dog also grown old, and maybe she would be too old to drop tabs of Pink and frolic on the beach with Junie, too old to dance through the surf with the Pink tickling her funny bone until all she could do was roll on the sand and shriek with helpless pink laughter, pink toes, pink surf, pink moon . . .

The bath provided the comfort that the cat and Will's photo couldn't. The hot water filled Junie's aching lungs with steam, injected her muscles with the heat they needed to fight off the Sleeper's cramp. In order to avoid painful Madge-thoughts, she contemplated pouring the sweet vanilla bath oil down the drain in the washbasin—maybe pour Madgie-memories down with it. She considered throwing the bath pearls away as well to avoid their cheerful pinkness—did.

*A dog. Good lord.*

•••

All of the assistants (dressed in functional gray, all of them called Mrs. Mac or just *girl*) were trained in the art of Keeping Up With Fashion and Junie's was no exception. The true skill was not just in knowing what sort of a shirt to put with a micro-mini skirt, or when to brush the cobwebs from long unused go-go boots, but in how to pacify an appalled Sleeper who wakes to find out that his or her least favorite fashion has come back into style. Mrs. Mac with the lilac eyes always gave Junie a tab of Yellow to calm her nerves while bathing after a Sleep. And today she gave it over an hour to do its soothing, cheering work before she showed Junie the tall, honey-colored beehive wig. She told Junie not to worry, that the wig was the latest thing and wouldn't embarrass her or Mr. Carter at the Platinum Party.

Junie tried not to think of Will Carter and tried not to watch as Mrs. Mac negotiated the beehive onto her head. Instead, she searched the skin of her arms for that particular luminescence that some long Sleepers get when they've become well and truly hooked to the timeless oblivion of the bed. Her skin was pale, true, and her eyes were large and particularly blue, but the frightening signs of deep addiction were still thankfully absent.

*Don't forget, Junie June, about that rattle-drop, rattle-drop, that's your heart telling you a different story than the one showing on your flesh.*

Mrs. Mac smiled at her in the mirror and added some pins to the frothy golden hairdo. The pins were cunningly tipped with little honeybees that winked with diamonds. Beneath the wig Junie's own hair felt like an unpleasantly oily helmet, plastered to her skull with sweat.

It would be like murder to smile in such a getup.

It was past noon when Sandra Holliday from the Spouses' Society came to consult her about the Platinum Party. Sandra was wearing a beehive too, but in a startling blue black that matched her handsome, well-groomed eyebrows. Her square-heeled kid boots made a thumping sound on the marble tiles as she strolled into Junie's salon with a glob of folders and glossy-paged booklets clasped to her bosom. "Junie June June," Sandra said. "Your Mrs. Mac is right on top of things, anyway. Nice bumblebee pins."

Sandra stumbled a little on her tall bootheels, but managed to negotiate her way successfully to a divan where she spread out her items like a chemist displaying newly stamped tabs of Pink. She accepted a cup of tea from Mrs. Mac and spoke decorously between sips in the best high-society manner. "So we've booked the Starlight, anyway, thank God. That silly frilly woman who runs the big hall is thrilled to have a Serviceman's Platinum Party to plan. All she needs now are your colors, dear."

Sandra opened one of her brassy booklets and thrust it into Junie's limp hands.

Junie glanced at it with a grim smile and clapped the book shut on fifteen different shades of pink. "The guest list," she said. "Can we take Madgie off without causing the Apocalypse?"

Sandra's cup wavered in mid-sip. She set her cup into its saucer with a genteel clink. "What's the matter?" she asked, her voice a careful zero. "Has something happened to Madgie?"

"Madgie bought a dog." Junie admired her own carefully manufactured externals. Her hands stayed put in her lap. The silly, empty smile stayed put on her face.

Sandra added sugar to her cup with a studious tinkle of the spoon. "My God. A dog."

"That's exactly what I thought." *Pink toes, pink waves, oh Madgie, gone forever.*

"Does she know they sometimes pine away during a long Sleep?"

Sandra was being disingenuous. It was perfectly clear that Madgie would not Sleep again. Soon she would begin to grow flowers with her own hands, vegetables in her back garden. People didn't plant vegetables they didn't plan to eat, or sow flowers they didn't intend to show off in their own cut crystal vases. They didn't buy dogs not intending to love them.

Sandra fidgeted in Junie's silence for a moment before plowing on. "We'll put her in the back. You won't be able to see her around the ice sculpture."

"Ice sculpture. Goodness." Junie tried to imagine her Will, her Mr. Carter, carved in ice. It wasn't hard.

"Yes, his starship, don't you think?" Sandra's eyes became too bright. "Oh, Junie Carter, you're so lucky that Mr. Carter wants to have babies the old-fashioned way. He's so romantic!" Her eyes searched Junie for a reaction, hard little flints, searching.

"Is that what you call it?" Junie said, affecting a laugh. "Romantic."

"Neil and I," Sandra began, her flinty eyes scanning Junie's face for clues. "Well, when we went to pick out the baby's statistics, it just didn't seem very . . . hmm . . . but they *do* turn out some beautiful babies, don't they. I mean our baby's just charming, really." Her eyes were like beach pebbles, so smooth and hard. "The docs do such a nice job putting together all that lovely DNA. But yours will be beautiful too, no doubt! No doubt at all! Completely natural! Imagine that!" Sandra took up her tea again, simpering across the rim of the cup with steely eyes.

Junie lunged to her feet, her smile slicing across her lips like razor wire. "Mrs. Mac will do the details, won't you, Mrs. Mac?" She made a point to clutch at her temples, even dislodged a pin, which tumbled into Sandra's lap, gold and diamonds gleaming. "I feel a bit tumbly around the knees. Please pardon me, Sandy."

Her knees had begun to shake for real by the time she reached the gallery. Then a tooth-scorching tremor began pulling at her lower jaw. Luckily, she didn't fall completely apart until she reached her couch and drew the counterpane over her head. Soon Mrs. Mac was there with a cold pack for her forehead, a glass of strawberry cordial to fortify the mangled fragments of her mutilated heart. "Mrs. Mac," Junie whispered. "That Platinum Party is going to kill me. The spouses can be so terribly jealous."

Mrs. Mac laid a cool hand on Junie's brow, soothing, suddenly, so soothing. "That Sandra Holliday isn't worried about Mr. Carter's plans for those natural-born babies. She's not worried about Mr. Carter loving you like he does, about Mr. Holliday not loving her like he plainly doesn't." Mrs. Mac gathered Junie against her downy bosom and rocked her like an infant, breaking at least ten handbook rules. "Mrs. Holliday is only worried about her sheets."

Junie hiccupped. "Her what?"

There was a catty kind of smile in Mrs. Mac's velveteen voice. "Miss Sandra Snow married up, as you know. That girl grew up resting her fanny on cheap, scratchy linens, but now she does all her napping on two-thousand-count Egyptian cotton. And the only way she figures she can make the Spouses' Society forget all about those rough linens of her past is if she can get their tongues wagging about other things, like the William Carters and their plans for two pretty little natural babies."

"No test tubes for Will Carter," droned Junie. "The man loves me so."

Mrs. Mac said nothing to that. Only hugged Junie again and made her kick the cordial straight back. As per handbook rules, she put the cat onto the couch before leaving Junie to her rest.

The woman and the cat stared at each other in silence. When Junie stuck out her hand, the cat bumped it with its head, startled itself silly and scrambled away into the gallery. If her heart hadn't been quite so heavy with dread, Junie might have laughed at the way its feet scrambled for purchase on the slick marble floor.

Mrs. Mac's nonregulation hug lay like a mink stole across Junie's narrow shoulders, soothing away the numbness of fear.

•••

Junie took a short Sleep to bridge the weeklong gap between the afternoon of Sandra's visit and the eve of the Platinum Party. After the waking procedure was complete (checkup, cat, photo, etc., etc.) she staggered to her boudoir and examined the framed picture of Will that she kept on her dressing table. He was long-bodied and strong, everyone's idea of a model Service husband. Unlike others, Junie never had to hear about space-station affairs or wild planetside boondoggles. He wrote letters in a confident tone, never forgot an anniversary, made the other Service spouses swoon with longing, and intended to put his wife with child in the natural way right after the Platinum Party. With good planning, he'd be able to see the child a few times before it grew up and joined the Service.

*Platinum Party: a celebration of seventy years of marriage . . .*

Junie fled into the Sleeping room where she huddled in a forlorn heap against the foot of the bed. She tried to remember how many days she'd been awake since the wedding, tried to remember when Will's photo had lost the prime position in the center of her emotional universe. She couldn't catch hold of the Will-thoughts though; they leaked right out of her head and fluttered away like dead leaves in an autumn wind. Fantasies of summoning the quiet and understanding man with the Sleep virus turned her thoughts into a wildly seething storm of self-loathing and it took a long time for her to realize that Mrs. Mac was shouting at her, shaking her, insisting repeatedly that the Platinum Party was off. Off. That some idiot at Mission Control had twiddled his

Illustrated by Brian C. Reed

slide rule the wrong way or something and misjudged the launch window.

Sleep was like a breeze that comes to cool a heavy summer sweat. It embraced Junie, enmeshed her, cocooned her in delightful oblivion. She was safe and sound, a minnow in deep and secret waters, a chick in the nest. No more pink (*dog, Madgie, dog, bitch!*), no more clutching, strangling baby-edged thoughts and Will . . . who loved her so deeply and so well, was safely on the other side of the universe where he could father no children upon her, natural or otherwise.

•••

Sometime later, Junie was ripped from Sleep to attend the Spouses' Society Springtime Fete. While they all waited for Mission Control to open a recording session between the Aquillon team and the eager crowd of newly woken spouses, Junie avoided Madgie, dodged Sandra and found a safe haven behind a potted palm tree. She nursed a glass of bland white wine and watched the spouses maneuver around one another, comparing babies that were displayed like heirloom jewelry by loving Mrs. Macs. They danced the society dance, compared clothing, automobiles, vacations, domestic help.

Madgie sat off by herself in one corner, shooing away her hovering attendant in order to minister to her boy child who was trying to eat his lunch with stubby toddler fingers. She had, apparently out of common consideration for the others, left the dog at home. But the chattering, preening spouses avoided Madgie anyway; it was as if she were carrying a plague rat under one arm instead of a chic Ferragamo handbag. Her skin was starting to loosen and her hair was starting to dull, but the smile she directed at the boy child was of soul-penetrating sweetness.

As soon as communications were established with Aquillon, Junie recorded her piece to Will and went home. She couldn't stomach the jolly blond earnestness of his projected image or the too-eager faces of the spouses, their searching, probing eyes scavenging for drama like carrion crows picking the brains from some poor beast's fractured skull.

Oh, but he loved her so. And he'd be home soon to *celebrate.*

When she was back home and almost ready to lower the canopy, Mrs. Mac came in with the cat. Junie held it for longer than usual and was startled when the animal began to make a harsh noise deep in its body. She could feel a tremor in her legs that crept all the way to her toes. "What's it doing, Mrs. Mac?"

"It makes that noise when it's happy." Mrs. Mac waited until Junie was ready to give up the cat and took it to the door. Her lilac eyes were gentle and placid when she returned to Junie's bedside to hand her Will's picture. She pressed her lips together in her compassionate way and touched her fingertips to the soft skin of her neck.

"What is it, Mrs. Mac?" Junie held the photo of Will face down with fingers that still trembled with the cat's happy vibrations.

"I won't be here when you wake," said Mrs. Mac. Her soft, earnest face was pink around the edges and her eyes were brilliant with moisture. "Miss Mac will be ready to take over at the next waking."

Black and blacker. The crumpled up, dying thing in Junie's chest kicked up a breath-choking spasm. She reached, the first time ever, she reached for Mrs. Mac's hands and the photo of Will fell fluttering to the floor. "What's your name, Mrs. Mac? I've grown ever so fond . . ."

"Mrs. Carter," Mrs. Mac interrupted, bending to pick up the photo. "You know it's not right, this sort of thing. My girl, Miss Mac, she'll take good care of you. You can't get attached to this old thing, now can you? I'll be unfit for service soon." Again one hand crept to her neck where the skin had begun to lose its youthful firmness. "The next Mrs. Mac will be young and strong and she won't remind you of getting old."

"But Mrs. Mac, I can't do this without you!" Junie leaned in, her voice a raven's croak. "The waking days, they all run together . . . I'm losing track of Junie time and Standard time . . ." She groped, groped for the words to explain. "Mrs. Mac, Madgie's GONE, I . . ."

"You've finally taken to the cat, though, dear. You'll be . . ."

"The cat!" Fractured rainbows splintered Junie's vision. "Mrs. Mac, it's you I want to see when I wake! That cat's been a different cat at least twenty times!"

Mrs. Mac's eyes, now calm, now gentle and resolute, tipped up at the corners when she smiled. "Why yes, dear, and your good old Mrs. Mac has been a different girl at least a half-dozen times now."

And then all of the Mrs. Macs Junie could remember marched across her mind's eye as if in a military formation. Sometimes they had dark hair, sometimes light; sometimes their eyes were dark, sometimes light. Only one had eyes of lilac, and sometimes gentle, soft periwinkle purple. Those calming eyes had become a safety beacon. Which was supposed to be the role of the cat. The cat could be engineered to look the same, issue after issue, to be that beacon of light for the long Sleeper. A good docile breed of cat was always suggested, one that would not pine away like a dog.

The doctors were still looking for the biological source of dog love. They couldn't find it, though, couldn't breed it out, no matter how hard they tried.

•••

The new Mrs. Mac had eyes the color of the sea, a changing bluey, greeny gray. When she came into the Sleeping room, she had her medical case in one hand, and the cat in the other. When she put the cat in Junie's lap, the animal stretched a mighty, toe-quivering, tongue-popping stretch before landing in a limp heap on her legs. It began to rumble and vibrate immediately.

Junie put a hand on the cat and felt its fur, examining the purple halo that her melancholy mood painted on everything in sight. "Aquillon mission is coming back today." She tried to wet her lips but couldn't summon the moisture.

Earnest Will was coming back.

"No, Mrs. Carter," said the ocean-eyed Mrs. Mac. "Delayed again. They sent the waking order so you could read his letters. That man sure can write a pithy letter."

"Yes, pithy. That's Will." Junie felt a smile tugging at the corners of her mouth, a shockingly spontaneous contortion. Another reprieve from Will and the grueling farce of the Platinum Party! Strange longings stirred within her. "How's your mother?" she asked.

The new Mrs. Mac's lips twitched first to one side, then the other. People who sniffed for wine and found vinegar had such a pucker to their mouths. "She's well," she said, snapping her mouth shut with an audible clack.

"And is your 'Mrs.' a real title, or honorary?" Junie felt something akin to glee as the new Mrs. Mac fought to keep her face calm and smooth. Her sea-colored eyes were darting back and forth, up and down, no doubt scanning her memory for the handbook rules that covered "What to Do About Long Sleepers Who Ask Questions They Shouldn't."

"I married while you were Sleeping." Mrs. Mac opened her case and began to busy herself with the tools of her trade. She steadfastly ignored further questioning, her face growing tight, then pink, then an astonishing crimson red. Finally declining outright to disclose her spouse's name and occupation, she threw her implements back into the case and left as quickly as decorum would allow. She did, however, leave the cat.

It continued to purr in Junie's lap.

The new Mrs. Mac had forgotten to show Junie the photo.

•••

The Service order for Junie to return to Sleep came in the morning post along with a letter from Will printed on cream-colored paper. Before leaving on his first mission, Will had donated several hundred samples of his very own writing to the Mission Control communications team so his notes, when printed on paper for Junie, would always appear to be written in his hand.

He loved her so.

"Dearest Junie," he wrote. "I'll be delayed again. I know that the Platinum Party is very important to you (Junie snorted like a horse and startled herself) so I'd do anything to promise you that this is the last delay. If I don't come home soon, we'll have to do the Diamond

Party instead of the Platinum! These asteroid mining operations can be tricky though, so it's probably best that you Sleep while I work. I wouldn't want you to worry yourself to death about my well-being

*Don't you have to be alive to worry yourself to death?*

so you should just Sleep so the waiting won't do you in. I can't wait to come home so we can go through the baby stuff that Mother said she sent. Sleep sweetly, Junie . . ."

Junie stuffed the perfect Serviceperson's letter back into its thick Service envelope before her eyes could verify the emptiness of the carefully constructed note, wondering if the new Mrs. Mac could make spoon bread like the old one could, thick with currants and perfect with a cup of rich black tea.

The idea of slipping into Sleep, of easing into oblivion made her spine curve and her nerve endings pop like firecrackers . . . but first she would eat spoon bread, tease old Mrs. Mac's daughter a little more, and spend a little time petting the parti-colored cat who had taken to following her around the house on her long, silent strolls up and down the gallery.

•••

Junie was tucking into hot spoon bread and pawing through the rest of the mail when her hand fell on a little pink envelope that smelled of vanilla. She picked it up and hefted it in her palm; it was as light as a feather, as heavy as the Midgard serpent. If Will knew about it, he would undoubtedly urge her to burn the damned thing on the spot as a farmer might exterminate a viper in the vegetable garden, a rat in the corncrib. Instead, she slipped the rosy thing into the pocket of her robe, took her spoon bread into the boudoir and sat down at her dressing table, turning Will's picture to the wall. She ate bites of sweetness while she scanned her reflection in the mirror. If she were to stand next to Madgie she would probably look like a wraith, but she wasn't sick with Sleep—not yet. Not yet.

She had just slipped her hand into the pocket of her robe in order to run her fingers along the sharp corners of the little pink envelope when Mrs. Mac came into the boudoir holding a calling card. Her kind face was pinched into a carefully bland expression, but there was a storm at sea in her greeny gray eyes.

"Sandra Holliday's at the door with a gift box. Wants to see you."

Junie hunkered deep into her robe, watching the world dissolve into crinkling, purple-edged black lightning. She saw that her glorious reprieve, her tiny moment of relief and happiness, was about to be smashed under the square bootheel of a social-climbing bitch bearing a baby gift. Junie focused her eyes on the waiting Mrs. Mac. "Your mother once told me that all Sandra Holliday thinks about is her two-thousand-count Egyptian cotton sheets. Think that's true?"

Mrs. Mac barked with laughter, but corked it immediately. "That about says it all," she said, regaining her composure. "I'll send her off."

When Mrs. Mac returned, she was carrying a box garishly wrapped in a heavy foil-based paper that featured spectacle-wearing storks carrying bundled babies in their grinning golden beaks. Junie took the gift, admired the sheer repulsiveness of the paper, and took it to the nursery where a large number of such gifts had long been stacked, still wrapped, beneath the ostentatious Carter family crib. Mrs. Mac dusted the gifts every day on the off chance that Junie would suddenly feel like opening them.

*No test tubes for Will Carter, not for that long, lean, romantic example of virile Service manhood. Sleep sweetly, Junie June.*

She left the stork-spattered gift with the others and went to stroll the gallery and touch the corners of the clever pink envelope that sat heavy and warm in the pocket of her robe. Occasionally, she sniffed her fingertips, which began to smell like vanilla, like Madgie's vanilla-bean hair. A hiding place was what she needed before she could open it, a still place, a place big enough to contain the screaming vibrations of this secret message from the dead. It was abruptly clear that nowhere inside the stifling house would do. Junie flexed her bare toes, scuttled down the gallery to the service door and let herself outside.

Fortunately for Junie's eyes the clouds were over the sun, but the light overwhelmed her anyway. Not only the soft cloud-filtered light, but also the wind, the sound of passing traffic and the smell of dirt attacked Junie's senses, causing a deep thrumming sensation to ripple over the surface of her skin. Junie sat on the lawn, almost panic-stricken at the sensation of the cool grass tickling her bare legs. How long had it been (*three months, Junie, or seventy years, take your pick*) since she'd sat in the grass, bare-legged, Indian style?

She had her hand on the missive from the deceased when she heard Mrs. Mac's voice drift toward her from the open kitchen window. She was talking to someone on the telephone over the sound of running water and rattling dishes. ". . . can't say for sure, you know she's a terribly odd little thing like a lot of them are, but Mother misses her so very much. I told Mother about her new little habits, asking such questions and things and can you believe it, but Mother thinks it's funny! I'd think she would be worried about Mrs. Carter going on like she does nowadays."

Junie held her breath to fight off great gobs of loopy laughter, clenching the pink envelope tight enough to put a crease in the delicate paper. Mrs. Mac of the lilac eyes thought Junie June was funny! Missed her! *Missed her!*

"Of course I think Mrs. Carter might be losing it, but what do you expect of these poor things, left all alone. Why you know, they can't even raise their own little babies, it's back in the bed once the baby's born . . ." Mrs. Mac clattered pans and thumped cupboard doors. "Well of course it isn't fair, but those Service people, they choose those ugly little halfway lives for us, now don't they? Annabel, you should see this place, though, honey, marble and glass, and beautiful things all around, well, it's like living in a museum."

The pink envelope smelled so sweet and Madgie and vanilla-beany. When she held it up to the light, she couldn't make out any of Madgie's spider marks on the paper inside, just a darkish square of paper. The ugly, clenched-up dead thing that was the remainder of Junie's once-tender heart drank in the pinkness of the envelope, drank in Mrs. Mac's bird-chirpy gossip like a gloriously refreshing manna from heaven. It didn't curve her spine or turn down her toes like slipping into silvery crystal Sleep, but it smoothed her fevered brow, offered milk and honey for her parched lips, sang her a lullaby, soft and sweet.

She tore open the envelope with rosy fingers and yanked the contents into her lap. When she saw what Madgie had sent, she gazed and gazed, then fell back, laughed and laughed, rolling back and forth on the soft grass. Oceans of madness and pain drizzled from her pores, leaked from her eyes and ears, crept away on little insect feet to hide in deep shadows far, far away from her ecstatically beating heart. Before Will, before the Service, there had been a child named Junie who had once ridden on the Ferris wheel on Coney Island. Swift rushing, shushing, lilting LIFT. Slow tipping, falling, floating DOWN. Her heart remembered the pattern that her mind had forgotten. Madgie, dearest friend.

•••

Near dusk she began to get the shakes and Mrs. Mac blamed it on her unauthorized adventure on the back lawn. When she couldn't get Junie to let go of the couch frame long enough to be carried to the Sleeping room, ocean-eyed Mrs. Mac spat curses upon the handbook rules and called her own mother for help instead of phoning for the blank-faced Service doctors who would likely do Junie more harm than good. Junie was lurching and twisting, beating her face with ragged fingers, vomiting helplessly onto the couch, the floor, her robe, her hands. The young Mrs. Mac was strong, but in her frenzy, Junie was stronger, planted her feet, would NOT go to the bed.

The long Sleep called to her like all the trumpets of the angels. It sang Scheherazade songs, danced Salome dances. It seduced with whispers and tender touches, threatened with bone-breaking spasms, stirred violent, dark red sexual longings down Junie's helpless, twitching thighs. Sleep whispered vanilla pudding words and razor-blade threats, offered the comfort of her mother's bosom and the taboo of her father's carnal couch. It plucked at her, turned her skin to the outside, raped her thoroughly and left her a twisted, bleeding doll when at last the fever broke.

Junie saw Mrs. Lilac Mac come into blurry focus through a gap in her tangled, vomit-streaked hair. Mrs. Mac's eyelids were heavy and red, her face a mottled ruin of tears and melting cosmetics. She slapped away her daughter's hands and gathered Junie up as a mother cradles an infant not half an hour old. Junie tried to wiggle away, to protect Mrs. Lilac Mac from the filth that covered her, but the woman had arms like velvet-covered titanium and there was no other choice but to sink into them in a swoon of pure love and the sweetest kind of gratitude.

They placed a sunshiny tab of Yellow on her tongue before settling her into the bath and it swept her into a sugary, golden calm. The Mrs. Macs washed her hair twice, scrubbed her skin with sea sponges drenched in fragrant botanical oils until she was pink and luminous. They drained the water out of the tub twice during the process and left her to soak in clean, unscented water, expressing a quiet concern when they couldn't find the soothing pink bath beads Junie loved so well.

Junie, a bright, clean, sober Junie (*one with further horrors to come, oh yes, the shakes aren't so easily conquered as all that*) this newly bathed Junie began to giggle and draw soap pictures on the tile sides of the tub. "This is me," she said. "And this is you."

Mrs. Lilac Mac bent in close. "Will you go into the bed when you come out of the bath? If you don't, the shakes will only get worse." The ocean-eyed daughter hovered behind, twisting nervous white fingers into cat's cradle contortions.

"No, no. No bed." Junie fluttered her fingers toward the filthy robe that had not yet been taken to the incinerator. "Pocket, there."

Mrs. Lilac Mac tweezed the item out of Junie's robe, looked at it, flipped it over, read the caption and began to laugh in breathy, velveteen wheezes. The skin of her throat looked wrinkled and soft like tissue paper that has been used a dozen Christmases in a row. She was astonishingly, radiantly beautiful. Junie wanted to cover Mrs. Mac's tissue paper skin with soft, childish kisses.

Junie looked again at the photo of Madgie's fluffy little dog. It was wearing a tiny straw hat with holes cut for the ears, a melon-colored scarf tied around its fluffy white neck like an ascot. On the back, written in Madgie's squashed spider script was the word "Pinky" with a heart drawn around it in ballpoint pen. "Mrs. Mac," said Junie, her voice strong and serious, calm and imperious. "Please call Madgie over and tell her to bring Pinky with her."

Mrs. Ocean-eyed Mac watched her mother go, remained kneeling like a geisha at Junie's side. Without the handbook to guide her, she was far from placid, far from soothing and sweet. Her fingers mumbled over her curly platinum hair, twisting, adjusting. She had a crumpled tissue in her lap that she kept consulting. In her nervousness, her eyes were darting, silvery gray in the low light of the bathroom. "You'll really give all this up? And for what?" She sniffled, blew her nose. "What about Will? They all say he loves you so . . ."

"Out of seventy-something years of marriage I've been awake three years, maybe four—I can't remember," said Junie. Her voice was even; her nerves, calm for the moment. Soon they would begin to jiggle and hop until the shakes annihilated her again, but now she was Miss So Serene and she played with soapsuds, speaking from a place of great clarity. "From the dogleg of a twenty-year mission, he says he loves me, tells me to Sleep sweet, Junie June. Not to live, just to Sleep. Oh, yes. They call that love." Junie paddled her fingers in the warm water, watching Mrs. Mac's eyes turn greeny gray again with sudden fullness.

Madgie burst into the bathroom with her ridiculous dog held in the crook of her arm, a pillbox hat perched on her head in the best Jackie Kennedy style. "Junie, I missed you so much!" she said, holding her fist against her throat. Then she raised her hand and covered her nose. "Gack, what's that smell? Oh, you had the shakes, you poor thing, didn't you?" Madgie stopped nattering on and her face became sad and still and real. "Junie June, if you give up the long Sleep . . . Well, what about Will? They all swoon about him you know, about how much he loves you." Madgie's hand fluttered out to touch Junie's wet hair with a shy kind of longing.

Junie was giddy, both not herself at all and more herself than she had ever been before. Her voice contained the harmonic tones of dancing celestial spheres. "That William Carter loves an idea, not me," she said, watching the doorway, looking for Madgie's little boy. She was suddenly interested in knowing his name. "That ideal woman of his would sleep in a coffin her whole life and watch her best friend die of old age."

Madgie's boy child crept into the room and hid behind his mother's legs. He peered at her shyly, then began to examine the cat who was perched on the sink. The cat looked back at the boy with calm, half-closed eyes. Junie held out her wet hand and stroked the cat. "His ideal woman relies emotionally on a series of petri-dish cats and an old photograph of her photogenic husband." Junie looked at her friend and embraced herself with dripping arms. "And Madgie honey, there's not enough time in the world to dream of a happy ending to that story, even while Sleeping the long Sleep."

Madgie with the pink toes, pink cheeks, pink heart, who loved to dabble her feet in the cool surf on warm, sandy beaches, who had begun to cherish her thinning skin and graying hair, her blooming columbine and fruiting vine, smiled a smile to make the angels dance. She rummaged in her tote bag and pulled something out from beneath the fluffy little dog. "You know what beats the shakes, Junie June?" Junie expected a flashing tab of Pink, but instead Madgie brought out a colorful little envelope and shook it, eliciting a feathery, papery hiss. "Growing things and sun, friends you love and cool ocean waves, sticky children, chocolate chip cookies and a silly little pooch in a big straw hat."

The cat yawned wide and Madgie's little boy smiled at Junie in delight.

And Junie smiled back.

•••

"Dear Will," Junie wrote, using the back of an empty packet of wildflower seeds as a post card, knowing he'd never see the envelope itself—not caring a bit. Just outside, she could see Madgie's boy Bill playing with the dog on the lawn. The child had sunburn on his nose and chocolate on the side of his face from her first batch of brownies (underdone, but edible). "Don't worry about me pining away for the lack of you," she wrote. "I've decided to plant some flowers, make some friends and buy a dog. You might get sad when you read this, dear, but you shouldn't. You see, they say you can't breed the love out of a dog. Dog love is a profound and sacred mystery, as fathomless as the expanding universe. So don't worry. Sleep sweetly, Will Carter."

*The shakes are starting to abate and I'm learning how to cook. The long Sleep sometimes sings to me at night, calling and calling. I think it's gotten into my bones somehow and maybe the desire for it will remain with me forever. But anyway, tomorrow Madgie, the Macs and I are going to the beach. The Macs are still worried about fraternizing but they're starting to come around. Oh, and I picked out the puppy yesterday. I call her Dawn.*

*Private Journal 2303.11.23*
*June Anne Carter née Goldsmith*

# TWENTY YEARS!

*Written by*
**Robert Silverberg**

## About the Author

*In his youth, Robert Silverberg dreamed of selling just one short story to a science fiction magazine with the words* Amazing, Astounding *or* Thrilling *in the title. Now, nearly fifty years later, Silverberg has become one of the most prolific science fiction writers of all time, with hundreds of short stories, novels, collections and nonfiction books to his name.*

*Robert Silverberg published his first story in 1954 and his first novel,* Revolt on Alpha C, *in 1955. After writing prolifically for SF and other pulp markets during the 1950s, he "retired" to nonfiction and other genres in the early 1960s. He then returned to SF with greater ambition, publishing stories and novels that pushed genre boundaries and were often dark in tone as they explored themes of human isolation and the quest for transcendence. Works from the years 1967 to 1976, still considered Silverberg's most influential period, include Hugo winner "Nightwings" (1968),* The Masks of Time *(1968), Nebula winner* A Time of Changes *(1971),* Dying Inside *(1972),* The Book of Skulls *(1972), and*

*Nebula winners "Good News from the Vatican" (1971) and "Born with the Dead" (1974), among many others. Silverberg retired again in the late 1970s before returning with the popular science fiction/fantasy Majipoor series. More novels and stories followed throughout the next two decades, including Nebula winner "Sailing to Byzantium" (1985), Hugo winners "Gilgamesh in the Outback" (1986) and "Enter a Soldier. Later: Enter Another" in 1989, and many others. His latest projects include the novels* The Longest Way Home *(2002) and* Roma Eterna *(2003).*

*Silverberg has been been a Writers of the Future judge since 1984 and is a recipient of the prestigous L. Ron Hubbard Lifetime Achievement Award and the Science Fiction and Fantasy Writers of America's Grand Master Award.*

*He lives in Oakland, California, with his wife and collaborator, Karen Haber.*

Twenty years! That's hard to believe. It seems like just the other day that I was being invited to serve as a judge for a new-writers contest that L. Ron Hubbard was launching.

I didn't hesitate. I was a new writer once myself, after all, back in the Pleistocene. A very young one, who was adopted as a sort of mascot by the established pros along the Eastern Seaboard where I lived then, taken under this wing and that one, and treated very well. It was quite a crowd: names to conjure with in the science fiction world, people like Frederik Pohl, Isaac Asimov, Lester del Rey, Algis Budrys, Cyril M. Kornbluth and Robert Sheckley. They all knew how hard it was for a new writer to break in—for *they* had been new writers once, too—and they offered me every sort of help.

Some of them introduced me to the big New York editors, from John W. Campbell and Horace Gold on down. Some of them gave me tips about what I had done wrong in a particular story that was getting rejected all over the place. Some of them offered me advice about things I was doing wrong in my *published* stories, showing me that even though I had found some editor silly enough to buy them, I had begun them in the wrong place, or failed to squeeze all the juice out of a good idea, or used eleven words where three would have sufficed. And some, for whom I feel nothing but love, spoke roughly to me—very roughly indeed—

about my early willingness to take the easy path to short-range gain at the price of long-range benefit and what that was going to do to my career if I continued to go that route.

I learned my lessons well, back there fifty years ago, and I went on to have the big career as a science fiction writer that I had daydreamed about when I was just a starstruck boy. And because those older writers had so kindly helped me along my path, I have always felt an obligation to do the same for the writers who came into science fiction after me. It's an eternal cycle of repayment.

The great SF writer Cyril Kornbluth, who was one of those who was willing to teach me some tough lessons in the 1950s, put it that way explicitly: others had helped him break in when he was a kid, he felt that it behooved him to do the same for newcomers like me, and he hoped that I would follow suit in my turn. And so I have, working with young writers in one fashion or another over the decades, as Cyril (who has been dead for nearly half a century now) told me to do long ago.

There was nothing like the Writers of the Future Contest when I was breaking in. In those days what new writers had to do in order to find their way into the world of professional science fiction was to send stories in, get the first ones rejected (because they were so awful), eventually write better stories and get encouraging letters of comment from the editors, finally sell a few to the magazines, stories which perhaps were good enough to win the attention of readers and other writers, and in that laborious way clamber up the ladder. That was how I did it—but because I was lucky enough to be in New York, and to make a few well-connected friends in the business while I was still quite young, the whole process became a lot shorter for me than it was for some people.

But then, a little more than twenty years ago, I got a telephone call from Los Angeles about a contest for new science fiction writers that L. Ron Hubbard wanted to start. Hubbard too had been a young, struggling writer once, in the pulp-magazine days of the 1930s. He loved science fiction and he wanted to ease the way for talented and deserving beginners who could bring new visions to the field. His idea was to call for stories from writers who had never published any science fiction—gifted writers standing at the threshold of their careers—and to assemble a group of top-ranking science fiction writers to serve as the judges who would select the best of those stories. The authors of the winning stories would receive significant cash prizes and a powerful publicity spotlight would be focused on them at an annual awards ceremony.

I liked that idea. I agreed to be one of the original judges. So did such writers as Frederik Pohl, Jack Williamson, C. L. Moore, Roger Zelazny, Gregory Benford and Theodore Sturgeon. A more formidable panel of judges would have been hard to find. Other major writers joined the list of judges later on—Gene Wolfe, Anne McCaffrey, Frank Herbert, Orson Scott Card, Larry Niven and many more.

And here I still am, twenty years later, taking part in the search for the science fiction stars of the future by reading packets of photocopied manuscripts from which the authors' names have been removed. Some of the stories I read are not promising. I can see right away that I'm not dealing with a future Isaac Asimov or Roger Zelazny or Jack Williamson or Robert A. Heinlein or L. Ron Hubbard—that this writer, whoever he may be, doesn't have what it takes; is, in fact, an amateur who lacks whatever mysterious thing it is that allows certain writers to cross the barrier into professionalism, and will never be heard from again. (Of course, I have no way of knowing whether I'm right, since the manuscripts are anonymous when they reach the judges. But an old pro like me has a pretty reliable way of telling, from reading just half a dozen sentences, whether a writer does or doesn't have the spark. Perhaps some of the writers whose contest submissions have seemed pretty hopeless to me over these twenty years have gone on to achieve brilliant careers anyway, but I doubt that there have been very many.)

And then there are the other stories, the ones that immediately announce, "Here is a star." You know it right away, when you read one of those. You feel a certain electricity.

Now and then over the years I've taken time out from my writing to do a little editing work. I've been a consultant for certain book publishers, helping them dig up promising new talent, and I've edited some anthologies of original science fiction.

And so the Writers of the Future Contest, through the two decades of its existence, has served the purpose for which L. Ron Hubbard brought it into being: to provide "a means for new and budding writers to have a chance for their creative efforts to be seen and acknowledged."

A decade ago, when I wrote a short piece for the *Tenth* Anniversary volume of the Writers of the Future anthology, I had this to say about the writers whom the contest had discovered, a paragraph still relevant enough to quote here:

"I've been browsing through some of the early volumes of this anthology series, looking at the names of the writers who were published here for the first time, just to see how many of them managed to fulfill the promise of that initial achievement. Some of the names meant nothing at all to me. Those people had passed through the contest like meteors, providing one moment of bright light and then moving onward without a trace. Like many who 'want to write,' they had had their moment and had gone on to other things that evidently were of greater importance to them. But then there were names like these—

Nina Kiriki Hoffman
Karen Joy Fowler
David Zindell
Dean Wesley Smith
M. Shayne Bell
Martha Soukup
Dave Wolverton
Ray Aldridge
Robert Touzalin (Robert Reed)
Howard V. Hendrix
Jamil Nasir

"All of them were amateurs ten years ago, when this contest began. [Twenty years, of course, by now.] But you see their names regularly in print these days. Like you (and like Robert A. Heinlein, Arthur C. Clarke, Ray Bradbury, Isaac Asimov, and, yes, Robert Silverberg) they wanted very very much to be published writers, and, because they had the talent, the will, and the perseverance, they made it happen.

Will you?

Don't ask me. You're the only one who knows."

That's all still true today. The only difference is that the list of published writers whose careers began with an award from Writers of the Future is ten years longer. And the process continues. The amateurs of today are the Hugo and Nebula winners of tomorrow. The Writers of the Future Contest is helping to bring that about.

# CONVERSATION WITH A MECHANICAL HORSE

*Written by*
**Floris M. Kleijne**

*Illustrated by*
**Matt Taggart**

## About the Author

*Floris M. Kleijne was born in 1970 and raised in the Dutch capital of Amsterdam. He started reading science fiction and fantasy at a very young age, rearing himself on translations of Jack Vance, Roger Zelazny, Robert Silverberg and Stephen King.*

*Floris wrote his first publishable science fiction tale, "Illusie" (Illusion), at age sixteen.*

*He studied at the University of Amsterdam, majoring in biology. After graduating in 1995, he worked as a university researcher, marketer and programming trainer before switching to self-employment and working as a programmer, project manager and general commercial service provider.*

*Through the years, Floris kept writing short stories in the speculative fiction genre. In 2000 he sold his first story, "Deep Red," to* Futures Mysterious Anthology Magazine.

*When an American friend pointed out the Writers of the Future Contest in the spring of 2003, Floris wrote the following story in four feverish days. It is his first entry to the contest. He dedicates it to the memory of Tracy.*

## About the Illustrator

*Matt Taggart was born in Bountiful, Utah, and raised in a big Victorian house with an acre of land known by the locals as "The Haunted House of Odell Lane." He had lots of room to grow and adventure in. Trees of every description and a huge seventy-five-year-old ivy-covered swimming pool helped fill his imaginative childhood days with never-ending adventures from the Elvish forest of Mirkwood to the crumbling battlements of ancient castles and sunken cities.*

*After graduating from Woods Cross High, Matt held many odd jobs from warehouse work to two and one-half years as an armed guard for Wells Fargo Armored. Later, he attended classes at Salt Lake Community College where he was but a handful of courses away from an associate degree in illustration before the winds of change blew him and his wife south to the Lone Star State.*

*Matt won several art awards during his time at Salt Lake Community College, including two awards at the "All Utah Open," a show for all the colleges in Utah under one roof. His motto is, "Believing in the Unbelievable and Rendering the Fantastic."*

*He now makes his home in San Antonio, Texas, and is diligently working toward a career in book and magazine cover illustration. The following illustration should serve as evidence that that career is just around the corner.*

When I spotted the Automaton, I must have been three days up in the Squeeze. The sight had cheered me up—I could do with some conversation, and I knew just the way to get it to stop and talk to me. Animal Automatons were easily shocked.

I had seen its approach from afar, since the crossroads lay in a wide, virtually treeless plain of tall, cheerless grass and sad, thorny shrubs. In fact, the only tree in my field of vision was the one to my right, from whose lowest branch the Squeeze hung by a rusty chain. It was almost as if the tree was planted there to mark the crossroads. But that was a silly thought. Of course it was the other way around: the road connecting the city to the harbor had been aimed at the lone tree, as had the thoroughfare paralleling the coastline.

The horselike device was closing in on the crossroads. As I watched it trotting toward me, I cycled through the repertoire of half-inch shifts and muscle contractions that kept the worst pain and stiffness at bay. Thus far, my minimalist exercise regime seemed to be serving its purpose: to make sure I would not freeze up in my balled half-squat position. The Squeeze did not allow for much more than twitches and tiny movements, but we were counting on those to be enough.

Carefully, ever so carefully, I lifted my weight off my right butt-cheek by pressing my shoulders into the curved bars on either side and contracting my back muscles, all the while breathing in slowly. When I felt the tiny piece of board start to lose its balance, I moved to the right just a little and settled down again. Perfect. The immediate relief of pressure and pain in that cheek was a blessing. Most of my weight was pressing down there, and I knew that without the piece of board, the narrow edge of the bar directly under my butt would have quickly caused unbearable pain. I had tried pushing forward and down with my feet to provide some relief for my butt, but had discovered that that way, cramps lay. And cramps would surely mean the end of me in this hellish device.

I moved my feet just so, allowing a different part of my soles to press into the horizontal bars. I shifted my hands on my upper arms and rolled my shoulders. Finally, I bent my neck and let my head roll from shoulder to shoulder, welcoming the pops and cracks that told me my neck was still in good working order.

Then I urinated, closing my eyes to experience fully the relief of relieving myself. I had timed it well. As the steaming flow hit the puddle three feet below me, I heard the low whine of the Automaton stopping, and the mechanical discord of its consternation.

"Oh," it spoke, as close to stammering as an Automaton ever came, "I beg your pardon."

"Begged and granted," I murmured as the last drops splashed into the puddle. Opening my eyes, I took my time to admire the creature.

It would have been a gross overstatement to call it a mechanical horse. Automatons were amazing in many ways, but none of those ways involved beauty or physical grace. A mechanical donkey would come closer: a donkey constructed of tempered steel, pulleys, leather straps and wires. In this particular case, the Animator had gone to the trouble of designing a mouth, with a convincing set of rust-iron teeth. This attention to detail contrasted oddly with the almost complete lack of cover on its body; it was almost as if a metal donkey skeleton, partially muscled and bearing a complete metal head, had presented itself to me. Odd, yes, but it would have given away to me who the Animator in question had been, even if I *hadn't* seen it half-finished a few weeks before. There was a very sweet irony that it was *that* Animator's Automaton in particular that presented itself to me as I hung in the Squeeze, waiting for the end. Then again, it might not have been a coincidence at all.

"Thank you. What, may I ask, are you doing up there?"

"Waiting for death," I said, and then, trying to dismiss the subject: "I bet I can guess who animated you, Master Donkey."

It gave a passable imitation of a whinny, confirming the identity of its maker.

"I've always considered myself to be a horse, actually." It had been given a deep and not unpleasant voice that fitted its head remarkably well, though not its body. "But you can call me Barno. Who do you suppose animated me, then?"

"I'm pretty sure it was old Petar."

"Right you are," acknowledged Barno, nodding its—his—head for emphasis. "Petar was indeed my parent. Very perceptive of you, sir . . . ?"

"It has been quite a while since I was last in a position to be called sir, but my name is Markus."

Barno whinnied again and abruptly raised his head high. The illusion of a startled horse was eerie.

"Markus, did you say? *You* are Markus?"

I smiled. I could imagine the contrast between the grim image of the infamous Markus that had undoubtedly been painted by the Constabulary, and the sorry squeezed figure he saw before him. I was naked and bruised, with crusts of dirt and dried blood covering most of my body. With my brown hair tangled and beard gone wild, I must have looked more like one of the Wild Men of the Glens than like the much-feared highwayman. Even standing up, I would probably have surprised and disappointed Barno. At five feet eight inches, I would have been able to look Barno in his beveled-glass eyes, but not over his head. Nor was I the beefed-up bundle of muscles he may have expected; my build was more that of a professional dancer or a mountaineer, tightly packed and sinewy.

Then again, what counted most might have been the simple fact that he had come upon me as I was pissing.

"Yes, I am Markus, and before you ask, yes, I am *the* Markus."

"So it is true," Barno mused. "Markus is caught! There was talk of it in the city, but hardly anybody believed the reports. The constables were strutting around boastfully, but even they seemed caught by surprise, as if they had captured you by accident. Truth to tell, that is the word in the street, that a Constabulary patrol had stumbled over you lying asleep somewhere. I am one of the few curious enough to stroll out here for a look. And here you are."

"Yes, here I am," I answered with a smirk, indicating my circumstances with a quick turn of my head.

"If you don't mind my asking, Markus, how did you end up in that contraption?"

I thought a moment. I did not mind in the least that Barno asked, but I was loath to give too much away to an Automaton, even one animated by Petar. Barno seemed an independent, but for all I knew, Barno had been found—and taken—by Nico, and that would mean Nico knew whatever Barno knew. I settled for a single word, meaningful enough to preempt further questions, but too meaningless to really tell Barno anything.

"Fate," I answered.

Barno nodded knowingly.

"That makes sense. You have made sufficient enemies in your time. One of them was bound to catch up with you sooner or later. Now tell me, Markus, how did you guess that Petar was my maker?"

I thought for a moment. The truth would not do at all, but I could give Barno an approximation.

"It wasn't really a guess. Old Petar always pays special attention to the head and the voice of his Automatons. I consider him one of the great artists among the Animators. Even this Squeeze clearly shows his brush."

"His brush?" Two metal hooks above Barno's eyes contracted, expressing confusion. I would have slapped my forehead if I'd had that much freedom of movement. Automatons are notoriously bad at understanding symbolism.

"I mean, his touch, his style." I waited for Barno to nod, understanding, then continued. "See how the cage is shaped like a large head, with eyeholes in front of my kneecaps, and a nose where my legs just fit? The nostrils would be just where my feet are. Petar made this Squeeze."

Illustrated by Matt Taggart

Petar must have installed tiny candles or other lights behind Barno's eyes, because they lit up in sudden discovery. The corners of his mouth turned out to be articulated, because they curled up in what was unmistakably a smile of delight. Petar, you are a true artist.

"Oh, I see! How wonderful! So that must mean you were just . . . peeing out the chin?"

The laughter welling up in me hurt my body in more ways than I would have thought possible, but it was worth it. It wasn't even the out-the-chin comment in itself; it simply was priceless to hear the word *pee* from the mouth of one of the usually so well-spoken Automatons.

"Right you are, Barno, right you are!" I let another deep laugh roll before adjusting my position and cycling through another mini-workout, wincing at the extra pain. "Now, do you mind if I ask a few questions of my own?"

Barno inclined his head to one side, in a thoughtful pose that must have been entirely fake. I had never heard of any Automaton actually *thinking* about the answer to any question. Petar had had some fun with this one.

"By all means," Barno invited, sitting back on his haunches. "This is proving to be one of the more interesting conversations I have had lately."

"Okay," I said, discovering the first and only advantage of my position in the fact that it was easy to hide the sudden tension I was feeling. "Just a minute ago, you told me you were one of the few curious enough to come out here."

"Yes?" There was now a look of confusion in the glass eyes, as if Barno was asking me, Did I? I chose to plod on.

"Can you tell me who else is coming to see me?"

"As a matter of fact, I can. The only other one interested enough to come out here seems to be . . . Nico. He will probably be here in half a day, by afternoon's end."

Nico!

Only three days in the Squeeze, and already Nico was coming out to have his fun with me! Three days! I didn't have to feign shock and surprise—I felt them. Three days! The end would come much sooner than I had expected.

"I can see you are quite taken by surprise, Markus. I say, I was surprised myself that the Harvester took an interest in you."

"Well, I am mainly surprised that he is coming so soon. I did expect him to show up. You see, we have a bit of history behind us."

History. Daylia. Father, screaming in agony. A column of smoke rising from the keep. Blood streaming down the curtain wall. The smell of roasted flesh. History.

"Oh?" Barno arched the two metal hooks, inviting me to expand. Mentally, I shook of the memories that crowded to the front of my mind. I realized that I wanted to tell someone, anyone, the whole story. It would be a relief to get it off my chest, before Nico would arrive and end it all. It might even rekindle some of the old anger and make the final confrontation easier.

"I can tell you about it, if you like. It will help pass the time. But are you sure you want to hear the story? It is not widely known, and Nico doesn't exactly appreciate anyone hearing about it. He doesn't exactly take kindly to anyone who knows his secrets."

This time, it was Barno who chuckled, making his metal body chime discordantly.

"Probably not, but how will he ever know I know anything? Only you know you told me, and I don't mean to be rude, but you will not last much longer in there. Particularly with Nico and his *history* on the approach."

"I guess you have a point there. But before I start, could you give me some water? There's a water bottle down there between the roots somewhere."

Squeaking, Barno got up and ambled toward the tree.

"My, my, what's all this? Indeed, there's the bottle, but your clothes are here as well, as is your sword, and . . . what possessed your captors to leave all your equipment here?"

I shrugged as best I could.

"As I understand it, this is their standard procedure. They stripped me, put me in here and hoisted me up. Then they threw my clothes in that heap, and showed me the full water bottle before putting it down there. Over the last few days, I've been lucky with the rain, but in different weather, that bottle would have been torture, trust me."

Mentioning the rain was careless of me, but Barno just nodded.

"I see how they are. And the sword too, and such a beautiful weapon it is!"

"Please don't touch it!"

Barno, who had been about to nose the hilt, recoiled at my shout.

"Sorry, Barno, but that sword is very precious to me. A family heirloom, as a matter of fact. They left it here so any traveler can use it to pester and prick me, or simply steal it. That hurt me the most, that they would leave Shamlick out like that."

"Shamlick?"

"Yes, that's its name. And it is part of the story I was about to tell you. Be a pal and hand me that bottle, would you?"

Barno grabbed the bottle between his iron teeth and brought it up to me, but then hesitated.

"I say, I'm not sure I should quench the thirst of a squeezed prisoner of the Constabulary."

"Come on, Barno, please. There isn't another soul in sight for miles, and no one will ever know. Besides, I'll need a drink of water if I'm to tell the whole tale."

"Oh, I guess there's no harm. Here you go." He stretched his neck and brought the bottle to my lips. Uncorking it with my teeth, I drank deeply.

"Thanks, Barno."

He set the bottle back down between two roots, making sure it stayed upright. Then he sat back again and looked at me, expectantly.

I took a deep breath and told my tale.

There's a beautiful spot up in the North Plains, where the Lussy River exits foaming from the gorges and flows into the lowlands. The mountains rise up quite suddenly there, and the Lussy changes within a distance of less than a mile from an unnavigable whitewater rushing between cliffs and sharp rocks into a broad and calm flatland river. After rushing from the gorges, the Lussy embraces its newfound freedom and overflows its south bank to form a wide lake of swans, lilies and reeds. Fishing and boating are good there, if you stay well away from where the Lussy flows into the lake; up there, the water is churning and boiling, but the rest of the lake is quite calm.

There is a huge irregular spur of bedrock thrown out from the mountains on the north bank of the Lussy, shaped much like a splayed five-fingered lizard's foot. Rising from the middle of this rock used to be a castle.

"I say, I know the place," Barno interrupted. "I've seen the ruins there."

"That's the place all right."

A moat still circles the Lizard's Foot and connects the sheer cliff behind the castle and north of the spur to the Lussy south of the castle. Between the second and third fingers of the Lizard's Foot, a sturdy drawbridge used to span the moat, leading to a steep access ramp that curled over and around the fingers, over another drawbridge spanning a deep cleft in the first finger, and pierced the castle's curtain wall at the south gate.

The semicircular curtain wall used to connect the cliff face north and south of the castle proper. It sported five grand defense towers aligned with the five fingers, and enclosed a wide cobblestoned courtyard. In the middle of the courtyard, close up against the cliff face but not quite touching it, stood the keep.

The keep was my home for fifteen years. I played in the courtyard and behind the battlements topping the curtain wall; climbed the rocky fingers of the Lizard's Foot and sustained my first fractures; stole my first kiss in the irregular rocky alley between the keep and the cliff face. Tomaz the Swordmaster taught me my positions in the courtyard; I learned to ride, to shoot a crossbow, to dance, to read.

My father was master of the keep. For most of my life, I only knew him as Father, but his name was Jomez.

"Jomez? Your father was *Jomez?*"

"Yes."

"That's one detail never included in the tales about you, that you are the son of Jomez. How odd . . . Wasn't there a battle between Jomez and Nico's troops years ago, and a siege?"

"Hah! You could call it that . . ."

Master Jomez, as his people called him, was a good man. It was as simple as that. I may be a bit subjective about it, but as far as I could see, he was a just landlord, a fair master of the house, and a good father to my sister and me. There were never any serious conflicts between his tenants and him, and he made a point of being accessible to everyone and, more unusually, listening to the complaints and suggestions his tenants and other employees felt free to bring to his attention. I believe he was well-loved and respected.

Mother had died when Daylia and I were very young, but Father had never remarried and had somehow found the time to have a big hand in our upbringing. Even though he was occupied with ruling the surrounding lands a lot of the time, I have many memories of the three of us riding together, or playing games, or of Father teaching us to read and write. He was a cheerful, kind man with boundless energy.

For all his various occupations, he still found time for his great passion. Studying and working with old Petar, Father had developed himself into a skillful Animator in his own right. For five years of my youth, my inseparable companion was an Automaton dog my father had created for me. Daylia, my sister, had a pet owl that could actually fly. Both of us ended up wrecking our Automatons accidentally, but though Father gave us a good hiding for it, he was quick to forgive and forget.

Father was never the artist that Petar is. He had the will and a lot of the skill, but lacked the talent; he was simply not a mage. Even so, there were always any number of Automatons bustling around the courtyard and two Automaton guards at the gate. He had acquired some measure of fame for his animating.

That proved to be his undoing.

When I was fifteen and Daylia two years older, the first reports started coming in about a new and ruthless mage on the ascent in the south, between the keep and the city. His name was Nico, and he had acquired land and wealth at great speed by usurping or converting every lord and estate in a large radius around his original mansion. There were stories about destruction, widespread raping and killing, and . . .

"Do you even know why they call him the Harvester?" I asked Barno.

"No, although I suspect it is connected to the scythe he carries with him."

"Not the scythe in itself," I said, "though that's part of it, of course."

A very small number of refugees made it to the keep. Father gave them sanctuary without exception. Because Father was training me to be his successor, I was present at one of his interviews with these people. I remember sitting at Father's right hand, one step down from his throne, and listening in ever-growing horror to this man's tale.

His name was Mano, and he had been a villager a few dozen miles south of the keep, living peacefully until Nico's troops showed up and tore the village apart. Mano didn't even know what crime the villagers had committed in Nico's eyes to warrant such outrage. For all we know, the village was simply in the way of his expansion.

Mano had hidden in terror in a refuse heap, escaping certain death at Nico's hands, and hated himself for the coward he believed himself to be. He had hidden and seen how the people of his village had been rounded up by Nico's mercenaries, their hands tied behind their backs. These were the elderly, the women, the children; the men had been taken prisoner and deported. The mercenaries lined them up and stood guard behind them and at either end of the line.

Then Nico showed up.

Nico eyed the villagers cowering before him. He walked all the way down the line once and back, looking each of these poor people twice in the eyes, reveling in their fear. Back at the beginning of the line, he reached behind his back for his scythe.

The children did not understand what was happening, and that was probably a blessing for them. Some of the adults in the line had heard rumors, and at least one of the old men collapsed, sobbing hysterically.

The mercenary behind him jerked him upright by the scruff of his neck.

Then Nico proceeded to "harvest."

As Mano told it, by the time Nico was halfway through the line, one of his mercenaries had enough and ran. Without breaking stride, Nico motioned to one of the others. Ten seconds later, the fleeing mercenary crashed to the ground, a crossbow bolt in the back of his head.

After he reached the end of the line, Nico wiped the blade of his scythe on the tunic of the man lying bleeding at his feet. Then he motioned for the mercenaries to pack up and move out.

This was the greatest horror of what I heard that day, the thing that stuck in my mind and haunted my nightmares for weeks, months after that. Nico had cut down every single villager, and then turned his back and left them to bleed to death. It was a dishonorable and cowardly act, cruel and so shockingly unnecessary. I had a vivid imagination even then, and could picture the villagers in incredible pain, crawling around, bleeding from their shattered stumps, feeling their inevitable death slowly approaching.

Mano had been too terrified to crawl out of his hiding place for hours after Nico and the mercenaries moved out. Even then, he was shaking uncontrollably and felt like throwing up. The village elder saw him and called out, ordering him to flee to the keep and warn us against Nico. It tore Mano apart to leave his fellow villagers behind like that, but he ran anyway. He was incapable of doing anything else. He arrived at the keep the next day.

Father gave him the best guest bedroom in the keep and ordered a twenty-four-hour watch on him. It didn't help, though. Mano threw himself out his window that same night and fell to his death on the cobblestones of the courtyard.

"That's terrible!" cried out Barno.

"Yeah, and then some."

Father was deeply disturbed by Mano's tale. He was sensible enough not to blame himself for Mano's suicide, but the fact of it had underlined the fundamental horrible truth of his tale.

Father wanted to march on Nico immediately, but we had never been a warsome family, maintaining a force only strong enough for the defense of the keep. It was frustrating to be so powerless, so unable to act, but that was the situation. So Father kept taking in refugees, interviewing witnesses and listening to their gruesome tales. He could not act directly against Nico, but he was determined to help Nico's victims and to simply *know* of Nico's atrocities.

And then, six years ago, Nico came to the keep.

He came with a small detachment of his troops, supplemented by half a dozen clumsy and grinding mechanical warriors. By that time, he had already started to replace his unreliable and unduly sentimental mercenaries with Automatons of his own making. As he marched up the access ramp, we could see they were ugly and noisy and generally badly constructed, but it seemed they did their job well enough, according to the wide-eyed testimony of their terrified survivors.

Nico marched up the access ramp with his men and devices with the imperious arrogance of an evil king. The tower guard spotted him in time for Father to head him off at the south gate. He sent for me to join him, but by the time I made it to the gate, Nico had already arrived.

It was a strange and unsettling scene, between the open gate doors and directly under the oily black points of the portcullis. Father was flanked by two human and two Automaton guards. Nico had apparently ordered his bodyguard to wait out on the drawbridge.

My father had always been an imposing figure, not only tall, but with a barrel chest and a wide girth.

"It seems you have not inherited your father's posture, then."

"No, I take after Mother more."

Ruddy-faced and generously bearded, he had always been an imposing and powerful figure in any gathering by virtue of his physical dominance. He had been known to silence feasts in the grand hall by the simple and unconscious expedient of walking through the doors and standing at the head of the table.

Nico, on the other hand, was a scrawny figure, with a skull face, a mop of unruly, colorless hair, and narrow, birdlike shoulders. He was dressed in skintight breeches and a blue coat that emphasized his potbelly and his limited muscular development. Standing only to my father's shoulders, he might have been a beggar or one of the half-starved refugees we'd been welcoming—except for the blue clothing and the wild fire in his eyes, he should have been all but invisible next to Father.

But for a moment, as I approached Father and Nico facing each other under the portcullis, it seemed that Father was the smaller of the two. And did I detect a whiff of fear on him? Surely not, not Father! But as I got closer, I could hear a defiance in Father's voice that belied what should have been their power balance. It was disturbing and frightening. How could it be that my father was reduced to a show of defiance, even though he was standing at the gate as the master of the keep? Unconsciously, I slowed my step, but I couldn't avoid coming close enough to make out what they were saying.

"Consider carefully, Master Jomez," Nico was saying. His voice was like the layer of slime on the rough scaly back of a toad, like an ancient crone's wedding gown of satin and sandpaper, like the . . .

"Quite dramatic, Markus, and quite unlike you . . ."

"I know, Barno. But you have to imagine this voice—it seriously gave me the creeps, but saying that doesn't begin to convey how my skin crawled hearing him speak."

"Fair enough. I've heard the man speak myself, and I concur."

"Don't be too quick to reply. As an ally, I can bring you more wealth, more power than you can imagine. As your enemy, I would still have all that power to spread. But in that case, I wouldn't be sharing it . . ." He reached behind him and fingered the rusty blade of his scythe. Only it wasn't rust, of course, I realized, shuddering.

I stepped closer and touched Father's arm to let him know I was at his side. Father threw a quick glance, acknowledging me with a nod. There wasn't even the briefest smile, though—his face remained grim. If nothing else, that confirmed that things were deeply wrong between him and Nico.

Nico turned his face to me, pretending to notice me for the first time. I looked in his eyes, though, and saw a glimpse of the coldly calculating alien mind behind them. He'd been aware of me from the moment I came into view, I felt sure of it. He kept eye contact as he resumed speaking to Father.

"Think of your pups, too, Master Jomez. Think of what you might leave them after your demise. Of natural causes, of course," he added, making it sound like a casual afterthought.

His voice still sent shivers down my spine, but his remark had stung my youthful pride. Grasping the hilt of my sword, I started.

"Pups? I'll . . ."

Father, without even looking in my direction, stuck out his left arm, fingers spread, and shut me up instantly. Instead, he spoke, and his voice shook.

"Nico, I have met you at my door and held a civilized conversation. You have asked me a question and I've given you my answer. And now you stoop to threatening my children? I think this conversation is over!"

The last word thundered and echoed in the entranceway. Nico, however, didn't even flinch. He inclined his head to one side, then the other, his eyes trained on my father's face, as if he was examining an unfamiliar species of plant. Then he went on as if it was a conversation between friendly neighbors.

"Then there's also the matter of those few enemies of mine you've been so kind as to keep within your walls. I am now ready to take them with me. Please fetch them, yes?"

I heard Father inhale sharply through his nose, normally a sure sign for Daylia and I to apologize profusely for whatever trespass we'd committed, or run. He was shaking with pent-up rage. Then, incredibly, he drew his sword and held the point mere inches from Nico's chest. I heard the two human guards take a shocked breath at this unprecedented breach of the rules of hospitality. Almost without noticing it myself, I hissed, "Father!" Nico just smiled as if nothing had happened.

"I know all about how you deal with your *enemies,* Harvester! These people are under my protection, and if you want to get to them you will have to come through me. I said our conversation was over—don't make me add force to my words!"

Nico took his time smoothing his unwrinkled clothing and adjusting his immaculate cuffs.

"Very well, Master Jomez. I have posed my question and received your answer, as you say. You have chosen to be my enemy and not my ally. Unwisely so, I might add, but you are a free man, entitled to your choices and prejudices, be they the choices of a fool and the prejudices of an unworthy father. When next we meet, I'll not be in a mood for friendly chatter."

"More threats? GO!" It seemed I heard the portcullis shake with the thunder of Father's voice. "Guards! Show this . . . *visitor* out!"

The two human guards hesitated, but the Automatons were incapable of fear. They hefted their halberds and took a couple of perfectly synchronized steps toward Nico.

"Oh please, don't bother. I can find my way out," he mumbled airily, waving one limp-wristed hand. Then he subvocalised a short phrase that I didn't quite catch. It seemed to shimmer in the air before him, then suddenly shot toward first one, then the other mechanical guard. Turning haughtily, Nico didn't even wait to see how both Automatons halted with a confused grind of cogs, and returned to their positions.

"Nico!" Father shouted. "Nico! You will be stopped! You will never have the use of any of my Automatons while I draw breath!"

Nico strode off calmly, his bodyguard falling in behind him.

"Nico!"

Resheathing his sword, Father squeezed my shoulder. I could feel him shake.

After this incident, the south gate was kept closed at night, and both bridges drawn. Father intensified the guard and sent messengers out to warn his nearby farmers. He instructed the swordmaster to double the daily training regime for the guard, and for my sister and me. Pretty soon, Daylia and I spent a part of each morning and each afternoon fencing with the swordmaster or each other in the courtyard, sometimes under the approving eye of Father, when he wasn't meeting with his three captains and discussing defense strategies. For the first two weeks, he would not let Daylia and me out of the keep; after that, he assigned three-man bodyguards to both of us.

Over the next few months, things quieted down in the keep. The inflow of refugees, never more than a trickle, dried out completely, and with that our main source of news. Father sent out spies and messengers—volunteers—and most of them returned with stories of Nico consolidating his position, taking the reins of the city, ruthlessly murdering whoever opposed him. Some of our spies never returned at all.

Even with the knowledge of Nico's expanding mini-empire, his reign of terror, I think we slowly settled back into old habits. It was the start of what promised to be a beautiful summer, and the fields around the Foot were blooming in earnest. Many of our farmers had returned to their homes to tend to their crops and livestock. Some of the refugees went with them, choosing to build a new life as farm hands under the protection of Master Jomez. Though the guard was still on twenty-four-hour alert, it started to feel to us as if we had escaped the brunt of both Nico's expansion and his wrath over Father's defiance.

As it turned out, Nico was only toying with us.

I remember the day vividly. I remember fencing with Tomaz and can describe in detail the leather vest he wore, the way his moustache moved in the wind, the sunlight glinting off his sword. I can recall effortlessly the mixed smells of cooking, horses, hay. I still hear the pounding of hammer on anvil in the smithy, a horse whinnying, the almost musical clatter of our swords. Every detail of that day is burned into my memory.

I remember most clearly how I felt that morning. Uncharacteristically, Tomaz had been complimenting me over the previous few days on the speed of my attacks and the accuracy of my parries. We had been fencing for hours with only short breaks, but I felt invincible. The day was beautiful and I was pressing Tomaz back from the south gate; he was having difficulty fending me off even though I was fighting uphill. My sword was a blur and I was grinning constantly as I pressed on. So submerged was I in our swordplay that I barely noticed my sister riding past me with her bodyguard, out the south gate and over the drawbridge.

Daylia. For as long as I could remember, my sister and I had been as close as decency permitted. Two years my senior, she had automatically assumed the role of my protector, and had held on to that role until my physical growth made it too obviously unnecessary. And that was not the only way she tried to give Father unneeded proof that she was as good and strong as a son. She was all too aware that she was Father's firstborn, and nothing could shake her notion that a firstborn *daughter* had been a shameful thing to Father, despite my father's vehement denials. Even though there was never any doubt about my succeeding him, she insisted on participating in the same lessons, going through the same training regime, wearing breeches even.

It had worked out perfectly for the two of us. As far as I was concerned, I had the companionship and rough playfulness of the brother I wanted, as well as the beauty, kind-heartedness, and sheer grace of a sister. For most of our childhood we had been all but inseparable, exploring the Foot together, boating the lake, accompanying Father on his visits to the outlying farms.

Lately, her development into a young woman had become more and more evident, and consequently my feelings for her more confused; this had affected our closeness in a way I was not sure I appreciated. But in general, ours was one of those deep, unwavering sibling friendships most common to twins, and we could almost read each other's minds.

She rode off past me for a leisurely tour of the sun-drenched lands, and as far as I can remember, I did not even greet her. This haunts me still, that my sister went away and I was too focused on battling Tomaz, reveling too deeply in my physical prowess, to even raise my hand to her in goodbye.

The sound of their hoofs beating on the drawbridge faded as Tomaz signaled a break. We lunched off light bread and fruit, sitting in a natural recess in the haystack by the stables, and drank deeply of the water one of the maids brought over. No beer, no wine—we had more training to do that afternoon.

Father ambled over, grabbed one of the apples, and started discussing some points regarding the training of the guards with Tomaz. I climbed higher up on the stack, and drifted off to the sound of their softly rumbling voices, hay tickling my neck, its fresh, earthy smell in my nostrils. And slid into a dream.

In the dream, Daylia rode past me as she had an hour earlier. I called out to her and rode with her, my mount materializing under me as happens in dreams. We galloped down the access ramp, her bodyguard disappearing, and rode our favorite race, clockwise along the moat, until we reached the little glen at the foot of the cliff, panting and laughing. Then the scenery shifted and we were exploring the deep shadowed valley between the third and fourth Finger, discovering stagnant ponds, deep cracks in the rock, snakes. Daylia turned to me and touched her hand to my shoulder, pushing softly.

The pushing turned to shaking.

"Master Markus! That blasted boy falls asleep everywhere!" Tomaz's voice, and Father's laughter, had trouble piercing my dream, but Tomaz had reached up and grabbed my shoulder, and that did the trick. I struggled awake and laughed with them.

"I know, Tomaz. I remember the cook finding my boy curled up in a cauldron, and startling poor Arthur out of his wits, as he had been about to pour gallons of water into the pot!"

As he got up and grabbed his sheathed sword Tomaz laughed, though he must have heard that story dozens of times before. He seemed off guard and had his back to me. I jumped off the haystack, one hand around my scabbard, the other on my hilt, unsheathing the blade as I landed. This time, at last, I almost beat Tomaz to the draw. But he wasn't swordmaster of the keep for nothing. With incredible speed and dexterity, he dodged without looking around, correctly predicting the direction of my attack, and drew his own sword in time to parry my second attack. Locking my blade under his for a second, he looked me in the eyes and grinned.

"Not bad, young Master, not bad at all!"

I flicked my wrist, freeing my blade, and our exercise resumed under Father's approving eye. After another hour, Tomaz's greater experience and endurance began to tell. I signaled end-of-training and withdrew to one of the embrasures in the curtain wall to watch Tomaz work with the guard, demonstrating some techniques for fending off multiple attackers at once.

Then the breakpoint came, and nothing was ever the same again.

First, it was a sudden look on Tomaz's face, a look of shock and fear that I had never seen on him before, that I had never even dreamed possible on Tomaz. Then it was the way he kept fencing, but stopped moving his feet or even looking at his attackers. Instead, he stared in the direction of the gate, wide-eyed. Then there was my complete and insurmountable reluctance to move a single muscle in my body that might cause me to see what Tomaz was seeing.

Finally, I looked to my right and saw.

Daylia's bodyguard wore white tunics over their chain mail, bearing three embroidered lilies, the emblem she had chosen for herself. One of them was riding through the gate and toward us. One side of his tunic was bright red, and the blood obliterated most of the lilies. He was wavering in his saddle, leaning to one side. A crossbow bolt stuck deep between his ribs.

He was alone. He was crying.

Tomaz barked orders. Guards helped the man off his horse; others ran to find Father. Very slowly, forcing each foot forward by sheer force of will, I approached the group gathered around the wounded man. Tomaz was feeling around the bolt as the man bit on a leather strap. His name was Geral, I remembered, vaguely.

"Where's Daylia?" I whispered. No one heard me. I spoke louder.

"Where's Daylia?" Heads turned, but no one answered. A dam broke inside me.

"WHERE'S DAYLIA?" I shouted, and threw myself forward onto my knees, grabbing a fistful of blood-soaked tunic in each hand, bending over the bleeding man. "WHERE IS SHE?" Then, my anger dissipating as quickly as it had come, I whispered: "Where's my sister?"

"Let me tend to his wound, Markus," Tomaz said, putting his hand on my back. I shook him off as the bodyguard said:

"Nico . . . Nico took her. Forgive me, my lord."

Galloping at full speed through sun-sprinkled fields, specks of foam flying from the horses' mouths, bent deeply in the saddle, Father led us, Tomaz at his side, and I was close behind them. We led a column of sixty, and all of them wore full armor and weaponry. For the first time, there was no joy in riding, only urgency and rage. And fear.

They had been ambushed two hours' riding from the keep, crossbows dispatching the bodyguard with ruthless efficiency, killing the other two instantly, probably missing Geral's heart by an inch. Daylia had dismounted with drawn sword, ready to do battle, but she had been knocked down by cloth-covered hammerhead bolts. They had bound her onto her horse and ridden off.

"Where to, man! *Where* did he take her?" my father had asked Geral. The despair in my father's voice would have broken my heart if it hadn't already felt like it was being torn apart.

"To his fortress, my lord," Geral had breathed, panting. "He wants to hold her hostage . . ."

So we assembled as large a force as we could muster and rode on to Nico's fortress. The sun was only hours from setting. Anything could happen in the time it would take us to reach the place where Daylia might be suffering unimaginable torment even as we rushed to her rescue. So we rode, pushed by the gods. Our horses' hoofs pounded a war drum's rhythm and threw a trail of dust behind us. We did not speak.

As dusk set in and lights came on behind the windows of the farms we passed, we penetrated deeper and deeper into Nico's realm. For every farm with the flickering yellow light of a hearth, we saw two that had been reduced to smoking, blackened patches with only the chimneys standing. Fields were burned or downtrodden, livestock killed and left to rot. Mercifully, it was too dark to identify rows of things that looked like shoes in the deepening darkness.

Stars were blinking on in the eastern sky, the western sky an ever darkening indigo, as we finally came to the fortress. There were torches burning all along the outer wall, but otherwise, all was still. I wondered vaguely what the large pale cross might mean that was painted over the enormous double doors. Then I heard Father's choked-off sob, Tomaz sucking in a shocked breath, an audible shudder going through our column.

It was Daylia. She was dead.

The next moment, the three of us dismounted by the gate. I have absolutely no memory of spurring my mount and covering the intervening distance. Giving no heed to the danger we might be exposing ourselves to, sparing no thought for cover, we approached Daylia's body, nailed spread-eagled to the doors, still dripping blood from her ankles, pain and terror in her faded eyes.

Father broke. He collapsed onto his knees in Daylia's blood, his fists balled, head thrown back and veins standing out, screaming in agony. I realized my mouth was open to scream with him, but no air escaped my constricted throat.

Tomaz kneeled and pulled out the nails through her calves, then reached up gripping the nail through her right hand. There was a horrible wet squeaking sound as the nail came loose of the blood-soaked wood. Sliding an arm behind her waist, he pulled out the last nail and let her body fall over his shoulder. Then he laid her down, gently.

There was something stuffed into her mouth, a wad of fabric, and a wide ribbon of it trailed down from her lips over her chest. Tomaz grabbed the flapping end of the ribbon so we could read the words written on it in red: FATHER, WHO IS GUARDING THE KEEP?

We took the three strongest, freshest horses on our mad race back, but by the time we reached the access ramp, the three animals were foaming at the mouth and shivering with exhaustion. We dismounted and left the horses; they couldn't have carried us up the ramp to the south gate. I felt half-mad with powerless grief and rage.

There was smoke rising from the keep, and broad lines of a black-looking liquid were running down the walls. As we climbed to the gate, we saw vague shapes hanging from the battlements, shapes from which the black lines flowed. It was too dark to make out faces, but there were so many bodies. So many.

Drawing our swords simultaneously, we passed between the Automaton guards and stood at the edge of the courtyard.

The keep was in ruins, destroyed by fire and what must have been magecraft. Smoke was everywhere, and flames still leaked from the upper stories. There were bodies strewn around, still more bodies, and the smell of burned flesh. And along the south wall, lit by flickering yellow and orange light, a row of small, oddly shaped objects, as if everyone had left their shoes and boots there. The smell of blood was sickening.

"Gods," whispered Father.

And even among the carnage and ruination of all that had ever been precious to me, something nagged at me. Something was not right. Even within the horror, I felt a deeper wrongness that chilled my spine. Suddenly, I knew with absolute certainty that we were in immediate danger.

And then Tomaz gave words to what I felt.

"How did they come in?" he whispered.

And as he said it, I knew.

"DUCK!" I shouted, raising my sword and spinning around. Tomaz was with me, moving faster than I ever could. But the Automatons were too close. They struck simultaneously, bringing their halberds down and thrusting forward. I just barely managed to parry the first stroke of the one on my side. Tomaz, at a disadvantage, was forced to parry with his unprotected left arm. The halberd gouged deeply, spilling blood. As I struggled to keep my footing against the swinging weapon in front of me, the second Automaton smashed an arm into Tomaz's head and went for my father.

He never had a chance. Exhausted and numb with grief, his swordsmanship rusty with age, he half-deflected the Automaton's first stroke. But a second before Tomaz managed to strike out and decapitate the device, it struck for the second time. The halberd's point plunged deep into Father's throat. By the time I felled my opponent, Father had already died in Tomaz's bleeding arms.

"Dear, oh dear," Barno mumbled, shaking his head, "that is all quite a bit worse than I imagined. And then you became a highwayman?"

I opened my eyes and forced myself back into the now. I had managed to hold in my tears, though it had been harder to tell the whole story than I had expected.

"You make it sound like a choice profession, Barno," I said, smiling grimly. "We gave the victims a decent burial, and buried Father and Daylia in the family crypt, sealing it afterwards. I wrote Nico a letter; then we took to the roads."

Up went the two metal hooks. "A letter, did you say?"

"Yes, a letter."

"What did it say?"

"I suspect you will find out in just a little while. There's movement on the horizon."

"Nico?"

"Who else? And he'll be sure to bring my letter and read it to me, to gloat. Would you mind moving to my left?"

Barno gave me a wondering look, but complied, trotting around the Squeeze and settling on the other side. Then he fell silent, and I was grateful. I needed the quiet to regain my composure, relieve myself, do a last exercise cycle. And to offer a small prayer to Father and Daylia.

Half an hour later, the approaching group was close enough to recognize Nico and make out his Automaton bodyguard. As Petar and Tomaz had predicted, he had dispensed with human soldiers altogether. The Automatons were under his constant mental control. They marched in unison, triple-file, and Nico lead them to the crossroads.

It was time for the end.

Nico halted three feet from the Squeeze, close enough to spit in my eye but far enough to avoid the puddle.

"I see you've made a friend, pup," he said. "How nice."

"It's not one of yours, *pig*—this one works."

Nico smiled, ignoring my taunt.

"It looks like Petar's work, doesn't it? So good to see the old imbecile is still working. You wouldn't happen to know where I could find him, do you?"

"Hah! Even if I did know, what would you offer me in return? My freedom? Just have your fun and get it over with, Nico."

Nico reached into his blue coat and drew out a folded piece of paper. I knew what it was; I had written it.

"I got your letter, after that unfortunate business with your family. How kind of you to inform me of your feelings, pup. However, you seem to have overestimated your capabilities just a little. Can I read you a few of your own words? 'Next time we meet, it will be on my terms. And on that occasion, you will die.' And look at you now. Naked, locked in a cage, filthy and helpless, with a mule for company. Are these your terms, pup? Is this the occasion you had in mind?"

"Yes," I said.

"Forget it," Tomaz said for the thousandth time. "There is no way. Nico is a coward. If anything is obvious about him it's that he will only approach the helpless, the unarmed. He kills women and children, the wounded, the sick. You can't come within a mile of him with a weapon. There is no way."

"There *must* be a way! We can't let it go, not like this! What else is there? Do you want to just let it go? Leave Father's death, Daylia's death, unavenged? Never! There must be a way to get close. We just haven't thought of it yet."

"Have you heard what happened to the last assassin? His dagger was hidden in a walking stick. He was disguised as an old man. He had dyed his hair and creased his face. He even had his legs injured on purpose to limp convincingly. He had the perfect disguise, but he was captured at the city gates and executed on the spot. How are you going to achieve what a trained assassin could not? You are Markus, by the gods! You'll be recognized immediately!"

From behind his workbench, Petar cleared his throat. We both fell silent immediately. Petar tended to keep his peace during our discussions until he had something to say, but when he was ready to speak, he was always right and often brilliant.

"You are both right, my friends," Petar said. He sounded like he was holding in laughter. "Tomaz, yes, Nico is a cowardly man, killing only those who cannot defend themselves, approaching only the unarmed, hiding from any danger. And yes, of course Markus is Markus, and Nico will recognize him. Markus, yes, there is a way."

"Do you have an idea?" I asked, excitedly.

"Oh, yes," Petar cackled, "do I ever!"

"I should really have you on my staff, pup. A tactician like you would be invaluable. If these are your terms, I much prefer them to mine, I must say." Then he laughed, a high chuckle that grated on my nerves.

"Oh, why don't you just kill me and get it over with?"

He inclined his head first to one side, then the other, as if he was considering my suggestion.

"I don't think I will just yet. In fact, maybe I will just wait here a while and watch you die."

I tensed every muscle in my body.

"Or maybe you won't," I hissed, folding the fingers of my left hand around one of the bars and tugging at the latch Petar had installed.

"Again," Tomaz said as I repositioned the sword against the absurdly accurate replica of the gnarled tree by the crossroads. Tomaz had insisted on making it as true to the original as possible. "You need to live and breathe the maneuver, Markus. You need to be familiar with each branch, each leaf."

"Yes, yes, and who will have to recreate those branches, those leaves?" But we knew Petar hadn't really minded.

"Again?" I protested. "Come on, Tomaz, it's been enough now. We just went through it perfectly at least two-dozen times. I'm ready. I can do this."

"NO!" Tomaz thundered. "You are ready when I say you are! We will try it again and again, and when I'm satisfied, we will put you in there for a day, and then two, and then three, and then a week if I think we need to. Then we'll splatter you with mud and pig blood, and practice some more. And frankly, I am sick of having to tell you this again and again. Get in there, and we'll do it again!"

I sighed, but I knew he was right. I positioned myself under the opened Squeeze and pressed my shoulders in place. Then I crossed my arms in front of me and grabbed the bars on both sides of my shoulders, careful to stay clear of the quick-release latch. I pulled up my feet and folded my legs into my chest as Tomaz closed and locked the bottom half of the Squeeze. Then he took a step back and untied his pants cord.

"What are you doing?"

"I am satisfied that you have the basic maneuver programmed into your bones and muscles. Now we're going to add a realistic touch."

"What do you mean?"

"You may be in that thing for days, and you'll need to relieve yourself. There will be a puddle under you. I will not let this fail because you recoil at the last moment from the feeling of warm piss under your feet."

And so for the next practice run, there was a steaming puddle of fresh urine under the Squeeze hanging from the replica tree in Petar's workshop.

Petar's work was perfect as always. With a loud clang, the bottom part of the Squeeze swung down and backward, and the cheek sections sprung up past the temples. I was already uncoiling and on the way down, landing in a half-crouch, left foot in front of me, right foot behind me. I fell half to my right, catching myself on my right hand and reaching across with my left, grabbing my sword. As I straightened my legs and spun toward Nico, I heard Petar's litany in the back of my head: "Nico is a vocal mage, Nico is a vocal mage."

I knew I had been incredibly fast, and as I struck, I could see in Nico's eyes that he only half comprehended what was happening. That suited me fine. The point of my sword sunk into his throat, aimed perfectly to cut his vocal cords. His eyes widened in shocked surprise.

"Don't call me pup," I hissed.

Too late, the first few of his Automatons moved toward me. Only one of them could move around Nico and get close. Barno spun around and lashed out with his hind legs, hitting the device midsection and demolishing it.

I pulled my sword free, twirled it above my head two-handedly and swung it across Nico's neck. His head toppled down, his body staying upright a moment longer. When it crumpled, I saw that Petar had been right: Nico's bodyguard crumpled with him.

"Oh my," Barno said behind me, but there was delight in his voice. "I thought you said you were waiting for death?"

"Not my own, Barno. Not my own."

"What is next, Markus?" asked Tomaz. It was three days after the confrontation with Nico, and we were riding up into the mountains toward Petar's workshop, to tell him of the success of his ruse.

"Next? You know as well as I do what needs doing. We have a castle to rebuild, repairs to make, damage to undo. When that is underway, I want to erect a statue to my father at the crossroads. And a shrine to my sister. After that, I would very much like to root out every mercenary we can find and chase them as far away as possible. And in the meantime, I want to visit each of our farmers and restore some measure of safety and order to their lives."

"I wasn't really thinking about your own estate, Markus. I was thinking of all the lands Nico had in his grip, and the city. Can you imagine what is happening in the city?"

"They're probably wondering what happened to Nico's Automatons."

"Wondering? They'll be cheering, Markus, celebrating! Right now, I bet there's a pile of Automaton parts in the marketplace and people dancing around it. It's not just our revenge, Markus—we've *freed* them. Do you know what will happen when they discover who killed Nico?"

"They'll hold a celebration in our honor?"

Tomaz laughed, shaking his head at the same time.

"You realize they'll ask you to be king, don't you?"

I halted my horse and turned to him. Tomaz and Barno stopped as well.

"King?"

"Oh yes, I'm sure of it. Petar expected as much from the start."

"Hmmm. I hadn't thought that far, not at all. King, huh?"

I smiled bemusedly, and nudged my horse gently, resuming our road. I'd have plenty of time to think about all that later. For now, it was enough to ride as a free man again. I felt the wind in my hair, the sun on my back, I smelled the blossoms, and I knew a fresh start lay ahead of us. Spurring my mount into a gallop, I raced ahead up into the valley, hoofbeats echoing and multiplying and announcing to Petar our imminent arrival and our success.

# THE WEAPONS OF THE LORD ARE NOT CARNAL

*Written by*
**Andrew Tisbert**

*Illustrated by*
**Fabrizio Pacitti**

## About the Author

*Andrew Tisbert grew up on a dairy farm in Vermont, the second to last child of a large family. He started college in New Hampshire where he studied with novelist Russell Banks and the late poet Joel Oppenheimer. He attended several colleges on and off over the next ten years and along the way had two children with a talented but struggling folksinger. She died of Hodgkins Disease while the children were still young.*

*Andrew stopped writing for many years to focus his creative energy on establishing a rock band called Attic of Love. The band has released an extended length album entitled* Lessons, *and continues to travel and perform.*

*In the fall of 2002, Andrew took serious reappraisal of his priorities and decided his return to fiction writing, his first love, was long overdue. He has been writing furiously ever since, has entered and won the Writers' Contest, and has completed a draft of a novel. He currently lives in Schroon Lake, New York, with his children.*

## About the Illustrator

Fabrizio Pacitti was born in Rome, a sanctuary of art. It was quite natural for him, therefore, to incline toward the magical world of fine arts. His father always told him to study and understand Italian art, because in art lies the past, the present and the future of a nation.

Fabrizio considered it a major breakthrough when he laid eyes on a Spiderman comic book. That day, when he was nine, changed his world forever. After a while, it came to him that if he studied art and practiced every day, he would be able to draw like that in the comic books.

In high school, he started reading comic books from Argentina and France. After the movie Alien came out, he became interested in science fiction illustration and in the world of fantasy. He then went on to the university, studying mainly history and philosophy. While in military service, he again started to read comics and took up drawing again.

In November 1994, Fabrizio's girlfriend, Loredana, came into the picture. They moved to Costa Rica and then to Panama, where Fabrizio now holds the position of Vice Academic Rector in a private university of arts and graphic design.

Fabrizio states Loredana "pushed him back to the drawing table" and even submitted his first and only entry to the Illustrators' Contest. His profound desire is to become a professional illustrator. This publication is a dream come true.

The first time Brother Jon saw the metal head he was deeply ashamed of the human race. How could anyone do such a thing to God's temple? It was—almost—unimaginable to him. Brother Jon had been on Mars with the other New Franciscans for almost twenty years now—their dome had been one of the first, a decade before the International Initiatives (the I.I.), to save the world really began colonization. In that time he had borne witness to many wonders. He had stood at the very foot of the great Mons Olympus. He had survived dust storms comparable to his vision of Hell. He had watched as the population grew on these deserts. Now more and more metal heads ran around, without suits, without air masks, or so they were saying on the web. Martian domes were still isolated, and the two men who normally took care of supply deliveries to the Franciscans were still the human kind, requiring human supports. So it was difficult for Jon to believe the metal heads existed. But there it was, running in front of the deliverymen as they approached the monastery in their rover.

Jon watched them from the observation deck that served as a hall between two of his gardens. It was early morning—just after matins—and he had stopped to look out across the Lake of the Sun. It was still far too cold to be outside without a suit and yet there was the metal head in the front of the rover with nothing on his back. Brother Jon stepped closer to the windows and pressed his fingertips against the cold glass. At least the head should have had the decency to cover himself, he thought. Then he scowled and got an odd feeling in his stomach. Of course. With a manufactured body, the metal head would no longer have any reason to feel the mortification of the flesh. Jon thought on this as he pulled his fingers slowly down. Then he said, "Darken," and the windows opaqued as he left the hall to greet the coming guests.

Brothers William and Peter were already waiting at the hatch with the abbot. They stood there casually, with Abbot James at the hatchway controls. It seemed to Jon they had no idea anything out of the ordinary was about to invade their quiet sanctuary. Jon stood in the side doorway and nodded to the others and only William acknowledged him with a sweep of a hand, as if brushing at a fly. Air hissed into the chamber, its door slid aside and the visitors stepped out. The metal head was like a pillar standing there. The humans—for that was how Jon distinguished them in his mind from the head—were suddenly clumsy and uncertain in comparison as they walked in front of him.

"Hello, my sons," said the abbot to the two men in that rich, oiled voice of his that contradicted his frail, bent frame, his dry, papery flesh. He was a palimpsest, Jon mused, on which was written . . . the years. "Welcome once again to our little friary."

Jon tried not to roll his eyes. The abbot continued to call this place a friary, but it was an affectation. They were not itinerant; who on Mars did they preach the gospel to? They were monks and researchers, they held solitary monks' vows. Only the abbot pretended to be waiting, presumably, for all the multitudes who would surely inundate the planet—and who would surely require saving—when more mirror satellites were flown and terraforming began in earnest. He never explained what he thought might change for the International Initiative's administrators to allow the exodus. Right now Jon was like everyone else on Mars: desperate to stay there. Earth below was freezing winter and storms, floods and lost cities and drought, famine and the bloody march of fundamentalism and ethnic cleansings. Earth was taking its last breath. Only the very rich made it to Mars now. Or the very indispensable. Or those who could make binding deals of a very different nature.

Jon ignored his own unease long enough to enjoy the taut expressions on Peter and William. The shorter of the two delivery men—an elderly French career astronaut the monks called *Mon Pere*—looked around the room to include everyone, ending with the abbot. "We've got your supply shipment outside," he said. "But we've come to ask a favor, too. Our friend"— and now he indicated the metal head—"has requested leave from the polar station to study the Franciscan order. I realize this might be an inconvenience to you—"

It was Brother William who interrupted. "Inconvenience? It might be an inconvenience? Are you serious? We won't have anything to do with a cyborg here!"

"That will be all, Brother William," said the abbot softly. William's face reddened. "What," asked the abbot—his gaze had not strayed from *Mon Pere*—"precisely does the . . . metal head intend to accomplish with his studies?"

"His name is Thomas," said the other man, Miller.

The metal head spoke then. Really, it was silly to call it a metal head—there was so much high-resistance plastic. Its voice was soft and reasonable, with almost a hint of laughter about it. "I am on a spiritual quest."

"Surely your kind is not disposed to things of this nature," said the abbot. Then he looked squarely at the head. "What kind of desperation turned you into this thing? You have denied the sanctity of Creation. This is no better than suicide. And I don't care to hear your philosophy on the matter, all this talk of an emancipation from the weakness of the flesh that I've heard on the web. You seek immortality, but want it for free."

"Free!" *Mon Pere* held up a thick, dirty hand. "You don't understand anything." He glanced at the head, and Jon saw deep affection in his pouched gray eyes. "More and more of us are forced to leave Mars or go through the transition. The I.I. finances it for you, and then you have to work it off. It's the only way to stay in space for most of us. The pioneering lease keeps going up and up.

"But Thomas didn't have to do it. Only three months ago I was still trying to talk him out of it." He edged toward Thomas and tapped the back of its smooth head. "Now I think he's uneasy about his decision."

"Not uneasy," said Thomas. "Rather, I've developed an appetite to learn something I've denied all my life."

Brother Jon stepped out of his doorway. "I don't understand why the I.I. would want people to make the transition—"

"Better pioneers, better astronauts," said Miller. "Stronger, faster, low maintenance. No suit, no air. And you can interface with all kinds of machinery. We would have been changed over and sent out mining the moons this year if it hadn't been for Thomas's help."

"I had no idea the disease had spread so rapidly," said Brother William. Beside him, Peter coughed.

Miller raised a fist and thrust his index finger at William. "Thomas didn't come here to be insulted by—"

"No, of course he didn't," said the abbot. His expression had changed, as if he had reached a new understanding. "And we would be delighted to take him on as our guest for a few days, to determine what it truly is he seeks."

Brother William jumped from his chair, but Peter was already clutching at his friend's arm, and it was clear to Jon the abbot's mind was set. The friar always in need of a subject to convert—no matter how pathetic.

Miller lowered his voice. "Thank you, Abbot."

"And I will be happy to make a substantial contribution to your dome, Abbot James, for any inconvenience," said the head.

Peter frowned and looked at the abbot. "What kind of contri——"

"Don't you see, Peter?" The abbot smiled. "Really, you must come out of your lab once in a while. This metal head used to be Thomas Eidelman, the billionaire. He financed the first pioneers. He owns half the equipment on Mars."

•••

The second time Brother Jon saw the metal head, his feelings of shame were far more specific. He had occasion to speak with the head during vespers before dinner, while he was outside taking his usual walk at Martian noon. It was a time of day when the temperature could be as high as twenty degrees Celsius and all that was required for the itinerant's survival was

Illustrated by Fabrizio Pacitti

an oxygen mask. And of course the goggles, lotions and tunic to protect against ultraviolet. Brother Jon enjoyed the slicing winds that caught at his tunic, the dust, the salmon tint to the sky, the buoyancy of his feet. He'd always been heavy—on Earth it had been all the more distracting. Now the rising wind put a sharp chill in him as he set out through the rocks of rust, the dome growing small behind him. To his right and the west Olympus Mons swelled up like the worn pate of God himself. Jon grinned at the notion. Then he looked down and kicked the orange dirt. There was still frost under the stones. He felt a pang of yearning to be able to walk out across the desert forever. Free of oxygen, of goggles, the cold. Just walk out. To the poles, to the canyons, to the face of God.

He heard the footsteps approaching behind him but didn't turn. Frankly, he resented any intrusion on his walks so continued along his path as if to deny the reality that he was no longer alone. It was probably Brother William come to complain about the abbot's decision to accept their visitor. Or worse, it was Peter. Peter had taken it upon himself the task of keeping Brother Jon's conscience in functioning order—even as a child he had apparently dreamed of poverty and slavery to the will of Christ. His vigil over Jon's private thoughts was insufferable. When Jon saw the metal head come up beside him, he enjoyed a moment of relief. But that was soon concealed by surprise and he stopped. "May I help you?" he said.

He found himself studying the head with an intensity beyond any natural curiosity. Part of him was astute enough to wonder why—though not self-aware enough to know the answer. Really, the head was quite pleasing in appearance, a revelation that appalled him.

The smooth face was molded to a generalized beauty that threatened to insinuate the delicate power of the Jesus of so many Catholic portraits of him on Earth. Of course there were no actual nostrils beyond purely cosmetic clefts in the nose, and the eyes moved with far too much precision. But these differences served only to strengthen the impression of some divine puissance. It was not right to have such a notion, Brother Jon thought, and recognizing his own thoughts caused him to close his eyes in disgust. Shame on humanity for creating metal heads? Shame on himself! He could just hear Brother William, stumbling on the hidden room of these thoughts. William scowls and cries out a prayer to return Jon to the true path. And what if it was Peter walking into this room? Peter's patent understanding, his silent charity and unspoken condemnation—that would be far worse than William and his bluster. Jon opened his eyes again. Of course the object of his discomfort still regarded him.

"I'm sorry to disturb you," said (whirred? laughed?) the metal head.

"It—" Jon turned and started walking again, then shrugged. "I suppose you came outside for a breath of fresh air."

There was a pause, during which Jon hoped the head would display some humanity by interpreting his sarcasm as a joke or an insult. When the head did neither, Jon wondered if that could also be the result of some humanity. And why did he care?

"Actually I wanted to escape the abbot and his stooges. You seemed rather levelheaded for a monk so I . . ."

That got Jon. He momentarily forgot the oxygen feeds in his nose and laughed until he began to asphyxiate. "I suppose we do seem eccentric if you aren't used to us," he said.

"Yes, I suppose you do. Tell me. How many are there of you in the dome? The abbot talks as if you are God's army on Mars."

Jon smirked. The head was rather outspoken for a piece of hardware. "It's a pathetic army, if that's what it is. There's about a dozen of us—fifteen exactly. There used to be twenty-six. This area was claimed before the International Initiatives, so it's American territory, and I.I. has been trying to shut it down for years. We're outdated, really. If it weren't for our study of the dust storms we'd already be gone. Who besides a dozen monks want to live out here when they can live in the canyon settlements? Then again, we could be shut down any time."

"I spoke to your abbot about that," said the head. "Those men who brought me here did me a favor once. That is why I sponsor them to stay on Mars as long as possible. I could do this for the dome as well. It's not a guarantee they won't kick you out, but it would help."

Jon looked up at the sky again. There was just the hint of vermilion edging the sun, and the dead volcano in the distance was a color like blood. The multitude of shades that were still orange and rust amazed him. For a moment he wondered what the others would think to see him strolling with the cyborg. "Thomas," he said. "Why have you come to us?"

"Your abbot was right about one thing. Most people who opt for the transition to metal *are* desperate. Desperate to stay in space, desperate to change their poverty, or their life. Some, I believe, would have committed suicide in another era. Cyborg design has interfaces now for any number of applications—

operating shuttles, mining equipment, direct tight feed of data, you name it. You are suddenly more useful. I admit there is a lot of coercion these days to make the change. But some extremely well off people, like myself, have done it back on Earth. People who have tired of their bodies, grown sick of their functions, their vulnerability and weakness, people who see transition as surcease. An escape."

"What of God?"

"Does he really exist? And the spirit. Can you define that for me? Do you really believe the soul to be a supernatural entity not connected to physical laws and existence? Or is it your mind, a sum of a map of your neural activity? I thought most theologians in the Vatican, anyways, had given up on the first idea before the end of the twentieth century. It doesn't matter. I believe I am the man I always was."

"You still haven't answered my question."

"What I asked you about God was not entirely a rhetorical question; I am not here to argue with you. Before my transition I knew God was myth, an artifact of primitive thought. Now I am no longer certain. That is what I am here to learn."

The metal head was so dispassionate as it—he—spoke. There should be the smell of fear, thought Jon, accompanying those words. But of course fear didn't really have a smell—especially if one was compiled of metal and plastic. And it was true that with the feed in his nose Jon couldn't have smelled it in any case.

"You don't have to accept my humanity to understand me, Father. Even a computer can be driven by a kind of yearning—to reach a solution to some paradox of logic, to compute the ratio of a circle's circumference to its diameter. . . ."

"But why now?" said Jon. "Why do you seek to compute the ratio of God's circumference to the diameter of the circle of the world now, in the absence of your body?"

"I'm not sure. Sometimes I feel I've forgotten something, yet I have no idea what it is."

Yes, thought Jon. There should be the smell of fear.

•••

The third time Jon saw the metal head it was in a dream, so perhaps it shouldn't be counted along with the others. Still, it had a great impact on his later behavior. Call it, then, an honorary meeting. It was during daysleep, evening by Earth Eastern Standard clocks, but afternoon still on Mars. In the dream there was a young woman who stood naked before him. It was unclear whether they had kissed, but Jon's fingertips were moist and there was a warmth and a dampness on the dark edges of his memory. Brother Jon was powerfully aroused and he was trying to conceal this fact under his tunic. Juxtaposed against this circumstance was the metal head, seated at Jon's computer terminal, studying scripture. The insinuation of laughter in the head's speech was greatly magnified to great bellowing fits, monstrous guffaws, magnanimous chuckles. The metal head recited scriptures between bursts of mirth as Brother Jon knelt beside him in terror: *For ye must be born again—being born again, not of corruptible seed—all flesh is as grass and will withereth away, but the Word of the Lord endureth forever—and the weapons of our warfare are not carnal.* Jon's own carnality stuck out like a sore thumb. And the woman in the dream was not some Greek form of beauty he could easily forget when the salmon dust of morning ensconced him and clouded his consciousness. No, Jon knew the woman. Even in the dream he ached with the knowledge he would have to remember her when he woke—or was that something he'd imagined in transition?

When he did open his eyes it was to the sight of that woman, not to the prevailing darkness of his room in nightmorning. Jill. He dropped his feet vertically through the bed field and sat up, then cradled his forehead in his thick hands. He dreamed of her often, much to his chagrin; and not always in his sleep. Still, after so many years, he longed for her. There had been no heavenly indiscretion; he had no sin to repent. They had met at university on Earth. He had recently become a monk and was finishing his postgraduate work in astrophysics and xenometeorology. She, oddly in this era, had been seeking matrimony, and so her plans excluded Jon. Besides, he was married to God—he did not want to marry her. What he had wanted was raw, uninhibited and repeated sex. They had remained friends through college, a relationship that had been, secretly, all too painful. The fight to control his lust had brought him, it sometimes seemed, to Mars.

The unrequited nature of his attraction strangely made his yearning—and subsequently his conscience—ache the more profoundly. That seemed a contradiction, yet it was true. It involved him in daydreams when he played with his body which amounted to a kind of psychological rape, for wasn't it rape when only one of a couple lusted and sated one's lust? And what actions he imagined to sate himself!

One reason Brother William had come to the monastery was to escape a certain admitted propensity for boys, a taste he had failed to restrain on one occasion. It had become the fashion to openly admit this weakness before the authorities and so absolve oneself. Jon imagined William's episode of moral indiscretion actually made it easier for him to abrogate his own sense of guilt: the act had occurred, but it was past. For this, Jon envied him.

The only light in the room was the blue glow of the computer terminal under his wooden crucifix. He'd forgotten it and left it on after reading scripture. He rose, stepped out of the bed field and told the lights to come on. He swept one of his robes up from the floor with a foot and pulled it on and commanded the bed field off. Then he spoke to the computer. "Find me references to carnality in the New Testament. Visual scroll."

He watched the screen until he found it. Yes. *The weapons of the Lord are not carnal.* Second Corinthians, chapter ten, verse four. Carnal, of the flesh. Jon sucked at his teeth as he went into the bathroom cubicle.

Even in two-fifths-Earth gravity he sometimes felt sluggish in the morning. He sat himself on the toilet and spent the next ten minutes frustrated with his body. First there was the effect of his dream to overcome before he could sit with any ease; then he found he had cramps. Then of course he was too hairy—this morning, cleaning himself was an annoyance he positively could not abide. It occurred to him to find this humorous, but he did not allow laughter to intrude upon his discomfort. He was tired of his body, of eating and defecating, pain and lust, the effort of moving, of feeling. He was tired of his carnality. His body wearied him. Was this why he had experienced such intense resentment when he saw the metal head approaching his monastery? Had he recognized himself?

•••

Jon spent nearly all the day in prayer, alone in his garden. He kept the wall panels opaqued to the Martian nightday and abstained from his meals. By compline, his stomach was a hard, burning knot. He finally commanded the eastern walls to transpare and watched the end of the sunrise. The moons were ghosts near the zenith. The sun, touching the desert, was edged with bright green. To Brother Jon's left, the door opened and William entered. "Beautiful, isn't it?" he called.

As he crossed the garden toward Jon he inspected the hybrid trees and vines. One might even think he knew what he was looking at, Jon thought. "The meat from these will be plenty when they mature," said William, patting a plum tree from which Jon had already harvested the porklike balls of meat it produced. He patted Jon's shoulder with the same gesture when he'd reached him, then said, "Could I speak with you openly, Brother?"

They sat beneath a squat orange tree and, for a time, William only stared at him. As if searching his face for the shadow of sin, Jon thought. He recalled the year William had found a letter Jon had written to Jill, even though he'd had no intention of ever sending it. William brought the letter to Abbot James in outrage, and Jon had been forced to suffer penance for its frank and intimate nature. That season Jon had set aside a special plum tree that yielded fruit resembling adolescent boys. When these found their way into William's dinner bowl, William was too embarrassed to bring this further transgression to the abbot's attention. But from that day forward William left Jon alone. William never wished to speak with Jon—openly or otherwise.

"How can I put this nicely?" William said. "We are all worried about you, Brother."

Sometimes, Jon told himself, it was as if he hated Brother William.

"Brothers Peter and Jeremy saw you outside with the cyborg. You shouldn't be spending time with it. It is an evil abomination and can only serve as a stumbling block to you."

Jon leaned his head back against the tree. "Surely I am not the only one to spend time with the metal head."

"Jon. You *are* the only one to speak to it. You and the abbot."

William seemed proud of that statement, and Jon was disgusted. "Even Peter has no charity?"

"We've discussed it and agree that the head is a corrupting force here. You and the abbot are suffering a trial of faith. The abbot was a fool to let it into the monastery. He is blinded by the need to preach the Word, and by the desire to use the cyborg's influence to keep his ministry on the planet. I would hope you dispense your charity with more care."

Anger was welling up within Jon now; he was annoyed by the way it made him tremble. "I appreciate your sense of responsibility for my soul, Brother. Really, I do. You wouldn't mind leaving me so that I might give your words the meditation they deserve?"

William practically leapt to his feet. "Certainly, yes. You will excuse the intrusion."

Jon forced himself to smile sweetly.

William began to go, but turned on an impulse. "I know you, Jon. You revel in standing on the edge of what is acceptable. You fancy yourself a bit of a Rabelais, I think. You should beware your own desires."

"An interesting lecture from you of all people."

William turned crimson. "I have atoned my sin." Then he stormed out of the garden.

Jon took deep breaths and stared at his shaking hands. He was aware that part of his anger stemmed from the fear that William was right. He reminded himself how shameful the metal head was. Yet he'd spent the day combating his desire to be quit of the flesh and praying to God for guidance.

So far, God had been reticent.

•••

It was only the fourth time Jon had seen the metal head, yet something had changed between them. Jon had left the garden finally, and had just gotten into his bed when he heard the door buzz. He rose and let the head in.

"I spent another afternoon in interview with your abbot," it said.

"And?" Jon sat back on the bed field.

"I'm afraid I've left him flabbergasted. It appears he thought he would teach me scripture. My access to the Word, however, is far more thorough than his could ever be."

Jon wondered if the whirring laughter in the head's tone hadn't suddenly gained amplitude. "I don't understand. Didn't you come here to study scripture?"

"Of course not. Hasn't it occurred to you that I'm permanently interfaced? I downloaded the Bible weeks before I came here. I'm here to study your spirits, not your books."

"You," said Jon, "are a walking scripture reference."

"I am the Word. Not to mention the way, the truth and the light." The laughter had indeed grown in amplitude.

Jon recalled his dream. *"For all flesh is as grass, and the glory of man as the flower of grass. The grass withereth and flower thereof falleth away: but the Word of the Lord endureth forever."*

"First Epistle of Peter, first chapter, verses twenty-four and twenty-five."

"Very good. How about Second Corinthians, ten, four?"

Jon spent the next hour quizzing the head on Bible verse.

It was only the fourth time Jon had seen the metal head, yet something had changed between them. They were allies. It didn't even occur to him to feel ashamed until after Thomas had left his room.

*And there be eunuchs which have made themselves eunuchs for the kingdom of heaven's sake* . . . That was somewhere in Matthew. *Marvel not that I said unto thee, Ye must be born again. That which is born of the flesh is flesh. That of the spirit is spirit.*

*And the weapons of the Lord are not carnal.*

•••

"I've caused you trouble with your peers," said the head, and Jon did not deny it. They were outside the dome at Martian noon again; their walks had become a regular practice. Wind scattered sand around them in a haze, but the head sat on a rock, oblivious. Jon was aware of Olympus Mons in the distance even though the sand made it almost impossible to see. It was a presence—God's face, he reminded himself.

Two weeks had passed and the metal head had become Brother Jon's full-time companion. Nearly the entire monastery had turned away from him, at Brother William's urgings, he was certain. Peter still spoke to him, but with a tone of such condescension that Jon was soon avoiding him. The only person in the dome who seemed without disapproval was the abbot himself. Jon did not understand the old man.

"I'm sorry my quest has caused you strife," the head continued. Jon had to strain his ears to hear over the wind.

"It isn't your fault," he said. "We should go back to the dome, Thomas."

"No. Wait. I want to speak with you with assured privacy."

Jon frowned.

"You are tired of the flesh. You want something I have found here." The head touched his own chest with a plastic fist.

Jon paled. Suddenly he could hear the head clearly, as if the wind howled all around but never touched them. They were in the eye of the storm. Or the head was the focal point of the storm, immune to everything about him. "I don't understand what you mean."

"I see it in your eyes, Jon. If a monk deigns to lie, he should do it with more conviction. Listen to me. I like you. Go to Valles Marineris. Make the transition to metal. You can credit it to my account. Don't be afraid."

"I must do what is right in the eyes of God, " said Jon. His eyes stung. "I pray and await his direction." He paused. "It is so logical—the transition, becoming one with the Word, leaving behind the world of the flesh . . ."

"'What he desires,'" said the head. "Has it ever occurred to you that your faith is nothing more than pride?"

Jon glared down at the head through his goggles.

"A religious man asserts that he is 'saved' not through anything he has done, but through the grace of his god. His only proof is his own faith that he is saved. That seems to be an act of pride, not to mention a paradox. And then there is this phenomenon of speaking to God in prayer . . . and getting an answer. How does a man recognize among the multitude of voices in his head the true voice of God? He must assert himself that the voice is God's. Religious pride. *Vanity of vanities, saith the preacher, vanity of vanities; all is vanity.* So you wait to learn what He desires, in spite of what you desire."

"I don't have to stand out in this storm and listen to your insults."

"I speak candidly because I am your friend."

"No. You are hardware." Shaking, Jon turned and started back to the dome. The wind was suddenly upon him again, and roared in his ears.

Later, in his room, he prayed angrily. Lord, do not withhold the wisdom of your flaming tongue from me. What should I do? I believe the transition could be good in spite of Thomas. What is the path you would choose for me? I want to be the instrument of your will. A pure instrument. Incorruptible seed.

•••

The next morning Jon's computer awakened him early. He heard it load something then switch off. He rolled out of the bed field and told the screen to light. Thomas had sent him a message. "I am sorry to have distressed you," it said. "I have decided to leave this morning. I believe I have found what I seek, as much as that may surprise you, and I am at peace. Thank you for your friendship despite diversity. In case you need it, I have cleared your identity with my credit account. Thomas."

Jon pulled on a tunic and ran out the door. He hurried down the hall and cut through one of his gardens to get to the front hatchway.

The abbot was standing by the hatch with the wall beside it transpared. Outside it was Martian dusk, rust and salmon deepening to a green-flecked sky and blood. There was a figure growing smaller on the desert.

"He's just going to walk out across the desert?" said Jon.

The abbot nodded. "I must admit that's something I've wished I could do." Then the old man turned to Brother Jon and smiled. "I believe we converted him, my son." He rested his papery hand on Jon's shoulder. "I am very old. I almost wish I had the nerve to become a metal head."

Jon felt as if his own desire was scrawled across his face for the abbot to see. Perhaps it was. The abbot squeezed his shoulder, then let his hand fall. "Abbot," said Jon. "May I have your permission to visit Valles Marineris?"

The abbot's eyes focused somewhere far away. "Thomas and I have spoken on this before," he said softly. "You must abide by your own conscience. And the will of the Lord."

That afternoon, Brother Jon took the monastery rover and headed for the canyons.

•••

The colony at Valles Marineris was a series of interconnected enclosures built into the canyon wall, with a total population in the mere thousands. To Jon it was a stifling metropolis. What afflicted him first—even before the motion of machinery and humanity, the colorful bustling of busy men and women with desperation in their eyes, dizzying him to the point of nausea—was the smell. A mixture of sweat and stale breath, oils and disinfectants. He had grown used to the incense and dim light of the monastery. These halls were too bright, too corybantic. The cybernetics center was three city segments from the air-lock port where he left the rover. He was barely able to breathe as he rode the beltway there.

The process was too simple. A counselor helped him choose a body much like Thomas's, although the face was thicker. He was led to a classroom where another counselor explained the procedure to him and about five other men. The counselor had the pale skin of a man who never left his dome, and his endless smile, Jon thought, was overly reassuring. "We came to change Mars," he said, "but found it might be easier to change ourselves." He said it as if it were a clever joke. "Your synapses are the channel by which information is transferred and stored. Your 'self' is the combined sum of these connections in your brain, and the patterns created by past connections. We begin your transformation by creating a holographic map of what we call your synaptic self. This image is plastic; just as the original is shaped by your genetics and interaction with your environment, so too can this paradigm continue to learn and grow. 'Awareness continuity' is a gauge we use to judge whether a cerebral representation is merely a copy or a genuine continuance of a person's self. Generally speaking, awareness continuity of ninety-seven to one hundred percent is considered a true transference of the self."

Jon was under the surgical lasers within an hour of the orientation. Most of the transference was accomplished under sedation, but there were moments of lucidity during which he forced himself to think of anything but what he was allowing to happen. He found himself thinking of Jill: memories of her hair, the softness of her skin beneath the light, nearly transparent dresses she wore.

After exposing his brain, they transferred the image of his mind. As the mind became convinced it was in the proper body, it slowly assumed control of the metal-head hardware. His organic body was incinerated and Jon was tested for cognition and motor responses.

When he left the center, Jon saw a metal head among a crowd waiting to mount the beltway. "Thomas?" he said. The whirring of his voice still surprised him. When the head turned Jon realized it was not Thomas; it was just another head, like him.

•••

When he returned to the monastery, Jon did not expect the monks to welcome him. But William stood at the hatchway, looking alternatingly at his shoes and somewhere behind him.

"Brother Jon?"

Jon felt like a pillar standing before the soft man. William began to approach, but stopped short. Jon watched him sweat and force a swallow.

"It isn't contagious, Brother," Jon said without sarcasm, and William blinked. "You were here to greet me. That's enough."

William frowned. "No, it isn't. Jon. I was sincere in my concern before. Now," he looked around the room, the opaqued windows, as if to find words, "you just frighten me. For that I ask your forgiveness. I know you desire to follow the Lord's will. That should be enough, and I'll do my best not to question your faith any longer.

What else could this transformation be but an act of faith? I am sorry I did not identify with your struggle sooner."

"There's nothing to forgive, Brother." William stepped closer, hesitated, then finally gave Jon's artificial body a one-armed hug.

Days passed in the dome and Jon found himself efficient and untiring in his duties in the gardens and the geological lab. The abbot interviewed him daily, apparently curious about the state of his mind. What James learned from these sessions was not clear, until it began to dawn on Brother Jon what he had become to the smiling old man. He was as incorruptible seed. He could stay on Mars for as long as he wished. He was as immovable as the will of God, as Olympus Mons. James had his perfect apostle to carry on his ministry, and James was content. It no longer mattered if the dome was shut down.

Jon still thought of Jill from time to time but the memory of her beauty no longer tormented him. He came to realize, in fact, that nothing really tormented him anymore. This epiphany induced in Jon the sense that something was missing. Something had been lost. Pain, torment, temptation, all were symptoms of his soul. Jon's symptoms had been cleared away.

He remembered his agonized prayers for guidance during Thomas's visit. I only want to carry out your divine will, he had prayed. To be a pure vessel of your will. It puzzled him now to scrutinize the Lord's silence. Why had God not told him? Why had he not answered his prayers? It didn't seem possible that the Lord would require Jon sacrifice his own soul.

For this is what he now believed, without any doubt. His soul had been destroyed forever.

*For God so loved the world, that he gave his only begotten son, that whosoever believeth in him should not perish, but have everlasting life.*

*—John, 3:16*

# SUNRUNNERS

*Written by*
**Matthew Champine**

*Illustrated by*
**Beth Anne Zaiken**

## About the Author

*Matt Champine was born in Oklahoma City, and has spent most of his life in Tupelo, Oklahoma.*

*In the sixth grade Matt met Robert A. Heinlein's Stone family and he's been a science fiction reader and wannabe writer ever since.*

*For the last quarter of a century he's raised kids, taken care of family and made decisions essential to keep things moving ahead.*

*One thing Matt has done very well is gamemaster, the art of guiding a half a dozen virtual adventurers through game scenarios. He is also known as Lord Direwolf in the Society for Creative Anachronism, once famed throughout Ansteorra for his skill and ferocity on the field of battle with the two-handed sword.*

*Matt now resides and carries the mail in Ada, Oklahoma, where he happened to meet Leslie, his wife, who has helped him seriously try his hand at writing and he thanks her wholeheartedly for her encouragement and support.*

## About the Illustrator

*Beth Zaiken was born in Germantown, Maryland, about eighteen years ago. Soon after her birth, the family moved to Rochester, Minnesota, where they live today.*

*Beth's great love of nature and the natural world has kept her feet firmly on the ground, while her equally great love of all things fantasy has stuck her head in the clouds. She has been drawing, painting and sketching since she was old enough to hold a pencil.*

*Her parents have always been supportive of her artistic endeavors, and for that she owes them a great debt. She would also like to thank Charles Pearson, a local wildlife artist and grandfather figure, who has been her art mentor since she was twelve.*

*Beth has been winning high honors in several significant competitions in visual art throughout her middle school and high school career. She is also very active in service to her community and to her school, creating designs and posters for organizations as diverse as the local nature center and the school drama program. She looks forward to further exploring her talents at the Rhode Island School of Design this fall.*

*Upon entering the contest, Beth was surprised to find out that she was a winner. Nevertheless, the following illustration—rendered by one of the youngest winners of the contest—was done by an artist who aspires to a long and successful career in illustration.*

Colonization of an extraterrestrial body began June 6, 2017, as construction crews cast the first foundation bricks of the Joint Venture Lunar Base (JVLB) . . . a temporary staging and support base for construction of the Very Large Permanent Earth Orbit Space Station, supplying structural glass, atmospheric gasses and other important lunar materials . . . Certainly nobody guessed that almost two decades later JVLB would become so commercially successful or such a pivotal point in modern civil rights. . . .

—*Manned Space: A Study of Sociological Development, Introduction*

"C'mon, Frans, you can't go by yourself. This is too late to start a run anyway. The dark will catch you!"

"What should I do, Peter?" Frans looked at me through those bushy eyebrows. "Wait here for two weeks until next sunrise while the rent and docking fees add up? Let the company impound my rig, slap a debtor's lien on me, and put me out of business?" Frans shook his head emphatically while continuing to stuff his personal belongings into a duffle. I didn't have an answer for that, at least not a helpful one. The old fellow was right.

"What about Ray? What's he gonna do?"

"He and I have discussed it," Frans said as he finished packing. "The doctors will get his diabetes under control, the company will sue him for the bills, then force him into a work contract. Then, if some things go right, we will pay him out soon." He sighed. "Ray is, or was, a good partner, but he doesn't need to be Out There. Not anymore. It would endanger us both." He sounded like he was trying to convince himself more than me. I didn't blame him. Frans was about to do something everyone thought was crazy; he was headed out on a solo run across the lunar outback.

Frans had taken me under his wing the day I arrived at Lunar Base. He had wasted his valuable run time to help a lost, towheaded California college student get his bearings and had happily taken my first survey. Now Frans was in a bind, and I felt like I wasn't doing enough to help my friend. I bet he was feeling the same way about Ray right now.

"Ray will be fine," he said, but wouldn't meet my eye. He strapped the bag securely.

"Yeah, I'm sure he will." I couldn't make it sound very positive.

He looked at his watch. "I'm late."

I looked uncomfortably around the bare little Temporary Occupant Quarters as Frans shouldered the scuffed gray duffel bag and slid the door open. Like my own T. O. Q., the rough walls showed the welded-lunar-dust bricks of the original Lunar Base construction. A mattress pad on a low brick shelf was the bed, and courses of offset bricks were storage shelves. Kind of ironic, I thought. I'd never lived in a place as rough as this, even as a poor freshman. Now I was a postgraduate sociology student, a thesis away from earning my masters, working on an interplanetary research project for my university, and living in a bare-brick, no-bathroom single. We were quite a pair, Frans and I. We made our way through the gray Lunar Base corridors in silence.

Frans was a founder of the growing group of independent prospectors. The SunRunners or just Runners, were folks who didn't want to return to Earth after their contract was up or when retirement time came. They raced lunar sunset with their hand-built, solar-powered rovers, trying to keep ahead of the dark, stopping only to process prime lunar dust into glass, water and air with their solar furnaces. When the night caught up with them, they packed their equipment and sped west again, leapfrogging their way around the Moon until they were back at Lunar Base a month later with a load to sell. This isn't as hard as it sounds, since the sunset terminator advances at just over ten miles an hour on the Moon. The catch was that between driving, setting up, processing, and tearing down, there was hardly enough time on a run for two men to rest. Without atmosphere to bounce radio transmission, and no relay satellites, communications were limited to line of sight; even a minor accident or breakdown could turn into disaster. I thought it was a miracle only one Runner team had ever been lost. Trying a run alone seemed almost suicidal.

We had to walk through the common central hub of the residential structure to reach the docks. I liked the Common, and not just because of the vending machines. Paint, murals, handmade furniture and other homey touches showed the combined efforts of Lunar Base tenants over the years. The Common was never empty, but there was quite a crowd when we walked in. As we crossed the Common, faces turned and conversations stopped. Most Runners were already gone, but it looked like a lot of the permanent base personnel were interested in what was happening with Frans. He walked to the central residential kiosk to log out of his T. O. Q., stopping to exchange greetings and shake hands along the way. Judging by all the handshaking, Frans could have been elected mayor of Lunar Base, if the company had dared to allow elections. I scanned for some good snapshots of the party with my PDA, and noticed a gleaming cap of short red curls. There was Patty, standing back from the press in a base jumpsuit. She always tried to hide her redheaded good looks behind loose work clothes and lots of attitude. She looked beautiful . . . and upset. I headed her way through the crowd.

Shortly after I'd come to the Moon, Frans had asked me to sit with Patty in the hospital. Frans told me he had happened to be in his surfacesuit on the docks when the crash alarms sounded; he'd been the first to the flipped lander. It hadn't been much of a crash, but cabin integrity had failed and Frans had found her unconscious and suffocating. Patty was returning from some martial-arts event on the space station, and had her helmet unsealed while chatting with the lander crew. The disoriented crew had been unaware of her distress and the emergency response team hadn't reached the crash yet; she might have died except for Frans. She'd been lucky and only had a concussion with some minor vacuum exposure burns in her lungs.

She was watching Frans intently when I stopped beside her. Lucky Frans.

"Uhm . . . hello, Patty." What a dork I was sometimes.

"G'day, Pete." She didn't look at me. "Did ya hear? The bastards contracted me."

"What?" I pushed down my sudden anger. "I thought they couldn't do that 'til you were recovered and released to duty?"

"Apparently they can. Soon as I filed a claim for lost pay they declared me insolvent and delinquent, then filed a lien. It was contract or get shipped back home in irons. I can't even trek up to the space station for a meet."

"Ouch. Sorry." My anger faded into frustration. The personal lien clause of the Lunar Base Accord had been intended to protect the company from freeloader and welfare cases, but instead it had allowed a form of slavery to arise. An outstanding debt to the company became a debt to society, which allowed the company to file a lien on future earnings. This resulted in a due-process choice of immediate payment, forced contract work without pay, or being returned Earthside to prison. A good quarter of the people in the Common now were under contract, working for room and board until their debt was settled. Lunar Base had been in political limbo since Lunar Development Corporation took over two decades ago, leaving the contracted with no higher authority to appeal to. The few who opted for a return to Earth got out of jail soon enough, but were often sued into ruin. I was supposed to be a neutral and objective scholar, but this subject was spoiling that.

"Sorry, mate." She finally looked at me and her glowing smile parted the sea of freckles. "Didn't mean to be such a gloomer. How are ya, Peter? Ya been hangin' 'round the medical center much lately?" We laughed together; I had visited her a lot. I watched her gaze return to Frans.

"Worried about him?" I put my hand on her shoulder.

"Yeah." She turned toward me and hooked her finger in my shirt pocket. For a while in the hospital she could barely whisper, and this was a signal for me to listen closely. "Somethin' is goin' on, Pete," she whispered, "and I'm damn worried." A tear trembled. "I gotta go."

I watched the most beautiful woman on the Moon hurry away. The space-born were elfishly tall and slender, an effect of very low gravity on hormone patterns. The look was, to risk cliché, otherworldly. I had never told her how I felt about her, though. No matter how I tried, we'd never really seemed to click. I knew she liked me, but all the clicking seemed to be me.

"Sunset in thirty minutes," blared the overhead, "all rail-launcher maintenance teams report for rail-launcher shut down."

Frans threw up his hands as the message repeated.

"There is my cue, everyone," he said after the announcement. "Time to go, thank you all." We left amid a storm of farewells and well-wishes.

I wasn't surprised to see Patty waiting for us at the dock air lock when we got finally got there. I tried to come up with some witty greeting, but as usual, my mind went blank instead. It didn't matter; her attention was on Frans. Lucky Frans.

"Hello, Frans," she said. She nodded to me, and took Frans's arm, "I heard about your mate, tough go. You got more troubles waitin' for you on the docks."

"Nothing I didn't expect, my dear," he said to her, "but thank you for the confirmation." He patted her on the arm in a fatherly fashion, then opened the air lock.

"This is loony, Frans." She put her other hand on his arm, holding him back from entering the air lock. "You can't go out alone. What about your heart? Let me fetch my kit. I'm goin' with you."

"Absolutely not, Patty dear," he said gently, "you are not ready to go back Out There yet, and you have obligations here besides."

"I'm better now! And my contract can go straight to hell for all I care! You need a partner, and I'm goin', and that's it."

Damn, she was awesome. Something stirred in me, that feeling of uselessness again. Surely I could do more than watch as Frans drove off to his doom while Patty suffered for it? Frans took Patty's face in his hands. Looking at his wrinkled hands, I realized just how old Frans must be.

"Patricia, tell me, has your doctor released you back to full duty yet?" Frans was very serious.

"No, he won't, the bloody company quack, but I feel . . ."

"So," Frans interrupted her, "you want me to risk your health also? Perhaps even your life? And help you become a contract jumper? Is that what you want?"

She sniffled, but held her head up. "If that's what it takes, too right," she said.

"No, I won't allow it. I am sorry, my dear."

"It's my choice, and I want to," Patty said, and sobbed.

This clash of wills was making Frans even later, and I had no idea what to do about it. I just knew I was sick and tired of being useless.

"I'll go," I blurted out, surprising myself more than them. They just looked at me, stunned, I guess. Frans was the quicker on the uptake, though.

"Well, then it's settled. Peter goes with me, and you can do me the favor of making sure Ray is well taken care of, my dear." He kissed her forehead. "Goodbye,

Patty." Patty still stared at me, streaks of tears on her wonderful freckles. I could see respect growing in her eyes.

"Pete," she said quietly, "you are a twit," and stormed off, which I thought was quite a trick in lunar G.

So maybe it wasn't respect.

I was still vacantly staring in the direction Patty had disappeared when I heard the air lock close and seal behind me. The polished aluminum of the door reflected my dumb face when I turned. Standing alone in the corridor, I considered the vagaries of life, friendship and the disadvantages of having an opposite sex. I grabbed a docksuit off the rack and donned it while Frans cycled through to the docks, then jumped into the air lock as soon as Frans got out. It took me a moment to get oriented when I cycled through; I didn't come out here on the docks much.

The dock was a long loading platform, running east from the center of Lunar Base, roofed and walled with thick concrete for radiation protection, but not sealed against vacuum. The twenty vehicle bays were open to the surface, facing north and south to keep direct sunlight off of the docks. With the crates, stowed parts and forklifts scattered along the main dock, the place seemed chaotic and disorganized to my unfamiliar eye. I walked around the obstacles and searched for Frans's long-range lunar rover, which he'd whimsically named *Luna-bago*. With all the Runners out it wasn't as bad as it could be, but it still took me a minute to find the craft, and the trouble Patty mentioned.

Frans was down in the bay beside the *Luna-bago,* confronting three men; their surfacesuits had security division markings. I saw them gesturing, and realized I hadn't turned on the docksuit com, a breach of company safety regulations. I fumbled with the wrist controller.

". . . try to make this clear," I heard Frans say, "I'm not a company employee, and am not obligated to the charter or the fascist edicts of company management. Is that clear enough, Alan?" I could see to whom he was talking now, Security Division Coordinator Alan McMahon and two of his security division goons. Everything else on the docks had stopped as people listened.

"If you'll let me finish?" S. D. C. McMahon asked with a tight-lipped smile.

"Certainly, if you can do so in the next five minutes, Alan," Frans calmly returned. I could tell Alan didn't like that, but he plowed on.

"I'm sure I can, sir. As I was saying, part two of the company charter empowers the company to protect the safety of employees and property, and more specifically, section D allows the company to safeguard itself from spurious and malicious legal action. Pursuant to part two, section D of the company charter, I hereby place you into protective custody until a court decides if the company is liable for your willing self-endangerment. Please come quietly."

"Not yet," Frans said and held up his hand. "Surely I have the right to know just what self-endangerment you are keeping me from suing you for."

"Mr. Gould, you have no rights here. I will, out of courtesy, answer your question, and then you will come with us. You failed to file a trip plan, but information my office has acquired leads me to believe you are taking your rover out without a crew, an obviously dangerous act. Now . . ."

"Reporting for duty, Captain Frans," I yelled, and performed an exaggerated British-style stamping salute. Since I forgot we were in lunar G, this launched me off the dock, and down into the group of men. With curses and grunts, we finally got untangled.

"Take him into custody, now," Alan snapped when we all regained our feet. One officer stepped toward Frans. Frans stepped back beside the prow of his rover.

"Hold on, Alan, what are you arresting me for now?"

"It doesn't matter now, Gould, you ARE going in. Cuff him."

Frans reached behind himself while Alan talked, into the open-nose storage bay. At the officer's next step, he whipped out a long metallic object.

A sword?

Frans brandished the jagged-edged, wickedly curved weapon like some B-movie pirate. The security officers scrambled back, one of them leaping up from the bay to the main dock.

"Not before I say a few things, Alan. First, remember I have rented this bay from the company, and as a customer I have every right to defend it and my property from illegal seizure. Second, since I'm not violating any of your precious charter clauses, you have absolutely no reason or right to arrest or detain me. Third, if you DO insist on violating my civil rights by detaining me without due process, you make yourself and your company liable for civil and criminal charges. Or maybe Lunar Base Director Moshya would like to invite the United Nations to investigate human rights crimes here?"

I had to choke back a laugh at that. The UN had been fighting for years to have Lunar Base and all the rest of the Moon declared United Nations territorial jurisdiction and would love to have more ammunition for that cause. Some clear human rights violations might force many of the member nations to stop ignoring Lunar Base. Alan waved his men back and talked quickly on another com channel, then was quiet as he nodded and grimaced. Frans watched carefully, and I stood there wondering what next. Finally Alan finished his other conversation and looked at me.

"Mr. Laggar, I have been told to inform you that your disruptive activities will be reported to your project manager. Furthermore, if you leave the environs of Lunar Base, we are no longer responsible for your well-being and your occupancy contract will be revoked." He turned to Frans.

Well, how about that? It sounded like I had just got kicked out of town.

"Mr. Gould, you are free to go. You're lucky I don't arrest you on weapons charges."

"Don't be such an idiot, Alan," Frans laughed and struck the sword against his rover. The "weapon" shattered into dust. "It was just glass, scrap glass; you people need to clean up around your forges."

I couldn't hold the laughter back this time, even though I knew better than to harass the local cops. Frans almost gave me the slip again then, moving into the cabin of the *Luna-bago* while I was enjoying my mirth. I scrambled quickly to the copilot's side, showing my lack of lunar G skills again and giving the watching security division officers something to laugh about in return. I had to knock forcefully and repeatedly before Frans would unlock the door. Apparently the duties of a security division officer included hysterical laughter at unfortunate grad students.

Finally I got settled into the airless cabin and turned off the com. For a long uncomfortable minute, Frans ignored me as he manipulated the surprisingly simple controls. I had expected dials and readouts, but there were only twin control sticks and a blank touchscreen between them at my station. The pilot station seemed identical, and a shared bank of access connectors and cup-holders on the low console between our seats completed the simple cabin. I was going over all this for the third time when Frans finally reached over and slid a com access cord out of the console. He handed me the plug and motioned at the wrist controller on my docksuit. With a little effort I located the access port and patched my com into the rover's com net.

"Thanks, Frans." Lame, but better than blurting out the other things I wanted to gripe about.

"Thank you too, Peter. Your timely escapade helped a lot. Now I'll let you return to your study."

Maybe just a little griping.

"Look, I just made a fool of myself more in the last five minutes than I had in the previous whole semester, and probably risked my career, too. You're not just gonna blow me off, Frans. I mean 'Mr. Gould'. I'm going Out There with you." I could see amusement in his face.

"I don't think your attire is appropriate, Mr. Laggar."

Crap. I was still wearing the docksuit, which belonged to Lunar Base. Designed strictly for temporary use, it lacked the features of a true surfacesuit.

"Like you gave me a choice. Give me ten minutes, I'll go get my surfacesuit and some other stuff. You have to promise to wait here, though." He frowned at that.

"Peter. Pete. This is not a game. The lunar surface is one of the harshest environments man has ever faced. It is devoid of all the basic necessities of human life—no air, no water, no food. It will be difficult, boring, and, above all, dangerous. You've helped me more than you know so far, but your impulsiveness must end now. If you go Out There with me, you will risk your life."

"And you won't be? Alone, no backup, and what else, some kind of a heart condition?"

"I've been doing this for many years, Pete. My risk is minimal. And medication completely controls my arrhythmia problem."

"Frans, are you gonna wait for me or not?"

He watched me, still frowning. I knew this look; it was the look of someone trying to say no when they wanted to say yes. All grad students learn to recognize that look. Finally he broke down and grinned.

"Pete," he said cheerfully, glancing at his watch, "my rent on this bay expires in seventeen minutes, and that's when I start my run."

"Cool. Keep the door open," I said, and unplugged the com. Before I could get out, Frans tapped my arm. He gave me a hand-com, then smiled and waved me along. I was more careful how I maneuvered this time and gave nobody a reason to be amused. Before I had cycled through the dock air lock into Lunar Base, the little hand-com beeped.

"Frans?"

"Of course, Peter. I am moving the rig out of the bay so there is no question about docking fees. Take what time you need, but try to keep it under half an hour please."

"Thanks, Frans, I will."

"And Peter?"

"Yeah?"

"If you have any second thoughts, just call me and tell me. There would be no shame."

"Frans, you're wasting my packing time."

He was laughing when he keyed off.

I left the docksuit on the deck of the air lock, and ran back to my quarters. I was glad for the extra time; my surfacesuit skills were almost nonexistent, and the lunar butterflies in my stomach didn't help. This was what I was supposed to be doing here, studying and learning, but making a rover trip circumnavigating the Moon wasn't part of the standard curriculum. I was supposed to be here researching the social implications of lunar colonization for my thesis and for the department's research project. What I was doing now was throwing away my objectivity and risking my graduation.

It was less than thirty minutes before I clumped back through the Common with my duffle over my shoulder and my surfacesuit helmet under my arm. While no crowds waited to see me off, I was beginning to feel very much like the "right stuff"; then I noticed the candy bar vending machine. I realized it would be a month before we'd meet again. I guessed it was just my day to be ridiculous, so the big brave astronaut stopped at the candy machine and dug through his bag for his credit card. I was trying to use my gloved pinkie to punch in my selection when someone came up behind me.

"Need help with that, mate?"

Not just every woman could call me a twit, then make my heart pound minutes later.

"Thanks, Patty, I got it now. I figured I'd be craving a candy bar before I got my first thousand miles out . . . haha . . ." Sure enough, I missed the button I was trying for and selected "cancel transaction" instead. Cursing under my breath, I waited for the machine to spit out my card so I could stick it back in.

"Here, let me," she said, then put her arm around my neck and leaned into me so she could reach and push my card back in. "What'll it be, mate?"

I could only point dumbly. Her breath was sweet; I smelled coconuts and flowers from her hair. I imagined I could feel her body through my suit.

"Good choice. I fancy those myself. You think ten will do for you?"

I nodded. Her arm was warm on my neck, warm enough to make me sweat.

"One," she whispered and held down the button. She gazed deeply into my eyes as the machine whirred and dropped the candy bar into the hopper. Ka-chunk.

"Two," she murmured. "I wanted to tell you something before you left." Ka-chunk.

"Three. If you take good care of Frans . . ." Ka-chunk.

"And make sure you both get back safe from Out There . . ." Ka-chunk.

"Then I'll be waiting here to make it worthwhile for you . . ." Ka-chunk.

"Six," she mouthed and kissed me. Ka-chunk. Ka-chunk.

"But if anything happens to Frans . . ." She leaned back and looked at me. Ka-chunk.

"Then I'll be waiting here for you . . ." Her eyes narrowed. Ka-chunk.

". . . to make you suffer for it the rest of your life." I could feel the fire in her gaze.

Ka-chunk.

I have no idea where I got the will to pull myself back from the brink of hormonal meltdown. Patty let go of me and started to leave, but I dropped my duffle and put one arm around her waist. She didn't protest as I drew her back to me and put my face an inch from hers.

"Patty, if Frans doesn't come back, I won't be coming back either, because I'll be dead before I leave him out there. Will you marry me?" My heart sounded like it was dropping candy bars. Before she had a chance to answer, I lifted her with one arm and kissed her. When I put her down, she seemed paler than usual.

"Don't answer now," I said, "I'll be back in a month, so you got plenty of time to think about it." I stooped and snatched my duffle back to my shoulder. You have to love lunar G when you're trying to act big and strong. I took a couple of long strides toward the docks, stopped and looked back over my shoulder. All those late study nights watching the Classic Movie Channel, I suppose.

"And wear a dress, 'cause we're going out as soon as I get back," I said, and smiled my best pirate smile. I don't remember reaching the dock air lock, but I do remember my hands were shaking so hard I had trouble putting on my surfacesuit's helmet. And I didn't remember the candy bars I left in the machine until we were an hour Out There.

## Chapter Two

> Another unexpected factor in lunar colonization was the appearance of SunRunners. The need for air and water to replace JVLB recycling losses was a constant drain on base finances. . . . These hardy souls cashed in savings, retirement and even the cost of transport back to Earth to buy large solar-powered rovers and . . . were pivotal to Lunar Base's growing economy.
>
> —*Manned Space: A Study of Sociological Development, Introduction*

I'd been in eighty-mph-bumper-to-bumper traffic in Los Angeles. I never thought half that speed in a locomotive-size lunar rover could be any worse. It was.

The rover seemed to barely touch the regolith, uneasily swaying and bounding across the mare. Occasionally a larger crater would cause a tooth-jarring bump. Vibrations from the motors and suspension seemed to be transmitted straight to my seat despite the surrounding soundless vacuum. I had expected a quieter, calmer ride, not this crazy low-flying-power-saw routine. The cab of the rover made it worse; slung low and forward, my butt seemed just inches from the lunar surface racing by. What a rush.

An hour passed before I began to pay attention, and it was another hour before I got used to it enough to relax my grip on the seat belt. Frans didn't say a word the whole time, just sat there with a hand on the right control stick, occasionally touching the screen. Finally comfortable enough to look around, I could see the front segmented rollagon wheel blurring by just to my right. I was morbidly fascinated that I could see through the blur. Each of the eight giant rollagon wheels was made of curved alloy struts, with heavy rubber "feet" along the tread-line; in dock, they looked ridiculously mundane, but Out Here, they seemed almost magical. Sunset gilded the spinning struts, and the dust kicked into arcs of glittering diamonds. I was hypnotized.

I woke up later when Frans tapped on my helmet. We were still rolling across the lunar surface, though not quite at the breakneck pace of before. Frans motioned for my attention, then reached down beside him to operate a control, which allowed him to swivel around and face backwards. I fumbled beside my seat until I found the knob and released the lock. When I turned the seat around, I saw a small hatch to a rearward area. Frans was already climbing through on his side, and I couldn't keep from looking uneasily over my shoulder at the lunar surface passing by. Frans stuck his head back into the cab and motioned at me to "Come on." With a mental shrug I slid the hatch open and stepped through, finding myself in a small air lock with Frans. I managed to close the little hatch behind me, then Frans hit an equalizer valve by the third hatch. In just a few minutes we were relaxing in the tiny dining area, steaming dinners in front of us, watching a video view from the front of the rover. A portable joystick let Frans make adjustments as we dined.

". . . knew he was developing diabetes, the signs were there, but we agreed that what the heck, how bad could it become in less than a month? Which shows just how smart we were." Frans smiled. "Eat, eat. We don't want you getting skinny Out Here."

"But," I said around a bite of meatloaf, "just what was so darn important anyway?"

Frans stared down at his green beans for an extra moment or two, then looked at me.

"What do you mean?"

"Frans," I said, then swallowed, "look, I may not be too bright, but this seems obvious even to me. Ray risked death by diabetes for that run, and you have a heart condition, and were ready to risk it by yourself. The company made a big deal, looked like to me anyway, over some matters that seemed trivial. Is this beginning to add up?"

He nodded, and I continued.

"Something important is happening, something mostly secret, something potentially valuable. Wanna tell me what is so important to you that you were willing to assault those officers?"

Frans shook his head and laughed.

"Unbelievable," he said when he was done laughing, "unbelievable. I wonder how many others have deduced what you have?"

"I don't know. Everybody is just guessing now, but it was the company that got everyone thinking." I pulled out my PDA and showed him an image of a memo.

TO: DIRECTOR, LUNA BASE
FROM: DIRECTOR, LDC
SUBJECT: INDEPENDENT EQUIP PURCHASES

PLEASE DETERMINE THE INTENDED USE AND/OR DESTINATION OF THE ITEMS ON THE ATTACHED LIST. THESE ITEMS SEEM IN EXCESS OF PROJECTED NEED. PLEASE CONTACT ME OR MY STAFF UPON YOUR QUICK DETERMINATION OF THIS MATTER. TAKE IMMEDIATE ACTION IF NEEDED. USE SECURE COM AND MAIL FOR ALL INFORMATION REGARDING THIS MATTER.

"I see," he said.

"Yup, this caused quite a stir," I said and snapped the PDA shut.

"Tell me, Peter, how did you get that memo?"

"A printout was pinned up on the Common's bulletin board yesterday." I smiled. "I think Patty did it. Never piss off your computer expert by enslaving her."

"So this isn't an original?"

"C'mon, Frans, you're a century behind, there's never an original anymore."

"Of course." He thoughtfully watched the regolith passing by on the screen. We sat and finished our meal quietly. I knew better than to interrupt his thoughts, another skill learned by grad students.

"Well then," he finally said, "I think there is no reason not to tell you."

I saw a lecture coming. As I tucked my PDA into my pocket, I keyed on the digital voice recorder—just in case there was a test later. Frans leaned as far back as the tiny dining area would allow.

"What do you know about the American frontier, Pete? Do you have any special insight on how and why civilization finally overcame the wilderness? No? I have, or at least I think I have. It was because of the mountain men. Many think they were simply asocial, desiring or forced to live away from civilization. Whatever their reasons, these men embraced a harsh and solitary lifestyle. They showed the rest of America that the western frontier was not deadly, that a man could make his way alone. In fact, it even seemed possible to prosper. Without this example I wonder if the American West would have been settled so quickly."

"Are you trying to say you're a lunar mountain man, Frans?" I asked with a smile.

"No, I'm not. I'm the second wave. I'm the outback station, the wilderness trading post, the frontier general store."

"You mean an independent lunar base," I said with disbelief. Frans nodded. This was getting crazier all the time.

"How long will this take, Frans? Especially with the company on to you now?"

"This is my last run, Pete." He sat up straight. "They won't realize it until I put in a bid to supply air and water for the space station, the V. L. S. S."

"Wait." I paused to think, not easy with my head spinning. "You already BUILT this base? And we're going there now?"

Frans nodded.

"Okay. You aren't going back to Lunar Base? Ever?"

"Don't you think they will be more prepared next time, Peter? They must have had an inkling that something is happening, although I find it odd that they then let me go. I imagine there is already some kind of warrant for my arrest." Frans smiled gently.

"Crap. I promised Patty I'd get you back to Lunar Base in one piece, too."

"I know. You forgot to turn off the hand-com. When I tried to call and check your progress, you were . . . busy." I could see that, by the time this was over, I'd have no sense of embarrassment left.

"Frans, I hope you have some way in mind to get me back?"

"Certainly," he chuckled, "but are you sure you want to go back? They don't like you anymore, either."

"Dammit, Frans, I have to go back. My research project, my degree, my thesis, my . . ."

"Patty?"

I nodded morosely.

"Well, that's a good reason, Peter. Women are always a good reason. Don't worry. I'll get you back. You may have to walk a bit, but I'll get you back." Funny how prophecy makes you feel better.

We drove straight through to Frans's base station, taking turns driving and resting, and I've never been so bored in my life. I had trouble staying awake; the lunar surface rolling by at a steady thirty miles per hour was like a sleeping pill during finals week, after a six-pack. Coffee didn't help, so we finally had to get into Frans's medical supplies and amph me up; then I didn't sleep enough. Mostly by luck, I didn't drive us off a cliff or flip us into a crater. When the terrain began to get up and down a lot, Frans wouldn't let me drive much anyway. We were heading into the northern lunar polar regions, where a couple of large meteor strikes had gouged a valley in a mountain range a very long time ago. Frans showed me on the survey map, and it really didn't seem much different from the rest of the Moon.

It took us a week of steady driving to reach the valley, including some painstaking mountaineer driving at the end. Even though the sun was now high in the lunar day, the valley remained in near darkness, lit only by reflections from the surrounding mountain peaks. In the overall dimness, I could just make out a darker streak meandering through the valley, like the dark river Styx winding through the land of the dead. Despite that depressing image from some literature class, I thought it looked cool.

"What's that creek running through your property, Frans?"

Frans laughed. "Pretty close, Pete. That is where I get my water, anyway."

"Really? Frans, are you pulling my leg?"

Illustrated by Beth Anne Zaiken

"No, Peter, I'm not. What you see is a crevasse, a stress crack from the original impacts that formed this valley. It has been here for millions of years, gathering dust."

"Ha! You'd think it would be full by now."

"Probably it was," Frans grunted as we jolted through an unavoidable crater, "but vulcanism or perhaps another nearby meteor strike caused a sinkhole. That's how Ray was able to spot it on the survey maps." He didn't say anything else until we reached the valley floor. We finally rounded a ridge and the rover's lights fell on the station.

"Welcome to Mirkheim," Frans said quietly.

"Whoooa . . ."

It didn't seem real. They hadn't used forged bricks to build sunken bunkers like Lunar Base; instead shimmering purple bubbles seemed to grow out of the base of the mountain, throwing off glassy buttresses. It was almost too much; I was beginning to feel a little lost, but Frans got me back on track.

"First let's unload, then I will give you the tour."

"Wait. Is that the station?"

"Yes," Frans said as he unbuckled, "that's the station."

"How . . ."

"We used old solar furnace reflectors as forms, foamed the glass with carbon dioxide as we poured. We used explosives to dig the chambers, then capped them with the glass hemispheres. A little cutting, a little grinding, and a lot of sealant got them fit and airtight. Ready to help me unload now?"

We went straight to work then. Frans was still being quiet, and I didn't press him about it—I guessed Ray was on his mind. They'd been partners a long time, and

I think Frans was missing Ray now that we were here. I knew I was missing Patty and I hoped she was missing me, even just a little.

The work helped. The rover cargo section was packed full of crates and pallets, as well as some large wrapped pieces, and each one had to be unloaded and stowed just so for Frans. On the Moon a thousand pounds of mass weighs about as much as my normal one hundred eighty pounds on Earth, so the unloading wasn't difficult, even though we had only a basic hand truck and a come-along. In a couple of hours Frans was his old self and declared it was dinner time. We ate in the rover, since it was still powered up and all the food was still there. In celebration, we splurged on turkey and dressing.

"Okay. I got a bunch of questions; you ready, Frans?"

"Of course, ask away, my friend," he said as he sawed the reconstituted turkey breast.

"First, why purple?"

"That was unplanned. The dust we used had some cobalt or iridium in it, something that colored the glass when we smelted it." Frans chuckled fondly. "I remember Ray wondered if we should build a brothel instead of a general store."

"Cool. Okay, why bubbles?"

"You should know that, Peter. The best shape for a pressure vessel is a globe. The old reflectors we got for scrap. We layered pure glass with foamed glass, to make them lighter and more insulating. The results were, well, eye-catching."

"That's an understatement. Now for the big question—why here? How did you find this place and why is it so special?" Frans chewed thoughtfully for a minute.

"I got the idea from a science fiction story written by an author named Poul Anderson. I'm sure you know there are ice deposits at the poles, but the poles are not a good place to have a base. There's not enough sunlight for a base to be full solar, and the energy for living and processing the deposits would have to come from nuclear power plants, or some other expensive alternative. I started seeking closer, easier to reach spots years ago. I'd hoped to find deep dust layers with ice or frozen carbon dioxide, insulated from direct solar heating by the layers of dust above, like the permafrost of Earth's arctic tundra. I failed to find a widespread layer, but instead there are scattered patches, hiding under ejecta mounds and crater ridges."

"Ah," I interrupted, "that's why Runners keep their charts and logs a secret, so nobody can spot their patches."

"Correct. I theorized that if there were patches, there might be super-patches easier to utilize than the polar deposits. Basically I needed to find a deep valley on the polar side of shielding mountains, but not so close to the poles that we couldn't get access to solar power. It turns out you can't have mountains too close behind your site, the reflected light and heat keep the temperature too high. And you must be able to drive in, of course." He paused to sip his coffee.

"Sounds like a hell of a research project to me."

"Indeed. It took four years, including some exploratory runs. But we were working on the station the whole time, gathering the things we needed, working out how we'd build it."

"So this is the super-patch, this valley with a crack running through it?"

"One of them, anyway. There are others, less accessible, not as much ice. There are likely others we didn't find, but there can't be many with as much material." He finished his coffee.

"How much ice?"

"A lot. Hundreds of tons."

"What? Tons? Hundreds of TONS? That's possible?" I barely kept myself from jumping up and doing a lunar newbie bounce off the ceiling. Frans cleared the table while I fidgeted.

"Possible? Yes. Likely? No. We got lucky. Somewhere close, perhaps even one of these craters, there was a comet impact, or maybe an icy asteroid. The crevasse might have twenty thousand tons of material, about one percent of it ice."

"Two hundred tons of ice," I pulled my PDA, opened the calculator, "two thousand pounds per ton, ice goes for what, about a thousand dollars a pound?"

"Twelve hundred last run," Frans said while putting the dishes in the washer.

"Uhm, uh, that would be . . ." I looked up, jaw hanging, to see Frans smiling at me.

"Almost half a billion dollars, Peter. Of course, there may not be as much ice deeper in the crevasse, and the fraction may drop to as little as one tenth of one percent."

"Only fifty million dollars then, how sad. Frans, you and Ray are RICH!"

"Hardly."

"I don't get it. Even if the rate goes down, you're still a multimillionaire!"

"Get your surfacesuit on, and I'll try to explain."

And explain he did. For the next few days we talked about it and worked on getting the station operational. Sunset was coming soon, and Frans had a lot for us to do while we talked. The station had no independent power when we arrived; they'd run it off the rover when they were here, so we installed several fuel cells for power. To recharge the fuel cells and supply processing power for the station, we ran cables up the slope of the shield mountains, and installed solar panels there. With power on, we installed lighting, heaters and the "outhouse," a specialized organic waste recycler.

Two weeks after we'd left Lunar Base, I finally got to sit and relax in the station with Frans. We lounged in the station's main dome, surfacesuits still on, cold brews in hand, just gazing up at the inside of the glittering purple dome.

"This is very cool, Frans."

"Thanks."

"Okay, let me try and sum this all up," I said. "If you try and sell your ice to the company, directly or through other Runners, the market will crash and put the rest of the Runners out of business. You'd have to take up the slack, and the company would eventually find out what was going on. They'd roll the security division in here and take your station, since there's no law Out Here. Right so far?"

"Yes." He kept looking up at the dome as he sipped his beer.

"If you try to sell to someone else, which could only be the space station, you'd have to use the company for your transport, and they'd roll in here and take your station, and put all the Runners out of business. You could go to the UN and apply for some kind of legal help, but as soon as the company finds out they roll in and take your station, since the UN doesn't actually have anyone here to help you. In fact, nothing we can think of will stop the company from rolling in here, taking the station, and putting the rest of the Runners out of business as soon as the company finds out about what you have here."

"We."

"Huh?"

"We. You are a partner now, my friend."

"Hmm. Frans, I don't deserve it, I must protest—okay, since you twisted my arm like that." At least it brought a smile to his face. "Thanks. I don't know, Frans, I don't know; I'm no lawyer, but I think we're missing something here. What did the guy in that science fiction story do?"

"They ended up preserving their secret. Since they had their own space transport that was enough. We don't have that option." Frans peered intently at the dome.

"Well, that's too bad. The good news is we have a couple of weeks to work it out. Don't worry, Frans . . . Frans?" His attention seemed riveted to the dome. Suddenly fear ran through me.

"There!" Frans lunged to his feet. "Did you see that?"

"No, what?" I frantically searched the inner surface of the dome, but I saw no breaks or cracks. "What is it?"

"The rover," he yelled as he jumped to the air lock.

I squinted up, trying to see anything through the sparkling dome. I thought I could make out a flicker of light outside.

"I see it, Frans, did we leave a light . . ."

A bright flash lit up the dome, my beer jumped and spilled, and debris pounded the glass. By the time I recovered from my confusion and put my helmet on, Frans was already cycling out of the air lock. I hurried out, but it was too late; we were both too late. I joined Frans as he watched the quick dying flames. Blue light from the dome behind us showed the *Luna-bago* was a total wreck; the whole rear deck was gone down to the axles, and the cabin was a scorched shell with gaping windows. Frans walked silently around the wreck. My fear rose, and I started to feel short of breath. Would I ever see Patty again?

"Frans . . . Frans, what do we do now?" He ignored me and stooped to examine some piece of the wreck. My emotions were getting the better of me; waves of dizziness hit me. "Frans, I . . ." Afraid I'd fall, I sat on one of the crates. Frans looked up at me then, and I could see his pale face. His lips were moving as he watched me, then he raised his hand and tapped his helmet. I stood up to go see what was wrong with his helmet . . .

I woke with a start and grabbed for the rover controls before I remembered where I was. Then I realized I didn't know where I was. Then Frans leaned over me, and I did remember, kind of.

"Peter, can you answer me?" His face was filled with concern.

"Uh, sure. Man, I got a headache." Even as I said it, the pain was easing.

"Understandable. Anoxia does that. I'm sorry, Pete."

"Sorry? I'm not sure what you mean, Frans." I sat up and looked around; we were in the main dome again.

"We got in a hurry, and you didn't open your regulator, and I didn't wait to check you. That was stupid, and stupid kills." He sat beside me and shook his head.

"I forgot to turn on my air?" I closed my eyes as my stomach did a barrel roll, and I clenched my teeth against nausea. I had made a near-fatal error. I remembered Frans tapping his helmet; I'd forgotten to turn on my radio too. Breathing only the air in the helmet, I would have been dead in ten minutes, but passed out in just two or three. I'd never thought of myself as stupid, but that was scary. I realized that maybe I wasn't taking this seriously enough. Hell, even that thought was understated. I would have to either be more careful, or be very dead.

"Sorry I'm such a putz, Frans." I put my head in my hands.

"We were both at fault. I just need to remember how new you are to this. You've done very well so far."

"Glad to hear it. Any idea what happened with the rover?" Our eyes met, and we mutually, silently, agreed it would never be mentioned again.

"Yes," he said. He rose and stepped to the crate we used as a work table. He picked something up, and handed it to me. "This."

"This" was a blackened and twisted piece of plumbing, one end melted away, the other still attached to a fitting. Something else was wired to the remainder of the pipe, something that was out of place.

"What is it?"

"It's a welding flare. It was used as a detonator, with the gas storage tanks as the explosives. There must have been a timer to ignite the flare."

"A bomb? How?"

"Liquid oxygen is very flammable. The flare burned through a feed pipe from the liquid oxygen tank, burned the shutoff valve, too. I saw the fire through the dome, but it was already too late by then. When the hydrogen tank ruptured from the fire, well, you saw what was left."

"Someone tried to kill us." It was beginning to sink in.

"Yes. The timing was perfect for us to be halfway through our run. We would have just never come back, lost somewhere here on the dark side of the Moon."

"Wow. You think they know about Mirkheim?"

"Not the location, but maybe the idea? I don't know." Frans shook his head.

"But, why? Why kill us at all?"

"Half a billion dollars?"

"Oh. Right. No, wait." I paused a moment to gather my thoughts. "To collect, they'd need to know where we were and what we had. Then it would be easier and safer to come out here after we left, wouldn't it? And even if we were here, why risk blowing the place up, when they could just bring a few friends and toss us out? No, they don't know or don't care about the ice, don't know where we are."

"Very logical, Peter. What motive is left, though?" Frans sat wearily beside me.

"Well, aren't you the only man on the planet with an independent lunar base? The only competition for Lunar Base Corporation?"

He slowly straightened, his face becoming hard and angry.

"What kind of trouble are we in, Frans?"

"I'm not sure yet. Are you up to finding out?"

I stood up and reached for my helmet. "Nothing I'd like better."

We carefully checked each other's surfacesuit this time before entering the air lock. We spent about an hour briefly checking the wreckage and tallying what we had to work with for our survival. We spent another hour finishing the six-pack, then we went to bed. The terminator rolled over us as we slept. Mirkheim was in total darkness when we woke.

## Chapter Three

> As independent operators, they took the risks that the Lunar Development Corporation was not willing to take. Isolated by lack of communication and the search for scattered resources, some paid the price of their risky endeavor, losing everything to misadventure. A few paid with their lives, building a frontier-hero mythology around the Runners. Whether heroes or gypsies, the Runners were essential to the success of JVLB. Eventually . . .
>
> —*Manned Space: A Study of Sociological Development, Introduction*

"Peter, that is too risky, I cannot allow you to endanger yourself like that. You can't travel like that in the dark, anyway."

"What, wait here for your medication to run out so I can watch you die? Or maybe we just starve to death together? Uh-uh, Frans, no way." I had to smile at the deja vu this conversation was giving me. "No radio, no rover, most of our stuff is gone, even most of your medicine. No way we can just wait. Anyway, you were willing to take off by yourself."

"I was willing to take an acceptable risk for my future and the future of my fellow Runners, and the future of my family. That's not the same as hiking off into the lunar night, Pete, not even close. You would be risking certain death against a slim chance of a rescue."

I had to gripe a little.

"First of all, who says it's certain death, and second, a slim chance is better than none. They won't think we're late until sunset reaches them in a couple of weeks, and then they'll have to wait two more weeks until sunrise to start a search. If by some miracle they drove straight here, it would be two more weeks before they could reach us, and two weeks back home. How long until Ray decides we're in trouble Out Here?"

"I told him I would contact him within two months." Frans looked bleak. "He would probably tell a Runner where to find us, but he might give the company our coordinates so they could send a lander."

"So, they can't possibly help us for six weeks, at best, and it might be more than two months. How long will the medicine you have left last, maybe two weeks?"

"A month if I split my dose in half. I'm sure I can survive long enough after it is gone."

"There you go, practicing medicine with your head up your butt. Didn't Ray almost die over that already?" Dammit, I just have to be stupid sometimes. "Uh, sorry, that's not what I meant to say." His answer surprised me.

"No, no, that is fine, Peter. You are right. In trying to protect you, I'm risking us both. Let's talk about your idea."

"Really, I'm sorry it came out that way. . . ." Frans interrupted me with a wave.

"Peter, you must learn to be graciously correct, however clumsily you get there. Now, your idea?"

"Right. Gotcha. Okay, I was figuring how long it would take to hike back to Lunar Base, just as a baseline."

"Too long, I assume?"

"Way too long. But I got to thinking it would be much closer to reach a Runner as he passed by. If I could average just forty miles a day, I could make it six hundred miles south not too long after sunrise. Then I could just sit in the sun, keep the suit-com open, and wait for a Runner to come by."

"Forty miles a day? How are you going to manage that with a hundred air canisters strapped on your back?"

"I'm gonna take your backup compressor unit instead."

"Oh? How will you power it in the dark?"

"With your backup fuel cell."

"That is ridiculous. You might be able to handle their combined weight, but they are far too bulky to attach to your surfacesuit. Wait. You thought of that, too."

I smirked at that. I just couldn't help myself.

"A sled? No, a wagon or cart would be more efficient. Not the rollagons though, they are too heavy. . . ." He started to pace as he worked it out. All I had to do was make encouraging sounds now and then while my PDA recorded it all.

"You sound like an engineer, Frans," I teased.

"I am," he shot back, still pacing, "Lunar Base chief engineer at one time."

I knew Frans had retired from Lunar Base, but hadn't realized he had been management. That sounded familiar. I opened my research files to the early personnel records and found what I was looking for. The second director of Lunar Base was Vera Gould, and Frans Gould was her chief engineer.

"Frans," I called. He looked up from the paper he was sketching on.

"Yes?"

"Were you married to Director Vera Gould? Back when you were the base engineer?"

"She was my wife, yes. She was married to her job, though. Why do you ask?"

"I connected the names just now. I was thinking what a small world it is when I remembered something Patty said to me. She mentioned that her grandmother had connections on Lunar Base, and pulled strings for her to get the programmer-analyst job. Well, then I thought you'd need some darn high-ranking strings. Like a former director?"

For the first time, I saw Frans uncomfortable about something. I didn't let him off the hook; I kept watching him expectantly. After a considerable internal struggle, he grinned sheepishly.

"Peter, that figuring out of people's secrets is a bad habit. Patty is my granddaughter. I had to promise Vera I wouldn't tell anyone before Patty could come. Now you have to promise."

My God, what a relief! Frans was my friend, but I'd been a little jealous of how much attention he gave Patty . . . and she gave him.

"Sure thing, Gramps. So, is that why you were waiting at Lunar Base when I landed? Waiting on her, but you got me instead?"

Frans nodded.

"And that is why I was there when she crashed," he continued, "to see her before I left on a run."

"Why the secrecy?"

"Vera doesn't want Patty to know that grandfather is a Runner bum. It was why she left me in the first place. Vera decided Patty should never find out who I am." He smiled, a little grimly.

"Ouch. Well, we'll get back at the old witch."

"Peter! That's rude." He chuckled. "How?"

"When we get back, I'm gonna talk Patty into being my wife, so she'll be married to a Runner bum." We found that very amusing.

It was the only amusing thing for the next twenty-four hours. Frans designed a human-powered long-range rover using the materials from the station. I froze my butt off searching in the lunar night, gathering the materials he wanted. Frans measured, calculated, and made adjustments while I grunted, sweated, lifted, moved, and froze some more. It was important though, even more now that I knew Frans was Patty's grandfather. I probably could make it here at the station for a couple of months; I wouldn't be in good shape, but alive. Frans probably wouldn't survive.

Frans woke me when he finished with the various hookups, and we went out to inspect the device under the glaring work lights.

"There you are, Pete. One Human-Powered Long-Range Lunar Rover, ready to go."

"Damn, that's a good-lookin' piece of work, Frans. Mind if I borrow it?"

"Well, it's the last one I have on the lot . . . but for you, sure." We made manly humor to buck up our confidence in the face of imminent danger; I had the hilarious urge to scratch and spit.

My idea had started simply. The plan was to hike south until I found a Runner's rover tracks. If I could get there not too long after sunrise, a Runner should be along within a few days, and even if the Runner didn't come close enough to see me, the suit-coms were good for ten or fifteen miles. The big problem was that surfacesuits were only good for about eight hours before needing a fresh rebreather tank and battery recharge. This meant I had to take along a truck full of tanks, or some way to recharge them. The station used several rover-style recycler/recharger fuel cells. Given electricity, water and air the fuel cells would make and store fuel, or could produce electricity, air and water vapor by catalyzing stored fuel. Combined with a gas storage and compressor unit, I could recharge tanks and batteries as I walked.

Both units were as light as technology could make them, but the fuel cell weighed about four hundred pounds on Earth, and the compressor half that. But that wasn't all, it turned out. I needed some way to recharge the cells, because there was no telling how many days I'd have to wait after sunrise. I couldn't just sleep on the ground either; in the night I'd freeze to death, and in the day I might overheat. We added a short solar panel for the fuel-cell charging, and to be a shade for resting under, and put one of the *Luna-bago*'s scorched bucket seats under the panel, facing forward. In the end, we had built a huge rickshaw, including a harness for my upper body between the grip rails. The whole thing massed nearly half a ton, but in lunar G it lifted like one hundred and fifty pounds, which I intended to drag across six hundred miles of airless, extraterrestrial desert. I felt tired just thinking about it.

"Well," I said as we finished our inspection, "I guess there's no time like the present."

"Indeed. Here, let me help you strap in. Remember to use the handles; you are the stabilizing system."

"And the motor, and the driver, and the in-flight entertainment too. Thanks, Frans."

"Don't worry, Pete. It's a good plan. Good luck."

We solemnly shook gloved hands.

"Remember, Pete," Frans said as he stepped out of the way, "the mass is still there, so it will be difficult to accelerate, but with the friction coefficient down, the momentum will help your progress."

"Got it. Hard to start, hard to stop." I reached up and pulled down on the handles, leveling the cart behind me. The handles kept pressing upwards, making me unstable.

"Frans, the balance seems off, can you see how?"

"I will adjust it, just a moment."

"Okay," I said.

The cart bobbed, then the handles settled into my grip. "There, that's it, that got it. See you in a couple of weeks." I turned to wave to Frans.

He was sitting in the seat on the cart, a big smile on his face. I couldn't help it; I burst into laughter. Frans did too. We laughed together for a few priceless seconds.

"It's a good idea, huh?"

"Yes it is, and I even improved it a little."

"Well, I like your improvement, and I'm glad you're coming. Buckle up. Your chariot is about to launch."

I set my feet and leaned into the harness. I had a flash of concern; the cart didn't seem to react much to my effort. Despite my worry, it eased slowly and smoothly forward until I was moving at a brisk march. I guided us out of the station area, and then turned on the afterburners. In moments we were moving at a jog, five or six miles an hour.

"Steer left some, Peter," Frans called to me, "there is another way out of the valley."

"Good. I wasn't looking forward to pulling this thing up that pass we drove through."

"Just a habit. Runners try not to retake the same path to a good spot."

As we rolled off down the valley, I looked back at the station. Sparkling purple domes edged everything near them in neon, framed by the starlit valley. The stars themselves burned clear and clean, not coy and winking as I remembered them from Earth. The beauty of the scene cut itself into my memory. I blinked back tears and felt something change in me; if I survived, I would be back Out Here.

## Chapter Four

> . . . conflict between the Runner community and the corporate entity of Lunar Base Corporation led to actions both sides came to regret. However, those events and the circumstances that arose from them were inevitably to lead to a new sociological dynamic on the Moon. . . .
>
> —*Manned Space: A Study of Sociological Development, Introduction*

I could hear my father calling me to wake up; I must have overslept.

"Wake up, Peter!"

My head was filled with cotton and I ached all over; no way I was going to school today. I rolled over to tell him, and my left knee exploded with pain. When I could think again, there were tears in my eyes, and I was back on the Moon. Frans was holding his helmet against mine and yelling my name.

"Okay, Frans, I'm up, just gimme a sec to . . ."

"No, just listen to me, Peter. Your plan worked! Someone heard me on the radio." Frans was almost boyish in his elation. Despite my own rush of relief, I tried to be cool.

"Damn, I'm glad of that. I'm tired of walking. I'd like to ride awhile." I flopped back on top of the cart, and watched Frans start a lunar Jewish jig. My sprained knee ached, my muscles burned with fatigue, the inside of my surfacesuit smelled, and I had a headache from the stale breathing mix, but I was as happy as Frans. Despite my earlier confidence, the odds had not been with us. Frans had guided us to a wide corridor of relatively smooth lunar surface, a hundred-mile-wide highway often used by Runners. However, often isn't always, and Frans guessed we had a fifty percent chance someone would use this path on their run. We had positioned ourselves in the heaviest concentration of old tracks, but our twenty-mile-wide radio range covered perhaps half of the well-used part of the path, which gave us an optimistic twenty-five percent chance of a rescue.

My radio was off to help conserve the battery, but I figured it wouldn't be a problem now. Funny, to get air from the fuel cells we took electricity, so to conserve air, we had to conserve power. I switched the radio on.

". . . so let me tell Pete to get his radio on." It was Frans's voice.

"I'm on, Frans, thanks," I interrupted.

"Peter?"

Strange, it sounded like . . ."Patty?"

"Peter, I brought your bloody candy bars." She laughed.

My pains disappeared, and I was suddenly sharply aware of everything around me: the beauty of the lunar vista, the warmth of the still-rising sun, the sea of stars. I could even see the gleam of a satellite arcing overhead.

"Uh, Patty?" I felt extra stupid, too.

"Yes, Patty, ya twit. Who else would trek out here after you?"

I couldn't think of a good answer; my attention focused on the moving point of light. It seemed bigger. Fear stirred in my gut.

"Peter? Pete? Frans, is Peter okay?"

I waved at Frans and pointed; he looked at me, then into the sky. Something was flying toward us, and on the Moon that meant a lander, and a lander meant Lunar Base had found us.

"Okay, mates, if you don't want to talk to me, I'll just turn around and . . ."

Frans shut off my radio and leaned in to touch our helmet faceplates again.

"This could be trouble," he said.

"Trouble? Someone tried to kill us, Frans, and that someone is probably on that lander. We have to do something."

"Certainly, I agree. Do you have any suggestions?"

"Well, we can't call the Space Patrol . . . wait. I may have an idea." My mind was racing, clicking over like no sociology final had ever made it race. "All right, listen to this and tell me what you think. We can't let them catch us both together. It would be too easy for us to have an unfortunate accident that way. And we have to get Patty out of the way, too. And we can't all take off together; the three of us together would be easy targets if they are armed."

"Armed, Peter?"

"Guns. If Patty picked us up before the lander gets here, they could change course, shoot a few holes in the rover, and POW! another unfortunate accident."

"I find the idea of guns on the Moon hard to believe, Pete, but better safe than sorry. Go ahead."

"Better safe than dead, you mean. Switch your com back on."

We turned our radios back on in the middle of a blistering string of curses. I looked at Frans's and we shared embarrassed grins while Patty explored the possible lineage and sexual habits of someone. Probably me. When she paused for breath, Frans jumped in.

"Patty, dear?"

"Frans?" She responded instantly. "Is everything all right? You stopped transmitting, Peter stopped talking and . . . what happened? What do YOU want?"

"Uh, we had a change of plans," I answered, a little confused by that last part. "Patty, I need you to stop where you are, one of us is going to come to you. Something has come up, something we'll explain when we get time. Frans, how long until the lander is here?"

"If we can see it, we probably only have a couple of more minutes."

"Lander? Hold on. There's a lander? Why?" Patty sounded confused.

"Yes, a lander is almost here, and I don't know why, and we can't wait. Frans, grab the spare pack and start toward Patty." Something bothered me about Patty's answers, but there was no time to stop and figure out what.

"No." Frans sounded grim.

"Don't have time, Frans. I have to stay here and get captured, and you have to go to the rover and escape."

"No. I'm out of medicine. The lander is the fastest way back to the base, and whoever this is can't afford to kill me or let me die while you are still free and alive."

"Kill? Die?" Patty was clearly getting worried. "What's going on?"

"So, you and I are each other's insurance?" I nodded, ignoring Patty for the moment. Frans nodded back.

"That's it then. Patty, I'm coming to you, Frans will be the only one talking now; we can't transmit anymore, or the lander might find you, too."

"But, Peter . . . NO! You sonnofa . . ." There was a pop as Patty was disconnected.

God, I felt stupid.

"Frans, did you ask Patty how she happened to be Out Here in a rover?"

"No." He looked bewildered.

"They are with her, too."

My head whirled as I tried to fit it all together, but I knew we were running out of time. Frans was beginning to get it, I could see. I decided I didn't have time to actually figure out who or why. I really had to act now, DO something, before that wasn't an option anymore.

"Frans, we gotta hurry." We both glanced up at the descending lander.

"I'm . . . at a loss, my young friend."

"Someone has to get away, so the rest of us have a chance."

"Well," he said, "if that is our only chance, then we go together."

"Your heart," I said. His hand touched the surfacesuit over his chest absently, then he nodded.

"Right. And I daresay I'm the better negotiator. Let's do this."

Seconds later I was back in the harness. The silence was bothering me; I expected melodramatic threats, crafty negotiations or warrants for our arrest, anything but silence. No time left to consider that, though. My heart pounded, I was chilled but sweating, and my fear threatened to make me puke. Com off again, we touched helmets. Frans must have noticed my distress.

"Peter, this isn't a suicide mission. Calm down." He sounded sure of himself.

"Well, I don't see any other options here, Frans. Do you?" My voice was far more in control than I felt.

"Do you have your little computer handy?"

"Uh . . . " I felt quickly through the outer pockets of my surfacesuit. "Yeah, right here."

"Turn the voice record on, and hold it tight to my helmet."

Frans started reciting coordinates, locations on the lunar surface. I should have paid attention, but all I could think about was Patty. Surely they wouldn't risk hurting her if a witness existed. On the other hand, I didn't really know who it was holding her, and might have a hard time proving anything. Suddenly I didn't like my idea. Maybe I'd be better off trying some heroic rescue attempt. Before I could totally freak out, Frans spoke to me.

"Those are some of my best spots, Peter. You'll have to travel from spot to spot. Just shovel the dust into the outhouse, that'll process out what you need. You might make it home before sunset." Debris from the lander exhaust blast started to rattle on our helmets. "Go, hurry."

My panic faded as quickly as it had risen.

"Okay. Good luck, Frans."

"You too, my boy."

We shook hands in silence, a moment I felt could be our last. I leaned into the harness as we were pelted by dust and rock. Between the dust and my tears, I didn't see the lander touch down.

I moved quickly for half a minute, then bumped down into a good-sized double crater. The twin ejecta mounds threw a hard, black shadow across the bottom of the crater, mostly hiding the cart. The lander was still bouncing on its landing gear when I peeked back over the crater rim. Frans shuffled toward the lander and waited while two men in security division surfacesuits unloaded. I switched my radio back on; I hoped it wouldn't give me away, but felt I needed to hear what was happening. Frans blustered at the men, but they didn't say anything, at least not on our channel. They ignored his protests, grabbed him, switched off his com, and dragged him bodily to the lander. Suddenly I noticed my trail; the cart track and my footprints were quite visible in the high relief of the morning sun. The only footprints for about a thousand miles. Crap.

I was just a hundred yards away from the lander. If I waited in hiding, only the most incompetent search since Stalag 13 would miss that trail. I needed a head start, but they'd be even more incompetent if they didn't start searching for me right away. I looked around the mare; if I ran, there was no way the men wouldn't see me. Movement caught my eye. The rover was close, closer than I'd thought, only a mile or so. Well, there went most of my chance of sneaking off. Still, it was my best hope, so I waited and watched.

It was less than ten seconds before incompetence struck.

Both men were reentering the lander with Frans. It would take a minute or more to cycle the air lock going in, and another minute to cycle back out. Even if they were just checking in for instructions, I had two minutes or more to make my getaway. A quick glance told me the rover was still speeding straight for the lander; with a little luck, whoever was driving wouldn't see me run for it. I didn't bother strapping in, just threw the harness over my shoulders, grabbed the handles, and let adrenaline power me out of the crater. I hardly felt my knee as I turned away from the oncoming rover and put everything I had left into a burst of acceleration. Within half a minute, I was running down a slight slope at about twenty miles per hour. My radio fizzed static and popped. NOW what? I thought.

"Peter, this is Patty. Is that you hopping along like some bloody outback kangaroo?"

In a few seconds, the wreck was over. Shocked to hear her voice, I had slowed my pace slightly, and the cart's momentum simply pushed me off my feet. My first reaction was to hold myself up to catch my balance, which pushed the handles down. I might still have recovered, but my injured knee gave then and I fell, my faceplate and the cart handles plowing into the dust. Still, I'd been lucky. If the handles had lifted again, the cart might have rolled over me and dragged me to my death. Instead, the handles dug into the dust and struck a hidden ridge or crack, and physics did the rest. I plowed to a stop in the dust, but the cart spun starward, catapulted over the suddenly lodged handles, flinging loose items in all directions. The cart, or what was left, was still tumbling across the lunar surface when I wiped the dust off my faceplate, struggled to my feet and turned to limp back toward the lander.

"Peter! Are you okay?" The concern in her voice twisted my heart.

"Yeah, I'm all right," I said with a grim smile, "my stuff is scattered for a mile, but I got lucky. How are you?"

"Never mind me; is Frans okay?"

"They have Frans on the lander. We decided he should surrender. Patty, Frans is out of his heart medicine, has been for more than a week."

"Well, where in the hell were you going, then?"

"Doesn't matter now. What do we do about Frans?"

"You don't worry, Pete, I'll take care of Frans, you just get back to that lander if you want a ride home."

"On my way, thanks," I said with some relief. She didn't answer, and her voice had seemed sharp. I guess I'd said something to set her off.

I started trotting, favoring my knee. Something was still bothering me, so I decided to risk her wrath further.

"Patty, we thought something had happened to you, like maybe someone attacked you?"

"Something like that, mate," she said, and laughed. "The big, brave bloke is locked in storage B."

"Isn't that the . . . ?"

"Freezer. He's a lucky bugger; my first thought was to send him vacuum diving. Now please hush, Peter. I need to get busy. You people in the lander, I know you're hearing me. I'll be there in thirty seconds. If I don't see Frans outside when I get there, I'm gonna roll through ya at seventy-five kph, then reverse on the wreckage and play moon rugby with your heads. Com out."

I broke into a sprint, or as much of a sprint as I could manage. This was not going any way I could have imagined, and I wanted to be at the lander. I had no plan, but if I was close, maybe I could do something to help. I could see the rover barreling straight at the lander, and I'd bet the guys inside could see it too. I knew Patty meant what she said, and I hoped whoever was in the lander believed too.

The slanting sunlight made the dash across the lunar surface almost easy; craters, loose rocks and dust usually made running harder. Still, my head was down as I watched my path when the lander lock cycled open.

"All right, lady, here he is." I looked up in time to see Frans being dragged from the open lock by one of the kidnapers. I was coming from behind them, and they must not have seen me. I could also see another one of them hiding in the shadowed air lock, secretly observing the oncoming rover. They were going to ambush Patty's rover; it was time for me to do something. What, I didn't know, but I was almost there and it would come to me.

Then the guy in the air lock swung out and started shooting a pistol into the cab of the oncoming rover. I saw glass and plastic fly, and a surfacesuited figure jerking . . . and I went a little crazy.

I leapt at the man with the gun, catching him dead-center, and we went skittering across the ground. I was acting in rage, and had no plan, simply the desire to kill him. I rolled to my feet on the first bounce, and was on him before he could recover his balance. Unlike TV, he hadn't dropped his gun, and didn't bother fighting back, just turned the gun on me as I uselessly tried to punch him through his surfacesuit. The gun blasted once, close enough for the muzzle blast to thump my helmet, but the shot missed in the struggle. We fought for a few seconds more, then the muzzle touched the middle of my faceplate. I distinctly heard a click as he pulled the trigger, and I was shocked into motionlessness. Desperately, he pulled the trigger again and again; we both realized the gun was empty about the same time. I drew back a bit, and he rolled away, shielding his attempt to reload with his body. His backpack was now to me.

I grabbed the main air feed hose like a suitcase handle, and jerked him to me. The hose and fittings were "accident proof," but not built to survive the kind of abuse I applied. I stood up and shook him violently, until the helmet fitting split. Like any drowning victim, he forgot what he was doing and panicked when the next breath didn't come. I stepped back and watched, fascinated for a moment by his death struggle; had I just done that?

"Peter, dear, get outta my way!"

My head jerked up, and I saw the rover bearing down on me. Without further thought, I grabbed the panicked thug and jumped clear of the rover's path. I didn't see the impact; the guy was completely freaking out, and we struggled several more seconds. Finally he blacked out, and then I spent the next half a minute sealing the hose fitting with the emergency goop from the surfacesuit emergency kit. I'd ruined the helmet, but he'd live.

When I turned to see the crash, it was already over. The rover had crashed through two of the lander's legs and spun to a stop a few yards further on. The spacecraft had toppled to the ground, a plume of dust and gas mushrooming around it. My heart was pounding, my hands were shaking, but my vision was very clear. Frans and his captor had leapt clear, but were just standing there, apparently too shaken by events to do more. I limped to the rover, hoping that by some miracle Patty had survived the gunshots and impact, but my guts twisted at what I saw.

The cab was mangled and flattened. I could only see a patch of surfacesuit in the crumpled wreckage. I ignored the sick feeling and hurried as best I could to the main air lock; if I could get inside and open the cabin air lock, I might be able to free her. Before I got there, the outer door popped open and an unsuited figure tumbled out, followed by someone in a surfacesuit. It was Patty. She saw me there, standing dumbfounded; of course she had to laugh.

"Peter, do this chump a favor and help him into a lifeball. I need to check on Frans." She pulled the activator on the package she was holding and tossed it to me. Reflexively, I tried to catch the slowly arcing lifeball, but it deployed into an unwieldy giant pill. By the time I'd quit juggling it, she was gracefully bouncing toward Frans and his former captor, a black pistol in her left hand. I turned my attention to the guy asphyxiating in front of me. It was Alan, Coordinator of Security Division Alan, mouthing and flopping like a fish out of water.

"Patty, what . . . ?"

"Had to use his suit to decoy the bugger with the gun, and couldn't leave him alone in the rover, could I?"

"But, didn't he have a gun?" It seemed to take forever to get him in the oblong lifeball. I grunted as I struggled with Alan.

"Yup, and he stuck it too close to me, so I took it and twisted his arm for the trouble. Teach him to lie to me about rescuing my friends. Going com off for a bit."

"Huh." Alan was still conscious when I zipped it and popped the $O^2$. He gasped and glared as the lifeball pressurized.

He might as well have been locked in a vault, so I started over to Patty and Frans. They had their helmets together, and I turned to check on my thug instead. He was still unconscious, with a trickle of blood from his nose. He'd certainly sucked too much vacuum, but his breathing seemed fine to me, better than the breathing he'd wanted for me. I looked until I found his pistol, then dug the spare clips out of his surfacesuit pockets. He must have been expecting some kind of war; he had nine more clips besides the empty one. My search complete, I dragged him toward the rover, my knee throbbing with every step.

"Peter," Patty called, "are you—oh, never mind, you're ahead of me, I see. I left the duct tape on the dining table; be a dear and tie him off?"

My answer was somewhere between a grunt of weariness and a groan of pain. The adrenaline must have been wearing off. I was smiling, though. She'd called me "dear" twice already.

Halfway to the rover, my thug started to struggle. I dropped him, stepped back, fumbled the pistol out of my pocket, and pointed it at him. Then I remembered it wasn't loaded. Cursing, I found a clip, got it shoved in just as the guy stood up. I could see his face, an ordinary face, a face you could see anywhere. He saw me working the slide, trying to cock his gun, and his face changed. His hand snapped out, a gleam of steel suddenly appearing, and he lunged at me. I felt the slide close on the pistol, and a fierce rage rose. The gun bucked, the only sound a faint thump from the recoil in my glove. Icy pain numbed my arm as he slashed at me, but I felt the gun thump again and this time he staggered back, his face twisted and dark.

"Bastard!" I yelled. Thump. He regained his balance and surged toward me again. I stepped coldly into him, burying the pistol in his chest as his knife swung into me. Thump. Thump. He fell limply then, in lunar slow motion. I went to one knee beside him and pressed the muzzle of his pistol to the faceplate of his helmet. All I could think of was that he'd tried to kill Patty. I willed the pistol to shoot, to put a bullet through the ordinary face, but my anger had abandoned me. I could hear Patty calling to me on the com, see her gloved hand on my arm; I trembled with the effort of trying to pull that trigger.

I didn't actually lose consciousness, but things grew confused and flat. Frans and Patty walked me to the rover and dressed my wounds. The thug had cut my arm badly, as well as a couple of other minor slashes. It was about half an hour before I felt even close to normal.

I sat up in the bunk, putting my head down as a wave of nausea came and went. Patty glanced up from wrapping duct tape around Alan's ankles. The rest of him was already well taped.

"Hey, Pete, be careful," she said gently. She ripped the tape off the roll and came to squat beside me. "Maybe you should lay back down?"

"No." I shook my head, still looking down. "Just let me get my bearings. I'll be all right. I just had a thought, did you check the lander for crew?"

"The little one was the pilot. Everyone accounted for."

"Good. How did you find us?" I felt the rover lurch, and realized we were moving.

"Alan. They orbited a lander to listen for you when you were late, but I insisted we take a rover for backup. Alan came with me, to coordinate the rescue, he said." Her freckles twisted into a frown. "Pete, Ray died. They said it was an accident."

I couldn't find any surprise, although I hadn't considered it consciously.

I nodded. "Patty, I know you know that Frans is your grandfather. Frans knows about you, too; he has all along."

She sighed and reached out to squeeze my hand.

I cut my eyes sideways at her. "That guy, is he . . ."

She met my gaze. "Yes. Dead. Thank you, Pete. You saved our lives, all of us." I didn't know how to feel about that and turned my face back toward the deck. Patty saw my confusion.

"Peter. Look at me." She hooked her finger in my shirt pocket. "You didn't make the decision that someone had to die. He did. You saved lives. You saved your life, you saved Frans, you saved me." She held my eyes with hers. "Right now you're tired and hurtin' and lost some blood. You just remember, Peter Lagger, you are a hero. My hero. Someday, our children's hero."

I guess heroes cry.

## Chapter Five

. . . finally resolving the political ambiguity of Lunar Base . . .

—*Manned Space: A Study of Sociological Development, Introduction*

We hurried to the main air lock just in time to meet the soldiers. Thankfully, my limp was mostly gone. The inner door gimbaled open, and a young lieutenant stepped out of the air lock first, his armored spacesuit jarringly out of place. We stood blocking the way, and he had to stop halfway out. The rest of his squad stood at ease behind him.

"Excuse me," he snapped.

"Certainly," I said, "but sorry to see you go so soon."

He raised his eyebrows at that. After a moment of thought and a deep breath, he tried again.

"Excuse me, sir, but I need to see the administrator."

"Ah, I see. I can arrange for you to see prisoners." I watched his eyebrows climb another notch.

"Prisoners?"

"Prisoners. Most of the former administration is being held on various charges, including attempted murder. We're hoping to convene a proper court next sunset." I'd been surprised how easy it had been to just walk in and kidnap the bosses at gunpoint. Two more of Alan's thugs had surrendered, too. It was becoming clear most of company management had not been involved with Alan's operations. Then again, they were all slavers in my eyes.

"Well, who is running Lunar Base, then?" The poor officer seemed bemused.

"Let me make introductions. This is Frans Gould, Luna City mayor; I'm Sheriff Lagger, and this is Deputy Sheriff Lagger." I stuck my hand out. "You are . . . ?"

"Lieutenant Shaw, sir." He shook my hand out of reflex, but he was looking at Patty.

"G'day, Ron," she said, "been keepin' up your Jiu Jitsu practice?" He shook her hand with a small bow.

"Yes, ma'am, but I doubt I could take you yet." He released her hand and turned back to me. "You got a good deputy there, sir."

"She's some kinda wife, too."

"You married Patty the Python? Congratulations." Several of the soldiers snickered.

"Uhm. I guess so. Anyway, to what do we owe the pleasure of your visit, Ron?" I rolled my eyes at the Python. She appeared very innocent.

He straightened himself up, trying to regain his sense of purpose. "Sir, I have been ordered to ascertain why Lunar Base Corporation has stopped supplying Glenn Space Facility, and to restart those supplies ASAP." Sounded like they'd finally named the space station. The first thing we'd done after our coup was shut down the big rail launcher. We had been ignoring daily calls from the space station since then.

I shook my head. "Well, there's your problem, right there. This is Luna City now. Lunar Base Corporation is out of business." That set him back a step. He turned to his communications man. They tried fruitlessly to contact the space station for several minutes. Finally, Lieutenant Shaw turned back to me.

"Sir, I need to use your com room, please."

"Sure, no problem. Just hand over your firearms. We don't allow guns in the city limits."

"Oh, for Chrissake," blurted out one of the soldiers. Shaw spun on his heel and stared at the offending soldier. The soldier looked down, and Shaw turned back to us.

"What's to keep us from just marching down there?" He let anger harshen his voice.

"Me and the Python, that's our job. You may want to reconsider that, though." I smiled.

"Why?"

I turned to Frans. "I'll let Mayor Gould explain that. Sir?"

Frans stepped up and shook Shaw's hand. "Son, I'm sorry you're in the middle of this. Will you give an old man two minutes to try and straighten this out?"

"Sure, Mayor. Go ahead." Shaw glanced back at his squad. "Peeps, record this." The young soldier bearing the com set adjusted some controls.

"Yes sir, recording."

"Great. Good thinking, son. Let me get right to it. Lunar Base is no longer owned by Lunar Base Corporation and hasn't been associated with any Earth government for quite a while, which raises the question, under whose jurisdiction do we fall? Are we now our own country, or are we territory of one of the original coalition countries? If you step through that door with your guns, you are setting an irrevocable precedent. Either you will be a military force illegally invading a free and independent country, or you will be willfully breaking the laws of the municipality of Luna City. Either you start a war here, or you go to jail here." The same loudmouthed soldier guffawed. Lieutenant Shaw winced, but stood firm, silently pondering what Frans had said. We all waited.

"Uh, sir? Are we still recording?"

Shaw closed his eyes for a long moment. "Did I order you to stop recording, Peeps?"

"No, sir!"

"I didn't think so." Shaw turned to his men. "Sergeant. Form the men up."

"Yessir." The men exchanged salutes. Shaw turned back to us.

"Excuse us." He stepped back and closed the air lock.

As soon as the door closed, Frans laughed and turned to face us.

"I do believe Lieutenant Shaw is destined for great things."

"Ronnie's a bright cookie," agreed Patty. "We're lucky it was him they sent down."

"Patty the Python?" She shrugged at me. I had to kiss her to wipe the smirk off her face. I saw some heads stick around the corner of the corridor; people couldn't resist the urge to peek. I flashed them an OK and waved them back. It was less than two minutes before the air lock door reopened. Finals were over, time to see our grades.

Lieutenant Shaw stepped through the door, seeming a little older now. One of his men closed and locked it behind him. The exit cycle immediately started. Shaw cleared his throat.

"Mr. Gould, I've sent my men back to the lander. I'm sure you understand that I can't authorize the surrender of their weapons."

"A good decision, Lieutenant Shaw. What about yourself?" Frans pointed at Shaw's side arm.

"Sir, this pistol is a part of my uniform, as an officer and a gentleman. It is also a symbol of my military authority, much as Sheriff, uh, Lagger's side arm is a symbol of his civil authority. I hope you will recognize and accept this."

"Well said, son. No." Frans crossed his arms. Shaw didn't seem surprised at the refusal. "Son, when do you wear your side arm?"

"Sir?"

"Do you wear your side arm when you are off duty, Lieutenant? When you are performing your normal duties on your base? Or do you only wear it when invading your neighbors?"

Shaw looked over at Patty.

"Is the mayor here some kin to you, too?"

"My grandfather," she said with pride.

"I knew it. Mr. Gould, if I surrender my side arm to you, will you let me contact my superiors with your communications equipment?"

"Certainly. Peter?" Frans turned to nod at me, barely controlling a grin.

I pulled a receipt book from my shirt pocket, flipped to the right page, and handed it to Shaw.

"Just sign at the bottom. The pink copy is yours. Come by my office anytime to pick it up." He carefully filled out the receipt, removed his copy, and handed me the book, followed by his pistol.

"Mr. Gould, will you come with me?" Shaw gave a crooked smile. "I'm sure there will be some questions I can't answer without your help."

"Glad to, my boy. Will you still need Pete to arrange the visitation with the prisoners?"

"No, sir. I'd rather not get involved with that. Speaking my own opinion, I'm sure they are just where they belong." He winked at me and Patty. "After you, sir." They walked away from us, already deep in conversation. I grabbed Patty's hand and we watched until they turned out of sight. It seemed important.

> Patty is pregnant again, and the doctors think the new dietary supplements will prevent another miscarriage. We have every hope you'll be grandparents by Christmas. Yes, Mom, I'm still working on my thesis; I figure when time comes

to retire and settle down somewhere it would be nice to be called Doctor Lagger rather than "that old looney." Dad, the boom is well and truly started. There are a few working sites now that are quite similar to this one, the original that Frans Gould and Ray Davis discovered. We named it Daviston, after Ray. Politics seems to agree with Frans; we just celebrated his sixty-ninth birthday. Then, of course, he had to race off to an important meeting with the UN team. Alan's appeals are just about gone, and we are pushing for extradition. The Moon's first murderer should have to pay on the Moon. The rotten thing is that the people who ordered Alan may get away.

The new transceivers and satellites let me talk straight to ham operators on Earth and I'm not wasting time watching the furnaces. Dad, a Chinese boy named Liu downloaded his design for an asteroid belt rover to me, and I'm searching the markets for components. If I can put it together, I'll need you to sponsor him to Luna City. If he can cut it up here, then we may try Out There. . . .

—VoiceLetter to Parents, August 8, 2039

# STATE OF THE ART

*Written by*
**Vincent Di Fate**

## About the Author

*Vincent Di Fate has been cited by* People *magazine as "one of the top illustrators of science fiction." The many awards he has received for his paintings would attest to that, including the Frank R. Paul Award for Outstanding Achievement in Science Fiction Illustration, the Hugo Award for Best Professional Artist, the Chesley Award from the Association of Science Fiction/Fantasy Artists for Lifetime Artistic Achievement and the Arondo Award for Best Cover Art. He was also Guest of Honor at the 50th World Science Fiction Convention in 1992.*

*His work has been exhibited at the Hayden Planetarium in New York City, the National Air and Space Museum of the Smithsonian Institute in Washington, D.C., and the Kennedy Space Center.*

*In addition to providing us with his own art, he has written numerous articles on the topic and published four major books:* Di Fate's Catalog of Science Fiction Hardware, The Science Fiction Art of Vincent Di Fate,

The Art of Science Fiction Films *and the award-winning* Infinite Worlds: The Fantastic Visions of Science Fiction Art, *in which he collects works from many of the modern masters and discusses the significance of each artist. He continues to lecture extensively about the methods, meaning and history of his craft and has been a consultant for MCA/Universal, 20th Century Fox and MGM/United Artists. He is a professor at the Fashion Institute of Technology (State University of New York) where he teaches, among other things, a studio course in science fiction illustration. He is also a visiting professor in the Independent Study Degree Program at Syracuse University and is a recent past president of the Society of Illustrators.*

*He has been an Illustrators of the Future judge since 1996.*

As has been noted, this volume marks the twentieth edition of these collected award-winning stories. Not all of the past editions have included winners of the Illustrators of the Future Contest, however, as that competition was added a few years after the writing contest was launched and was well on its way to becoming an industry standard. By almost any measure, twenty years is something of a landmark and attaining landmarks is always a good time for reflection. So, what has science fiction been up to over the last two decades since the contests began? How has it changed? Where is the field of SF illustration headed? How does creating SF art differ from other forms of the illustrator's craft, and does it still offer exciting challenges to those sufficiently gifted with the imagination and artistic talent to do it?

Stories of the fantastic have always been with us, but the kind of stories we call science fiction really took shape in more recent times, when there was a credible accumulated body of science to support these kinds of speculative tales. In fact, although there were precursors that go back to ancient Greece and before, science fiction developed gradually in eighteenth- and nineteenth-century European literary circles in response to the Industrial Revolution. Mary Shelley's 1819 novel *Frankenstein* is frequently cited as an early example of what would be called, by the end of that century, "the scientific romance." Today we know these stories as *science fiction,* a term derived from "scientifiction," coined in the 1920s by Hugo Gernsback, publisher of *Amazing Stories,* the world's first SF magazine.

I mentioned stories of the fantastic, but what does that mean? Well, fantasy, supernatural horror and science fiction comprise what is collectively called fantastic fiction. Their mutual bond is that they contain story elements that stray far afield of the common life experience. The SF story differs from its related forms in that it attempts to rationalize its fantastic content by using the generally accepted principles of science to sustain its premise. Fantasy and supernatural horror also strive for a kind of internal consistency so that they will seem credible to the reader, but while the rules pertaining to what a vampire can and cannot do may mimic those of science, they are decidedly *not* science. And, typically, science itself provides the source of conflict on which the SF story revolves: creatures from outer space arrive on Earth with territorial ambitions that throw civilization into chaos; a scientist turns back time only to unravel the reality he wants so much to improve. The science fiction story, by its very nature, is about change. Its central conflict customarily arises from the impact of dramatic upheaval brought on by the introduction of radically new technologies—the catastrophic collision of science with the comforting flow of the familiar.

Most historians agree that although it had its roots in Europe, science fiction really hit its stride in twentieth-century America where authors like E. E. "Doc" Smith, John W. Campbell, Jr., Jack Williamson and then, later, Robert A. Heinlein, L. Ron Hubbard and Arthur C. Clarke were defining the scope of the genre in terms of pre– and post–World War II science and technology. And they did so with such fervor, that SF is often erroneously thought of as a uniquely American art form.

However, one could certainly not ignore the monumental influences of France's Jules Verne and of England's H. G. Wells. Their writings in the last quarter of the nineteenth century established a dichotomy that still endures in the literature of SF. On one hand we have a nearly consistent vision of a future enriched by the wonders of science in the works of Verne, while on the other we are shown a darker and more cynical view—one in which humanity, despite its intellectual advances, is never truly free of its limitations as a biological species. The invading Martians of Wells's 1897 novel *The War of the Worlds*, for example, are not overcome by humanity's resourcefulness, but rather by the airborne presence of common infectious bacteria to which the aliens have no natural immunities.

In the midst of all of this development and expansion, illustration found its single most challenging role in providing the reader with a visual frame of reference to help him navigate his way through the unfamiliar waters of the technological future. Of all the specialized types of literature, nowhere is the link between art and story stronger and more meaningful than in science fiction. As SF evolved, great talents emerged and became specialists in the genre: Albert Robida and Fred T. Jane (both of whom *wrote* as well as illustrated SF), Warwick Waterman Goble (who illustrated Wells's alien invasion novel for *Pearson's Magazine*); Frank R. Paul, Howard V. Brown, Hubert Rogers, Earle Kulp Bergey, Edd Cartier, Frank Kelly Freas and H.R. Van Dongen.

Since the early 1980s when Writers of the Future and its picture-oriented counterpart came into being, we've seen a brief but impressive expansion in horror literature (which, through the writings of the likes of Stephen King and Dean R. Koontz, actually became the literary mainstream for a time), an expansion in the popularity of epic fantasy, an explosion of SF and fantasy ideas in film, TV and videogames, but also a small but steady decline in the sales of science fiction books and, most especially, in SF magazines. What accounts for this curious state of affairs—a growing popularity in mainstream markets and in visual media, yet a decline in category readership? There is much speculation on the matter but few concrete answers. The more precipitous decline in magazine circulations (and this holds for *all* magazines—not just SF) seems to coincide with the rise of the Internet. Thus, many of these publications have gone on line in the hope of finding a new and sustainable audience.

If you were to ask an established illustrator what the field is like these days, he'd probably give you the direst view of how things are and where they're headed. He'd probably wax nostalgic about the good old days and how there was never enough time to do all the work that was being offered to him. But the fact is that for the illustrator the sky is *always* falling—even back in the good old days of which he now speaks so glowingly. Illustration is largely a freelance profession and, unlike those who work regular jobs with reliable, steady paychecks, the freelancer feels every twist and turn in the economy and every bump in the road. This is why the Society of Illustrators was founded back in 1901 and why the Graphic Artists Guild came into being in the 1970s. The formation of these organizations corresponds with major changes in the copyright law, a significant document of both federal and international law that greatly impacts how creative people earn their livings.

But even more important than the law itself are the changes that are taking place in the print media—and most of those changes are the byproduct of a relatively new thing in our lives, the personal computer. The Internet takes up a good part of our time as well as our entertainment dollars, and we use a computer to access it. The computer is also a useful tool in the creation of illustration, what with software programs like Illustrator, Photoshop, Painter and the like. Some are foolish enough to believe that buying the appropriate software alone is enough to transform just about anyone into an artist. That's a little like saying that a better typewriter will turn the average Joe into an Ernest Hemmingway. Certainly these machines can make the job easier, can possibly even enhance one's skills, but it still takes talent and a modicum of training to be good at writing or illustration.

What we're really observing, I think, is not so much the death of print, as some would claim, but rather that the traditional role of print is changing. Taking on a lot of its former functions is cyberspace—that elusive place in the digital/electronic universe where people go to be entertained and educated and where most of us do at least a portion of our daily work. Some examples of this include downloadable novels, music and movies, online news and weather services, online magazines, interactive websites and video games.

In another common commercial outlet for artists, the film and television industries, there was a time when an illustrator might have gotten a phone call from a movie producer to create some pre-production art for a science fiction or fantasy film. The artist would diligently produce a series of character drawings, or designs for spacecraft, or robots, or what have you, and those drawings would be passed along to a makeup shop or a prop department where the makeup designs and props would be fabricated for filming. But today, instead of involving all of those different creative units in the process of making movie effects, there's a kind of one-stop shopping, where a single artist, or small group of artists, manning computers will generate all the art that's needed, neatly putting the fruits of their labors into computer files where they can be combined later with live-action film elements in post-production to make the mind-boggling films and TV shows that we watch. And film and TV are voracious consumers of artwork, employing many tens of thousands of artists—in fact, many times more artists than were ever supported by the print media. Today's illustrator can be expected to create character and prop designs, pre-production "talking paper" (art used to sell a project to a studio or to secure funding), set and production designs, storyboards, and matte paintings for direct, on-screen use. But unless you are one of the small handful of movie lovers like myself who sits patiently through the ten-minute credit crawl at the end of a movie, most of these artists' names will be unknown to you.

So, one critical casualty of all this progress is the star status of the illustrator. Gone are the days when consumers would go out of their way to buy a magazine simply because it contained illustrations by the likes of Charles Dana Gibson, Howard Pyle, C. Coles Phillips, Norman Rockwell, or even Frank Frazetta. But, if the truth were told, those days were numbered nearly fifty years ago when commercial television was introduced and people turned to it for entertainment, information and news. In the now long-dead era before TV, reading books and magazines and making weekly trips to the movies were how most people entertained themselves.

The illustrators then were every bit the stars that the writers were in the magazines, and as many people knew who Dean Cornwell was and were familiar with his body of work as knew the name and works of Dashiell Hammett.

For me, my lifelong love affair with science fiction began in 1950 when, at the age of four, I saw my first science fiction film, *Rocketship X-M*. Soon after seeing that movie I discovered SF paperbacks and, eventually, the genre magazines. Over the intervening decades, few major books and films of the genre have eluded my attention. Throughout my life, as both a science fiction fan and a professional, I've spent a good deal of time noting the thematic preoccupations of the film genre as compared to the literature with which it shares its name, and the connection of both to the vast visual vocabulary that distinguishes the genre, sets it apart from other categories of storytelling, and draws to it its loyal following. Even those who would never dream of plunking down their hard-earned cash to see a science fiction movie or to buy a book know on sight, in all their widely varied manifestations, a robot, a spaceship, a ray gun and the plethora of other weird and fantastic objects that inhabit the science fiction universe.

As to the importance of science fiction in its many forms, these stories are first and foremost entertainment intended mainly to provide momentary release from the troubles of our daily lives. That some do far more than that—that they inform us, touch our hearts and give us pause to look beyond the obvious to matters about which we might otherwise be oblivious—speaks volumes about the influence and efficacy of the genre. Many of our shared values come from the collective experience of reading and moviegoing. On the silver screen and on the printed page, we learn of acts of heroism, of selfless sacrifice, of deep humanity, of altruism and compassion. We also learn of acts of heartless cruelty, but on few occasions are such acts glorified, no matter how gratuitous the violence may seem. Sadistic deeds, almost without exception, even in this most permissive of times, remain those of the depraved, the tyrannical and the despotic. The modern antihero, for all of his frailties, in the end behaves with moral conviction; or, having failed to do so, gives us pause to consider the fatal flaws in his judgment.

Informative and richly entertaining, yet in hindsight so many of the ideas of the SF genre, particularly of the mid-twentieth century, reveal the principal concerns and anxieties of their day. The somewhat detached nature of the science fiction story makes possible a kind of natural osmosis between real-world anxieties and their assimilation into the fantastic narrative. By happenstance, dumb luck or cunning design (and, in most cases, by virtue of all of these factors combined), SF books and movies hold a mirror to our culture that is at times far more revealing of the human condition than coexisting works of the mainstream set in the familiar world we all share.

The iconography of SF is another matter. So many of the images that litter the landscape of the science fiction universe hark back to the works of Hieronymus Bosch and before—perhaps to the very dawn of the human experience itself. There is the mandala, a Buddhist and Hindu religious and cultural symbol dating back to the sixth century B.C. and earlier—a disk-like object of concentric circles and other geometric shapes illuminated with the images of deities and of the cosmos. In the 1950s, at the height of the flying saucer scare, one could see in the phenomenon a link to this ancient symbol—this icon of ethereal beings who ply the heavens in a miraculous and mystical disk. The mandala was meant to represent the wholeness of the self: the supreme integration of mind, spirit and body. In the era of the cold war, with the fate of humanity hanging precariously in the breach, this desire for wholeness became a matter of widespread, if largely unspoken, wishful thinking.

I believe that the works of all visual artists operate on this deeper level—that beyond the manifest nature of art there is a latent order that enriches the artistic experience and is, in fact, its most durable aspect after the topicality of its apparent subject matter has at last faded away. But in the case of science fiction art, and due in large measure to its truly unique function, the art is never far removed from the concerns of the stories that it supports, regardless of the passage of time. Science fiction stories lie mainly in the future, in realities fabricated out of whole cloth and in which time itself is irrelevant and obsolescence impossible.

If there were nothing more to commend it, science fiction would still be a window on the potentialities of the future and a gateway to imagined realms. In this regard, it provides us with a sense of connectedness to the larger universe, which would be otherwise daunting and incomprehensible in its vastness. The sheer loneliness of such a concept is both terrifying and humbling, but through the imagination humanity attains not merely a sense of place, but of purpose. At the cutting edge of our dreams are the myriad manifest destinies of our possible tomorrows—boundless horizons to keep the wandering instincts of our species seeking to reach ever outward.

We each have a need to believe that what we do is important in the broader scheme of things. For me it comes in the heartfelt belief that, thus engaged with our place in the vastness and wonder of things, we have less of an inclination toward self-destruction. It is clear to me that imagination begins its journey from subjective rumination to shared experience by first being translated into pictures and words by those of us with a command of these communicative modes. What a glorious gift it is to be able to take the abstraction of thought and give it size, shape, color, dimension and the attributes of things real.

When I was young I used science fiction as a means of escape from the harshness of reality. It seems to me there is hope in the exercising of the imagination, for whether we have too little or too much, we can always imagine a better world in which all things are right and in their proper time and quantity and place. And having satisfied that fundamental need for well-being, we can then look to the horizon and at last come to the understanding that in our instinctive yearnings to go beyond, we can finally know no limits.

# SHIPWOMAN

*Written by*
**Roxanne Hutton**

*Illustrated by*
**Laura Diehl**

## About the Author

*Trained as an optical engineer, Roxanne (Roz) Hutton said she was very much her father's daughter growing up, building cars and rifles with him in Northern Vermont. "Studying and shooting WW II firearms gives me a feel for history very much reflected in the military science fiction I write."*

*"Warfare is a paradox engineers are especially suited to appreciate. We expend enormous amounts of rational creative energy in the service of the most irrational activity of all."*

*Her novel-in-progress is based on a story that received honorable mention in a previous quarter of the Writers of the Future Contest. "This is not my first attempt at a novel, but I think it's the best so far. I'd really like to make my name in short fiction first, so I'm taking my time with the novel."*

*Roxanne Hutton passed away before the release of this anthology. The publication of "Shipwoman" is the culmination of her dream, a dream shared by her fellow writers, and her family and friends.*

Redfar floated in her cabin, fuming at nothing and everything. She was tired of being treated like a baby when she'd qualified for every tech rating aboard. She was tired of the resentful looks from the men, since they had to wear clothes even when they were off duty. She was tired of talk about war, as if the buildup on the TallRock frontier was the only valid topic of conversation. She was tired of the other looks, reminding her she was the only female aboard, even if she only wore a breast-band for practice. But mostly she was tired of being far away from the city and her friends, even if *Quickray* was the best scout sub in the fleet. But more than anything else, she was tired of being bored out of her mind.

She sighed. The jet of perfluorocarbon fluid that left her mouth almost knocked her comp pad from her hands, adding to her sense that nothing was going right. She tried to focus on her lessons, as if she hadn't already studied diskrays and sea cucumbers to death. Even message traffic from Conn was routine and boring.

The next message on her pad blinked red. "BW: Sonar contact."

"TH: Altitude, bearing, range?" By the origination code, Turnhigh was watch commander. His typing came up on Redfar's pad quickly and smoothly.

Would it be worth it to leave the solitude of her bunk? Bigword was on sonar, and he had the best hearing in the fleet. If he thought a signature was significant, it probably was.

"BW: Bearing three three seven, distance five kliks, altitude 1020 and descending."

"TH: Sound?"

"BW: Odd. Quiet burbling, like batteries outgassing, lower in pitch. Creaking too, like metal strain, with a grating crunch to it."

"TH: Confirm descending."

"BW: Confirmed. Rate three meters per minute."

The "General Quarters" light flashed. Redfar saved her lesson and floated herself into a dutysuit, putting her comp pad in her pocket. If she waited until the crew was at their stations, she could probably swim up to the upper access to Conn without being ordered back to her quarters. She managed to sneak her way up there without being seen.

She was barely in position before Whiteleft arrived. From the grease clinging to his hands, her father had been back in propulsion working on that faulty fin motor.

"What is it?" he signed to Turnhigh.

"Strange sonar signature, descending. Might be a drift-bomb."

"In the middle of farming territory? Besides, drift-bombs are silent."

"Malfunctioning?"

"Too many coincidences. The truce has been holding. Breaking it with a faulty drift-bomb in the middle of nowhere is too absurd even for the TallRocks. Get us an intercept."

Widethumb was in the pilot chair. Turnhigh signed the order to him as Whiteleft put a soundbud in his ear, no doubt listening to the signature. He shook his head. His ears weren't as good as Bigword's, but he had more experience. Redfar wished she could hear too. She didn't dare call attention to herself. Commander's daughter or not, they'd send her to her room just when things were getting interesting.

There was a hum as *Quickray* turned and picked up speed. It was engineered to be as undetectable as possible, but there were times when speed was more important than silence, even in battle.

"WL: Time to intercept?" Whiteleft punched into his comm panel.

"TH: Three minutes fifty seconds."

"BW: What's that sound, Commander?"

Whiteleft flipped on the speakers. At full speed there was no point in bothering with soundbuds.

The sound was as Bigword described it, stress and strain in some rigid structure, plus an irregular, deep-pitched gurgle. But on top of it was a sound Redfar had never heard before. It reminded her a little of the herdbeasts they could detect swimming at very high altitude, but it was higher pitched and close. Redfar felt her hair standing up, even as perfluorocarbon flowed past her, and she felt her heart beating hard.

Terror! That's what the sound was. It tore at her ears, and worse, it screamed into her soul in a way she'd never felt before. Something human was in terrible distress, and somehow it . . . she . . . was making this horrible sound. Redfar didn't know how she knew, but she was certain something awful was happening.

"WL: Flank speed," her father punched. The hum of the motors increased. "And with all this noise we're making, we might as well go active."

The sonar pinged and screen 1 lit up.

"BW: It's huge," Bigword typed.

It was indeed one of the largest subs Redfar had ever seen, half the size of one of the cities. But the design was unfamiliar, and wrong. The fins were much too large, and it had strange vents and openings.

The computer was trying to get a configuration match, but contour images kept cycling on screen 2.

"TH: Look, the starboard stabilizer . . ."

The sub was tumbling slowly. As the starboard side came into view, the stern stabilizer was a mass of torn and crumpled metal. As more of that side appeared, more damage was visible. Something had torn most of the hull plating away, leaving a twisted frame over unfamiliar interior machinery. Haze drifted out, shifting quickly from sonar pulse to sonar pulse. Bubbles.

"WL: Prepare for crash salvage."

Salvage crews would already be suited, and with this command they would be sealing up, topping off the oxygen in their circulators, then purging the salvage hold and the escape locks. There was no way this giant sub would fit in the hold of a scout sub, but who knew what they might find? They might end up towing the giant home, and a tow cable was stored in the hold.

"WT: Stabilizing for intercept," Widethumb reported, and Redfar admired his skill as he slewed the *Quickray* to a stop with the escape locks facing the stricken sub. Whiteleft had barely reached for the "Execute Salvage" command before lock telltales turned red. Everyone was eager for the bonus a prize of this size could bring.

Bigword rapped on the sonar screen, a "Look at that" signal.

The top of the sub was stoving in, as if a giant thumb were squeezing it down.

"TH: It looks like the bow is imploding," Turnhigh punched, then gave Whiteleft an incredulous look.

Redfar found her mouth hanging open. How was it possible? A huge spate of bubbles poured from the hull.

"WL: They must have had a massive pump malfunction."

Bigword routed the messages from the divechief to the main comm screen.

"GD: Found crew lock. Power off, manual operational. Opening. What a mess. Blood in water. Bow crushed too deep to enter. Poor bastards. More rooms here. Deserted. No, one body. Woman. Crash revive?"

"WL: Affirmative."

"BW: Sonar contact."

Whiteleft gave Bigword a "What?" sign, rather than tie up the comm circuit.

"Ranging ping. I make it twenty or thirty kliks, out of the frontier."

"Will they risk it?" Turnhigh signed.

"Maybe not. But they had to hear us paint the sub. They won't get a picture, but they'll know something big is here. They might send a fast scout or attack sub to check."

"WL: Rig for silence as quickly as possible. In the meantime I want it to sound like there's a routine repair job going on out here. Make it sound like one of the big algae tanks broke loose. But get that sub ready for tow right away. Cut off those damn bubbles somehow."

Redfar kicked off toward the lower decks. A woman? If she'd been alive when the sub imploded, she could probably be revived. The water was barely above freezing, and if they got her breathing warm, oxygenated PFC fluid within four minutes she'd have a chance.

With all the divers either already out or leaving other stations to join in salvage duty, Dr. Finwall was going to need help down in sick bay, and Redfar had a revival qualification. A woman. Much as she liked the men, it was about time she had a woman to talk to, even if she was a foreigner. Whoever this strange sub belonged to, it certainly wasn't DeepReef.

Finwall was alone, waiting by the emergency revival lock when Redfar swam in. He gave her a relieved nod as she took the aide position.

They waited. The divers were coming as quickly as they could, but it seemed like forever.

"Any news?" Finwall signed. Redfar gave him an "About what?" shrug. "Your appointment?"

"No. Nothing."

He nodded sympathetically. "Don't worry. I'm sure you'll be appointed. And even if you aren't, you would make one hell of a shipwoman."

"I haven't been studying my brains out to end up as wife and mother to a sub full of horny crewmen."

Finwall gave her a chiding look and signed, "A shipwoman is highly respected, and the best are just as important to operations as morale. You'll have your choice of subs. God knows there aren't enough to go around."

"But I like *Quickray*. And I don't want to be shipwoman to my own father. If I can get through the academy, I could come back as an officer."

"Good point."

There were clunks from outside. The revival timer was almost up to two minutes. Turnhigh would have set it to start at the implosion.

The lock cycled. Water spilled in with the woman, settling toward the floor of sick bay where it would be sucked up automatically. Redfar grabbed the woman's legs and eased them onto the table as Finwall towed her body backward. Two minutes five seconds. She was nice and cold, a good sign.

The oxygen circulator was all ready, so Redfar intubated her as Finwall tried to rip the front of her uniform. It was some kind of very strong fabric, but it yielded to a pair of bandage scissors.

She glanced at the comm screen. Two minutes fifteen seconds. The divers were looking for someplace to hook the tow cable.

Finwall held defib electrodes in place. Redfar got the tube settled and the circulation started just in time for him to give her the "clear" sign. She pulled her hands away and he hit the discharge button.

There was a tingle in the fluid as the defibrillator discharged. Right away the monitor started to beep and a heartbeat showed, stabilizing within a few beats. Finwall centered an oxygen monitor over her radial artery, pressed it in, and readings appeared. She was picking up very nicely.

"Well, she's healthy enough," he signed, then he carefully removed the respirator tube. Her chest was rising and falling strongly. Redfar could see distortion in the fluid as it rushed in and out of her mouth. She was going to live. Finwall readied an injector. Stimulants and antiradicals, no doubt.

There was more traffic on the comm screen. The power system of the sub had gone active. Lights had come on, and there were assorted whirs from machinery. Just as suddenly the screen went crazy, as if the comp were dumping files. Redfar turned her attention back to Finwall and their patient.

He was checking her pupil response. He nodded. "Good. At this rate she should be coming around in a few minutes. Slender little thing, isn't she?"

The woman was very slender, her chest barely wider than her hips, although she seemed well-proportioned otherwise. Her features were delicate, with the tiniest nose Redfar had ever seen. Her hair was black, and there was something odd about her eyelids, an extra fold of skin.

They were cleaning her up and peeling off the electrodes when Whiteleft swam in.

"How is she?" he signed.

Finwall gave him a nod. "Heart kicked on the first try, good blood oxygen. We were under three minutes, so she should make a full recovery. I think she's fairly young, which helps. There were no other survivors?"

He shook his head. "Her sub collapsed like an aluminum can. It's possible there may have been someone in the bow who didn't get crushed, but there wasn't a way to get to them in time. We're still trying to figure out what made the damned thing squash. And we've had a couple of ranging pings. The TallRocks are sending out a scout."

"That's all we need."

The woman's eyelids were flickering.

Redfar waved her hand for attention and signed, "She's waking up."

Suddenly the woman started to thrash so violently that the men had to grab her arms and hold her down. Redfar tried to sign reassuringly, but the woman's eyes were wild with panic, and she seemed to be having trouble breathing. Her mouth opened wide and expelled a hard stream of fluid, then gulped more only to force it out again.

Not knowing what else to do, Redfar reached out and stroked the woman's face. Slowly the panic left her eyes, and her breathing settled down a bit. Gradually she relaxed, apparently realizing she was safe, even if she was among strangers. Finwall and Whiteleft released her arms and let her lie back.

She felt her throat, then strangely she waved her hand in front of her face.

"Are you feeling better?" Redfar signed.

The woman looked at her blankly. It seemed as if she recognized that Redfar was trying to talk to her, but didn't understand.

"Can she be from so far away that she doesn't understand Usign?" Redfar signed to her father.

"Everyone in the world uses Usign. The TallRocks use some pretty odd signs, but they can sign it when they want to."

The woman pointed at the comm screen.

"Where am I?" a message read. There was no origination code.

They gaped at her. "I'll be damned," Whiteleft signed. How had she done that? He gestured for the keyboard, so the doctor unclamped it and handed it over.

"WL: You're on DeepReef scout sub *Quickray*."

"The others! What about the others?"

"WL: You were the only one we could get to in time. I'm sorry."

She closed her eyes for a moment. "Thank you. Thank you for trying."

"WL: I'm Whiteleft, commander of the *Quickray*. Who are you?"

"Mitsume, shipwoman of *Faraday*."

"WL: *Faraday?*"

"The ship."

Redfar's brow crinkled. What kind of names were Mitsume or *Faraday?* She had no idea what signs to use for either of them. She caught a look from Finwall to her father. This was a shipwoman? She didn't seem pretty enough.

"WL: Your sub was heavily damaged. We're towing it to our base. Where is it from?"

"Colony 2721. We call it home. Or at least we did."

"WL: What are its coordinates?"

Redfar saw what her father was after. If there was an unknown country out there, with unknown craft and perhaps powerful weapons, DeepReef needed to know about it as quickly as possible.

"Green sector, segment 1001, Iota three. Is there a problem?"

Those were coordinates? They made no sense to Redfar, no sense at all.

Messages were coming in from Conn. The TallRock scout was getting closer, and the divers were reporting ready to tow. Whiteleft ordered Turnhigh to start descending as soon as everyone was inside. They'd rigged buoyancy modules to the foreign sub to stabilize it for towing.

"I have to get up to Conn. Can she come with me?" Whiteleft signed to the doctor. Finwall gave the monitor a look, then nodded. "She's recovering faster than I expected." The woman let him peel off the oxygen sensor. Redfar thought to get her a blouse, but then she noticed that the cut in the woman's dutysuit had disappeared. The fabric was unbroken. There was no sign it had ever been cut.

Before she could mention it, her father gestured to Mitsume and swam toward the hatch. The woman followed, swimming after him awkwardly. Perhaps she was feeling the aftereffects of three minutes of death? Certainly a shipwoman wouldn't be clumsy.

There was a lurch. The woman looked around nervously, but Redfar knew it had to be the tow cable at the end of its slack. Sure enough, when they got to Conn the knot-meter showed they were underway and descending, on course for the maintenance sub serving the farming zone. If the TallRock sub was going to chase them, it would have to negotiate the rough terrain of the seabed as well as DeepReef's defensive systems.

Whiteleft swam to the command station and belted in. "WL: What's the TallRock doing?"

"TH: She's coming in like she's got a torpedo on her tail, making about thirty-five knots. By the sound she's one of their fast attack subs. She's coming in active and noisy as hell."

"WL: Damn. That means there's another behind her running near silent. Looks like we can kiss that truce goodbye. How'd we make out silencing our tow?"

"TH: Fair. The creaking has died down, but she's making a lot of machinery sounds."

"Would it help if I took the *Faraday* down to minimal power levels?" Once again the woman was able to talk on the comm screen without touching a keyboard.

Turnhigh turned and stared at her.

Whiteleft typed, "WL: If it will cut down on the noise emissions. How can you do that with no one aboard?"

"It's done."

"WL: Bigword?"

"BW: We're still getting a little bubbling, but the machine noises are dying down."

"WL: You're in communication with your ship?"

"BW: We're being ranged again. The TallRock has closed to 5.5 kliks."

"WL: Damn. We're too slow. Prepare for crash dive."

"No!" the woman typed without typing.

"WL: Why not?" Whiteleft typed it as a simple query, but he turned and glared at Mitsume.

"My systems aren't designed to survive high pressure. We're too deep as it is. Go no deeper."

"WL: We have no choice. Execute crash dive."

"WT: Executing."

Widethumb pushed the control yoke forward, and Redfar felt a change in angle in the near weightlessness of the fluid. But she felt no increase in pressure on her ears. She looked at the altitude gauge. It hadn't moved.

"TH: We're not diving," Turnhigh reported, "I'm reading a buoyancy increase in the remotes." He sent a command through the auxiliary circuit, studying the screen. "TH: They're not responding. The tow is dragging us higher."

Whiteleft typed furiously at his station. Command override codes flashed across his screen, but the altitude gauge remained stubbornly at 972 meters. Then it went to 973. "WL: As soon as I reduce buoyancy it goes right back to max, as if someone is countermanding me."

"I am grateful that you rescued me, but you may not take me deeper."

"Flank speed," Whiteleft signed to Widethumb.

"The cable won't take the strain," Turnhigh signed back, and Widethumb hesitated.

"BW: Message from the TallRock, and we're getting painted," Bigword typed.

It was obvious the enemy sub was painting them. The *Quickray* was made to be as transparent to sound as possible, and the pings of the enemy sonar were close and clear.

"TRAS117: DeepReef scout sub: Release your tow immediately," the incoming message read.

"Damn!" Whiteleft signed.

"Why do they tell you to release *Faraday?*"

"WL: Isn't it obvious? They want to take it."

"Why? You've already rescued me."

Redfar wondered if this was a woman or a child.

"WL: They want to salvage it."

"Salvage? Systems are active."

"WL: So much the better."

"They would salvage an active vessel?"

"WL: Of course."

"Unacceptable. Are you at war with them?"

"WL: There was a truce, but they've broken it."

"Can you outfight them or outrun them?"

Whiteleft drummed on the edge of the keyboard. This was no time for a discussion. "WL: No. *Quickray* is a scout sub with two torpedo tubes, and we can't outrun them with your sub in tow."

"Is sonar their only sensing system?"

"WL: Yes."

"If you ascend to 1000 meters, I will activate my propulsion and disrupt their sonar. Agreeable?"

"WL: How will you . . . ? Yes. Do it."

Widethumb pulled back on the yoke and increased thrust. Immediately the knot-meter and altitude started increasing.

More of Mitsume's typing appeared. "There are two other subs, bearing three three seven and three two five. Recommend course of one three three."

Whiteleft turned around to look at her appraisingly. "WL: That will carry us on an intercept with the first one."

"True, which they aren't likely to anticipate."

"WL: They'll see us."

"We're invisible to their sonar."

"WL: That's impossible."

Mitsume shrugged. "I've set up a phased array of hydrophones to create an interference pattern and cancel our return echoes, as well as our source noises. Analysis of their signals indicates they don't have enough processing speed to compensate. It may be advisable to use your maximum speed."

Another message appeared on the comm board. "TRAS117: DeepReef scout sub: Surrender at once or we'll open fire."

"WL: Give us flank speed."

Widethumb nodded and shoved the throttle forward.

There was a faint hum, nothing like the usual muted roar of *Quickray*'s top speed.

"BW: I think her jammer's working," Bigword typed, "I'm not getting return echoes from us or the pings from the TallRock."

Suddenly there was a loud swoosh noise followed by buzzing.

"BW: Torpedo launch. I make two standard TallRock fish, probably high explosive."

There was a tremendous jolt, a pulse of pressure more felt than heard, then another. The horizon gauge swung wildly. Redfar was almost thrown from her handhold.

"WL: Report!"

"BW: Double explosion. Distance about five kliks. The damned TallRock fish blew."

"WL: What the hell? Malfunction?"

"BW: Two at once? Not likely."

"The casings were only steel. My low-frequency comm laser was sufficient."

No one typed anything. Widethumb made a sign Redfar had never seen before, to no one in particular.

Bigword clamped his hands to his ears, obviously listening to his soundbuds. Then he started typing. "BW: The TallRock is screaming for help. I think she's got some serious structural damage, judging from the alarms. There's also an encoded message, quite a long one."

"WL: Why don't you use your laser to finish them off?" Whiteleft typed.

Mitsume looked displeased. "Killing of humans is not permissible."

"WL: But they tried to kill us."

"A squandering of precious personnel and resources. Save it for the Delnaks."

"WL: Delnaks? That's a fairy tale. Stories to scare little children."

"A fairy tale that blew me out of the sky and into your infernal ocean? A fairy tale that killed my men, and that's killed trillions of humans in the last century alone? A fairy tale that's close to wiping us from the universe?"

"WL: The universe? You mean Oceanus? We get intelligence from everywhere in the world, and no one's even seen a Delnak. And there aren't more than two hundred thousand people anywhere."

Mitsume's eyes widened. "Two hundred thousand? Is that all? What is your rate of infant mortality from genetic disease?"

Whiteleft shrugged and shook his head.

"TH: Commander, the comp is acting up again."

The comp screen was a jumble of commands and file listings, the same way it appeared down in sick bay right after they revived Mitsume.

"WL: What the hell is it?"

"TH: Someone is downloading files. Looks like medical records and history files."

"I apologize. It's necessary." Mitsume wore a faraway look. Redfar shook her head. Of course. Somehow the woman was a swimming comm system, in communication with her ship. Since she could access the comm boards, she could certainly access the comp.

"WL: Stop immediately! How dare you!"

Mitsume's face turned grim. "Twenty percent mortality, despite screening and gene therapies. Your separate political entities are not intermarrying. Population is declining. Endpoint projected in six generations."

"WL: What do you mean, 'endpoint'?"

"Birthrate of zero."

"WL: Are you saying we're dying out?"

"I'm afraid so. Depending on how rapidly technical competence fails, you have barely a hundred years left." She shook her head. "Which is more than the rest of us. You need us, Commander Whiteleft, almost as much as we need you."

"BW: Sonar contact."

"WL: Now what?"

Bigword gave an apologetic smile as he typed, "BW: Two other sources have gone active, bearings three three five and three two three, right where she said they'd be. Now I'm getting ranging sources from all over the frontier. And return echoes. The interference system isn't working."

The woman shook her head. "Too many sources. It's an n-body problem that can't be solved without a very large quantum computer. I'm suppressing for the nearest targets, but I can't suppress them all."

"BW: The two nearer subs are in pursuit. Torpedo launch."

Despite the greater distance, the sound was much louder.

"BW: I make sixteen fish. They must have dumped all their tubes."

Whiteleft typed, "WL: Activate countermeasures. Can you handle this many torpedoes at once, Mitsume?"

"I don't know."

There was one explosion, then another, then another.

"I'm timing to maximize hit probability and minimize laser recycle time. Estimate success on fourteen out of sixteen."

Two more explosions in quick succession.

"WL: Up five degrees, ten degrees to port. Drop decoys."

"Will target foremost first."

"WL: Negative. Some may be wire-guided. Target rear torpedoes to destroy wires and force internal guidance."

"Complying."

There were more explosions. Redfar tried to keep count, but they came so fast she lost track. On top of the thunderous bangs was the buzz of their motors, getting louder and closer.

"BW: They're not buying the decoys. Four left and gaining."

"WL: Damn. The TallRocks have improved their ECM."

There were three more bangs in close succession. The lights dimmed as the shock wave shook them.

"One left," Turnhigh's nervous hands signed.

"Laser inoperative."

"BW: Twenty seconds to impact."

"TH: The tow is slewing to starboard. One of the buoyancy modules just detached."

"BW: I see it in the fish sonar. It's dropping right into . . ."

There was one last explosion, and it hit Redfar like the fist of God. Her brain seemed to go numb and dark. She saw Mitsume's face, then her father's. Slowly the Conn came into focus. One of the main lights was out, but the telltales showed green. They'd survived.

Whiteleft was out of his seat, looking closely at Mitsume. She looked pale, and a thin haze of blood colored her exhalations.

"TH: Is she all right?" Turnhigh typed.

She made a gesture, a reassuring push away. "Give me a minute."

"Get Finwall up here," Whiteleft signed. "WL: Did you say your laser is out?"

"Too much energy is reflected by the water. The lens heated up and cracked. Repair will take about ten minutes. Additional cooling for the lens will take twenty-five."

"WL: Dropping that module on the torpedo was good thinking."

"The Delnaks have taught us to adapt."

"WL: Well, we're in one piece. Sub status?"

"TH: Assorted outages, mostly lights. Heatpack output up and clean," Turnhigh reported.

"WL: TallRocks?"

Bigword let go of his soundbuds. "BW: They went silent as soon as they launched the fish. Not getting a thing."

"They're following our original course, but we're gaining distance. I detect more subs approaching from north and northeast. Six are attempting an intercept, ten are moving to cut us off."

"WL: How are you detecting them?"

"Deepscan. It was developed for asteroid mining, but it's a way to detect Delnaks at interstellar distances. I've adapted it."

Interstellar? Redfar knew Oceanus orbited a star, and there were many stars out there. The scientists had proven it ages ago. But it was impossible to go to such a high altitude. A sub would explode, no matter how strong it was.

"I've made some adaptations. *Faraday* is safe down to eight hundred meters. You may descend if you wish. It will be two hours before maximum depth adaptations are made."

"TH: Commander? We're completely exposed up here."

Whiteleft shook his head. "WL: We'd be just as exposed at eight hundred. Program a decoy to descend gradually toward the Terra Range, with a very faint recording of our weird sounds and a twenty degree reflector. No, make that three decoys, with one at altitude and a divergent course, and one descending right under us and divergent by one degree. Drop a message buoy with our situation, too. With any luck we can at least make the TallRocks split their force to chase echoes."

"TH: I'm on it."

Whiteleft turned his full attention back to Mitsume, and he switched his keyboard to a private channel. "WL: I don't think I have to tell you we'd be very interested in your weapons and scanning technology, especially your repair and adaptation systems. But why do you say you need us?"

"We're at war with the Delnaks, and we're losing."

"WL: Losing?"

"We encountered them nearly two thousand years ago. Ships started to disappear, then whole colonies. There was a science colony here on Oceanus, as a matter of fact. Destroyed over a thousand years ago. We had no idea anyone survived. The hyperdepth researchers must have rescued whoever they could and adapted their fluid breathing systems to long-term use. What I'd like to know is why the Delnaks haven't taken you out."

"WL: They don't know we're here?"

"Possible but unlikely. They're very thorough, we've seen too many times."

"WL: Why haven't I ever heard about this? Why isn't it part of our history?"

"I'm not certain. There are irregularities in your historical file systems. It appears as if files were deleted deliberately."

Redfar pulled out her portable and typed, "RF: They didn't want us to know."

"WL: Redfar, I think you'd better go to your bunk."

"No, let her stay. She's right, I think. They must have decided it was the only way they'd be safe from the Delnaks."

"WL: But we're dying out?"

Redfar saw what Mitsume was driving at. "RF: If the survivors were the remnant of a colony, the gene pool was too small. That's basic biology, right? That's why you wanted to know our infant mortality rate?"

"WL: But couldn't the Delnaks kill them . . . kill us by dropping bombs?"

"I don't know. I think it's crucial we find out. When we crash-landed I had no idea there were humans living down here."

"WL: And you would have died if we hadn't rescued you."

"I tried to adapt the ship, but there was too much battle damage."

"RF: What does this have to do with us?"

"WL: Good question. We need you to diversify our gene pool, if nothing else. What can we possibly do for you?"

"Refuge."

"WL: What? Bring the entire human race to Oceanus? Even with your technology, you've implied that there are trillions of people out there."

"No longer trillions, but hundreds of billions. You're right, obviously all of us can't come here. We've improved medical technology, so most of us should be able to adapt. But Oceanus isn't the only watery world. We could probably recreate your deep-fluid technology and sign language, although it would save time and millions of lives if we can use what you've already learned."

"RF: They need the idea."

"Precisely. We must hide a substantial portion of the human race in the depths of watery worlds. There were signs that the Delnaks were in decline when we first encountered them. I've heard a theory that the conflict with us has reversed their decline. If we 'vanish,' they may decline again. In time we can emerge, and this time destroy them before they can recover, or at least eliminate their interstellar capability. If hiding in the depths works, it could save us from extinction."

"RF: But if what you say is true, it could take thousands of years."

"Is oblivion better?"

"WL: Where do we go from here?"

"Repairs to my flight systems are almost done. The Delnaks generally don't remain nearby, once our ships are destroyed. I should be able to sneak back to my base with a copy of your databases. From there the information can be transmitted all over the human sphere in a matter of days, and I'm certain we'd start a crash program to set up colonies. You could expect colonists to begin arriving in a few weeks."

"WL: That quickly?"

"We're desperate. And we know how to adapt. Not everyone will think it's a good idea, but the ones who do will come."

Finwall was hovering nearby. Redfar remembered that he'd been ordered to Conn. He moved in closer and peered at Mitsume. "Commander, she doesn't look well."

She looked very pale, and the fluid she exhaled was tinged with red, perhaps more than before. Her lips looked awfully blue.

"My lungs are having trouble adapting, and my nanomechs aren't keeping up. Those shock waves . . ."

"WL: Get her to sick bay. Redfar, give him a hand. What's the status of the TallRock subs?"

"TH: I've got a tactical plot set up."

"WL: Damnation! They must have been preparing for an all-out attack during the truce. This prize has triggered it."

Redfar wanted to have a look at the plot, but she helped the doctor tow Mitsume to sick bay. She could put it up on the screen there.

"Let's get her on the table, and you set up the oxygen circulator while I examine her," Finwall signed.

They put her on the table and strapped her in place, and Redfar activated the oxygen jet. She positioned the nozzle of enriched PFC fluid so that it was directed at Mitsume's mouth and nose as Finwall put a new oxygen monitor on her wrist. The plot came up on the medical monitor.

"FW: No wonder she's cyanotic. Look how low she is. Okay, the circulator's helping."

Her blood-oxygen level was improving, but below normal. Her eyes met Redfar's.

"I have to get back to *Faraday*."

"FW: You're in no condition to travel."

"I have to go high enough to breathe air again. My nanomechs can't repair my alveoli fast enough."

"FW: Air? What's that?"

"A mixture of gasses. Humans evolved to breathe gasses, not fluids. What do you think vocal cords are for? We evolved to communicate by sound."

"FW: They're an evolutionary vestige, like your tonsils or appendix."

"You've never heard music, have you?" Mitsume asked, pity on her bloodless face.

Finwall shook his head doubtfully.

"RF: What if she's telling the truth?"

"I am. You have to get me back to *Faraday*. I only have about fifteen minutes left, even with your circulator."

The comm screen was still carrying the traffic from Conn. Redfar called up the tactical plot. The first large group of TallRock subs was getting close. She was relieved to see a group of DeepReef subs were on an intercept course, but then she saw that they were too far away. Time. What they needed was time.

A message appeared on the medical monitor. "WL: How is she? We need her up here to use her laser."

"FW: We're losing her. She says she has to get back to her sub, or she only has fifteen minutes left."

"WL: Do you believe her?"

Finwall studied the monitor for a moment. "FW: Yes, I do."

The comm screen turned red: battle stations.

"WL: Okay people, our only option is a backsack. Give me total silence. Cut us to quarter speed, give me a course of zero nine zero. Mitsume, can you cut your ship's noise to a minimum, and blind those two pursuing subs to us?"

"I can try. I must warn you: when I die, *Faraday* will lose power. It may snap the cable when the thrusters cut out."

"TH: We're at quarter, at zero nine zero. The TallRock attack subs are gaining fast."

"BW: I don't think they see us."

"WL: Can't you program your ship's comp to provide a steady thrust, even if you die?"

"I'm shipwoman."

"WL: I don't understand."

"I'm *Faraday* Mitsume. I am the ship, and the ship is me. When I die, it dies."

"WL: How can that be?"

"We've had to adapt."

"WL: Finwall, you have to keep her alive."

"FW: Damn it, I'm trying."

"TH: They're passing us, maintaining course. They missed us."

"WL: Program one of our fish for each. If we can take them out it will buy us a little time."

"Killing humans is not permissible."

"WL: We have no choice. Prepare to launch."

"TH: Program loaded."

"WL: Give them half a klik, then fire."

"FW: That's too close. The shock wave will kill her."

"WL: Any farther and we can't be sure of a hit, and they'll have a chance to return fire."

"Killing humans is not permissible!"

"WL: Okay, make it eight-tenths. That's the best I can do."

"FW: It's not enough."

"TH: Four-tenths, five . . ."

"WL: Come to parallel course."

"WT: Turning. Ready to fire."

"TH: Seven-tenths, and . . ."

"WL: Fire."

There was a whoosh as tubes discharged torpedoes, then the buzz of their motors. Mitsume looked up at Redfar, and she suddenly reached out and grasped Redfar's hand so hard that pain shot up her arm.

"Without a shipwoman, *Faraday* is dead."

A shock wave hit them. The lights dimmed, but Redfar managed to cling to consciousness this time.

Mitsume's eyes were open but lifeless. Thick red flowed from her mouth and nose for long, long seconds, then stopped. The grip on Redfar's hand relaxed.

"BW: The torpedoes exploded prematurely. The two subs are still intact, but I'm hearing alarms all over the place."

"WL: Damn you, Mitsume! Reverse course. Give us as much distance as you can, in case they manage to launch."

"WT: Turning. She's sluggish."

"TH: I'm not reading any thrust from the tow. She's dead."

"WL: Finwall?"

The doctor reached down and closed Mitsume's eyes, then reached for the keyboard. "FW: What the hell do you expect? She's dead. Total respiratory collapse."

"BW: We're being painted. The TallRock battle group is headed right for us. The tow is reflecting like a damn algae tank."

"WL: Give us all the speed the tow cable will take, and see if you can't get us closer to our subs. How soon will the TallRocks be in torpedo range?"

"TH: Maybe thirty minutes. After that, they can't hardly miss a target like the tow."

"WL: Take us fifty percent past the rating of that cable. We don't have much to lose."

"TH: Commander, why don't we cut the tow loose? We can't save it, and at least then we'll have a chance of getting out of this ourselves."

Redfar grabbed the keyboard from Finwall. "RF: You can't do that!"

"WL: Redfar, stay out of this. Help the doctor take care of Mitsume's body. That's an order."

The comm screen went blank. Redfar was sure her code was locked out of the Conn system as well.

"Damn you, Father," she signed in frustration.

Finwall's face was sympathetic, but she could see he had more bad news too. "I have to do an autopsy. If you don't want to help, I'll certainly understand."

"I don't think I could stand that."

"Just help me get her undressed."

She knew it was awkward undressing a body alone, so she nodded. Finwall reached for the bandage scissors, but when he touched Mitsume's dutysuit, it fell open easily. There was a seam where none had been before, and it parted readily down her arms and legs. Together they eased it from under her. The feel of the fabric was strange, soft yet resilient.

Mitsume's build was compact, but otherwise she looked like a perfectly ordinary woman. Redfar expected to see some electrodes, or some kind of device that connected her to her ship. Internal?

Finwall switched on the medical scanner, and an image of Mitsume's body filled the screen. "Well, she's certainly human, although her lungs are awfully small. No sign of computer implants. I wonder if they have telepathic technology, on top of everything else?"

Redfar shrugged. She could still see Mitsume's grieving eyes, and her last words on the medical monitor. *Without a shipwoman,* Faraday *is dead.* She stroked the fabric of the dutysuit.

"Can I keep this?" she signed.

"I think your father will want to give it to the scientists, along with everything else. If we get out of this alive." Finwall studied her. "She was only here for a little while, but she meant a lot to you, didn't she?"

She didn't know how, but this sad, brave foreign woman had touched her. Maybe it was growing up with nothing but men around. She'd always wanted a sister. She nodded.

Finwall smiled. "I'm sure it will be safe with you. Why don't you keep it for me, until it's time to pack it up?"

"Thank you," she signed, and at his nod she swam out toward her cabin.

Once inside, she slipped out of her dutysuit and let the warm fluid caress her. It was all too familiar. Home.

She couldn't let go of the suit, but kept running the silky fabric through her fingers. Without really thinking about it, she slipped it on. The seams joined themselves together quickly and smoothly. It should have frightened her, one little part of her thought, but instead she felt anticipation.

She was huge. She could see the inside of her bunk, but she could see all around her as well, the sleek tube of *Quickray,* the men inside, the enemy subs closing in.

Illustrated by Laura Diehl

She could hear their electronic voices, see their comm screens, hear the toneless buzz of the comp. She had a thousand hands, a thousand ears, a thousand legs, a thousand eyes. It was a sensation both exciting and frightening.

She could see words, but not with her eyes. They were just there, inside her head, in a way more like sound than sight.

"We have time to make one last recording, and one last attempt to save us. We're placing a compulsion on the suit, tailored to the young woman. We can only hope and pray that she's young enough to form the link, and that there's time to establish it. If this message is playing, then we have succeeded.

"It's up to you, Redfar. The compulsion is removed." Suddenly the suit was just a suit, even though she knew what it was. "Everything depends on you. More is at stake than the fate of DeepReef against TallRock. You know that. But if you accept the role of shipwoman, there will be no turning back. You will leave Oceanus and everything and everyone you've known, perhaps forever. If you do not, you will go on with your life. You won't live to see the end of the human race, or even the end of your own people. That's all we can do. Choose."

She hesitated, watching the TallRock subs inch closer.

She yanked open the hatch to the hallway. As she swam for the stern as fast as she could, she could see the message traffic in Conn.

"TH: I tell you it's powered up. We're picking up speed and we're invisible again. The woman lied to us."

"WL: I don't think it's that simple. Finwall, what's going on down there?"

"FW: Nothing much. The autopsy is showing a healthy young woman with ruptured lungs. What did you expect?"

Redfar reached the dive station. The divers were there, suited up, playing games on comp terminals while they waited for orders.

Gatedock nodded to her as she unracked her dive suit. "Wants you down here, does he? I guess it's as bad as I've heard," he signed.

"I suppose." If the sub was hit, divers had a chance of surviving if help came before their oxygen ran out. Capture was better than death.

She ran through standard suit drill, sealed up, and topped off her tank, moving closer to the lock as she did. As soon as she could she kicked inside and yanked the hatch shut.

Normally Gatedock would be able to override the controls, but she could see the operating program. She bypassed the necessary connection and toggled the lock cycle. Water flooded in.

The comm screen in her helmet lit up. "GD: What the hell do you think you're doing?" His face showed outside the inspection window.

"Sorry, Gatedock. It's necessary."

She accessed the screen in Conn. "Prepare for tow-cable release."

"WL: Who is that? Mitsume, we've got six subs on our tail. Are you alive in your ship's systems?"

"I'm sorry, Father, I have to go."

The outer door opened, turbulence from their fast passage dragging her toward the hatchway.

"WT: We're losing power!"

"WL: Redfar! Where are you?"

"GD: She's suited up and about to exit."

"WL: Get her in here. Override."

"GD: Tried that. Not functioning."

The turbulence dropped with their speed. As soon as she dared she kicked out, then restored helm control to Widethumb. A moment later she released the cable from *Faraday*'s nose and retracted the nose ring. Her ship loomed up to her, slowing. A touch of thrust brought the open outer hatch to her. Warm, rich fluid would be waiting. She kicked in and cycled the lock.

"Father, Mitsume is dead. Someone has to take over for her. Otherwise it's the end of everything."

"FW: It was the damned suit. I let her take it."

She fired the thrusters, altering course to carry her away from *Quickray*. She had to go up. But not too fast or her systems would be damaged. She wasn't designed for this.

The TallRock subs were following with forty-eight torpedoes, and in fifteen seconds forty-eight more. More than she could handle.

But her comm laser could penetrate sub hulls as easily as torpedo casings.

*Killing humans is not permissible.*

"WL: Redfar, wait. Let's talk about this."

"No time, Commander. I have to get to the surface. It's the only way. I have to tell Mitsume's people what happened and give them our data."

"WL: Redfar, you're my daughter. I order you to stand down and return to the *Quickray*."

"TH: There isn't any way to do that, sir. The TallRock subs are closing fast."

"TRAS201: DeepReef Subs: You are in torpedo range, and completely out-tubed. Surrender at once, or you will be destroyed. Respond."

"I'm sorry, Father, but I'm shipwoman now. You'll have to adapt to that. Will you help me complete my mission or not?"

She could see the enemy subs with her deepscan, hear the distant buzz of their comm systems and comps. If only they were close, so she could scramble their codes? No, there were too many. Even if she surrendered to draw them in, they could still destroy her before she could disable them all.

"WL: You're my daughter."

"Yes, but I'm shipwoman too. If *Faraday* dies, I die. If they capture me, they'll dismantle me. They'll destroy me as completely as the Delnaks would."

"TRAS201: DeepReef Subs: Stand down. Now. Respond immediately or be destroyed."

The inner hatch opened. The living quarters were pristine, newly repaired by the ship's horde of nanomechs. The bodies of Mitsume's lovers and companions had been absorbed. They were part of *Faraday* now, atom by atom. She removed her helmet and swam to her combat cell, well-protected in *Faraday*'s heart.

"WL: You haven't left me much choice."

"Sorry."

"WL: Yes, I am too. What's the plan?"

"I'm ascending, course one six zero. I can only ascend at ten degrees and twenty-two knots. You take a reciprocal course, and crash dive at sixty down. Let's see if we can't split the enemy force, at least. See if you can't evade their torpedoes long enough to get lost in the badlands until your guys arrive. I've got my laser, and as

I get to know my ship better, I bet I'll find a few more tricks."

"WL: Good luck. At least you won't have any compunction about using your laser on those bastards. Do it now, before they launch any torpedoes."

"Good luck, Father. I'll be back, I promise."

"WL: Good luck, Redfar. I love you."

"I love you, too."

*Quickray* turned to three four zero, and dived at sixty degrees. Two of the subs turned to follow, but their sonar returns were weak. A DeepReef scout sub was built for stealth. They'd have a heck of a time getting a targeting fix. She set up a routine in her hydrophones to track it and automatically cover its sounds. Turnhigh would figure out quickly enough that they could go to flank without losing stealth. But the two pursuers had enough torpedoes that they might not need a good fix.

On the other hand, torpedoes were expensive, and *Faraday* was the prize. She saw the two subs turn back to follow her. This maneuvering put them behind the pack, for all the difference it made.

"TRAS201: Large DeepReef Sub: You were warned."

There was a double pressure wave as the lead sub launched two torpedoes. She let them outdistance it by a tenth of a klik before she flicked out with her laser and detonated them. They made quite a satisfactory bang, and did some minor damage to the lead sub. None of the TallRocks slowed.

"TRAS201: Large DeepReef Sub: This new weapon of yours is powerful, but it has limits. You must surrender. Respond."

That was all too true. But her father had a saying, "If you can't dazzle 'em with brilliance, baffle 'em with goatshit."

"FDYRF: TRAS201: You are mistaken. I am no more DeepReef than you are. My weapons can be employed on your hull as easily as your torpedoes. DeepReef has offered to ally with us. We are considering it. Do you have a better offer?"

There was a pause. Her course was taking her away from the TallRock subs, but it was also taking her away from the DeepReef fleet. This was intentional, to put *Quickray* out of danger. If her ploy was successful, they might both survive.

"TRAS201: FDYRF: Identify yourself and your city."

"FDYRF: TRAS201: We are science sub *Faraday Redfar,* from the city of Mitsume."

"TRAS201: FDYRF: Mitsume? Never heard of it. What are its coordinates?"

"FDYRF: TRAS201: It's a floating city, at high altitude. We have only begun making contact with low-altitude cities. I'm not at liberty to divulge the coordinates."

She had been gaining altitude all too slowly, but still she was over eleven hundred meters and climbing. The TallRock subs were lower, but they would start to feel the strain of high-altitude flight before long. It would certainly give her credence.

"TRAS201: FDYRF: Analysis of your configuration indicates you may be telling the truth. Rendezvous with us and we'll discuss it."

It sounded reasonable, but dare she take the risk? From what she knew of the TallRocks, they were likely to salvage first and discuss later. She understood Mitsume's horror at dismantling a ship with active systems all too well now.

"FDYRF: TRAS201: If I rendezvous with you, what's to stop you from attacking me in close quarters?"

"TRAS201: FDYRF: You want us to trust you? Then shouldn't you trust us?"

"FDYRF: TRAS201: It's easy to talk about trust when you've got forty-eight tubes ready to fire."

"TRAS201: FDYRF: Quite right. This is your last warning. Surrender now or be destroyed."

Too late she saw her mistake. The TallRock subs were faster and had gone to flank speed as they'd talked. They weren't nearly as fast as *Quickray*, but they were barely two kliks behind her now, and closing.

Her father was right. She'd have to target their hulls.

She hesitated. They were configured much as *Quickray* was, with Conn an amidships bulge over a long tube. The comp and the heatpack were buried inside, as well-protected as possible. The most effective way to stop them would be to hit the comp, but it was a lot of steel to cut through. She had the power but not the time. The other way was to hit them in Conn. With no one to launch the torpedoes or guide the smarter ones, she'd have a chance. She identified the command sub, 201, and targeted Conn.

*Killing humans is not permissible.*

She was picking up comm signals, but more than that was coming through. She could see them at stations. The divers were in the ready room, playing games. Torpedo loaders were nervously checking finicky fish. The commander was at his central station, trading calming signs with his staff, while the sonar operator listened to his soundbuds. They were men, breathing the same kind of fluid as she did, blood pumping in veins just like hers. They had just as much right to live. They were just as precious as individuals. Couldn't they see that? Why were they doing this? How could she? The ship part of her saw farther, not just in distance.

*Killing humans must never be permissible.*

The commander reached out and hit a key on his panel.

Forty-eight torpedo tubes discharged, hurling a message of death as intolerable as it was inescapable.

She targeted as quickly as she could, blasting away with electronic speed and precision. She gave a quick pulse of her fusion engine. It drove her upward in a blast of superheated steam, but came within an eyelash of blowing her to bits. It gave her a little extra distance, gouts of bubbles confusing the torpedoes enough that some of them lost their targeting lock. She was over the path of the oncoming subs, so she flicked her laser through the space between them and the torpedoes, severing the remaining guide wires unreeling behind. Then she caught the first six, the new cooled lens Mitsume had created allowing her to fire rapidly.

It was much more effective. Out of the mass of torpedoes, there were only fifteen left. Eight too many, and headed straight for her. She only had time enough to detonate seven.

"DRSS3312: FDYRF: WL: Godspeed, Daughter."

A shadow came between her and hurtling death, *Quickray* at flank speed, a maneuver only Widethumb could have engineered. Three of the smarter torpedoes evaded, but the rest hit the scout sub amidships. The concussion shook her, safe in the cocoon of *Faraday*. The center of the sub disappeared in a cauldron of fire and bubbles. By the time the horror of it reached her, she'd already destroyed the stragglers.

"FDYRF: TRAS201: You bastards!"

She was closer to the battle group than ever. The maneuvers had placed her above them. She was well out of line with their tubes, which would increase the time of flight for the torpedoes but wouldn't hamper their targeting. The commander reached toward the key on his panel.

"No!" She targeted and fired.

The laser sliced through steel and hit the commander square in his head, turning it to vapor. Men wheeled around, jaws dropping in shock. Water gushed in, fluid and bloody bubbles gushed out, leaving a trail of gold streaming from the Conn of 201 in the eternal night. She targeted again, this time the propulsion system, barely damaging the hull but stopping the sub dead in the water. She hit them all, disabled them all, firing while her numb brain shouted into the night: "Not permissible! Not permissible! Not permissible!"

The disorganized subs launched a few torpedoes, but she detonated them easily, climbing higher by the moment. Even with working drives they couldn't follow her. Not now, not ever. They'd plug the holes, fix the drives, maybe even in time to evade the DeepReef fleet. She didn't care.

She'd killed. Just one man, but it was a pit, blacker than the ocean, blacker than her home. But it was lost in a bigger pit, a bigger ocean. Everyone she'd ever loved was gone, killed in one furious moment of fire.

*Never again. Never again.*

*Faraday* creaked. Internal pressure was stressing the hull as external pressure decreased with decreasing depth.

There was a program. Mitsume had created it. Much as it scared her, Redfar had to run it if she wanted to live. If she didn't live to complete her mission, the death of *Quickray* would have been for nothing. She gave the command.

Her ears popped as pressure dropped. *Faraday* was venting fluid in preparation for atmosphere. Air. How was she supposed to live in thin, tenuous gas bubbles?

A valve opened. A geyser of bubbles squirted into the room, rising and gathering in the ceiling. They joined together into one giant bubble toward the bow, a bubble that grew until the ceiling was lost in a writhing pane of silver. It descended, shrinking her world.

"No. I don't want to do this. No!"

There was no one to read her message.

She knew it was necessary, but knowledge was no match for the terror that seized her. Panicked, she swam to the floor. The air kept coming, vital fluid flowing away. She flipped face down so she couldn't see it.

"No!"

She pressed her face down, trying to breathe in a vanishing pool. It was too low, then gone.

She tried to hold her breath, but it was futile. Fluid gushed from her mouth, and despite herself she breathed in. The air burned. She coughed, chest heaving painfully.

Sound came.

She'd never heard anything like it. It was complex, exotic, and somehow there were words in it. She realized that it was part of the program Mitsume had wrought, her dead friend's message of comfort and reassurance. The sounds themselves had no meaning, but the words came to her through her connection to her ship:

> *Amazing grace, how sweet the sound*
> *That saved a wretch like me.*

*I once was lost but now am found;*
*Was blind, but now I see.*

It was music, and she knew why Mitsume had pitied them for the lack.

She tried to swim from the floor, but she was so heavy she could barely raise her head. Her face was cold, water running down it. She was crying and the tears dripped, instead of hanging onto her eyes as she cried. She cried because she was lost, her father and friends were lost, and she cried because the music was so beautiful.

She found she could make sounds with her own throat. She had no idea how to form them into words, but she could make them pitch the way the song did. Her music wasn't nearly as good, but it pleased her in a way that was new and interesting.

It took her hours to build enough strength to crawl up to the couch in her combat cell, but her ship provided food and drink in plenty. It took days to drift to the surface. It gave her time to grieve, and time to think of Mitsume, who hadn't been allowed to grieve for her own lost family.

At last the surface was above her, shining in streaks of light on the dark depths, huge, black and scary. *Faraday* broke through into air.

She saw the sky for the first time. It was so black! In the distance there were wisps of white. *Clouds*. The sky wasn't like the opaque blackness of the deeps, but filled with brilliant points of light.

*Stars,* her *Faraday* part knew. Distant suns with distant people. And distant enemies.

She knew how to listen for the drives of the Delnak ships, and knew better than to scan for them and risk their finding her, alone and inexperienced. The sky was quiet, the path open. She energized null-gravs and lifted clear of the water, warming up the fusion drive. There was a hyperdrive to calibrate and a course to set. What she didn't know, *Faraday* did. They did. One person, one shipwoman, *Faraday Redfar*. Her course wouldn't be elegant, but it would take herself and *Quickray*'s database to where they could both do some good. Take her to strangers who'd never breathed fluid, who communicated by sound, with tiny noses and flaps on their eyelids. Who made music.

She was alone and afraid, but in a way she didn't understand, she was going home.

# LAST DAYS OF THE MAHDI

*Written by*
**Tom Pendergrass**

*Illustrated by*
**Matt Taggart**

## About the Author

*Tom has been a science fiction fan since reading Andre Norton and Robert Heinlein novels as a boy. He has only recently begun writing fiction and has completed a novel. This story, "Last Days of the Mahdi," combines Tom's two great literary loves, science fiction and espionage fiction. It is his first sale.*

*Tom worked as an intelligence officer and terrorism expert for the U.S. government for twelve years, which has given him a unique window into the seamy underside of humanity.*

*He drew his inspiration for this story from his extensive international travels in the Middle East. He is an experienced globetrotter, having spent substantial time in Europe, Asia, Africa and South America. He speaks Russian, as well as some French and Arabic.*

*Tom lives in Huntsville, Alabama, with his wife, two sons and two Dalmatians. He is employed by a major international corporation, grows bonsai trees and is active in his community.*

The detritus of three millennia are piled beneath my feet behind the sun-warmed glass of the Mahdi's pyramid. I see the Nile stretching in an endless cocoa stream north to the Delta, where al-Iskandriya sits as the mud-daubed flood waters mingle with the azure of the Mediterranean. Beneath me, al-Qahira, site of ancient Memphis, sprawls in an endless warren of dust-colored alleys, punctuated by the whitewashed steel spires of the modern caliphate.

The caliphate, the incarnate dreams of a nation long suppressed, finally resurrected two hundred years after the last pretender to that title was washed away by European wars. The caliphate, whose lands spread in a crescent from the Atlas Mountains to the Shat-al-Arab, teeming with millions of malnourished, impoverished souls, stricken for centuries by their lack of leadership and education, bankrupted by the technologies that had stolen from them their birthright, the oil that had driven the industrial age. But when water became the key to world power and the coin of commerce, the caliphate found itself destitute.

And poor it had been, not just in riches but in spirit, until the Mahdi appeared to fulfill the prophecies and dreams of his people. But I know a secret about the Mahdi that they do not. I know the secret that must die with him . . . or with me.

For the Mahdi and I are two sides of the same coin, created by the Organization to be wanderers in this world, always familiar, yet strangers. We are chimerae, genetically engineered spies, designed to blend in to our roles, our DNA telling our lies to protect our identities. We are a lie, we have no identity.

I am called Loki. That is not my real name. My birth name is classified information; no more than half a dozen souls within the Organization know it. To the rest of the world, the person that I was is dead, killed long ago in a senseless act of violence. I, we, were named after the gods of our ancestors in an act of hubris by our creators. For like the gods, we can become what we need to be.

The golden sun of ancient Egypt streams through the glass walls, feeling warm on my face. I see myself in the glass, a ghostly reflection. I am a thin man, with café-au-lait skin the color of the Nile, a deeply creased forehead, and a fringe of thin graying hair that nests around my bare scalp. The blood of the Mamelukes courses through my veins, the blood of the tribes that followed the Prophet, peace be upon him, and then the righteous caliphs out of the desert and into this land. But it is not my blood.

I can scarcely recall what I looked like in the days before the transformations. Not that it matters. What once was cannot be again. I made my decision as did Dagda before me.

Dagda, that is the god-name that they gave to the man who has become the Mahdi. He was created and trained by the same men, the same Organization, which created me. And he was not of the blood of the Prophet, peace be upon him. He was not even of the blood of the sons of Shem—but his blood now is borrowed, and who is to say whose it is, or once was?

I turn from the window and look across the sunlit glass and mirrored corridor. The heat of the sun prickles my back through my thin cotton shirt. The great door opens, its intricate carved and inlaid arabesques flash in the afternoon light, and a man, as insubstantial as a wisp of smoke, appears.

"The *Sa'id* will see you now," he says in a voice like frayed papyrus.

I pick up my bag by its worn leather strap and walk slowly toward the door. The two guards flanking the door like epauleted djinn stiffen as I walk through. I nod to the man, who I know is the Mahdi's vizier, his advisor and confidant.

"*Shukran*, thank you," I say, careful to look down from the wizened visage.

"The Mahdi is afflicted by the curses of the heretics. I have heard that you can melt away the cares of the world. Is that true?"

"So I have been told, my lord. But it is a true honor to be able to share the gift given me by Allah with his most righteous servant." The words come from my lips like honey. The imprinting has been good; I feel the weight of a thousand years of traditions lie lightly on my shoulders.

"It is good that you can share Allah's gift. The Mahdi is in pain." The corridor ends in a brilliant room. The walls are covered with brightly colored mergoums, the carpets of the Berbers of the Arab Maghreb. On the floor, dressed in a plain robe of spotless white, sits the Mahdi with legs crossed. I fall to my knees, almost without my conscious control, and touch my head to the floor. I wait to be spoken to.

I feel the Mahdi's gaze rest on my bowed head. "You may rise."

I lift my eyes to look upon the face of the one who has been promised in the hadith. His eyes are dark, nearly black, and his nose is sharp and curved like a scimitar. But his voice is like a spring in the desert.

"Honorable Healer," he says, his Arabic as beautiful as the words from the mouth of the Prophet, peace be upon him. "I have heard tales of your skill. I am sorry I must trouble you. I have need of your services."

"It is an honor, O Reverent Master." My Arabic is the language of the delta with its harsh consonants in dissonance to the elegance of the Mahdi's speech. It is like a common crow next to the scarlet ibis of his voice. "How may I assist you?"

"Since we returned victorious from al-Quds—Jersualem—I am afraid Satan has placed a thorn in my flesh so that it will distract me from the work of the All Powerful. My pain prevents me from standing or from sleeping. The doctors seek to give me drugs, but those would dull my senses, and that is what Satan wishes for most of all."

The vizier speaks in his thin voice behind me. "The Mahdi was astride a tank when a Zionist bomb exploded. It was not his time, thanks be to Allah. But when the Mahdi fell, he injured his back grievously."

"My lord, I will help you, if God wills it. My art is ancient but effective and has been passed down in my family for generations. I need you to undress and lie down."

I pull a cotton towel from my bag and turn my head as the Mahdi struggles out of his clothing, helped by the frail old man. He lies down on his stomach and I cover his nakedness with the towel. My hands tremble in the presence of one so holy. In my conscious brain I know that he is nothing more than I am, that he is not the

Promised One; but deep under my consciousness, in the recesses of my soul where the imprinting has taken hold, I am a follower. And I know that he is the One.

"My lord, I will need to feel your back to see what can be done. The treatment may hurt, but I can assure that you will sleep soundly when I am done."

The vizier now stands and motions to the stone-faced guards. The guards step closer to me, and I understand that they will be watching my every move. There have been attempts on the life of the Mahdi before, but Allah has not yet chosen him, praise be to God. I silently pray that he not be fated to die at my hands.

My fingers are strong, the gift of the genes the Organization grafted into my body during the transformation. The skills are new, learned over intense months of training, but they are effective. I feel along his spine, my fingers kneading knots of tightened muscle. I find what I am looking for, and as my hand pushes deep into his tissues, the Mahdi cries out. The guards rush and grab me by the shoulders.

"No," the Mahdi whispers through clenched teeth. "Let him finish. Satan's work is not dismantled without pain."

I am released and I continue, more cautious now. The spine is bent, as if the walls of Zion had fallen on him. I lift his shoulders and push against his back until I hear it pop. The Mahdi exhales now. His breathing grows deeper.

*"Sa'id,"* I say, "I have adjusted your back but your muscles are still at war with your body. I will rub you down with oils—sandalwood and rose and fragrant clove—and your pain will subside. And you will sleep. But the damage is deep. I must return."

"So be it."

I open my bag and pull out a handful of small glass jars. I carefully remove the stopper of the first and gently pour the oil onto his back. My hands spread the thick fluid over his back, pausing to separate the fibrous tissues. He stiffens and then relaxes as I knead his tense muscles, working his shoulders and then his back.

He is still now, and his breathing is heavy. I whisper to him, "And sandalwood to help you sleep."

I open the stopper of the third jar and reach inside to scoop the creamy paste. I feel the needle hidden in the paste and I squeeze it between two fingers. I spread the paste on his back, then lift the skin, pinching and slapping it to desensitize it. Quick as a snake, the needle flits into the fleshy skin at his waist. I pinch so he cannot feel the pain and I tap the needle to send its contents into his skin. I reach into my jar for more sandalwood paste, and as I scoop, I deposit the spent needle back into the jar. I quickly screw the lid on.

As I gently rub his back I look back at the guards. They have drifted back to the far side of the room, obviously deciding that I am innocuous. In a moment, the drug will take effect and the Mahdi will be relaxed and compliant.

I lean over the Mahdi and whisper, *"Dagda. Dagda, restoris."*

The Mahdi lifts his head briefly and looks at me with blank eyes. "What did you say?"

"Nothing," I say. His face still uncomprehending. "Just a prayer for restful sleep in a long-dead tongue."

He grunts and lowers his head back onto the thick pile of the mergoum. I cover his body with another towel and stand. The guards step toward me.

"I am finished," I whisper. "He should sleep well now. Do not wake him, for he needs his rest." They nod and escort me to the door.

The streets of the ancient city are filled with dust, coating everything in fine powder and dulling its colors. I wander from the great glass pyramid that lies along the Nile toward the east through narrow lanes. I see my reflection in the glass of a passing bus, belching its diesel fumes into the khaki sky. The caliphate has not switched to the hydrogen that powers the rest of the world. But now, only the caliphate uses the oil that could have driven the greatness of the nation had it not been squandered by petty tyrants. In the glass, I see the dim reflection of two men in dark leather jackets. They have been with me since I left the pyramid.

"Good," I say silently to myself. "The vizier is having me followed to see where I will go." But it is obvious that these are not the best men the vizier has. Their posture is careless, as if this were a chore for them. And their manner is reckless. I would be a fool not to notice them. Clearly I am not under suspicion, but I am careful not to look at them or show recognition. For how would a poor Egyptian masseur know how to detect surveillance, no matter how sloppy?

I walk slowly, trying to look as if I am the age that everyone assumes me to be. My skin and hair were prematurely aged by the doctors, but my muscles are young and my reflexes have been heightened to exceed those of normal men. For sixteen months I have trained day and night for this mission—the surgeons have sculpted me, the linguists have tutored me, the behavioralists have imprinted the behaviors of an ancient culture on me. Through it all, the genetic manipulation, the settling in an alien body and struggling with a personality that is at once me and not me, I have focused on one thing: Dagda.

I know him as well as I know myself, though before today I had never met him. He was the fourth of my kind, the fourth to have been transformed from who he was to someone else. He was sent to be a mole, living deep undercover in the most insular of societies. He was to infiltrate into the power structure, and had been gifted by the geneticists with the intelligence and charisma to do so. But he succeeded beyond all expectations. He became the power structure. He became the Mahdi, the messiah who brings Allah's will to the world in the last days.

It was in Mecca when the women had fallen at his feet, shouting "Here is the Righteous One," and the men had shouted, "He is chosen by Allah" as foretold in the hadith. But it was a lie. It had been engineered by my superiors, who were not content with assuming God's role in Creation, but also wanted to assume God's role in directing the affairs of men. And it succeeded, for a time.

Dagda had taken his direction from the Shrink, who heads the Organization. It was the Shrink that made him the Mahdi, and the Shrink that sought to rule the caliphate. For four years, Dagda had led his people with the interests of my government at heart. He had been a good ruler, fair with his people, but he had not been what they assumed he was.

Then the messages had stopped. The Mahdi had begun to beat the drums of war, and the tribes had swarmed from their heartland as they had done centuries earlier to overwhelm their neighbors and carry the crescent banner to the ends of the earth.

That was when I was chosen. To become one of the Mahdi's people, to get close to him, and to discover what has happened. And, if need be, to kill him.

My feet take me to the tenement which has been my home for the last four months. The door is heavy and metal, with thick flakes of paint blasted by the wind-borne sands that have plagued al-Qahira for these many years. I pull it open and am greeted by the coolness of the dark. I walk in, and I see the two leather-jackets take positions on either side of the street, looking bored.

I place my bag on the floor and sit on my carpet. The muezzin calls the time for prayer. I face toward the east and pray. I see the leather jackets are doing the same outside my window, and I know with certainty the entire caliphate is on its knees. "He will unite the Muslims," I say, reciting the hadith of the Mahdi.

I remain on the floor, sitting in the cool dark of my room as I watch the surveillants grow restless. After an hour, they leave. I turn to prepare for the evening's work. I open the trunk that sits against the far wall and lift its false bottom. I pull out a wooden box and place it on the floor. The tools of my trade, makeup, disguises, poisons. I open the box and lift out a small flat mirror. I stare at my features, and then with the tools in the box, I begin my work.

I streak my face with dirt, darken my complexion, but that is just the beginning. I glue a great black mole on the side of my nose. I reach into my mouth and snap out my teeth with a pop, one by one—the surgeons have done their job well. I place my teeth in a formed shell, each in its place. I look in the mirror and my cheeks are sunken. I take molded plastic prostheses from the box, and glue them on my arms and hands, blending the makeup along the edges so that they look like weeping sores. I reach back into the trunk and retrieve a torn and soiled robe, threadbare at the knees and gleaming with the salt of long-dried sweat. I pull a stained *khaffiyeh* onto my head and fit it with a frayed rope. I pull from the box a contact lens that is white and filmy, and place it in my eye so that I will look half-blind.

I look outside. There are no street lights in this part of the city, and the darkness is falling quickly. Almost time. I walk across the room to the small refrigerator which sits, unplugged, alone against the mud-colored wall. I open the door and am overwhelmed by the stench. I fight the bile rising in my throat and force my stomach to remain calm. On the rusted wire rack is a small chunk of goat flesh, ripened for the past weeks in the heat of the unplugged refrigerator. Flies buzz into the room, streaming in endless profusion from the surface of the meat. I reach in and pick it up, shutting the door quickly.

The goat has turned gray, and its surface is alive with writhing white maggots. I feel myself retch and turn away. Once my stomach is calm again, I look back to the meat. I scoop the maggots into my false wounds and rub my arms with the rancid goat, making sure that the smell permeates me. I place the rotting flesh inside my robe and open my door into the night.

I limp along the streets of al-Qahira, headed toward the central mosque where I will sit on the steps to collect alms. The great dome seems to spring upon me as I step out of the maze of alleys. I take a position on the steps leading to the entrance, and I spread out a purple cloth for the worshippers to place their money on. I am joined by the refuse of the city, the poor and the lame, the crippled and the blind, who litter the steps of the mosque like the maggots on my goat.

Illustrated by Matt Taggart

The good men of the city come by, clutching their *khaffiyehs* to their noses to ward off my smell, and drop their generosity on my cloth. A man, well dressed in a fez with a gold tassel, comes up and throws a heavy gold coin on the cloth.

"May the blessings of Allah be upon you," I say, my voice scratchy and the words slurred by my missing teeth.

"And on you, *inshallah*," the man says. He pulls another coin from his pocket.

"And what will you do if I give you double my alms for today?" he asks. It is the recognition sign of my contact. I remember the response.

"I will likewise give to those in need," I say. I have given the countersign.

"Then I shall give you thirty dinars," he says, and throws paper money on my cloth.

The other beggars look at me in awe. It is a code: the meeting will be in thirty minutes. I wait for ten minutes before I fold the money into my cloth and stand unsteadily, walking back down the steps with a noticeable limp, before disappearing into the darkness of the streets.

I glance behind me as I enter the cool afternoon shadows of the old city. The mud-daubed walls seem to engulf me in their stillness. I look to be certain I have not been followed. It is not necessary, my genetically heightened senses alert me to danger that no normal man could sense. But I am a cautious man; it is what has kept me alive through these many missions and many assumed identities.

Keeping my limp, I stumble through the narrow streets that emanate spokelike from the central mosque. I stick to the shadows as much as I can, but in the hot afternoon sun, so do the rest of the masses who crowd the streets. The stench from beneath my robe clears my way, and people turn away from me, as if my presence offends them. It is good, for though they may remember my passage, none will remember my face.

A fruit-seller's stall straddles a narrow alleyway. I see behind it an ancient covered van, a petrol burner like those that are still so common in the caliphate. The fruit seller sees me and nods almost imperceptibly. He turns and spills a tray of figs across the roadway and begins screaming curses in Arabic, curses reserved for the worst of criminals.

"Get the boy," he screams pointing down a dark street. "He is a thief." The fruit seller jabs his fat fingers in the air at the back of the phantom thief. All eyes are staring into the darkened shadows opposite the alley and none see me as I slip noiselessly into the back of the van and pull the dusty doors closed behind me.

The back of the van is vacant save a small rug that provides only limited padding against the hard metal floor. On the rug lies a small vid screen attached with a wire to the side of the vehicle. I sit, my legs crossed, and pick up the vid screen. There is a man in the driver's seat. He does not look at me, only cranks the van and pulls away from the commotion at the fruit stand.

There is an earplug dangling from the vid screen with a microphone attached to the wire halfway down its length. I place the speaker in my ear before I activate the screen.

A dark image, blocky from the scrambled digital transmission, jumps to life. The man on the other side of the screen is bald and has the pudgy face of inherited wealth. He is not an Arab, nor is he a Muslim. He is the man known to me only as the Shrink, the man who is both my master and my nemesis.

"Loki," his voice crackles in my ear. "I assume you have made contact." He looks at me and his lips turn upward in a sneer, almost as if he can smell me from halfway around the globe.

"Indeed," I say. The Shrink recruited me, engineered me, imprinted me, trained me, manipulated me. He made me into what I am today. He created me . . . and he created Dagda; he created the Mahdi.

"Well?"

The Shrink was not accustomed to being kept waiting. "I made contact with Dagda. He was unresponsive, and did not recognize any of the code words. Nor did he recognize his codename when I mentioned it to him."

The bald man rubs his soft chin as if in thought. "Any ideas?"

"It appears that Dagda has succumbed to both the genetic manipulation and the imprinting. He no longer remembers that the identity he assumed is not his own. I am afraid that you did far too good of a job."

The Shrink does not take notice of my jab at him. "What will he do?"

"He believes he is the Mahdi. He will do what the prophesies say. He will destroy all those who are infidels and who oppose the will of Allah. He will pave the way for the end times."

The Shrink pauses in thought. "You almost sound like you believe he is the Mahdi yourself." He laughs from deep in his throat. "But that is only a superstition. He is Dagda, a chimera like you, a man, a spy, nothing more."

Do I believe Dagda is the Mahdi? How could I? I know who he was. But in his palace, the aura he emitted was almost palpable, as if the presence of Allah was on him. But Dagda couldn't fulfill the prophecy, could he?

"Can you answer one question for me?" I ask.

"Certainly."

"When you altered Dagda's genetic patterns, whose did you use as a model?"

"Some descendant of an Arab king. Sharif Hassan was his name."

I inhale slowly. "Sharif?" I say, muttering the Arabic honorific. "So then he was descended from the Prophet Muhammad?" I refrain from adding the traditional "peace be upon him" in the Shrink's presence.

"I suppose. Not that it matters." The Shrink shrugs.

"And he shall be of the house of the Prophet," I mutter just above my breath. The prophecies *are* correct. Dagda is the Mahdi and the heir to the house of the Prophet, peace be upon him.

"I am under a lot of heat over here," the Shrink continues. "Our subject has turned very dangerous to us. We must rectify the mistake. You must remove Dagda from his position." The Shrink's eyes narrow, and he seems to be peering through me.

"It will be difficult to kidnap him."

"I do not want him kidnapped. I want him removed, eliminated. Do you understand?"

A chill descends on me. To kill the Mahdi? The imprinting is strong and the thought sends shudders through my body.

"Loki, do you understand?" His voice is strident now.

I nod. "It is what I am trained to do. Do you have evacuation plans in place?"

"Affirmative."

"Then I will do it *inshallah,* God willing."

I pull the plug from my ear and a sick feeling settles in my gut. I signal the driver, and he pulls over into a garbage-strewn alley. I slip silently from the van and into the filth of the city.

Kill the Mahdi? No, I mustn't think of him as the Mahdi—that is my imprinting speaking; I was trained to become a believer so that I might pass for one. I know he is not the Mahdi, he is a man like me. I have killed men before, this will be no different. But he has the blood of the Prophet in his veins. He is the Mahdi.

I struggle within myself. They had exposed me for months nonstop to Arab culture and politics, assaulting my senses with the tastes and smells of North Africa so that I would seem at ease here. But they also indoctrinated me in the religion, and were successful in ways that no missionary could be. I was designed to appear to be a believer, else I couldn't have gotten close to the Mahdi. But they had designed Dagda in the same way, and the imprinting had overwhelmed him. He had lost his self and become the Holy One.

I make my way through the trash-strewn streets in a daze. My mind is a jumble as if I am privy to someone else's thoughts and decisions. And in a way I am. Am I thinking as Loki, the elite assassin, or as Farid, the folk healer, the good Muslim who honors his leader, sent from God to purify the faith?

The streets are black in this neighborhood, and I use the cover of darkness to strip off my disguise. I drop the rotten meat on the street, and I feel the buzzing presence of the carrion flies leave me as they chase it into the drain. I pull the filmy contact from my eye and quickly shove it in my pocket. If the plan works, then I will have no further need for my disguise.

I am in my neighborhood now, and I walk a circuitous route around my door to make sure that none of the Mahdi's men are still lurking. I am alone. I open the door and enter, dropping on my thin pallet exhausted.

When I awake, the late morning sun is streaming through my window. I already feel the heat of the day building. The stench of carrion still clings about me and I undress, throwing my robes in a bag and sealing it tightly. There is no bath. I wash myself with tepid water from the sink in my kitchen. I have patients to visit this afternoon, and then, perhaps, the Mahdi will call. I sit on my pallet, doing little except struggling within myself. My imprinting wrestling with my training, my id against my ego.

On the third day, an abrupt knock on the door awakens me from my afternoon slumber. I pull my robe around me and answer. It is the Mahdi's man.

"Farid, the healer?" he says. He is tall and thin, with a fine mustache and obsidian eyes.

"Yes, I am Farid," I say, feigning puzzlement.

"His eminence, the Mahdi, may God's blessing be upon him, desires your immediate attention. I have come to take you to him."

"*Ahlan wa Sahlan,* you are welcome here. Please step inside while I gather my things."

I offer him a cold glass of *karkadeh,* the sweet syrupy hibiscus drink popular along the Nile. I turn my back on the Mahdi's servant as I ready my bag of ointments and salves and essences of rare plants. Finally I pull into my bag a small green vial made of thick opaque glass. If I am to kill the Mahdi, then this will be my weapon.

Many years ago, shortly after I had been recruited by the Shrink, I had been instructed in the mixture and use of poisons, in *chaumurky* and *chauturgy*, poison in drinks and in food, poison by contact and injection. I had learned all the methods of silent death known to man. There are poisons that leave no trace, poisons that disguise themselves as disease, poisons that act quickly and poisons that take days to kill. But I prefer the classics: ricin, nightshade and cyanide. And it will be one of these, the essence of monkshood, that will end the Mahdi's reign.

I close the supple leather of the clasp and pull the bag's worn handles together. "I am ready," I say, and the Mahdi's herald rises to his feet and bows.

"We must hurry, the Mahdi is in pain," he says.

I nod and pull the door closed behind me. The air is still as if waiting for something. I feel the struggle within myself again—the twin urges of my training, which has turned me into a cold killer, a trained assasin who will follow orders, and my imprinting, which tells me that to kill the Mahdi would be the gravest of sins, and ensure my eternal damnation.

I follow the Mahdi's man into the dusty street where we are joined by half a dozen men armed with rifles. They are in the bright green uniforms of the Mahdi's household, and I feel the awe-stricken gazes of the crowds as I pass among them.

The great glass pyramid gleams in the bright sun as we walk toward it. It seems to beckon me, pulling on my imprinted self saying, "This is the glory of the age, behold it and be moved."

My trained psyche, the cold assassin, struggles to reassert control, to fight back the urge to confess all to the Mahdi. I know now how Dagda could relent to his imprinted ego, to become something he was not. The imprinting is strong, and the process of transformation has torn down so much of what had been my *self*, that some personality, no matter how alien, is seeking to fill the void. It must have been the same with Dagda. For how many years had he lived the lie before the lie consumed him? For three years before he was named the Mahdi, then for five years before he ceased being Dagda. And then the final two years, the years I had trained to kill him. Ten years living this life, seven years as the Mahdi.

I catch my breath. The words of the hadith come to me. *He will reign for seven years. After his passing will come the Day of Judgment.*

Seven years. If I kill him now, will I bring about the last days? It is the imprinting welling up within my soul again, fighting for dominance. My disciplined self forces the thought back deep into the recesses of my thought, suppressed but not defeated. The Mahdi's man mistakes my silence for reverence, and leaves me to my thoughts.

The guards around the entrance of the pyramid step out of our path as we walk through the immense stone gates. They avert their gaze from the Mahdi's servant and bow as we pass. We walk through the great entrance of the pyramid, up the immense stone steps, to the gilt elevator that rises through the center of the structure.

The vizier meets us at the top of the building.

"Honorable Healer, praise Allah that you have arrived. The Mahdi is once again in need of your services. Satan has once again set his servants to torment the Holy One."

"I am your humble servant," I say, bowing deeply to the old man.

The heavy carved doors are open, and the vizier leads me through them. Once again, the Mahdi is dressed in a plain white robe and seated on a plush carpet. I drop to the floor and prostrate myself before him.

"Rise, O Man of Faith. I am touched by your devotion. *Allahu Akhbar*, God is great."

"*Allahu Akhbar*," I reply. "O Merciful One, I understand you are in pain. I am but a poor excuse for a healer, but I will do my best." I am overcome by the holiness of his presence.

"And I will be grateful," the Mahdi says, his voice a refuge from the oppressive heat and stench of the city. He undresses himself and lays face down on the carpet.

I begin to rub his knotted muscles, slowly, carefully working the tangled fibers apart. He inhales sharply as I begin work on yet another mass of inflamed tissue.

"Healer," he says. "After your last visit, I slept a peaceful sleep. But in this sleep, I had a puzzling dream. I was in a green valley, more green than any I have ever seen. Everywhere was water. And the buildings were clean and white. Everyone there knew me, and the called me by a name, it was the name you called me. Dagda. And I felt that I belonged there. Healer, do you know what this dream means?"

Perhaps the drugs and the code words had finally awakened some brief memories in Dagda. His dream was of the Organization's campus, nestled in green hills where hundreds of streams met in a shining blue lake. If he remembers, must I still kill him?

"*Sa'id*," I say. "I am not wise as are you. What do you think is the meaning of this dream?" Perhaps I can awaken Dagda inside the Mahdi's person. Then I will not commit the unforgivable sin of killing God's servant.

"I think it is Paradise, where the rivers run freely and the servants of the faithful feed us figs and dates."

The Mahdi's imprinting is too strong for Dagda to overcome. "Perhaps you are right, O Gracious One. Would that I could see it with you."

The Mahdi's back relaxes as he relives his glimpse of Paradise. And I know then that I must send him to find it. I have my orders.

My imprinted self makes a last desperate attempt to stay my hands from their appointed task. *If you kill the Mahdi, the days of the world will surely end,* I hear in my head. But the superstitions of an ancient people cannot deter me. My training is supreme. I have my mission.

I reach for the green vial. The death will come swiftly and painlessly. "Your Eminence," I say, "I have more powerful medicines that will help you sleep and will end the pain in your back. Perhaps you will dream of Paradise again."

The Mahdi nods his head and smiles the all-knowing smile of the enlightened. "May the blessings of Allah be upon you," he says.

I spread the salve across the Mahdi's broad smooth back and pinch and slap the skin until it tingles. I feel in the green vial and locate the needle. I plunge it into the loose skin at the top of his hip and inject its lethal contents into the hero of the age. The Mahdi's body relaxes and I feel his breathing become shallow. My body sags and I fight the tears that I feel welling to my eyes.

With shaking hands, I place my vials back into my bag and whisper to the guard, "He will sleep for a long time tonight. It is very important that you do not wake him until morning, else the medicines will not help him."

The guard nods and looks toward the Mahdi, lying face down in silence, calm and still as the dew on the reeds. I step past him feeling the heat of his breath as his head follows me toward the exit.

The immense carved door opens and I step into the glass hall. The windows open to the four corners of the caliphate, and the walls seem to glow rose as I see the city sprawl underneath me. I feel a gust of wind tickle the hairs on the back of my neck and I shudder—my imprinted mind tells me that it is the soul of the Mahdi gone to Paradise. I hear the door shut and my trained mind knows it is but the breeze from the immense door.

Beneath me the city is alive with the commerce and filth of millions; Earth has not stopped turning. Allah has not descended to sit in judgment. I laugh at my superstitions. The imprinting can be removed, I think, to be replaced with something else. I am not Farid, the healer, after all. I am Loki of the Organization, and I have accomplished my mission.

I turn toward the elevator to descend to the city, and to escape from the man I have become. Back to the surgeons and the psychiatrists. Back to the Shrink. I can feel my id overcoming the imprinting and the superstition as if I were home already.

And then it catches my eye. I turn and stare toward the west and the pyramid of the heathen Pharaoh Khufu. The sun is an immense red orb touching the western desert, and the words of the hadith come to me.

*The sun will be as blood and the world will end as all souls are judged.*

Beneath me the lights of the city wink out one by one.

# ASLEEP IN THE FOREST OF THE TALL CATS

*Written by*
**Kenneth Brady**

*Illustrated by*
**Beth Anne Zaiken**

## About the Author

*Kenneth Brady likes to think of himself as a storyteller. He's a writer, director, producer, actor, musician and sometime singer, but all of those activities serve his pursuit of storytelling. Formerly a student of theatre arts, he's now working on a degree in linguistics, focusing on studying Japanese, Thai and French. He credits his wide range of interests to his ethnically diverse background—Irish, Japanese, German, Swiss, French, Polish and Choctaw.*

*He has written screenplays, stage plays, poetry, music and a few novels, though short fiction is his first love.*

*He is deeply indebted to The Wordos, the writing group in Eugene, Oregon, to which he belongs, for helping him to develop his short fiction writing skills and for supporting him without exception.*

*Though he currently supports himself as a software technician, Kenneth plans ultimately to see his work occupy a space on bookshelves somewhere between two of his favorite storytellers: Ray Bradbury and David Brin.*

People descended in gleaming metal, fire burning bright across the cloud-streaked sky. They touched down and they stayed. They built, they charted, they named names, they changed the composition of the air. They explored with sensors and unmanned aircraft. When they found the planet safe, they bred. The first child, Pietor, was a test.

It was essentially a desert planet, and so they named it Mohave, but there were stands of trees, and places of lush vegetation, oases in the shifting red sand and baked playas. Most of these places were mapped and developed early on, all except for one.

The Tall Forest was the one place the people never went, because it was unwelcoming, solid, impenetrable. The forest spoke of things better left alone, and those who tried to explore it never returned. Against human nature, it was not cut down or burned to the ground, but instead left alone.

In the forest, the others watched. They knew the people's children would someday do more. The children would explore the ground. They would change more things than just the air. They would remake everything.

Pietor was the first, so far the only. He was brown-haired, dark-skinned. He showed no signs of deformation but a tendency toward narcolepsy. After ten years it was decided that children were safe, and the floodgates were opened. In two more years there were dozens. There would be many more children someday.

So for twelve years the others stalked and waited, planned and prepared. Mostly they slept.

Pietor slept too.

•••

"Come to the forest of your dreams," Marina says. She leans over, hands pressed flat on her thighs just above the knees. White-blond hair falls loose across her pale forehead and covers one eye, leaving one bright green iris shining, only inches from the young boy's face. Her smile glows, teeth parted just slightly to show the pink tip of her tongue.

"I have some things to show you, Pietor."

He watches her hair move in the wind. Behind her the trees bend and blur away, seeming to leap and play, to climb. The ground rumbles softly, soothingly.

"How do you know my name?" Pietor says. "I don't really know you."

Marina smiles wider, stands, then collapses cross-legged onto the ground in front of Pietor. She tosses her hair behind her, then strokes the soft, tan mossy ground in front of her.

"You do know me," she says.

"Marina," Pietor says, and he doesn't know how he knows. It's the same way he knows that though she may look like a young girl his age, really she is as old as anything he's ever seen. The same way he knows the ground around him is not ground at all, but fur. Tan fur that vibrates when he strokes it. That the distant trees moving in the wind aren't trees at all but tall cats on hind legs, stalking birds, rodents, people.

He knows lots of things.

Illustrated by Beth Anne Zaiken

He has always dreamed of Marina, of this place. Of a world beyond the colony. But each time he awakens, he remembers only parts of the dream, individual elements of this place he visits.

"You know everything about this place," Marina says.

Pietor wants to believe her. He wants to know that the world around him is knowable. He wants this girl—this Marina, this world—to be his. He wants the real world to be more alive, more interesting, more *real* than it really is. He wants to be in a place where he feels welcome, where he fits in.

"I want to," Pietor says.

"I know what you want," she says. And she reaches out her hands, slowly, softly. He thinks maybe this time she will put her hands to his throat and squeeze until the life is gone from him. But she doesn't. When she touches his eyelids they fall, they close.

"I'm coming," he says.

"Finally," she says. She kisses him lightly on the forehead. He feels the rush of her touch and wants to reach out to her, but instead he drifts off.

And he wakes.

•••

The Allen family buggy left in its wake a trail of broken green saplings, and smashed red volcanic rock turned to dust beneath titanium roller tracks. Nearer to the forest the underbrush flourished. The mingled fumes of burning alcohol and disk coal followed the buggy down into the valley and toward the band of hardwood forest the colony's sensors could not penetrate.

Twelve-year-old Pietor Allen brushed his brown hair away from his eyes. He pushed his glasses up the bridge of his nose. They were too big and slipped down again. The lenses were made here, but his mom had brought the frames from Earth to fit him when he was older; the frames had once belonged to Pietor's grandfather, and his mom told him he would have to grow into them, that they were his grandfather's. Pietor put up with the big glasses because they were a tie to a planet he had never visited.

He had often wondered whether he would have felt normal on Earth, or just as much of an outcast. He had always felt a little abnormal. On Mohave he was an experiment, and he knew it. The focus of studies to see if he would be a normal kid, if he would have problems because he was born on an alien planet. And he was always treated less like a person and more like a test subject, even by his parents. But now that there were more children—little, cute children—even that minimal amount of attention had subsided. Now he was just the kid who fell asleep at inopportune times.

He pushed the glasses up again and watched out the rear window as the red dust drifted and seemed to hang in the air. The gravity of Mohave was only slightly less than that of Earth—hardly enough to notice when walking—but it affected the little things, and the dust settled as if in slow motion upon the rough pathway the buggy made through the underbrush.

His parents were in the front of the buggy. Xavier checked their course on a map while Leticia operated the controls. They whispered back and forth about what they might find, what the forest would look like.

Night descended in sheets, skeins of dark grays and browns and finally black until the only thing Pietor could see were the blinking lights of the company colony, miles off, just shy of the horizon.

"How long, Dad?" Pietor asked.

Xavier, never looking up from the map, said, "Soon, Pietor. We'll let you know."

"I think we're close," Pietor said.

Xavier looked up then, and turned. Leticia looked too. "How would you know?" Xavier said.

Pietor looked at his mother and father, not sure if he should say. They had never believed him before, so he had no reason to think they would now.

"It's just like in my dreams," he said. "This place feels close."

Xavier shook his head and focused his attention back on the map.

"Pietor," Leticia said, "you know that those are just dreams. This is the real world, and dreams are nothing but your imagination acting up. You'll need to learn to tell fantasy from reality if you want to survive in the real world."

Pietor looked away, out the back window.

"My dreams are better than this," he said, mostly to himself.

"Everyone's dreams are better than real life," Leticia said. "If they weren't, no one would pursue them."

The buggy rumbled onward.

They had left the relative safety of the colony two hours ago to check out the forest. Xavier was convinced they would find something not yet recorded, something new. If they were lucky, they would find new forms of life that could be farmed and shipped back to Earth. Something that would show Mohave as more than just a desert world with a few spots of vegetation. Something more than a terraformed world. Something to show it was special.

Pietor was sure they would find nothing.

Nothing but trees and rocks and darkness. Pietor hated that part about this place. The planet seemed lifeless, even among the underbrush. Trees and plants might be alive, but to Pietor they were boring. No scurrying rodents, no bugs, no birds. Nothing like Earth, like everything his parents told him about their home. Nothing like the wildlife vids he'd seen growing up, nothing like the Disney toons, little creatures running everywhere, talking, having adventures.

The Pointless Forest, he decided to call it, after watching an old Earth toon. The whole planet seemed pointless to Pietor, and the forest would be the same.

But in the dreams it was different.

•••

Marina trails her fingers in the black water as the little boat drifts downstream. Where her nails touch the water it lights up. Phosphorescent fish rush to the surface and swirl around her hand.

Pietor leans back against the bow and tilts his head to the side to watch her play in the water. Here he doesn't need glasses; his vision is perfect. He smiles.

"They like you," he says.

"Of course," she says. "They're my friends."

"There aren't any fish in the real world," he says.

"Yes, there are," Marina says. "You just haven't brought them yet. Here they are what might be, essence of the world in all its possibilities. You are part of that, and all of it is tied to you."

"Me?" Pietor says. "I'm not tied to anything."

He moves his hand to the water, swirls it around just as she is doing. The fish swim to him, encircle his hand. Then one of them darts in, brushes his finger. And bites.

He pulls his hand back, and the blood runs from the bite in his finger. When the droplets hit the water, the fish cluster around, feeding on the nutrient-rich liquid, swishing their tails rapidly, darting all around the boat.

"They like you, too," she says.

"No, they don't. They hate me."

"They're afraid of you," she says.

Pietor wraps his good hand around the bloody finger to stop the bleeding, pulls it back into the boat. Marina swirls her hand around in the water and the blood disperses, then is gone.

"Should they be afraid of you?" she says.

"No," he says. "I wouldn't hurt them."

"They don't know that. They don't know you."

"You don't know me," Pietor says, annoyed. He stands quickly and the boat rocks violently until he sits again. Marina sits, faces him. Her face is impassive.

"You're different than the others, you know," she says.

"Everyone says I'm just like everyone else. I don't feel like everyone else, though. I have these dreams. I dream about you, about this place."

"You are different."

"Am I?"

"You're the first of your kind. Think about it. The first human born on Mohave."

"And that means I'm different how?"

"People are reactionary, from what we've seen. You're subtle, reserved, not prone to violence. For example, would you hurt me?"

Pietor steadies himself on the sides of the boat.

"Not on purpose," he says.

She stares at him, her look exploring his entire face, from the top of his forehead all the way to his chin, scanning left to right, then back again.

"See, I do know you," she says. "But I don't know all of you. Not every one of you. And neither do the fish. But someday we will all know each other, and all get along as it was meant to be. You're the voice of your people as I am the voice of mine."

"I don't think I am," Pietor says. "Nobody likes me."

"Not those people," Marina says. "The new people that will be someday. You're the first."

•••

Pietor's view through the windscreen showed the Pointless Forest in all its impenetrable glory as far as the buggy floodlights could reveal. It was like a fortress, close stands of trees wrapped around and woven through other trees, creating a solid wall that stretched upward toward the sky. Sensors had mapped the forest as a big circle with a diameter of five kilometers.

The properties of the wood made it impossible to detect what was inside the circle of trees.

"There's an opening," Xavier said. "Look over there. There's a way in."

"Are you sure?" Leticia said.

"Look."

"Okay, I see it. Why was that never picked up by the colony sensors?"

"I don't know," Xavier said.

"Because it wasn't there before," Pietor said.

Again, his parents looked at him, quizzically, as if he were some sort of nasty bug that needed to be squashed.

"It had to be," Leticia said.

"It opened for us," Pietor said. "Maybe you shouldn't go in."

"Like hell," Xavier said. "Might be our only chance to see what's inside."

"I don't know what might happen," Pietor said.

"Of course, you don't, Pietor," Leticia said.

"I don't think you should go," Pietor said.

"Then stay here," Xavier said.

"Xavier," Leticia said. "What are you talking about?"

"I'll go," Pietor said.

"Of course, you will," Leticia said. "We wouldn't dream of leaving you alone out here. Right, Xavier?"

"Right. Of course not," Xavier said.

Pietor looked away.

Xavier drove the buggy toward the opening, a gaping hole in the trees that looked as if they had been grabbed by a set of huge hands and pulled to each side, anchored at their roots but bowed outward in the middle of the trunks. The opening dwarfed the buggy as it stopped near the base of a tree.

"These trees are like giants," Leticia said. "You know? Like creatures from some fairy tale or nightmare."

As they drove through the opening, only Pietor looked out the back window to see the trees once again closing up, sealing them in. He thought to say something, maybe to warn his parents more strongly—as if they would be warned—but instead he faded off to sleep.

•••

Pietor floats on his back in the lake, naked, his toes poking above the surface. From the shore are sparkles of light, like reflections of mirrors or broken glass on the rocky beach. Little fish swim around him and bump his feet, hands, head, but this time they do not bite.

Pietor reaches out and lifts one of the fish from the water, and it doesn't struggle. But when it is out of the water it flops a few times, then stretches, elongating down both sides of Pietor's palm, then drops both ends back into the water. It looks like an eel now, or a sea snake, and it slides up and around his palm, then again into the water, and Pietor never sees the end or beginning of the creature, just its endless slithering body. He drops his hand in the lake and the creature falls away into the depths to join its brothers and sisters.

"There are so many things you have yet to see in this place," Marina says. She swims up behind Pietor, then past him, and slides fingertips along his arm to his hand. For a fleeting moment he sees that she too is naked, and he tries to get a better look. It is his dream, after all, isn't it? She moves a bit closer, but instead of revealing herself she uses his body to push off.

"Not yet," she says.

"I'm in the forest," Pietor says. "In real life, I mean."

"I know. Maybe you should not have brought your family, though."

"Why not?"

"They're not like you, Pietor. They wouldn't understand the things you understand, the things you see. Some things are meant for you alone."

Then she flips around and goes under the water head first, arching her back. In the glittering light from the shores Pietor watches the skin of her back, her buttocks, then her legs glide away and under the surface.

Again he is alone in the lake, and he feels the sea snakes or eels which were once just little fish swirling around the lake in an ever-tightening spiral toward him. And he remembers that even the little fish were capable of biting; who knew what the sea snakes would do.

One of the snakes leaps from the water, and in midair changes to a small kitten, which plummets back into the water, then dives out of sight.

He wonders if he should trust the planet, trust the forest of his dreams, trust anyone or anything to take care of him. He thinks of the dozens of babies back at the colony, also born of Mohave, and he wonders if they are here, too, dreaming as he is. They may be the fish, the sea snakes, the kittens.

He trusts this world, his dreams, even the tall cats, more than he has ever trusted people and real life.

He floats, lets the water surround him more and more until everything but his nose is under water.

Then he sleeps.

•••

"Pietor," said Leticia. Pietor blinked a few times to clear the sleep from his eyes and glanced up at his mother. He stood and took notice that the buggy was stopped, no longer bouncing through the underbrush. They had to have arrived.

"Are we there yet?" he asked.

"You know we're inside the forest," Leticia said. "You going to sleep through your father's big discovery?" She turned back to the front of the buggy.

Outside the windscreen, the bright floodlights lit a clearing. Trees thrust up and out of the illumination all around, and Pietor recognized the shapes of the swaying giants, and above in the distance the canopy of branches at the top of the trees. This time Pietor looked from a viewpoint with which he was more familiar, and he knew they were definitely in the right place.

"The forest has been here a long time," Pietor said. "No one discovered it."

"Come on," said his father, and he opened the door of the buggy into the night of the forest.

•••

"You should have come alone," Marina says.

The clearing is different in the luminance of Marina's hair, her phosphorescent glow lighting the trees like white fire. She moves toward Pietor, loosing her hair from its tie behind her head.

"I know," Pietor says. "They wouldn't stop."

"The tall cats will come for them now, Pietor. The tall cats who walk beyond the edge of your vision, then stalk around through the trees over your head."

Marina reaches Pietor and lays her hands flat on his chest, then presses, pushing him backward, down onto the ground. Before he can react she is straddling him, her face above his, her eyes reflecting brilliant green light.

"The tall cats drop down from the trees, silent, and sink teeth deep into your skull. They tear off the back of your head while you're still alive."

She sneaks her fingers around the back of Pietor's head, runs them through his hair, nails tickling his scalp. She moves her face closer to his.

"You hear the crunch of bone, the sucking sound as the skull pulls away. You feel the air touch your brain, licking its folds with a chill wind."

She brings her hands back around to the front of Pietor's face, slides her fingers over his forehead, down his temples, then to his eyelids.

"Then everything goes black."

She closes his eyes with her fingers.

"But they're not coming for you, Pietor. They wouldn't have bothered you. You should have come alone. It was you I wanted. It was always you."

Pietor sees nothing, but feels her lips as she kisses him, softly, on the lips.

"And I'll have you," she says. "Only this once."

•••

Pietor opened his eyes to conflagration. The Allen family buggy lay in pieces, the largest chunk of it the frame, which sat broken and twisted a dozen feet in front of Pietor. Flaming piles of disk coal pushed up black smoke into the night sky and the tendrils snaked among the trees. Where the smoke hit the canopy of branches the trees have withdrawn, and Pietor looked with astonishment at the opening that led up to the sky. People would now be able to get in.

The broken, shredded bodies of his mother and father lay on the ground, skin stripped and blood pooling around their eviscerated remains. Whole chunks of meat were missing, bones snapped, skulls shattered as if their brains had been sucked through the bone and out.

Pietor knew he should be upset, should care, but here in the real world he never felt those sorts of things. It was too bad his parents had died, and he had a pang of regret, but he had only a vague understanding of what was going on around him. Here was life and death in its grim reality, and Pietor felt almost nothing.

Still, it was interesting to him because it was something new.

•••

Marina moves her arms behind her back, unbuttons her dress and lets it fall to the ground. Pietor watches as each inch of skin is exposed, slowly, the skein of cloth drifting downward in the low gravity. As she stretches her arms up in the air, her fingers reach for the tops of the trees, and her muscles flex, her body arching, lithe, beautiful, feline. Pietor's gaze goes to her nearly flat chest, her breasts just beginning to develop, her nipples, then down between her legs and to her feet. Her toes curl into the ground.

"This is your discovery," she says.

He wants to ask her to touch him, to kiss him again, but something keeps him from doing it. He doesn't understand it, the feeling of wanting her nor the feeling of not wanting her. And then white hair begins to sprout along the sides of her neck, then around her nipples, between her legs, along the tops of her feet. Her toes curl into claws and her nose elongates. She pokes her tongue out between her teeth as her upper canines plunge lower, pointy and brilliant white.

When the transformation is complete, the lithe white cat settles down onto all fours and extends her nose toward Pietor, tongue still out, sensing, tasting the air.

"You're beautiful," Pietor says. There is no fear, no sense of danger. He feels only adoration, awe, maybe even love.

Marina lowers her body to the ground and puts her head on her front paws. Her body erupts into a purr, a soft shaking that grows until it massages Pietor's body with its relaxing rumble.

"Thank you," she says. The feline form doesn't alter her ability to speak, nor to send shivers through Pietor's body with a glance.

"Not as tall as the others," Pietor says.

"I'm not yet full grown."

"And when you are?"

"I'll be a great hunter," she says.

"And when I'm full grown?"

"You're the first of your kind."

"What?"

"You're not like the others, Pietor," she says. "I've told you that. You're born of Mohave, and you are an integral part of it. Everything born here is."

"And what of the other people?" he says.

"We do want you here. All of you. You'll tell the others at the colony about the lake and they will send to Earth for creatures to stock it. There will be fish in this water, and people will eat the fish. And we will eat the fish, too. And maybe the people as your civilization grows. You'll help me, won't you, Pietor?"

"You want to eat us?" Pietor says.

"Not you, silly," Marina says. She stands, so quickly that Pietor could not have moved away if he had wanted to, then brushes a claw lightly across his temple. "You are my brother. I'd never hurt you."

"Your brother?"

"Of course. We were born together, at the same time, of the same world. You breathe the same dreams in your mind that I breathe. That makes us siblings, as in tune with each other as twins born of the same mother."

Pietor knows this is true, knows that his own feelings of longing for Marina are deeper than just a simple attraction of the flesh. There is mystery certainly, but more than that there is familiarity.

"I've known you my whole life," Pietor says.

"You know everything about this place," she says. "As it knows everything about you. Help me."

Pietor knows as he knows everything in his dreams that there is no way he could ever refuse Marina. And he doesn't want to refuse her because she is everything he thinks of as good in the world. She is more than just his sister. She is the other half of Pietor himself, the half who belongs only to the planet Mohave, not at all to the planet Earth. He fits with her.

"I will," Pietor says. "But not everyone will know you as I do. Others will come to kill you."

"Let them come," Marina says. "The hunt is so much more enjoyable if there is a fight."

"You'll eat everyone?"

"No. Other children will be born to your people. And with them, others will be born to ours. Someday we'll all be a family. Everyone else will be selected out. You call it evolution, but we select for the survival of the planet. Not all creatures are good for the planet."

She stands on all fours, then arches her back, a shiver moving from tail to nose. Then she moves toward Pietor, rubs her body slowly along his arm, then goes around his back and around again. She moves in close toward the back of his head, and Pietor wonders once more if she will rip open the back of his skull and suck out his brains. He feels her breath, hot and strong on his neck, then his ear.

"As it is in dreams, so it shall be in life," she says. Her tongue darts out to lick Pietor's ear briefly, then she is gone into the trees.

Pietor scratches at the fine brown hairs pushing out of the skin of his groin, then lays down to bask in the warm rays of the sun.

•••

The colony's canary-yellow lander drops through the hole in the canopy and circles the smoldering wreckage of the Allen family buggy a few times, then sets down at the edge of the burned forest. Pietor sits cross-legged on a patch of burned underbrush, his eyes tracking the noisy craft as it crunches charred branches and plants beneath its weight.

The doors to the lander open and several armed men step out, cautiously walking toward Pietor. They reach the bodies of his mother and father and stand, looking toward him. Pietor knows the kinds of questions they will ask, and he knows how he has to answer if he doesn't want the forest burnt to the ground. There will be time afterward to show them the lake, ripe for fish. Then, someday, the forest will grow its own biosphere, and it will expand to change the world. And people will be just one part of that grand system.

Pietor buttons his shirt up to cover the brown hair which has sprouted on his chest overnight. He walks toward the armed men. They relax a little when they see he appears unhurt.

"I have some things to show you," Pietor says.

Now he wakes.

# FALSE SUMMITS

*Written by*
**Kevin J. Anderson**

## About the Author

*Kevin J. Anderson was born March 27, 1962, and raised in small town Oregon, Wisconsin, south of Madison—an environment that was a cross between a Ray Bradbury short story and a Norman Rockwell painting.*

*He first knew he wanted to create fiction when he was five years old, before he even knew how to write; he had seen the film of* War of the Worlds *on TV and was so moved that he took a notepad the next day and drew pictures of scenes from the film, spread them out on the floor, and told the story out loud (perhaps this is what led him into writing comics nearly three decades later!)*

*At eight years old, Kevin wrote his first "novel" (three pages long on pink scrap paper) on the typewriter in his father's den—"The Injection," a story about a mad scientist who invents a formula that can bring anything to life . . . and when his colleagues scoff, he proceeds to bring a bunch of wax museum monsters and dinosaur skeletons to life so they can go on a rampage.*

*At the age of ten, he had saved up enough money from mowing lawns and doing odd jobs that he could either buy his own bicycle or his own typewriter. Kevin chose the typewriter . . . and has been writing ever since.*

*He submitted his first short story to a magazine when he was a freshman in high school, and managed to collect 80 rejection slips for various manuscripts before he actually had a story accepted two years later (for a magazine that paid only in copies). When he was a senior, he sold his first story for actual money (a whopping $12.50), but he never slowed down. He repeatedly submitted entries to the Writers of the Future Contest, valuing the need to meet the contest's deadlines, until he disqualified himself through professional sales. He sold his first novel by the time he turned twenty-five.*

*Kevin worked in California for twelve years as a technical writer and editor at the Lawrence Livermore National Laboratory, one of the nation's largest research facilities. At the Livermore lab, he met his wife, Rebecca Moesta, and also his frequent coauthor, Doug Beason.*

*After he had published ten of his own science fiction novels to wide critical acclaim, he came to the attention of Lucasfilm, and was offered the chance at writing* Star Wars *novels. Along the way he also collected over 750 rejection slips, and a trophy as "The Writer with No Future" because he could produce more rejection slips by weight than any other writer at an entire conference. When asked for advice about how to be a successful writer, he answers quickly: PERSISTENCE!*

*He is an avid hiker and camper, doing much of his writing with a hand-held tape recorder while on long walks in Death Valley, the redwoods, or the Rocky Mountains. He is also a great fan of fine microbrews.*

*His website is www.wordfire.com.*

I moved to Colorado six years ago and set up a writing office that looked out at the spectacular Rocky Mountains. The scenery, the fresh air, the lower cost of living, all were undeniable advantages. Then my brother-in-law gave me a book about the fifty-four peaks in Colorado over 14,000 feet high, along with maps and instructions on how to climb them all, if one were crazy enough.

Nothing thrills a goal-oriented person more than a List. I was hooked and immediately took up the hobby. Over the next five years, I did indeed summit all those peaks. I learned a lot about mountain climbing . . . and its relationship to writing.

I grew up in the Midwest, a place not known for many lofty and craggy peaks. Without first-hand experience, I had the rather distorted impression that "mountains" were pointy gray triangles with a zigzag of snow on the top, as depicted in Bugs Bunny cartoons. Since then, though, I've become an expert of the ins and outs (and ups and downs) of mountains, and I've realized that climbing these complicated and often difficult summits offers a useful parallel to a writing career.

•••

Peak 1

First submission

First personal rejection
First publication in a small press magazine
First professional publication

•••

Caution: Metaphor Ahead. As anyone starting out knows, a writing career is a very steep path to follow. The terrain is complicated, the trails not clear, and often forests block your view until you actually get to the top. While struggling up a tough grade, you keep your eyes only on the summit immediately ahead, forcing yourself to push on just to reach the top of that ridge.

It wasn't until I began mountain climbing in earnest that I understood the frustrating and heartbreaking frequency of what are called "false summits." You can glimpse the apparent high point of the trail, barely seen through the trees, and you expend all your energy focused on the goal. The top is there, getting closer—

And when you finally arrive, you see that what you thought was the top of the mountain, your hard-earned destination at last, is only a small subpeak. Right after that ridge, the trail continues farther and steeper toward a much taller and tougher point. You just couldn't see it because the false summit in front of you got in the way.

For many writers starting out, that first hard-to-obtain summit may be getting published, even in a fanzine, or receiving a personal rejection note from a professional market. But once you've achieved that, you have to catch your breath, take in the view . . . and see that you've merely managed to reach a crest of the surrounding heavily forested foothills. The majestic snow-covered mountain peaks are much farther away.

•••

Peak 2

First novel sale

Qualification for SFWA membership

First photo or review in a science fiction news magazine

•••

Many writers at this point simply turn around, enjoy their pleasant day hike, and go home. Others push on to the next ridge, closer to the treeline. From your new vantage atop the foothills, that treeline peak certainly looks like the summit.

From then on, you struggle to reach that point, and once you've succeeded—your first professional sale, qualification for SFWA membership, a novel sold to a publisher—you'll have a better view. You can see more of the surrounding terrain. But you also realize that this still isn't the actual summit. There's another ridge up ahead even higher, up in the rocky tundra with a few patches of snow.

Again, some writers stop here. The true mountain climbers, though, eat their beef jerky, drink some Gatorade, and keep going.

•••

Peak 3

First multiple book contract

Quit your day job and become a full-time writer

First major award or nomination

•••

Anyone with experience in the mountains knows there are plenty of pitfalls and dangers. I've sat on the top of 14,014-foot San Luis Peak watching the approach of angry thunderclouds, but when I took my hat off to drink from my water bottle, every strand of hair on my head and arms stood straight upright and the air crackled with static electricity. Needless to say, I beat a hasty retreat as the lightning moved in.

I've been caught a quarter mile from the top of Columbia Peak in a white-out blizzard in early September, where I huddled shivering for an hour until finally, experiencing the first stages of hypothermia, I trudged out into the snow and blindly stumbled down the slope to lower and warmer altitudes.

I've crawled across cliff ledges that would have made Indiana Jones proud, and rapelled down a sheer (six hundred meter) dry waterfall, the only way down from the top of Little Bear Peak, Colorado's most difficult Fourteener. I've even encountered a black bear on the summit of isolated and rarely climbed Culebra Peak.

Similarly, in your "career climb" as a writer, there are plenty of pitfalls—some that you can control and others that are simply forces of nature. Editors quit, publishing houses fold, you miss a deadline. A psycho serial killer announces that he drew all of his inspiration from your novel.

Proceed with caution so you don't slip and fall.

•••

Peak 4

First bestseller

First movie deal

Friends and acquaintances want to borrow money all the time

Other writers begin sniping at you for your "undeserved" success

Critics blast you because you're "too popular."

•••

I have found that each time I reach a peak in my career, there is a higher mountain visible in the distance. Once you set goals for yourself and reach them, you can either rest on your laurels, or try to climb higher. Are Tom Clancy, John Grisham and Michael Crichton comfortably perched and satisfied on lofty Mount Everest? Or do even they see more challenging summits in the distance?

Even though I've climbed all the 14,000-foot peaks in Colorado, Denali in Alaska is 20,320 feet, the highest peak in the United States. Kilimanjaro in Africa is 19,340 feet, and Everest is 29,028 feet.

I may have seen a lot of summits, but there are still plenty of higher ones left to dream about. . . .

•••

Peak 5

?

# THE PLASTIC SOUL OF A NOTE

*Written by*
**William T. Katz**

*Illustrated by*
**Luis G. Morales**

## About the Author

*Bill Katz has always marveled at the spectrum of human innovation, everything from novels and films to computer algorithms to business models. Three years ago he decided to pursue new fields of creativity. He left Varian Medical Systems, and became an entrepreneur and student of creative writing.*

*For most of his life, Bill has been fascinated with the brain and aspects of Artificial Intelligence. He helped pioneer a 3-D neurosurgical planning system and his brain was possibly the first one "printed" in plastic, lathed from a 3-D Magnetic Resonance image of his head.*

*It's not surprising that his short story idea grew from his work in virtual brains and anatomical reconstructions. He likes to ponder scenarios where scientists decide to take that next technological step, whether the world is ready or not.*

*Bill is currently building Writertopia.com, an Internet community of workshops that will help him revise his upcoming techno-thriller novel. He lives in Virginia with his wife, Jennifer. His website is at www.BillKatz.com.*

I stare at the pieces of flesh, detritus only given names like arm and hand because they're affixed to my worthless husk, and I am deeply ashamed. My gift, my reason for being, is utterly destroyed.

"Look at those people," Jessica says as our limousine slows near a crowd gathered before the ten-foot gates of the institute. "Don't they have anything better to do?" I read two of the signs that rise above a line of policemen: Each Human is Unique and Feed the Hungry First. A blond woman, thirty-something with wild eyes, swings a baby doll above her head and screams at us, the words barely audible where I sit. An old, bearded man holds a poster with an image of me in a tuxedo, smiling, sitting on a bench in front of a Steinway grand. Around the portrait, he has printed in black letters: We Love You John! Please Go Gently Into That Good Night!

It takes a few minutes for the limousine to travel from the iron gates through a forest of hickories and oaks, leaves turning yellow, maroon, before stopping in a circular driveway. Jessica scrambles out first—always the eager employee—unfolds my wheelchair and offers her hand, which I ignore.

How did it come to this? It's a question I ask incessantly, but I never receive any answers, just condolences and false hope and unwelcome surprises like the jagged pain that shoots through my left shoulder as I force myself into the wheelchair. I'd have found some way to excise myself from this world years ago, if not for the tantalizing vision that Dr. Turnbull revealed to me. Now, I'm simply a living donation to science.

"How are you feeling today, John?" Turnbull asks from the lip of the ramp that ascends to the institute's glass facade. His cherubic face seems misplaced on that gaunt frame.

"Miserable, as usual," I say as Jessica pushes me past the doctor. In my fantasy world—the world that I've been forced to live in—I'm Turnbull, standing there in a white lab coat, stethoscope around the neck, while a stream of even-pitched words spill from the decrepit, middle-aged pianist rolling past, the lilt in the tones like the falling scream of a train flashing by. I can only imagine an existence of sharp senses, dexterous fingers, fulfillment.

"Now, now," Jessica says in her best patronizing voice. "You should be excited. You've been waiting for this day." She wheels me into the foyer, seemingly all crystal and marble in a contemporary, opulent statement. In the middle, bathed by light filtering through a stained-glass dome, sits a circular, floating staircase that rises the full twenty feet to a second floor. We move to the right, down a long hall toward the main research lab before Dr. Turnbull passes us and punches a plate on the wall. Two large doors swing open and Jessica steers me into a bright room packed with whining computers. I see the donut again behind the thick glass at the far end of the room. Turnbull showed me a picture of it when we first met, his rosy cheeks doubly infused with color when he talked about his baby.

"It'll take a snapshot of your brain down to a few nanometers; that's exceptionally precise," he said back then, crowing like a newly minted father.

It looks larger than I expected—not the radius, because I knew my dwindling body would have to fit in the hole, but the mass—the solidity of the object is impressive.

"Without the active magnetic shielding, many items in this room would fly toward the glass," he says. "You'll have to remove your jewelry and put on a gown over there." He points us to a regular-sized door that is dwarfed by a steel and glass contraption—some huge, rectangular air lock—placed into the wall ten feet down.

Jessica pushes me into the changing room and helps me shed my clothes. I wear no jewelry. No need for a Rolex when you don't care about time. No need for a wedding ring when you have nothing left to give, when you're barely alive.

"This will be over before you know it, and there's a batch of Stella's great stew waiting back home," she says as she wraps the long gown over my body. I feel the softness of the cotton along a stretch of my back, the left shoulder, the right hip. First, you only notice the senses you lose, then after years of decline, you relish the few you have, like some child nursing his last, precious bits of candy.

She steers me in front of a long board with an egg-shaped device mounted at its edge. Turnbull unlatches the egg along its right side and swings it open, the front half revealing a contoured space that appears to be customized for a narrow nose and prominent chin. That explains the plaster of my head they took a month ago.

"Let us know if you get claustrophobic in there," Turnbull says. "We're going to start with your head, then we'll remove the head coil and do your spine."

They lift me onto the board, the back of my head sinking into the gaping egg, and fasten wide, nylon straps across my shoulders and wasted biceps. "We'll give you some play by your hands," he says and I cringe at the choice of words, "but it's important that you minimize any movement."

Minimizing movement is what I do best. I am a slab of meat served up on this long dish, and if they wait a few more years, maybe I won't be moving at all.

"All right, we're going to close it up. Don't worry about the air supply or anything," he says. "We've put redundant systems into the head coil, and there's a mike and speaker so you can talk to us if you have to."

I close my eyes as they swing the front half of the egg over my face; it's warm and snug but I have no problem breathing.

"Can you hear me?" Turnbull's voice is tinny.

"Yes."

For some time, I feel the board bounce and imagine they carry me into the gaping hole of the donut, its inner, ceramic surface forming another cocoon around my head.

"We're starting now. Try to relax and don't move."

Close my eyes. Relax. Visualize a peaceful scene. I see Carol in her opal bikini lying in the cabana, staring at the surf rolling in from the Pacific, piña colada on the small wooden table. I'm there, basking in the warmth of the sun and the refreshing breeze, listening to the surf while an attendant spritzes my hot face with Evian water.

"You're going to hear some loud noises," Turnbull interrupts. "Don't worry. That's the way the machine is supposed to sound."

Almost immediately, thunder booms through the thin strip of space between my encased head and the donut, like railroad workers hammering steel rails with sledges, the haphazard beats offering no musical interpretation. I think this sound would bother me if my ears weren't already less sensitive and wonder why the engineers couldn't make the clangs into an interesting pattern, perhaps a syncopated rhythm. Add in some thumps at the appropriate times even if they serve no function other than making the donut's occupant more comfortable, letting him listen to some perceptible rhythm instead of a senseless, mechanical insult.

But that's usually the problem with engineers. They get the job done but the aesthetics, the form, aren't a priority. Turnbull is different.

I saw that the first day I met Turnbull. He kept an elegant office with mahogany and green velvet chairs in front of an expansive, lacquered desk—a throne fit for the "king of his field," as the doctor who referred me called him. Turnbull was dressed in a sharp double-breasted suit, a Brioni perhaps, and exuded more confidence than most of the presidents and prime ministers I'd met.

"I think we can offer you a solution." Those were the first real words he spoke to me and I liked his sense of directness. "We're working on a system that can preserve your art. That's what this is about."

He talked about the accomplishments of bioengineers over the last decade: artificial eyes, substitute hands, figuring out how to hook them into the human nervous system. The *pièce de résistance* was his research, a way to take a snapshot of the brain down to the smallest detail and get it running on a computer. Of course, he didn't say it that way, and if he did, I might not have trusted him. Instead he said they could perform "noninvasive imaging at a near-molecular scale" and the computers could "process the image voxels to construct a three-dimensional blueprint" of my brain. So I believed him. What could I have lost?

I had multiple sclerosis, a disease that stripped my nerves bare of an essential coating, and even among those who had MS, I had it particularly bad. At first, symptoms came and went—eye problems, tremors—but then there were fewer remissions and I developed "atypical symptoms"—that's what the doctor called the pain that was present some of the time. The pain was the most delicious affront as if the devil himself wondered why I should not enjoy pain even as I lost all other sensation. The disease progressed steadily, unaffected by the experts, until I got on the one experimental protocol that worked. It halted the deterioration but, given the course of my disease, most of the doctors said I probably wouldn't regain what I'd lost. The new steroid had stopped further loss of the coating, the myelin, but they didn't think they could bring back the affected nerves. And so I cursed everyone for letting things get that far. Turnbull, though, offered me hope.

"The computer doesn't care if your nerves have myelin or not," he said. "When it simulates, it only cares about the way your nerves are connected." After he finished describing the procedure, I pretended to reflect on it for a moment before signing the contract.

I'm thinking about this and it's relaxing, maybe even more comforting than my memories of Carol and our honeymoon in Maui, because that day with Turnbull was the rebirth of hope. I have no children, no part of me that lives on past this closing movement. What do I have to lose?

Now the hammering sounds come in a steady cadence—thump, thump, thump—and I'm trying hard not to fidget. I decide to empty my mind, imagine space that's vast, dark, silent. And at some point, the world just winks out.

•••

"John!" Turnbull's voice is vibrant, loud. "John, can you hear me?"

I feel like I'm being pulled from a wonderful dream by a nagging alarm clock. "Yes . . . I hear you." My words sound distorted, somewhat more baritone with a strange reverb.

My head isn't in the egg any longer and I'm lying down on something soft and it's not the cushioned board. I can tell because I sense the pressure behind my head and along my back and legs . . . *all* down my skin and there are no absences—*no* islands of sensation—it's just all there and I feel like my heart should be racing because that's what happens when I get a shock like this but there's nothing, *nothing,* just an odd tingle instead of the jolt of adrenaline and there's no pain—absolutely no wretched pain *anywhere*—I can't believe it because my senses are so clean and so pure and completely unpolluted by the ache there or the throbbing over there.

"We're going to remove the blindfold and you can open your eyes."

I feel a cloth lifted from my head and there's no period of adjustment. I just see so clearly and there's Turnbull standing over me, that beautiful cherubic face staring down with fluorescent lights overhead and two nurses in chartreuse surgical scrubs standing behind him, one next to a boxy gray gadget emitting a low-frequency hum with wires that fall in my direction and now I feel the straps on my ankles and wrists and arms and forehead and the only perception, the *only* sense that isn't brilliant exciting breathtaking is the muted smell of the place.

"Calm down, John," Turnbull says. He's staring at a monitor down by my knees—are those my knees?—and I see the screen fill with crisp dynamic splotches of colors that dance frenetically.

"Rest easy," he says. "I know it's odd for you, so we have to tune things up. Bear with us." I have an urge to reach up and hug him but the pressure from the straps tells me I'm not going anywhere. "We'll just sit here for a while and let you adjust. Just listen to my voice . . . and don't think about anything . . . listen to my voice."

I try to relax, take deep breaths, but there's no sensation of breathing. I'm not suffocating but no air brushes past the skin of my nostrils.

"Splendid," Turnbull says as he leans over me again. I hear *his* breathing—slow, steady. "Splendid."

•••

I'm still a little disoriented. We've spent my first day tuning or, as they told me in techno-speak, adjusting "the sensorimotor interface from the neural simulation to the neuroprosthetic devices."

Now I'm slated for my first PR gig.

Three media crewmen scurry about the lab, fussing among themselves and adjusting the overhead lights. Occasionally, they peek at me before quickly averting their eyes.

Turnbull strides in, wearing an immaculately white lab coat with the words, "Peter Turnbull, M.D., Ph.D." stitched in red just above a chest pocket. After our initial interview, after I signed the contract, I almost never saw him with a tie, just a dress shirt underneath the lab coat. Today, he's sporting a glistening, cyan silk tie and not a strand of hair is out of place.

"Let's get ready," Pham says. I've seen some of his interviews even though he reports on the scientific not the artistic scene. Pham wears a blue oxford shirt, khaki pants, and gold, wire-rimmed glasses that sit near the end of his flat nose. He appears quite comfortable. I'm not. I'm sitting on the exam table, legs dangling over the side, wearing nothing but black shorts, and thinking how I'm going to be broadcast through the entire net as the naked patient.

Turnbull takes a seat next to Pham and a crewman places a sausage-shaped microphone above our heads. We are surrounded by six tripod-mounted cameras that look like coffee cans sprouting rectangular visors around the lenses, the equipment painted a disgusting shade of lime.

"Where do you want me facing?" asks Turnbull as he smoothes the front of his coat.

"Don't worry," Pham says and points at the ring of cameras. "We shoot the entire footage and our editor reconstructs whatever angle she needs later. Shall we start?" Pham turns a few sheets of notes sitting on his lap and then focuses on Turnbull.

"I'm here with Dr. Peter Turnbull, the founder of the Institute for Neuroprosthetic Research," he says, then turns to me, "and the *new* John Neri who is widely regarded as this century's greatest pianist." I try not to wave, a small flip of my hand like the Queen of England.

"Dr. Turnbull, what was the biggest problem in building John's new form?"

Turnbull strikes an exaggerated, contemplative pose. "Well, I would say it was power. Evolution has created a fairly elegant solution. The human body handles every reaction—the molecular computations necessary for thought and control signals, the mechanical work of muscles—we do that using only the energy supplied by daily meals." Turnbull starts wildly gesticulating as he gets into his rhythm. "Add the problems of distributing the energy source and disposing the waste, whether its heat or metabolites, and it's a tough nut to crack.

"The core operation of the human brain takes about ten watts," he adds. "That's pretty power efficient and better than any man-made equivalent before modern nanotube computers. So this was a problem we had to address in the design phase: how to design a mobile, self-contained system that's very power efficient. In fact, an original design placed most of the computation out of the body, in stationary computers. Those computers could be as big as we wanted and draw as much power as necessary, and they got the sensory and motor I/O by wireless from the body."

"So why didn't you go with that design route?" Pham asks.

"Our early experiments used that technique, but for the final product, our sponsors wanted a more mobile, self-contained body and—"

"Are you talking about the Department of Defense?" Pham leaned forward and cocked his head. "We saw that a fair portion of your funding comes from DARPA special programs."

"Well, that's true," Turnbull says, looking like Custer's scout at Little Big Horn. "But we draw funding from a lot of sources, not just the military, and DARPA has a track record of funding progressive work like the early net. There are many applications that DARPA brought up: space exploration, disposal of hazardous waste, medical care in hot zones. So we're certainly happy to work with a variety of research agencies."

Pham smiles but there's a slight twitch at the corner of his mouth. "Will the androids have superhuman capabilities?"

"For our first attempt, we decided not to put in any sensors or features that were functionally dissimilar to human physiology. In fact, we purposely tried to limit everything and make it as similar to human analogs as possible, from a functional not a structural perspective. In the future, we can augment parts in a very controlled environment, with people like John here as the baseline. The other reason we're sticking with simple human analogs is the power consideration."

The interview continues *ad nauseum* until Pham finally turns his questions on me. What is it like? Are you eager to start playing again? Has the prospect of immortality changed your thinking? The questions keep coming and I give pat answers. I'm glad he doesn't bring up any sexual topics, but maybe with the magnetic limbic stimulators on the market for the last three years, he doesn't think it's an interesting question.

"Final question . . . Why do you think you were chosen?"

The institute had some unknown selection committee for the lottery of immortality and, as expected, there was no shortage of volunteers. Ultimately, neither scientist nor politician was chosen; it was an artist. Clearly, the institute, or maybe Turnbull, wanted to make a statement.

I know there are plenty of reasons for my selection. Turnbull claims he's a big fan, and I never question it, but that's simply fodder for the press. There's a huge public-opinion battle between those who want the technology and those who fear what it could do to society. Turnbull makes great efforts to separate his research from the cloners, and that's a smart move. There's always something reprehensible about making biological duplicates; maybe people feel they could be replaced—nightmares of *Invasion of the Body Snatchers.* Androids, though, aren't biological and certain groups, especially Turnbull's friends in Defense, thought the benefits far outweighed the problems. And who better to be the first android than a popular musician, especially one incapable of performing anymore, one of the walking dead?

"I think Dr. Turnbull was a fan and realizes how beneficial this technology would be for furthering the arts. Imagine preserving the next generation's Mozart or Michelangelo? I'm hardly the stature of either of those giants," I say, pausing just briefly in case he wants to object, "but I can help Dr. Turnbull work out kinks in the system. We'll see if this android body can reproduce nuances in performance art."

Afterwards, Pham approaches me, sheepishly, while his crew disassembles the ring of cameras. He gives me a DVD package emblazoned with my picture, head down over the keys of a grand, the Berlin Philharmonic Orchestra filling the background. Under the title, I see my signature hastily written in sprawling, gold letters.

"I just loved your rendition of Beethoven's second piano concerto," Pham says and hands me a black marker. "I managed to get one of the signed copies. Would you mind signing it again?"

I smile and meticulously write "John Neri, Second Movement" at the bottom of the case. The new autograph is precise, and small.

•••

"That's turning out pretty good," Turnbull says. "The electroactive polymers are functioning perfectly."

We're in an exam room and he's watching me flex my fingers. The silicone exterior looks natural, right down to sculpted fingerprints and skin pores. It's been two days since I woke in this new body and although I still feel off, the tuning has removed the weirder sensations. I shouldn't moan about the differences; the engineers have done an amazing job mapping the body parts into familiar sensations. After all, if I were still human, even small changes like swollen feet or sunburn would make me feel different too.

"How is he doing—the flesh and blood version?" I ask. "I thought he'd be at the interview, kind of assumed they'd want him there."

I've always been known as a perfectionist, a tough critic of all things musical and, according to my ex-wife, most things nonmusical. So it's particularly ironic that after the interview was posted, the majority of e-mails I received were complaints: how I only saw the coming of androids as blessing not blight. None of the e-mails mentioned the old me.

"He's stable. He said he wasn't feeling well enough to attend."

"Yes, I can guess what he's thinking." I turn my hand over and look at the palm; there are a few creases but no life line, no health line. "Just how close is my brain to his? Do the thoughts happen exactly the same way?"

Turnbull scrutinizes my face, as if he's trying to decide how much of a prognosis to disclose. "Down to a certain level of detail, both of your brains operate identically. But at the very lowest levels, there might be small discrepancies, the tiniest differences, since the computational mechanisms are very different."

"Does that mean I don't think the same way?"

"Well, to tell you the truth, we don't know. We ran simulations and the outputs looked great as far as we could tell, but we don't know if the differences accumulate over time. Maybe there's a divergence between you and your human form. But that's just the brain simulation algorithms. There's plasticity in our nervous system—we adapt. Experience shapes what we think, how we think, and you two are certainly having dissimilar experiences these days." He grins and writes something on a digital notepad.

I think perhaps that's not such a bad thing—to have some uniqueness.

"My perspective has certainly changed—maybe it's being able to feel, being so mobile again. Before the brain imaging, I was all wrapped up in a blanket of grief. That's probably why I didn't—I mean why *he* didn't—show up to the interview. To him, I'm just a wild shot at a living legacy."

Turnbull listens intently, cradling the thin, aluminum notepad with his arms. "So he doesn't think this will work?"

I try to choose my words carefully. "He doesn't have much vested in this. I do. He thinks if the experiment works—fine—but deep down, he doesn't think I'll be able to play."

It feels incredibly odd to confess how I felt about some *thing* that would be created from my body, but knowing that thing is now me. I am a virtual mirror into my own self-centeredness, and it's an ugly sight.

"And you," Turnbull asks, "what do you think?"

"I don't know. I'll do everything I can to make it work."

I want to tell him the truth, that I have serious doubts. After the brain imaging, the path of our thoughts split apart, but we saw things the same way until then. Old biases don't disappear.

"Follow me," Turnbull says and we leave the exam room and walk down a hall, arriving outside a curved wooden wall decorated with vertical grooves. The words *John Neri Hall* are engraved on a gold plaque to the right of four oak doors.

He opens a door and waves me in. "I hope you like it."

We pass the threshold and the ambient noise from the hallway nearly disappears. The auditorium is warm, personable, stunning: unmistakably designed for performances, not only scientific presentations. Stylish patterns of dark and light wood veneer cover the walls of the triangular space as it slopes downwards, drawing all eyes to the oak parquet stage. The seats, upholstered in black velour, are arranged on terraces that descend to the orchestra level like a tenderly manicured vineyard. Resting on the stage is a glorious Bösendorfer 290 Imperial grand with its top propped open, the black high polish softly reflecting.

"What do you think?" he asks and breaks my reverie as we reach the piano. I don't answer but run the tip of my left finger along the rim.

It takes about eighteen months of demanding, hands-on work to craft this instrument—a process that hasn't changed much since 1828 when the new Bösendorfer factory got an endorsement from seventeen-year-old Franz Liszt. The acoustics are shaped by parts made of seasoned Italian spruce gathered from thick forests in Val di Fiemme, the valley where Stradivari handpicked wood for his violins.

"It's beautiful," I say. I hadn't been specific in my requests for a piano and was pleasantly surprised at this development. "How long has it been here?"

"About four weeks, it's fully acclimatized." Turnbull grins. "We actually started inquiries on decent pianos after you signed on."

"Yes, it's a decent piano." I can't help but smile, overtaken by a rare giddiness. "Has Bösendorfer sent a technician?"

"He just tuned it yesterday. You're set to go."

I quickly sit on the bench, glide my fingertips along the cool ivory of the full eight-octave compass, and admire the exquisite workmanship. With my first strokes, a powerful, singing tone fills the space as I revel in the sounds, letting it flow through me and for a moment, the world resonates with iridescent beauty.

•••

There's a pristine courtyard in the middle of the research complex, complete with wooden benches, dwarf fruit trees—cherry, apple, plum—and a variety of ferns and azaleas surrounding a koi pond that runs the length of one side. A Japanese rock garden, its plane

Illustrated by Luis G. Morales

ruled with snaking furrows, lies on the far end of the pond.

Even though I practice day and night, I carve out a little time at noon to sit in the courtyard and watch the fat, vivid koi swim around their restricted world. I hardly need sleep. When I go into the lab to rest, the technicians speed up my internal clock and let the sleep simulations pass in a few minutes, unless they're recharging my internal batteries.

Today, when I enter the courtyard, I see one of the technicians parked on a bench by the rock garden, a paper bag in one massive hand. Nate is a bear, black with giant barrels for arms and a glossy, smooth head as wonderfully bald as mine. I sit next to him.

"I hope I'm not intruding on your down time," he says, the voice an impossibly deep and resonant boom that would fall in the lowest octave of a piano's register. Nate removes from the paper bag a thick double-decker sandwich that seems tiny in his hand and gingerly takes a bite. I marvel at the dexterity of his hands, the poetic motion, for someone of his size.

"No, I appreciate the company and," I say, with a sweep of my synthetic arm, "it's not like this courtyard is mine."

Three blue- and orange-painted koi swim by us and create an audible stirring of the water.

"You ever play football?" I ask. Nate must be well over three hundred pounds and almost none of it in fat.

His throaty laugh lifts my spirits and scares the koi away.

"No, sir," he says. "I get asked that a lot, due to my size and all. I do a little lifting but stayed clear of the football field . . . maybe it was my mother's influence. She was a teacher."

He takes a bite and the sandwich disappears, quickly replaced by another from the bag. "Yeah, I spent my time in the library—no long football practices for me—and that sure was tough growing up in Alabama."

I notice a worn copy of *How to Read an Unwritten Language* lying next to Nate on the bench. "Does your mother still live in Alabama?"

Nate's joviality diminishes and his deep voice returns more softly. "No, she died a few years back," he says, looks plaintively at me, and taps the left side of his broad chest. "Heart attack."

I nod but with a strange feeling of guilt, as if I am unworthy of this new body. I watch him take another bite and an old tune fills my thoughts, which I soon recognize is the beloved's theme in *Symphonie Fantastique.* When Berlioz wrote the piece, he used a thematic device, an *idée fixe,* where the memories of his love keep recurring in the form of a melody, although it's transformed each time. Unfortunately, instead of the charming tune at the beginning of the symphony, I hear the grotesque, vulgar dance of the Witches' Sabbath—the melody of the beloved twisted into the warbling clarinet in my mind.

"What's that?" Nate asks.

I look up, slightly puzzled, until I realize I'm humming the tune. I stop humming but the rest of my thoughts keep going, creating links between faint memories and present worries.

Since the changeover, the time I've spent in front of the piano has been a study in escalating frustration. My new body works. They've designed hands that look like my old ones, a head that passes as my mannequin, feet that handle the pedals appropriately. But I don't *feel* the same about my music; there's some subtle difference that I can't figure out.

I get up and walk to the edge of the pond and lean over to see my reflection staring back: a somber, artificial portrait of an artist. "I think I made a mistake."

"What kind of mistake?"

"Not really considering the consequences." I stroke my hairless jawline. "The world *is* going to be very different."

For a while, we silently watch the koi swim. I move closer, scraping the stone edge of the pond with my sneaker, and the koi stream toward me—strings of green, orange, blue, red, shimmering through the crystal water, each converging into a tiny grotto, waiting for the food that I didn't have.

Nate lifts himself from the wooden bench and walks over to me. "It always comes down to people. It's human nature to explore, and the technology that comes out . . . well, each of us uses it how we see fit. It's free will," he says, putting his large hand on my shoulder, "and you have it too."

Nate ambles away, pausing by the door to say, "Have a nice day, John." When he's gone, it occurs to me that for most of my life, before my new body, I haven't *genuinely* talked to people outside my insular musical world.

•••

The trace of notes lingers in the open space of the auditorium after I pause to review the phrasing of a run. It's been over a month and it still isn't right. Sometimes, I feel the breath of the composer's ghost on the back of my neck. Even now, in this body with synthetic skin, I feel the breath and sense Chopin's intense, brown eyes staring from their position astride a finely curved, aquiline nose.

I remember my mother, a supremely gifted pianist, pacing about our family's cozy music parlor, floor-to-ceiling shelves spilling over with sheet music, the fresh scent of flowers by the Steinway blending with the musty trace of leather-bound volumes. She made me listen to recordings of the masters, and now and then, she frowned during a passage. "You see. This piece was well played, very nice," she said, "but it is dead. There is not a single note that is alive, so how can he expect us to appreciate it?"

One day, she told me how she breathed life into every piece she played. She said that the creation of music is like the dance of two lovers: the performer uses her techniques, shaped by her own desires, while still paying heed to the subtle and occasionally forceful cues relayed by the composer. The balance between individuality and subservience shifts over time with the whims of the cognoscenti. Some years see the performer as merely a trained concubine to the force of the score; others see the pianist ignoring the pleas of the ghost while she sates her own needs. It is in the middle ground that art, like love, is made more fulfilling to everyone.

I chuckle when I remember my answer to her poignant lesson. "But mother," I said, then a strapping sixteen-year-old, "I'm a man and most composers are, well . . ." She grunted and narrowed her eyes and pursed her lips. "Honestly," she said, "why do I bother?" She stormed out, only to return an hour later, lured by my attempts at apology through a Debussy prelude. As these memories return, I think of Nate and try to imagine a world filled with immortal mothers.

A dry cough breaks the silence and I turn to see Turnbull in a seat almost obscured by darkness. "Please don't stop on my account," he says.

"No, I'm having problems and could use a break." I push away from the piano and hear the scraping of the bench on the stage echo through the auditorium. "Sometimes I forget that I don't fatigue, so my usual six-hour practices keep going and going."

"It sounds amazing, like your recordings a decade ago."

I'm irritated by his analysis, his inability to see the flaws so rampant in my playing. "Thank you," I say.

"I have a question. I didn't want to ask it while you were ill."

"Go ahead."

"What's it like?" Turnbull asks and he hunches forward. "How does it feel to be a top concert pianist?"

My first thought is how he used the present tense in his question: How *does* it feel? As if I am a top concert pianist. Then I recall that glorious moment when I felt the weight of a gold medal around my neck, the winner of the Tchaikovsky competition, a young man who had so passionately rendered Rachmaninov's Third.

"It feels good to have climbed the heap," I say. "There's maybe four hundred international competitions churning out new talent, but there aren't enough venues for performance. The supply is so much larger than the demand, especially here in the United States." As I'm speaking the words, it occurs to me what my existence will do to the equilibrium. What will happen to those children, the ones like me, that dare to accept the challenge and find their lives inextricably drawn into music?

"I actually came to ask you if we could have a recital," he says. "Just a short one to kick the tires, nothing long."

"How many people will be in the audience?"

"A handful of dignitaries. Ones that were instrumental in making this research a success."

"I'm not ready, you know."

"When do you think you'll be ready?"

"I don't know if I'll ever be ready."

"Don't you think you're being overly critical?"

"I've always been hard on myself. That's how I am, but I *know* when playing is great and when it's marginal."

"Well," he says, drawing out the word, "the few people coming are fully aware this is a work in progress . . . and some outside opinions might give you a little perspective."

I sit there on the bench a few feet from the Bösendorfer. Turnbull is asking me, but he doesn't have to ask. I'm fairly sure it's in the contract and my memory, at least, has never been better.

"How long has it been since you've given a concert?" he asks.

"A little over five years." I think for a moment and add, "Vladimir Horowitz used to retire now and then. He was gone for twelve years once, and when he came back, he gave an amazing concert at Carnegie Hall."

Horowitz created magic when his fingers touched the keys, giving every piece a unique character. I look down at my meticulously sculpted hands and suffer a rush of panic, a hollow sensation in its wake. How could I invoke his name when discussing my absence, as if the two of us have any similarity?

"It was a stupid thing to mention," I whisper.

I am just a minor echo of my own talent, a machine. Tantalus made real by nanotechnology. While I can execute with precision, faithfully reproducing the composer's intention like a billion-dollar music box, the result is mechanical and musically uninteresting, so very different from the completely human interpretation of Horowitz *or* the twenty-year-old Neri.

"What did you say?" Turnbull asks. His expression reminds me of my ex-wife's as she watched me receive the initial diagnosis over the phone.

"Schedule the recital at your convenience," I say and exit the auditorium. I'd been so cavalier with this experiment, so blasted egocentric, as usual, that I never thought about anyone else, *even me*, now trapped in this fresh, plastic shell.

•••

The day of the recital, I wander about the center, eventually drifting into the lab. Nate is sitting in front of two flat panel displays, and I watch with amazement how he touch-types with those massive fingers.

"How's the practice going?" he asks while continuing to type.

I sigh and it sounds real but I know there's no air behind it; I have no lungs. All of my vocalizations seem like they have air behind them, even if they truly do not. Sounds without substance, like my playing.

"I feel . . . artistically bankrupt."

Nate stops and studies me. "When's the last time you slept?"

"I think maybe two days ago. It's harder to keep track when you sleep only a few minutes."

He nods. "Let's get you set up."

The sleep station consists of a bed, which I lie down on, and a tall steel rack filled with blinking computers stacked like pizza boxes, fibers leaking out the back. I pull the right side of my sweatpants down slightly and draw aside a tiny flap on my hip, baring two circular ports. Nate deftly inserts transparent fibers into the holes and moves back behind the displays. I hear a few mouse clicks over the steady buzzing of the rack-mounted computers.

"You see *Groundhog Day?*" he asks.

"No. They celebrate that in some town in Pennsylvania, right?"

His wide face expands into a powerful grin. "It's a movie, Mr. Artiste," he says. "It's about a not-so-nice guy trapped in a single day. Every morning he wakes up and the world is the same as the day before. At first, it gets to him, and he tries to kill himself—lots of times—but he keeps waking up on the morning of Groundhog Day, the same as always."

Nate's shiny head bobs as he slides his rolling chair over to a black box and throws a few switches. "Then the man decides to deal with it and starts to work the system. He uses the time and learns all kinds of things like French poetry and jazz piano. By the end of the film, he's a real Renaissance man, helping the town folk and making that day something special."

"Does he ever break free of that day?" I ask. "How does it end?"

"How's it end." The bass pitch of Nate's voice drops with each successive syllable in mock incredulity. "It's a Hollywood film, man. There's always a happy ending. Now get some shut-eye."

I close my eyes, welcoming the onset of the sleep simulations. For a few minutes, I dream of groundhogs and free will and men with the gift of infinite time.

•••

Those who truthfully dedicate themselves to an art don't do it for money or glory. In the end, they do it because they have to; it's a palpable, visceral need that must be satisfied. Writers have to write. Painters have to paint. And pianists, they have to play.

As I stride to the Bösendorfer, I hear no applause and try to clear my mind of doubts, particularly since I have chosen to perform Chopin's difficult cycle of Preludes: twenty-four ingenious compositions that are linked but exist as separate pieces at the same time, each with its own spirit. I'm sure that some would question my selection, my impetuousness for starting with a work that will reveal any faults, but if I'm to be exposed, I'll go out with drama.

And so it begins with the first prelude in C as my hands glide, effortlessly, over the beckoning keys, creating a pulsating, agitated texture. The first prelude gives way to the forlorn, sluggish second and then the delicate melody of the third with its light, rippling figure for the left hand.

One by one they pass as I move from vigor to cheerfulness, a rain of sadness to tranquility. My beloved has returned, gleaming and whole and slyly transformed, all the sweeter from her absence, lent power and voice by my polished instrument.

My spirits soar as the intensity builds in the last prelude, the tension finally dispersing in a burst of double chromatic thirds and octaves, and it is done. I withdraw from the keys and soak in the very last remnants of the sound, relishing the gift.

After a moment, I stand and peer into the auditorium but there is only silence—a void—absent any signs of life save a rustling in the middle of the auditorium where my audience, hidden in darkness, must be recoiling. Doubt then loathing intrudes on my bliss. I am imbued with artificial hubris, hearing majesty where there was only mechanical precision.

The lights over the audience brighten and there is only one man in the audience, wheelchair-bound. I see he is young, in his late thirties, despite the slow, halting movements of an octogenarian, and I move to the edge of the stage. His unruly, sandy hair sits on top a handsome face with piercing blue eyes, a fine patrician nose, and strong chin. We are together for the first time since the imaging, and my view of the crippled, young man through distant eyes is starkly unlike the subhuman images of his, and my, memory.

I want to shout at him, force his colored perceptions, his idiocy to wither away in an onslaught of words. What did he expect? Did he actually think some man-made artifice would suffice? Did he ever stop to think what life would be in this android body without our music, or was the imaging procedure too short, too simple *not* to do it?

I'm sure he'll judge me, now that I'm trapped in this immortal body. This exceptionally flawed critic, who accepts no faults in music, especially from me, will deem me unworthy and retreat into the tepid embrace of his grief. Despite the half-buried instinct to address the outrage sweeping through me, I will not lash out. I will not sift my memories to find some insult, some club to bludgeon this man.

We watch each other, a reunion of talent lost and promise unfulfilled, until I see rivulets fall down his tired human cheeks.

I nearly walk away, to deprive him of yet another target, when I notice the most peculiar event. He begins to smile, not a mocking grin or a disguised scowl, but a heartfelt, welcoming gesture so infrequent on that cynical face that its presence compels me to stay and stare. Then slowly, passionately, he lifts himself to a standing position and claps, shouting with as much force as he can muster, "Bravo! Bravissimo!" While I numbly stand on the stage, he applauds for a precious eternity before collapsing back into the wheelchair.

"Jessica!" he says. Jessica enters the hall, smiles at me, and strolls to the wheelchair.

I want to talk with them, return to our warm, antique home, let him know what it's like in this new body, but I see his proud astonishment has been replaced by an overpowering melancholy. I know he wants nothing more than to leave this place . . . and me.

"Thank you," I say, unable to find proper words, and watch them disappear through the closing doors.

# THE YEAR IN THE CONTESTS

*by*
**Algis Budrys**

*Algis Budrys, editor of the anthology, was born in Königsberg, East Prussia, on January 9, 1931. East Prussia (now the republic of Belarus) was at that time a part of Germany, but Budrys is a Lithuanian from birth, because his father, the Consul General of Lithuania, was merely stationed in East Prussia at the time. The family came to America in 1936.*

*Budrys became interested in science fiction at the age of six, when a landlady slipped him a copy of the* New York Journal-American *Sunday funnies. The paper was immediately confiscated by his parents, as being low-class trash, but it was too late. Shortly thereafter, Budrys entered PS 87 in New York. There, he was given a monthly publication called* Young America, *which featured stories by Carl H. Claudy, a now-forgotten juvenile science fiction author, and such serials as "At the Earth's Core" by Edgar Rice Burroughs. He was hopelessly lost, and by the age of nine was writing his own stories.*

*At the age of twenty-one, living in Great Neck, Long Island, he began selling steadily to the top magazine markets.*

*He sold his first novel in 1953, and eventually produced eight more novels, including* Who?, Rogue Moon, Michaelmas *and* Hard Landing, *and three short-story collections. He has always done a number of things besides writing, most but not all of them related to science fiction. Notable among them was a long stretch as a critic.*

*He has been, over the years, the editor in chief of Regency Books, Playboy Press, all the titles at* Woodall's Trailer Travel *publications, and L. Ron Hubbard's* Writers of the Future, *where he works now. He has also been a PR man for various clients, including Peter Pan Peanut Butter, Pickle Packers International and International Trucks. His favorite client was Pickle Packers International, for which he participated in a broad variety of stunts; but his most challenging client was International Trucks, for which he crisscrossed the country for four years, from the Bridgehampton Race Track on Long Island to the sin palaces of Long Beach.*

*In 1954, he married Edna F. Duna, and is still married to her, an arrangement that suits both of them. They have four sons, now scattered over America and the world. Life is good.*

The judges in this year are named on the cover of this book. They are amazingly prestigious and knowledgeable contributors to L. Ron Hubbard's original (and still growing) vision. This has been true from the very beginning, though some names are, sadly, no longer with us and others, happily, have stepped forward to take their place.

We have been pleased to welcome judge Brian Herbert to our stellar panel of judges for the L. Ron Hubbard Writers of the Future Contest.

Sadly, Hal Clement has been taken from us and from SF in general.

The enterprise goes ever forward, and the authors and illustrators in this volume will, in due course, take their firm place in the history of speculative arts. For the 2003 year, L. Ron Hubbard's Writers of the Future Contest winners are:

**First Quarter**

1. Jason Stoddard
   *Kinship*
2. Bradley P. Beaulieu
   *Flotsam*
3. Andrew Tisbert
   *The Weapons of the Lord Are Not Carnal*

**Second Quarter**

1. William T. Katz
   *The Plastic Soul of a Note*
2. Luc Reid
   *Bottomless*
3. Gabriel F.W. Koch
   *Cancilleri's Law*

**Third Quarter**

1. Matthew Champine
   *Sunrunners*
2. Roxanne Hutton
   *Shipwoman*
3. Tom Pendergrass
   *Last Days of the Mahdi*

**Fourth Quarter**

1. Blair MacGregor
   *The Key*
2. Joy Remy
   *Sleep Sweetly, Junie Carter*
3. Jonathan Laden
   *Monkey See, Monkey Deduce*

**Published Finalists**

Kenneth Brady
*Asleep in the Forest of the Tall Cats*

Eric James Stone
*In Memory*

Floris M. Kleijne
*Conversation with a Mechanical Horse*

L. Ron Hubbard's Illustrators of the Future Contest winners:

Yancy Betterly
Robert Drozd
Luis G. Morales
Douglas Pakidko
Brian C. Reed
Beth Anne Zaiken
Laura Diehl
Shawn Gaddy
Fabrizio Pacitti
Brian Carl Petersen
Matt Taggart

Our heartiest congratulations to them all! May we see much more of their work in the future.

# CONTEST RULES

1. No entry fee is required and all rights in the story remain the property of the author. All types of science fiction, fantasy and horror with fantastic elements are welcome.

2. All entries must be original works, in English. Plagiarism, which includes the use of third-party poetry, song lyrics, characters or another person's universe, without written permission, will result in disqualification. Excessive violence or sex, determined by the judges, will result in disqualification. Entries may not have been previously published in professional media.

3. To be eligible, entries must be works of prose, up to 17,000 words in length. We regret we cannot consider poetry or works intended for children.

4. The contest is open only to those who have not had professionally published a novel or short novel, or more than one novelette, or more than three short stories, in any medium. Professional publication is deemed to be payment, and at least 5,000 copies or 5,000 hits.

5. Entries must be typewritten or a computer printout in black ink on white paper, double spaced, with numbered pages. All other formats will be disqualified. Each entry must have a cover page with the title of the work, the author's name, address and telephone number, an approximate word count and e-mail address if available. Every subsequent page must carry the title and a page number, but the author's name must be deleted to facilitate fair judging.

6. Manuscripts will be returned after judging if the author has provided return postage and a self-addressed envelope. If the author does not wish return of the manuscript, a business-size self-addressed, stamped envelope (or valid e-mail address) must be included with the entry in order to receive judging results.

7. We accept only an entry for which no delivery signature is required by us to receive it.

8. There shall be three cash prizes in each quarter: a First Prize of $1,000, a Second Prize of $750 and a Third Prize of $500, in U.S. dollars or the recipient's local equivalent amount. In addition, at the end of the year the four First Prize winners will have their entries rejudged, and a Grand Prize winner shall be determined and will receive an additional $4,000. All winners will also receive trophies or certificates.

9. The contest has four quarters, beginning on October 1, January 1, April 1 and July 1. The year will end on September 30. To be eligible for judging in its quarter, an entry must be postmarked no later than midnight on the last day of the quarter.

10. Each entrant may submit only one manuscript per quarter. Winners are ineligible to make further entries in the contest.

11. All entries for each quarter are final. No revisions are accepted.

12. Entries will be judged by professional authors. The decisions of the judges are entirely their own, and are final.

13. Winners in each quarter will be individually notified of the results by mail.

14. This contest is void where prohibited by law.

# CONTEST RULES

1. The contest is open to entrants from all nations. (However, entrants should provide themselves with some means for written communication in English.) All themes of science fiction and fantasy illustrations are welcome: every entry is judged on its own merits only. No entry fee is required, and all rights in the entries remain the property of the artists.

2. By submitting work to the contest, the entrant agrees to abide by all contest rules.

3. The contest is open to those who have not previously published more than three black-and-white story illustrations, or more than one process-color painting, in media distributed nationally to the general public, such as magazines or books sold at newsstands, or books sold in stores merchandising to the general public. The submitted entry shall not have been previously published in professional media as exampled above.

If you are not sure of your eligibility, write to the contest address with details, enclosing a business-size self-addressed envelope with return postage. The Contest Administration will reply with a determination.

Winners in previous quarters are not eligible to make further entries.

4. Only one entry per quarter is permitted. The entry must be original to the entrant. Plagiarism, infringement of the rights of others, or other violations of the contest rules will result in disqualification.

5. An entry shall consist of three illustrations done by the entrant in a black-and-white medium. Each must represent a theme different from the other two.

6. ENTRIES SHOULD NOT BE THE ORIGINAL DRAWINGS, but should be large black-and-white photocopies of a quality satisfactory to the entrant. Entries must be submitted unfolded and flat, in an envelope no larger than 9 inches by 12 inches.

All entries must be accompanied by a self-addressed return envelope of the appropriate size, with correct U.S. postage affixed. (Non-U.S. entrants should enclose international postal reply coupons.) If the entrant does not want the photocopies returned, the entry should be clearly marked DISPOSABLE COPIES: DO NOT RETURN.

A business-size self-addressed envelope with correct postage (or valid e-mail address) should be included so that judging results can be returned to the entrant.

We accept only an entry for which no delivery signature is required by us to receive it.

7. To facilitate anonymous judging, each of the three photocopies must be accompanied by a removable cover sheet bearing the artist's name, address, telephone number, and an identifying title for that work as well as an e-mail address if available. The photocopy of the work should carry the same identifying title, and the artist's signature should be deleted from the photocopy.

The Contest Administration will remove and file the cover sheets, and forward only the anonymous entry to the judges.

8. To be eligible for a quarterly judging, an entry must be postmarked no later than the last day of the quarter.

Late entries will be included in the following quarter, and the Contest Administration will so notify the entrant.

9. There will be three co-winners in each quarter. Each winner will receive an outright cash grant of U.S. $500, and a certificate of merit. Such winners also receive eligibility to compete for the annual Grand Prize of an additional outright cash grant of $4,000 together with the annual Grand Prize trophy.

10. Competition for the Grand Prize is designed to acquaint the entrant with customary practices in the field of professional illustrating. It will be conducted in the following manner:

Each winner in each quarter will be furnished a specification sheet giving details on the size and kind of black-and-white illustration work required for the Grand Prize competition. Requirements will be of the sort customarily stated by professional publishing companies.

These specifications will be furnished to the entrant by the Contest Administration, using Return Receipt Requested mail or its equivalent.

Also furnished will be a copy of a science fiction or fantasy story, to be illustrated by the entrant. This story will have been selected for that purpose by the Coordinating Judge of the contest. Thereafter, the entrant will work toward completing the assigned illustration.

572

In order to retain eligibility for the Grand Prize, each entrant shall, within thirty (30) days of receipt of the said story assignment, send to the contest address the entrant's black-and-white page illustration of the assigned story in accordance with the specification sheet.

The entrant's finished illustration shall be in the form of camera-ready art prepared in accordance with the specification sheet and securely packed, shipped at the entrant's own risk. The contest will exercise due care in handling all submissions as received.

The said illustration will then be judged in competition for the Grand Prize on the following basis only:

**Each Grand Prize judge's personal opinion on the extent to which it makes the judge want to read the story it illustrates.**

11. The contest shall contain four quarters each year, beginning on October 1 and going on to January 1, April 1 and July 1, with the year ending at midnight on September 30. Entrants in each quarter will be individually notified of the quarter's judging results by mail. The winning entrants' participation in the contest shall continue until the results of the Grand Prize judging have been announced.

12. The Grand Prize winner shall be announced at the L. Ron Hubbard Awards Event to be held in the year subsequent to the year of the particular contest.

13. Entries will be judged by professional artists only. Each quarterly judging and the Grand Prize judging may have different panels of judges. The decisions of the judges are entirely their own and are final.

14. This contest is void where prohibited by law.

MORGAN WALLACE
SEATTLE, WASHINGTON
FEBRUARY 19, 2005

# Voyage to the Furthest Reaches of the Imagination

buy & read

## *L. Ron Hubbard Presents Writers of the Future Volumes I-XX*

L. Ron Hubbard established the Writers of the Future Contest in late 1983, offering new and aspiring writers a chance to have their works seen and acknowledged. Since that beginning, the imaginative works from these exceptionally talented new writers in the fields of science fiction, fantasy and horror have been published in one of the *L. Ron Hubbard Presents Writers of the Future* anthologies and have provided readers an escape to new worlds ever since.

As was L. Ron Hubbard's intention, many of these talents have gone on to become established writers, including several *New York Times* bestsellers.

Now you can buy each of the volumes in the series, providing hours and hours of entertainment—your ticket to spellbinding adventures across the Galaxy.

Also included in each volume are invaluable tips on writing and art by such legends as L. Ron Hubbard, Frank Herbert, Frank Kelly Freas and more.

Order today! Each volume U.S. $7.99, CAN $11.99
Call toll free: 1-877-8GALAXY
or visit www.writersofthefuture.com or www.galaxypress.com
Mail in your order to: Galaxy Press
7051 Hollywood Blvd., Suite 200, Hollywood, CA 90028

THE NEW YORK TIMES BESTSELLER
BATTLEFIELD
EARTH
A Saga of the Year 3000
by L. RON HUBBARD

# Mission Earth

BY

# L. RON HUBBARD

The ten-volume action-packed intergalactic spy adventure

"A superbly imaginative, intricately plotted invasion of Earth."
—*Chicago Tribune*

An entertaining narrative told from the eyes of alien invaders, *Mission Earth* is packed with captivating suspense and adventure.

Heller, a Royal Combat Engineer, has been sent on a desperate mission to halt the self-destruction of Earth—wholly unaware that a secret branch of his own government (the Coordinated Information Apparatus) has dispatched its own agent, whose sole purpose is to sabotage him at all costs, as part of its clandestine operation.

With a cast of dynamic characters, biting satire and plenty of twists, action and emotion, Heller is pitted against incredible odds in this intergalactic game where the future of Earth hangs in the balance.